SPY IN THE SKY

Book 16 of the NEVER SAY SPY series

Diane Henders

SPY IN THE SKY

ISBN 978-1-927460-65-8

Copyright © 2021 Diane Henders

PEBKAC Publishing Inc.
P.O. Box 67, Station Main
Qualicum Beach, BC   V9K 1S7
www.pebkacpublishing.com

This book is a work of fiction. Names, characters, places and incidents are either the product of the author's imagination or are used fictitiously, and any resemblance to actual persons, living or dead, business establishments, events or locales is entirely coincidental.

First printed in paperback June 2021 by PEBKAC Publishing Inc.

v.3

Since You Asked...

People frequently ask if my protagonist, Aydan Kelly, is really me.

Yeah, you got me. These novels are an autobiography of my secret life as a government agent, working with highly-classified computer technology... Oh, wait, what's that? You want the *truth*? Um, you do realize fiction writers get paid to lie, don't you?

...well, shit, that's not nearly as much fun. It's also a long story.

I swore I'd never write fiction. "Too personal," I said. "People read novels and automatically assume the author is talking about him/herself."

Well, apparently I lied about the fiction-writing part. One day a story sprang into my head and wouldn't leave. The only way to get it out was to write it down. So I did.

But when I wrote that first book, I never intended to show it to anyone, so I created a character that looked like me just to thumb my nose at the stereotype. I've always had a defective sense of humour, and this time it turned around and bit me in the ass.

Because after I'd written the third novel, I realized I actually wanted other people to read my books. And when I went back to change my main character to *not* look like me, my beta readers wouldn't let me. They rose up against me and said, "No! Aydan is a tall woman with long red hair and brown eyes. End of discussion!"

Jeez, no wonder readers get the idea that authors write about themselves. So no, I'm not Aydan Kelly. I just look like her.

Oh, and the town of Silverside and all secret technologies are products of my imagination. If I'm abducted by grim-faced men wearing dark glasses, or if I die in an unexplained fiery car crash, you'll know I accidentally came a little too close to the truth.

I hope you enjoy the book!

Books in the NEVER SAY SPY series:

More books coming! For a current list, please visit
www.dianehenders.com
Or sign up for my New Book Notification list at
www.dianehenders.com/books

Humour by Diane Henders

For Phill

Thank you for being my technical advisor and the most tolerant husband ever. Much love!

To my beta readers/editors, especially Carol H., Judy B., and Phill B., with gratitude: Many thanks for all your time and effort in catching my spelling and grammar errors, telling me when I screwed up the plot or the characters' motivations, and generally keeping me honest.

To Allison and Gord from Skydive Vancouver Island: Thank you so much for generously donating your time and expertise, and letting me use your tandem harness to help me make the cover art and skydiving descriptions in this book as accurate as possible. (Any inaccuracies are completely my fault.)

To everyone else, respectfully:
Canadian English is an unholy hybrid of British and American English, so I apologize if spellings in this book look odd to you. But if you find typos, please send an email to errors@dianehenders.com. Mistakes drive me nuts, and I'm sorry if any slipped through. Please let me know what the error is, and on which page. I'll make sure it gets fixed as soon as possible. Thanks!

CHAPTER 1

Slipping into the server that had attracted my attention, I sent my invisible avatar burrowing through its files.

If I'd had a stomach in my current bodyless state, it would have clenched at what I found.

This couldn't be what I thought it was. Surely I was wrong.

Not for the first time, I cursed the fact that I couldn't simply grab the data and dump it into our own database. Instead, I memorized the worrisome words before returning to painstakingly recreate them in the Department's electronic file repository.

Had I gotten them right?

I couldn't afford to be wrong.

As I turned to follow the convoluted trail back through the internet, ever-present fear gnawed at the edges of my mind.

Would this be the time when a lost connection trapped me in electronic limbo, forever exiled from my physical body? Or worse, some signal failure amputated a piece of my consciousness?

Don't think about that. Concentrate.

It took far too long to find the server again in the ever-shifting data tunnels of the internet. It took longer still to rediscover the tiny snippet of conversation that had caught my attention.

But I hadn't been wrong.

I triple-checked the words before retreating to Sirius Dynamics, my attenuated consciousness snapping backward like a frightened elastic band. Safely inside our file repository, my invisible avatar sucked in a breath of relief.

Made it back. Thank God.

But now I had to face what I'd found. Pacing invisibly, I debated.

Maybe I was blowing the whole thing out of proportion. Those words could mean anything.

But I was pretty damn sure that was only a comforting fantasy. And the sooner I faced reality, the better.

I popped into visibility.

"Hey, Spider, I'm back," I said to the virtual ceiling.

"Aydan, thank goodness! I was afraid you'd gotten lost! I thought we still had our connection, but you weren't coming back." The relief in his tone gave me a pang of guilt over my dawdling.

"Sorry, I could still feel your anchor; I was just a bit slow." Steeling myself, I added, "What did you think of that data I dumped to the server?"

"I didn't like it." His usually cheery voice was grim. "Was there anything more?"

My heart sank. "Not that I could find around that date and time. I'll go back and look through everything in the month leading up to it, though."

"No, it's nearly lunchtime, and Stemp wants to talk to you. As soon as I saw what you'd found, I notified him."

My spirits sank even lower. "Um... okay. But if you need more information, it would be easier for me to go back in right away before the internet connections shift too much."

Pretty damn pathetic that I'd risk eternal exile in

cyberspace just to avoid a meeting with my director, but there it was: The lesser of two terrors.

"No, it's okay." Spider's reply interrupted my gloomy thoughts. "You need a lunch break to get your strength back before you try to breach another server." He still sounded worried. "Come on out."

"Okay." I trudged reluctantly down the virtual corridor, postponing my exit into reality as long as possible. At the portal I hesitated, braced myself, and then stepped through.

The usual pain crashed through my head.

Spitting obscenities, I hugged my temples and squeezed my eyes shut. When the worst of the misery had subsided, I dragged my eyes open and summoned a tooth-clenched caricature of a grin.

"God, I love my job," I growled. "That just never gets old."

Spider's face scrunched into a sympathetic grimace that made him look like a high school kid instead of the late-twenties computer genius he was. "I just hate how much this hurts you! I wish there was a way to make it better."

"There is," I reminded him, holding out my palm to display the tiny cube of highly-classified circuitry that allowed me to sneak invisibly into any network in the world. "I could use the other network key instead of this one."

"It's too risky." Spider's hazel eyes darkened with worry. "Just because our *very* few tests..." He paused to give me a severe look that was approximately as threatening as a puppy's growl. "...indicated a four-to-one ratio of network access time to unconsciousness, that doesn't guarantee you won't go into a permanent coma the next time you use the newer key. Passing out is definitely not 'better'." He made air quotes around the word.

"For me, it is. At least it doesn't hurt."

"But we don't have enough data to be sure it's safe," he argued. "Tammy is the only other person we can study, and she doesn't have any side-effects when she comes out of the network. What if losing consciousness is a sign that your brain is getting damaged?"

"Well, this pain sure feels like brain damage," I growled. "I bet Tammy gets away without side-effects because Brock is controlling her. And there's no way in hell I'm going to let *anybody* drive me around the internet like a cheap rental car. Especially not a self-important little shit like Brock." Relenting at the sight of Spider's unhappy expression, I sighed and added, "Sorry, I didn't mean to dump on you. You're the expert, and I trust you. I'll go and grab some lunch and be less cranky when I get back."

His bony shoulders relaxed, his usual boyish smile returning. "Thanks, Aydan. You aren't cranky at all."

"You're 'way too nice." Feeling several decades older than my forty-eight years, I hauled myself off my office couch and patted him on the shoulder on my way to the door.

A necessary detour to the ladies' room gave my cowardly rationalizations a chance to take over. I could sneak down the fire stairs and avoid Stemp just a little longer. A few more minutes wouldn't change anything.

By the time I had finished washing my hands, I still wasn't ready to face my fate. I stepped out into the corridor, instinctively turning toward the fire stairs.

"*Shit!*" The expletive burst from my lips as I jerked to a halt face-to-face with Stemp, who was apparently returning from the men's room. Just my damn luck.

He slammed on the brakes, too, and we both stepped back to create some much-needed personal space.

"Agent Kelly," he said with his usual cool composure. "There you are. Shall we?" He gestured toward his office.

I squelched the idiot impulse to tackle him to the carpet and flee. He was a former agent and a martial arts expert. If I took him on, I'd be the one who ended up on the carpet. Literally and figuratively.

I stifled a sigh and fell into step beside him.

In his office, Stemp closed the door behind us and waved me into the chair across from his desk.

I sat, working hard to keep my body language relaxed.

"Webb told me what you found," Stemp said in his usual emotionless tone. "So it appears that someone else has developed..." He hesitated, then clarified with his usual precision, "Or redeveloped... a lethal ultrasound weapon."

"Maybe," I equivocated, afraid that if I agreed out loud it would make the nightmare real. "Or I might have misinterpreted the words. It was just a little snatch of conversation from audio surveillance at the Frankfurt airport. It could have meant anything."

Stemp's reptilian features gave me no reassurance as he quoted the words that had burned into my brain. "...*just have to get within twenty-five feet. Nobody will ever guess what the bottle is.*"

I sagged in my chair with a groan. "Okay, to anybody who doesn't know the weapon looks like a bottle and is lethal up to twenty-five feet, it could mean anything, but to us..." A heavy sigh slipped out, fanning the glowing embers of my anxiety into violent irritation. "What the hell is *wrong* with people?" I demanded. "Seriously, who sits around thinking, 'Jeez, the world could really use a silent invisible death ray? *Another* fucking silent invisible death ray?"

Stemp's shoulders rose in a fractional shrug. "That is

what we must determine. Webb has already assigned it Priority One, and he has directed Brock to make it top priority as well."

I sighed. "Well, I guess I'll get back to digging, too, then."

As I rose, Stemp said, "One more thing."

My pulse ticked up and I did my best to hide my dread while I resumed my seat.

Stemp's unnerving amber gaze scanned my face in silence for a moment. Looking for secrets.

"How are you?" he inquired politely.

Every nerve in my body flashed to red alert. Stemp never made small talk.

I returned a bland smile. "Fine, thanks. And you?"

"Very well, thank you. I trust you have fully recovered from your difficult experiences of a few weeks ago?"

It was a trap.

If I said I was fine, he'd expect me to requalify and go back to active duty. If I said I wasn't fine, I'd end up in the psychologist's office again, and Dr. Rawling would worm out my guilty secrets.

I edged unhappily into the minefield. "Yes, I've recovered."

"Excellent. When should I schedule your requalification examination?"

Blam. My first step, and already I'd lost a leg.

I summoned what I hoped was a casual but confident tone. "Probably in a few weeks. We need to get to the bottom of this weapon thing, so I'll be spending a lot of time infiltrating servers and decrypting."

Stemp's gaze sharpened. "Brock and Mellor can handle that. Your primary value is as an active agent."

"Yes, but-"

"Is there a reason why you're avoiding your requalification?"

Blam. Now I didn't have a leg to stand on.

And that thought was completely inappropriate, considering the amputations my friend Reggie had suffered in a real-life explosion. I suppressed a shudder and tried a different tack: The truth.

Or part of it.

I scowled at Stemp. "Yeah, there's a reason. I hate being an agent."

He eyed me with the detachment of an entomologist contemplating a struggling bug on a pin. "That is unfortunate. You may, of course, choose to stay on administrative duty."

"Yeah, and get locked up in the secured facility for the rest of my life." I hid the wave of panic that swept over me at the thought, and kept my voice hard and level. "Thanks, but no thanks."

Stemp sighed, his legendary expressionless façade easing into resignation. "While I sympathize with your situation, the fact remains that your ability to infiltrate and decrypt any network makes you too much of a potential security breach to live any other way. The choice is yours: Active agent or secured asset." He raised a warning eyebrow. "And I suggest you choose soon. If you do not, Upper Command will decide for you."

And I knew which way they'd decide. They'd love to lock me in their secure research facility.

But if I opted to requalify, the mandatory lie detector test would reveal that I'd covered up a murder.

Some choice.

"I'll get back to you," I muttered.

"See that you do. By Wednesday."

"*Wednesday?*" I couldn't keep my voice from cracking. "That's only two days away!"

"Yes, and it has already been two weeks since you returned from your Christmas vacation. You should have requalified for active duty immediately. Unless there is a psychological issue preventing you from performing at peak efficiency in the field..." Stemp's voice softened. "Aydan, if you're having difficulties, I'll arrange some sessions with Dr. Rawling-"

"No!" I tempered my knee-jerk exclamation with a sheepish smile and added, "I'm fine, I've just been procrastinating. Sorry. I'll do my requalification."

Stemp eyed me without expression as he closed off my last avenue of escape. "Very well. Report for your physical test at eleven hundred hours on Wednesday, to be followed by your firearms qualification. Dr. Rawling will see you for your psych evaluation at thirteen hundred. As soon as you've finished with him, come to my office for your lie detector interview."

The interview I'd fail.

"Okay," I mumbled, trying to hide my despair.

"Also..." Stemp hesitated as though choosing his words carefully.

Uh-oh.

"Upper Command has asked me to inquire about the status of your mother's estate."

I couldn't prevent a probably-unattractive smirk from tugging at the corners of my mouth. "You mean, they want to know if I'm going to continue the lawsuit over the proceeds-of-crime seizure, so I can inherit Sirius Dynamics."

"Your decision is of great interest to them."

I grinned. "No doubt."

Stemp's cool formal expression didn't change, and my evil satisfaction ebbed away. As much as I wanted to stick it to the chain of command, they weren't the true cause of my problems.

I sighed. "I actually haven't decided what to do about the lawsuit. The lawyer is sure we can win, but... I feel kind of guilty about inheriting Sirius."

The rarely-revealed human side of Stemp replaced the robot across from me. He raised a puzzled brow. "Why would you feel guilty?"

"Sam was a traitor and my m..." The word 'mother' refused to leave my lips. "Nora..." I said instead, "...was a murderer. I know Sam built the civilian research branch of Sirius with his own money, and after he died Nora didn't have enough time to do anything criminal with it. But still, the whole thing just feels..." I squirmed. "Tainted. Not to mention it'll be a giant pain in the ass."

"A giant profitable pain," Stemp corrected with a quirk of his mouth.

"Yeah..." Another sigh slipped out. "But so what? I can't look forward to using the extra money for exotic vacations, because the Department won't let me out of their sight for that long. I don't like designer clothes and I don't need any fancy expensive shit. I don't have kids to inherit it. What good is money when I have to keep working until I get killed in action or get too old for active service and end up locked in the secured facility until I die?"

Stemp's frown deepened. "You wouldn't be locked in the secured facility. You would live and work there, but you would be free to leave whenever you wanted."

"Under escort," I pointed out. "And only when an escort with a top-level security clearance was available. And we're always understaffed. That's not 'free to leave', that's 'waiting for a day pass from life imprisonment'." He began to speak but I overrode him. "And anyway, the secured facility is in Calgary. Do you know how many years I dreamed of leaving Calgary and living out here in the country? Do you know how hard I worked for that dream? The secured facility doesn't have a garage where I can work on my cars, or a garden where I can grow flowers and veggies, or fresh air or open fields..." My throat tightened. I scowled at Stemp and held my voice under control. "The secured facility is not an option."

"I am very sorry to hear that."

He did sound sorry. For all the damn good it did.

I shrugged. "I'll let you know as soon as I make a final decision on the lawsuit. Was that all you wanted?"

His dispassionate business face returned. "One more thing."

God, how many 'one more things' could there be?

"Meet Agent Holt at the Calgary Airport tomorrow at zero-four-twenty for a flight departing at zero-six-twenty, arriving in Kansas City at twelve-forty local time. Holt will escort you to the United States Disciplinary Barracks..."

Pure terror blotted out the rest of his words.

My voice came out in a squeaky tremolo. "Y- You're sending me to *Leavenworth?*"

CHAPTER 2

Stemp's eyebrows shot up in a completely uncharacteristic show of surprise. Then he let out a strangled cough, his hand flying up to cover the smile he apparently couldn't suppress. A moment later he lowered his hand to reveal his usual deadpan countenance.

"I apologize for the misunderstanding," he said gravely. "Yes, I am sending you to Leavenworth. As law enforcement, not as a prisoner. Holt will be escorting you because you have not yet requalified for active duty."

All the air left my body in a whoosh as I fell back in the chair. "Oh, fuck! Jesus..."

The corners of his mouth were twitching again.

That was enough to spur me to speech. And fury. "You *dickhead!* You did that on purpose!"

The humour vanished from his face. "I promise I did not. However, it was enlightening. Is there some reason why you would expect to be incarcerated?"

"Hell, no," I lied. "But I don't trust Upper Command any farther than I could throw them, and I'm pretty sure the feeling is mutual."

Stemp frowned. "More to the point, you apparently still suffer from crippling claustrophobia."

I gave him a warning glare. "Don't start. I'm pretty sure

any sane person would freak out if you told them you were sending them to Leavenworth. As long as Dr. Rawling says I'm okay for duty, that should be good enough."

"True," Stemp agreed, but his too-sharp gaze was still trying to pry open the edges of my brain and peer into my psyche.

I managed not to shudder.

After a moment of uncomfortable silence, he went on, "Further to my earlier unintentional bombshell, I was about to add that I have scheduled a briefing for you and Holt at thirteen hundred hours today because ex-CIA agent Grandin has requested that you visit him in Leavenworth."

"What the hell for?"

"He swears he has been railroaded by the U.S. government. He wants you to investigate."

"What?" I gaped at Stemp. "Of all the fucking gall! He drugged and abducted me, murdered an FBI agent, and made a really damn good try at murdering an MI6 agent, too. I saw the whole thing, plus it was recorded on video. I'm pretty damn sure he's guilty!"

Stemp inclined his chin. "He does not dispute those events. However, he has never changed his original story. He still insists that he received official orders to eliminate Agents Dirk and Rand, and to capture you and deliver you to a drop point."

"For a big cash bonus. Because that's just standard procedure," I agreed sarcastically. "All agents get big cash bonuses when they carry out routine orders. I know I do. It's just that all my bonuses have been tied up in paperwork for the past year and a half, right?"

Stemp permitted himself a small smile. "Indeed." He sobered. "Nevertheless, our lie detector indicated that

Grandin was telling the truth."

"Yeah," I allowed reluctantly. "That still bugs me. We know our lie detector is infallible. If Grandin was lying, it would have caught him."

"Indeed. And Upper Command would very much like to discover who in the U.S. government knows enough about your secret decryption abilities to go to such lengths to acquire you."

I hid a shudder and tried to look on the bright side. "Or maybe it's just a question of who in the U.S. government can be bought. If there was a big cash bonus for Grandin to deliver me, there could have been a big cash bonus for somebody higher up, too, as a reward for faking an order."

"True." Stemp steepled his fingers and eyed me thoughtfully. "Or perhaps a more subtle reward such as a promotion or political backing."

"That's what I'm hoping for."

"In any case, it behooves us to investigate." Stemp sat back in his chair. "Full briefing in the meeting room at thirteen hundred. Dismissed."

My legs still felt wobbly half an hour later. Despite my best attempts to concentrate on the delicious grilled panini I'd bought for lunch, my mind whirled in fearful circles.

Leavenworth.

The thought of entering those gates and seeing those doors slam behind me was enough to make my pulse skyrocket. My chest tightened, inexorable bands of panic slowly throttling-

"Aydan!"

I yelped and made a grab for my concealed holster,

quickly aborted.

Margaret Young twitched in response, eyeing me worriedly from a few paces away. "I'm sorry, I didn't mean to startle you."

"Oh..." I sucked in a shaky breath and pasted on a smile. "That's okay. I was a million miles away."

She smiled. "You must have been. I said your name three times."

"I'm sorry. What do you w-" Belatedly remembering my manners as I realized she was holding a coffee cup and panini of her own, I bit off my rude question and gestured to the empty chair across from me. "Would you like to join me?"

Her smile gained a few watts, deepening the laugh lines around her hazel eyes. "Thanks, I'd love to!" She slid into the chair. "I'm lucky you were here with a free seat at your table. It's so busy today." A chime sounded from her purse, and she whisked her phone out. "Oh, sorry, I'll silence that." She dealt with the phone and returned it to her purse before unwrapping her sandwich, still smiling. "I can't believe how lucky I was to move to a small town with such a great coffee shop."

"Mmhmm," I mumbled through a mouthful, mentally calculating how many bites I had left before I could escape.

Margaret chattered on. "...so I'd like to invite you and Lola and Linda and a few other women over to my place for a movie on my new flat-screen TV, with wine and popcorn. There's a romantic comedy on NetFlix that looks like it would be fun to watch with friends. Would tomorrow evening work?"

Another damn invitation. Why wouldn't she just back off?

I suppressed a sigh. Be nice. She had only moved here nine months ago. Of course she was trying to make friends. And she seemed pleasant enough, but...

"Thanks, that sounds like fun," I hedged. "I wish I could, but I have to go out of town on business."

Her face fell. "Oh." Her smile came back as she added, "I hope you're going somewhere exciting."

"Nope. Kansas City." I couldn't utter the word 'Leavenworth'.

"Oh." She gave me a small sympathetic grimace. "Well, let's try for later in the week, or next week. When will you be back?"

"I don't actually know. I'll find out in my meeting this afternoon, but sometimes these work things don't go according to plan." I gulped down the last bite of my sandwich and rose. "I'm sorry to eat and run, but I have to get back to the office."

Margaret looked so crestfallen that my heart smote me. The poor woman was trying so hard.

I added, "How about if I call you when I'm back, and we can figure out something then?"

She brightened. "That would be great! Have you got my number?"

She'd only given it to me half a dozen times.

I gave her my warmest smile. "Yep, I've got it. And thanks again for thinking of me. I'll look forward to your get-together."

With that bald-faced lie, I fled.

Back at the office, I was just sinking into a chair in the meeting room when Greg Holt strode in.

His craggy face split into a grin. "Got your shiv and file packed for Leavenworth?"

"Don't even joke about it," I growled.

His grin widened, but his steel-blue eyes were intent. "What's the matter? Guilty conscience?"

"Up yours."

He dropped into the chair across from me. "'Up yours'? Christ, Kelly, that's so fucking seventies. *Nineteen*-seventies. The *last* century. I wasn't even born then."

"Oh, I thought you'd get it," I said sweetly. "You look a lot older than you are."

He barked out a laugh. "Look who's talking, you old bat. I'll always be ten years younger than you."

"And you'll always act like a ten-year-old," I countered, grinning.

He shrugged. "Aging is inevitable. Maturity is optional." His gaze sharpened again. "So what are you feeling guilty about? Hellhound finally confess that he murdered Richard Fitzgerald in cold blood?"

I hid my surge of adrenaline in a contemptuous snort and a flat-out lie. "I've got nothing to feel guilty about. And you need to lay off Arnie. You investigated him up, down, and sideways, and there wasn't a shred of evidence against him."

Holt hitched his chair closer and lowered his voice. "Come on, Kelly, we both know he did it."

I crossed my arms. "Bullshit. You can't seriously think that in less than nine hours he managed to drive twelve hundred kilometres in the dead of winter in the middle of the night, single-handedly infiltrate an enemy stronghold, and murder a crime lord; all without any prior intel and without leaving any evidence. You're nuts."

He was also right, but nobody could know that.

Holt leaned back in his chair, his steely gaze level. "I know damn well he did it, and I know you know it, too. I just can't prove it."

"Well, you're welcome to your delusions," I said lightly. "But you might want to have a talk with Dr. Rawling about the way you keep insisting on things that can't possibly have happened."

As Holt opened his mouth to retort, Stemp strode in. Holt settled for a sardonic smirk in my direction before assuming an attitude of alert interest for Stemp's benefit.

Hell, Holt probably wasn't faking it. He was a career agent. He was probably thrilled to be going back into action.

Unlike me.

Stemp was already outlining the facts he'd told me earlier, and I pulled my attention back to his briefing.

When Stemp finished, Holt demanded, "How does Grandin think we're going to investigate? We have no jurisdiction in the States, and if we try to interview anybody in Grandin's chain of command, they'll just refuse to talk to us. This is a complete waste of time. If Grandin wants to talk, tell him to call collect and we'll do a phone interview."

"You may be right," Stemp agreed. "However, we don't dare ignore the possibility that he might have valuable information that he is willing to disclose to us now that all his avenues of recourse with the U.S. government have been exhausted. And not all communication can be conducted over the phone." He rose. "Your itinerary and e-tickets have been emailed to you. Your arrival time in Kansas City is twelve-forty local, and the interview with Grandin is scheduled for fourteen hundred. You may be able to catch the 16:57 flight back the same day. If not, your itinerary package contains hotel vouchers. Kelly, if you're unable to return tomorrow, your requalification tests will be rescheduled for the same times on Thursday. Questions?"

When neither Holt nor I spoke, Stemp added, "Have a safe journey. Dismissed." He strode out.

Holt flopped back in his chair. "Fuck. Like I had nothing better to do than get up at two AM and drive two hours in the cold and dark to get to Calgary. Do you want to carpool down?"

"Um... no, I think I'll go down tonight so I only have to drive across Calgary in the morning instead of coming all the way from Silverside."

Holt smirked. "Who are you sleeping with tonight? Kane or Hellhound? Or both at the same time?"

I got up and headed for the door. "You're such a pig."

His parting comment followed me down the corridor. "Yeah, but I'm right."

He was, on many levels. And when I did my requalification interview, our infallible lie detector would prove it.

CHAPTER 3

Back in my office, I called my two remaining civilian bookkeeping clients, thankful that the Department had allowed me to keep my favourites to maintain my cover.

Both Lola and Eddy assured me that it was no bother to reschedule my usual Tuesday visit to Wednesday or later. As I hung up the phone after Eddy's cheerful, "See you when I see you!", a chill settled in the pit of my stomach.

If the requalification interview revealed my lies, I'd never see Eddy again. Never again tap my toes to the rollicking tunes he coaxed effortlessly from the saloon's piano. Never again enjoy his superb hot wings, ice-cold beer, and tangy Caesar salad. Never again relax at my usual table with my back to the wall, secure in the knowledge that Eddy would be keeping a watchful eye out for trouble.

Oh, God, if only I'd never badgered Hellhound into admitting he'd murdered Fitzgerald. If I had never heard him say the words, I could truthfully say I had no knowledge of a crime. I would have had strong suspicions, but I couldn't *know*.

Holt would pass a requalification interview with no difficulty. He could honestly say he had investigated every detail and found no evidence that Hellhound had done it.

But no; I had to keep prying until I forced Arnie to admit

something he hadn't wanted to tell me in the first place. Why, *why* hadn't I let him keep his secrets?

My gut clenched. Arnie would go to prison for life, too. I would never feel his arms around me again.

I was dialling his number before I even realized I was doing it.

When his brusque 'Helmand!' rasped over the line, my throat closed and no words came out.

"Who the fuck is this?" he demanded, irritation roughening his voice.

I gulped hard and finally managed to speak. "Hi, Arnie."

His tone softened. "Oh, hey, darlin', how ya doin'? Ya callin' from Sirius?"

"Yeah, sorry for the blocked number."

"No problem. What's up?"

"Are you going to be around tonight?"

I could hear a smile in his voice. "Hell, yeah. Ya comin' down?"

"Yeah. I have to be at the airport tomorrow morning at four-thirty AM, and I'd rather drive from your place than from Silverside."

"Ugh, that's 'way too fuckin' early," he commiserated. "Sure, come on over. Ya want supper?"

"No, I'll grab something here and plan to get to your place around eight."

"'Kay, darlin', see ya then."

"I love you," I blurted.

Most people wouldn't have noticed the tiny hesitation before he replied, "Love ya, too, darlin'. 'Bye for now."

"'Bye." I hung up and slumped forward to thump my forehead on my desk. Idiot.

He knew I loved him; I didn't need to belabour the point.

I had sounded desperate. Needy.

Had I reactivated his commitment phobia?

"Aydan?" Spider's cautious voice roused me from my funk.

Pasting on a smile, I sat up to see him hovering in the doorway. "Hi, Spider. Ready to hit the decryptions again?"

"Yes..." He hesitated. "Is everything okay?"

"Fine, I was just..." I abandoned my attempt at explanation. "I have a bit of a headache, that's all."

"If you want to take a painkiller, we can wait until it kicks in before we get started again."

I sighed. "No painkiller can touch this kind of headache. Come on in."

The drive to Calgary was two long hours of peering at the small bubble of featureless asphalt and dirty snow revealed by my headlights in the profound darkness. The welcome glow of Calgary's streetlights brightened the clouds as I drew closer, and at last I let out a breath and eased my grip on the steering wheel as I drove into the city outskirts.

When I tapped on Arnie's apartment door, he opened it with his usual caution, his foot barring the gap at cat-height.

Hooker's large furry body bounded effortlessly over the inadequate barrier while Princess's tiny white form rocketed underneath, accompanied by a cry of dismay from inside the apartment.

"Oh, Princess, no!" Despite the strain in her voice, I recognized Kathy's beautiful voice easily.

I corralled Hooker, and Arnie scooped Princess up. We stepped inside the apartment and Arnie swung the door shut behind us.

"Hi, Kathy," I greeted his sister, then turned my attention down to my armload of purring fur. "And how's my big guy?" I scratched under Hooker's chin and around his scarred and tufted ears. The big cat slitted his eyes with pleasure, his purr rivalling a motorboat.

Hellhound stroked his small white passenger before lowering her to the floor. "Okay, sweetie, the fun's over." He gave her another gentle caress, his hand dwarfing the tiny cat. She gave him a purring chirrup, but hissed and spat when I put Hooker down, too.

"Princess, no!" Kathy gave us a despairing grimace before returning her attention to Princess. "Hooker is your friend. And your host. Be nice."

If 'nice' entailed a paw full of claws across Hooker's nose, Princess obeyed. Hooker flinched and laid his ears back with a growl, and Princess turned and stalked back to Kathy, ears flat and derisive tail in the air.

Hellhound sighed. "An' that's what it's been like for the last coupla weeks." He crouched. "Ya dumbass furball, did ya let her get ya again?" He stroked Hooker and examined his nose, the gentleness of his touch belying his gruff words.

"Is he okay?" Kathy asked anxiously. "Oh, Arnie, I'm so sorry! I'm causing you so much trouble!"

"Nah, you're no trouble at all. I like havin' ya here," Hellhound replied. "Hooker's fine." He massaged Hooker's scruff with affection and spoke to the cat. "You're four times her size, an' she's only got one front paw. Figure it out, dumbass." He straightened, cuddling Hooker against his chest while he nudged me toward the couch. "Come on in an' sit down, darlin'. Ya want a beer?"

After a few hours of pleasant conversation, Kathy rose. "Well, it's been lovely to see you again, Aydan, but ten-thirty is my bedtime." She gave Arnie an anxious smile. "And please don't feel like you should be quiet on my account. This is your home, not mine. And you know I always wear my earplugs, so you won't disturb me."

"Thanks, but it's your home, too," he countered. "For as long's ya want." He gave her a reassuring smile. "An' don't worry, ya ain't crampin' my style any. G'night."

As she disappeared into the small bedroom that had formerly housed Arnie's home office, I yawned. Rising to skirt the computer desk that now crowded the living room, I said, "I need to call it a night, too. I have to get up at three-thirty AM so I can get to the airport by four-thirty."

A few minutes later I watched with appreciation from my comfortable nest in Hellhound's bed while he peeled off his T-shirt, revealing bulky muscles and the intricate montage of tattoos that decorated them. As he dropped his jeans, I winced.

His eyebrows went up. "What, darlin'? Don't ya like what you're seein'?"

I let my gaze dip to his crotch with a grin. "You know I always like what I see. But I was looking at that." I pointed to the yellowish-brown remnants of a huge bruise that extended from his lower abdomen to his upper thigh, still visible behind his tattoos.

He shrugged and lowered his voice to a whisper as he slid into bed beside me. "It's fine. Can't even feel it anymore. Don't say anythin' to Kath about it, 'kay?"

"You still haven't told her you got shot while you were trying to rescue her?"

"Shhh. Remember how thin these walls are." He placed

his lips against my ear, his beard and moustache sending a cascade of shivers down my neck. "I ain't told her, an' I ain't gonna. An' anyhow, I didn't get shot. My bulletproof vest did."

"While it was on you." I wrapped my arms around him, shuddering again at how close I'd come to losing him.

He cuddled me close, tucking my head onto his shoulder. "Okay, darlin', spill," he whispered. "What's wrong?"

I tried not to stiffen, but I knew I hadn't succeeded. "What makes you think something's wrong?"

"We promised each other 'no lies'," he reminded me. "An' I don't think somethin's wrong, I know somethin's wrong. I heard it in your voice on the phone."

So that was what his momentary hesitation had meant.

I let out a long breath and relaxed against him. I hadn't scared him off with my desperate 'I love you'. Everything was okay.

Okay-ish, anyway.

"C'mon, give," he prompted softly.

"No big deal," I murmured, conscious of Kathy only inches away on the other side of the wall. Good thing she wore earplugs. "I have to requalify on Wednesday, that's all."

It was his turn to tense. "Shit." He pulled back a few inches to frown at me. "I still think ya oughta tell Holt I confessed to ya. Long's ya tell him before your requalification interview, you're off the hook."

"And you're on it. Not happening."

"There ain't any evidence, darlin'. When it comes to the trial, I'll tell 'em I was just blowin' smoke, lyin' to impress ya. No way they'll get a conviction."

"Until they put the lie detector on you," I pointed out.

"Then you're sunk."

"They won't. It wasn't an official op so I'd get tried in civilian court. They can't use classified technology." His shoulder rose and fell in a shrug under my head. "An' the Department won't go outta their way to nail me. I'm still their best..." He hesitated, obviously looking for some word besides 'assassin'. "...guy," he finished.

"But you're still in the army," I argued. "They might get out the lie detector for a military trial."

"Nah. Official records say I'm retired, remember? An' they ain't gonna bust out classified tech in an open court-martial, either." Arnie's words were confident, but uncertainty lurked in his tone.

"But if they do..." I sighed and switched gears. "Anyway, it probably won't come up. I made it through my last requalification after you'd killed your father."

"Yeah, but that was self-defence, so ya weren't technically coverin' up a crime. But if they ask ya about this one under the lie detector..." He trailed off without completing the sentence.

My imagination took over effortlessly. Stemp would never ask mission-specific questions during a requalification interview, but even a general question like 'Have you done anything to violate your oath as an agent' would be enough to trip me up.

Arnie sat up in bed, his face grim but determined. "Shit, this's stupid. I'm gonna call the cops right now an' confess. Long's I turn myself in to the city cops, I'll go through civilian court. Piece a' cake."

"*No!*"

"Shhh!" He shot a worried glance at the wall beside us.

I lowered my voice. "Don't you see, if you confess now,

Stemp's first question to me will be 'Did you know about this', and then it's all over." Despair twisted my guts. "Face it, Arnie, it's too late. Even if I ratted you out to Holt and Stemp right now, it would bring up the same questions. It's been three weeks. Nobody's going to believe the whole thing slipped my mind until now, and if I tell them you just told me tonight, it'll show up as a lie. Our best bet is to say nothing and hope it doesn't come up."

"Fuck!" Hellhound fell back on the pillow and scrubbed his hands over his face. "This's all my fuckin' fault! I oughta go to jail for what I did, but takin' ya down with me... Fuck, Aydan, I'm so fuckin' sorry!"

"Shhh, it's not your fault at all. I'm the one who chose not to tell Holt you'd confessed."

"An' if I hadn't blabbed to ya, ya wouldn't'a hadta make a choice at all." He thudded the heels of his hands viciously against his forehead. "Fuckin' idiot!"

"No, Arnie!" I seized his wrists so he couldn't hit himself again. "You tried. I already knew anyway, and I'm the one who laid the guilt trip on you and made you say it out loud." His earlier words registered belatedly, and I added, "And you sure as hell don't deserve to go to jail."

He turned a troubled gaze to me. "When I get orders to kill somebody, I'm a soldier doin' my job. But when I decide to kill a guy just 'cause it makes my life easier if he's dead..." His face twisted. "I'm a fuckin' murderer. Plain an' simple. I oughta be locked up."

"Arnie, no!" I took his face between my palms and held his gaze. "Richard Fitzgerald was exactly the kind of person you would get an order to kill. Drug lord, arms dealer... he raped little girls, for chrissake! He abducted Kathy to torture and kill her, and one of his guys damn near killed you, too.

The only reason you didn't have an official kill order was because he wasn't a direct risk to national security... yet."

Arnie tried to speak, but I talked over him. "I've been doing some digging into Fitzgerald in the past couple of weeks. Do you know how many times he was arrested and charged with major crimes? Dozens. And every time, the evidence somehow got lost, or a witness changed their testimony or died in a mysterious accident, or the charges just magically went away. He owned people high up in police and government, and nobody could stop him. You did the right thing."

"It woulda been the right thing if I'd had orders." Hellhound's chest rose and fell in a heavy sigh. "It woulda even been okay if he'd been attackin' me an' I killed him in self-defense. But Aydan..." Demons haunted his eyes. "I sneaked into his house in the middle a' the night an' killed a helpless ol' man in his bed. That's just fuckin' sick."

CHAPTER 4

"Arnie..." I stared down at his anguished face on the pillow and drew a deep breath. "When you've got somebody in the sights of your sniper rifle, do they have a chance? Any hope in hell?"

His expression went flat and The Killer spoke with his lips. "Nah. I don't miss."

"So they're helpless."

He flinched but didn't reply.

"Have you ever killed someone in their bed before?" I persisted.

His gaze wavered and fell. "Coupla times." His voice was only a whisper.

"And I bet not all your sanctioned kills were young healthy men."

He said nothing, but I could see the answer in his face.

"So stop beating yourself up about those things," I urged. "Fitzgerald was no different than your usual jobs. You did the right thing."

He sighed and glanced at the clock, obviously closing the discussion. "Ya better get some sleep. Gonna be a short night." He tugged me gently down beside him.

I pillowed my head on his shoulder, and he turned out the bedside lamp and pulled up the covers.

His breathing was slow and even in the darkness, his chest rising and falling under my hand in its usual soothing rhythm.

I stared wide-eyed into the darkness.

I was pretty sure he wasn't sleeping, either.

Unwilling to relinquish his embrace, I held myself still and matched my breathing to his.

Blank your mind. Don't think, just feel. The roughness of his chest hair under my palm and the warmth of the skin beneath. The steady beat of his heart. The tickle of his beard against my forehead. The reassuring weight of his arm around me...

"Aydan, ya still awake?"

I sighed. "Yeah."

"Sorry. This was a shitty thing to dump on ya when ya gotta be up in..." He craned his neck to check the glowing digits of the clock radio before falling back onto the pillow with a groan. "...fuck, three an' a half hours."

"It's okay. It was on my mind anyway."

"So... I been thinkin'..." He hesitated. "I know you're a good person. An' I'm tryin' to figure out... if ya think what I did was okay, does that make me okay, too? Or are we both just completely fucked up?" He sighed. "Sometimes I wish I was Kane. He's got his head on straight."

"Um..."

"What, darlin'?"

"I, uh... don't know whether this makes things worse or better, but... remember, John killed a guy in cold blood, too. And we covered it up."

Arnie propped himself up on one elbow, peering down at me in the dim illumination of the clock radio's display. "That wasn't in cold blood. Kane'd just found out the guy'd killed his kid... well, he *thought* he'd killed his kid. Thank Christ he didn't."

"Yeah, and the guy was completely helpless," I reminded him. "He was on the ground, incapacitated, not a threat to even a newborn mouse. And John snapped his neck. Damn near twisted his head off. John didn't kill him to protect anyone, or in self-defence. He murdered him for revenge."

"The fucker'd just said he killed Kane's *kid!*" Arnie repeated, but doubt wavered in his voice. A moment later, he fell back on the pillow and clutched his head. "Aw, shit."

"What?" I quavered in sudden fear.

"Ya didn't just cover up one murder since your last requalification, darlin'. Ya covered up two."

I yanked the pillow over my face and screamed into it. "AAAAGH!!! Shit-*shit-SHIT!*"

After a few long breaths that unfortunately failed to smother me, I shoved the pillow under my head again and stared blindly up at the darkened ceiling. "I'm so fucked. Hell, we're *all* fucked now."

"Just you an' me," Arnie countered. "I just remembered Kane was still an agent then. He made the judgement call there, so you're in the clear. An' neither of us is gonna tell anybody anyway, so he's okay." He sighed. "Hate to say it, though, darlin', but if Stemp asks the wrong questions at your requalification, you an' me are goin' to Club Ed."

I turned to peer at his profile on the other pillow. "Club Ed?"

"Edmonton Institution. Military disciplinary barracks, an' maximum security civilian pen."

"Oh, God."

We lay in silence. Panic spiralled up and overflowed, turning my lips numb and my fingers icy.

Prison. Never to be free again. Never-

"Marry me, Aydan."

Sheer shock jerked me out of my terror and I bolted up in bed to stare down at Arnie. "*What?*"

He sat up, too, and turned on the lamp. We squinted at each other in the sudden brightness.

"Marry me," he repeated.

I gaped at him. "Are you on drugs or having a stroke or something?"

"Nah, I'm thinkin' ahead." He took my hand. "Listen, darlin', it's no big deal. We can fly to Vegas an' be hitched in a few hours."

"But I'm flying to Kansas City in a few hours..." I trailed off, my mind steadfastly refusing to comprehend this sudden insanity. "Who the hell are you, and what did you do with my commitment-phobic Arnie?"

"It's okay, darlin', I'm freakin' out, too, but nothin'll change between us, an' we can get divorced when this is all over. But it'll work if everythin' goes to hell."

"How? Spouses still have to testify against each other. There's no protection there."

"I know, but in federal prison ya can get private family visits every few months. So if we're both in Club Ed an' we're married, they oughta give us fam'ly visits. Conjugal visits, darlin'."

In spite of the seriousness of the situation and my residual panic, a smile tugged at the corners of my mouth. "Seriously? You're planning ahead so you can get laid in prison?"

"Hell, yeah. I might be an idiot, but I ain't stupid."

"You're definitely neither."

His logic slowly seeped into my overwrought brain. I

would still be in prison. It was still terrifying. But I would have something to look forward to. A respite. A few moments of comfort every now and then.

"Fly to Kansas City like ya planned," Hellhound urged. "An' then grab a flight through Vegas on the way back. I'll be waitin' for ya in Vegas an' we can get married an' be home again before ya do your requalification."

"Is a quickie Vegas marriage even legal in Canada?"

"Yeah."

"How the hell do you know?" I demanded. "You can't even say the word 'wedding' without breaking into a cold sweat."

He grinned. "One a' my PI clients had a quickie weddin' in Vegas an' then ended up hirin' me to tail his new wife after they got back to Calgary." He grimaced. "That didn't work out so good for him, but now I know all about marriage laws. An' a simple divorce only takes a coupla weeks down there. After we're out, we'll just set everythin' back to normal."

I swallowed hard. "I won't be getting out."

He frowned. "'Course ya will. All ya did was not report my confession. Ya didn't know I was gonna do it, an' ya didn't hide evidence or lie to the cops or anythin'. Even if they convicted ya as an accessory, ya prob'ly wouldn't serve more'n a few years before ya got parole."

"I won't be eligible for parole. Ever. They'll lock me up until the day I die."

A long silence.

When Arnie spoke, his voice was hoarser than usual. "Why, Aydan? What'd ya do?"

"It's not what I've done." I sighed. "It's what I am. I'm a giant security breach just waiting to happen, and if Command gets any hint that they can't trust me, I'll be locked up for the rest of my life. They'd lock me up even if I hadn't committed any crime."

His hands tightened on mine. "All the more reason to marry me now."

"I... I..." The magnitude of what we were discussing finally hit me. "Y-You and me?" My voice rose in a squeak. "*Married?*"

"Breathe, darlin'." Hellhound took a few steadying breaths of his own. Our still-clasped hands were sweaty. "It's just an idea," he added. "I ain't sayin' it's a good one. Let's sleep on it."

I let out a shaky laugh. "Like I'm going to be able to sleep now."

"Sorry," he began, but I interrupted.

"Don't be sorry. I... I need to think about it, but... it's not the worst idea I ever heard."

"Awright." He let go of my hands and lay down, holding out his arm to welcome me to his side. "Try an' get a bit a' sleep, then." He turned out the light as I snuggled back into his embrace.

We lay quietly in the darkness again. My mind whirled.

Nothing had improved. In fact, the situation was worse than I'd realized. But for some reason my panic seemed less intense.

Odd...

"Hey, darlin'." Arnie's gentle rasp woke me. "Time to get up."

I opened my eyes in the still-dark room. "Wha...? Oh. It's three-thirty. Why didn't my alarm... shit, I forgot to set my alarm! Lucky you woke up."

"Yeah." Whiskery lips brushed mine. "Go get ready, darlin'. I'll drive ya to the airport."

"You don't need to, I have my car. Just go back to sleep."

He let out a small grunt of amusement, or maybe resignation. "I ain't slept yet, an' I ain't gonna 'til after we talk. That's why I wanna drive ya to the airport. It'll give us half an hour."

"Oh." Reality weighed my heart down all over again. "Okay. I just need a quick shower and then we can go. I'll get breakfast at the airport."

I shivered in the icy passenger seat of Hellhound's SUV as he pulled out onto the dark snowy street. "So..." My shivering intensified. "What do you want to talk about?"

"Well..." Hellhound gave me a sidelong glance. "I'm still up for gettin' married if you are. But before ya decide, we gotta talk about Kane."

"What about him? If we don't go to prison, we'll get a quickie divorce and nobody will ever know. If we do go to prison..." I trailed off.

"Yeah," Arnie agreed. "If we do go to prison. Ya oughta think about whether ya want this deal with me or him, darlin'."

"I can't!" The words left my mouth before I even considered them.

"Can't what? Think about it, or marry him?"

"Both. Neither. I can't! He's too... he'd take it seriously, and then I'd be trapped!" A moment later I overcame my initial terror enough to consider Kane's feelings. "And he'd be miserable." I swallowed against the sensation of a noose closing around my throat. "You and I..." My hand rose and fell in a helpless gesture. "We both know it's just for convenience. If I explained that to John, he'd be insulted that all I want from him is sex while I'm in prison. And I can't even imagine how he'd feel when I told him I'd only marry him on the condition that we get a divorce if I stay free." I sighed. "He'd be so hurt."

"Any less hurt than if he finds out we got married behind his back?" Arnie asked softly.

I dropped my face into my hands. "Oh, God."

"Ya gotta decide, darlin'. An' whichever way ya decide, ya gotta tell him."

"But it's four in the morning and I have to clear international security and board my flight by six, and..." I gulped. "...if I'm going to get married to anybody before my requalification, it has to be today. And I can't have a conversation like this with him over the phone."

"Call him now. He can meet us at the airport."

"No!"

Arnie sighed. "Well, darlin', I didn't wanna do this, but..." He drew in another deep breath. "If ya don't talk to Kane, I'm takin' back my proposal. No matter how much it hurts you an' me, I won't go behind his back."

I stared at his resolute profile in the fluctuating illumination of the streetlights.

He meant it.

An aching band tightened around my chest.

"I'm sorry, Aydan." Arnie's voice was soft, pain vibrating in every word.

I held my voice steady. "Don't apologize. You're doing the right thing." He opened his mouth to reply but I added, "I'll call him right now."

I pulled out my phone and hit the speed dial for Kane.

He picked up after only one ring, his voice hoarse with interrupted sleep but taut with alertness. "Aydan, what's wrong?"

"Nothing." The instinctive lie caught in my throat, and I tried again. "At least, nothing life-threatening. Arnie and I are on our way to the airport. I'm going through Security in half an hour, and I need to talk to you before I leave."

"I'm on my way." Rustling in the background confirmed his rapid movement. "Where do you want to meet?"

"Outside the west entrance to the car rental offices."

"See you soon." He hesitated. "I love you."

It was the same anxious 'Am I losing you?' tone that I had used with Hellhound earlier.

My throat tightened. "I love you, too."

Kane disconnected, and I let my hand drop into my lap.

Hellhound drove in silence for a few moments.

"What're ya gonna tell him?" he asked at last.

"I have no idea."

CHAPTER 5

Far too soon, I spotted Kane's tall broad-shouldered figure striding toward us through the sparse pedestrian traffic outside the airport terminal. As he hurried up, his worried gaze scanned our faces.

"What's wrong?" he demanded as soon as he was close enough to speak without raising his voice.

"Let's walk." I guided Arnie and John down the icy sidewalk and checked my bug detector. The reassuring green light showed no audio surveillance, and I drew a deep breath and laid out the facts. "I have to requalify tomorrow. There are a few reasons why I might fail my interview. If I do, I'm going to prison for life."

"An' so am I," Arnie put in.

"No, you're not." I squeezed his hand. "I didn't think of it until just now, but you said it yourself earlier: If I don't say anything, nobody will ever know. You were talking about John when you said it, but it's equally true for you."

"But, darlin'-"

"If the wrong question comes up, I won't answer at all," I overrode him. "And Stemp can't make me. He'll know I'm guilty of something and I'll go to prison, but if he asks the wrong question I'm going to prison regardless. Giving up details won't change that. I can keep both of you free, and

I'm going to."

Kane stiffened. "Both of us?" His shoulders sagged. "Oh, no. I forgot that you'd have to deal with the fallout from my actions in your next lie detector interview. Aydan, I'm so sorry-"

"You don't need to apologize," I interrupted. "Like I said, there are a few reasons why I might get tripped up in the interview. Even if your situation hadn't happened, I'd still be in the same amount of shit."

"Because a' me," Arnie muttered.

"I don't want to hear any apologies or guilt from either of you," I admonished. "We all did what we thought was right, and I'm hoping that's what my interview will show. If not..." I swallowed hard. "What happens, happens; but neither of you is to blame."

"But-" Kane began.

I silenced him with a touch on his sleeve. "Please let me finish. I don't have much time."

He nodded, watching me intently. His clear grey eyes were worried, but the trust in them hit me like a punch to the gut. In mere seconds, that trust would turn to betrayal.

Swallowing hard, I braced myself. "You know how I feel about..." My throat went dry and I swallowed again. "...captivity." The word came out in a croak.

Kane nodded, sympathy brimming in his gaze. "You downplay your claustrophobia, but I know how severe it is."

"I'm not..." My throat was tightening, and I gulped hard and forced the words out. "I'm not brave enough to face life in prison alone. So I'm marrying Arnie. Tonight."

Kane jerked to a halt as though he'd run face-first into a brick wall.

I grabbed his hands, babbling out the words as fast as I

could. "I know it's a terrible shock, but let me explain."

His jaw clenched, his grey gaze desperately searching my face.

"I love you," I hurried on. "Far too much to marry you at a time like-"

"Wait, darlin'," Hellhound interrupted. He turned to Kane. "I proposed to Aydan when I thought we were both goin' to prison. I figured if we were married, we'd get conjugal visits. That was when I was figurin' we'd both be in for life an' you'd be safe on the outside."

"So..." My voice came out in a bare whisper. "Our d-deal's... off... if you're not going to prison?"

"No! Fuckin'-*hell*-no!" Arnie's arm came around my shoulders, holding me tightly. "I still wanna marry ya! I was just tryin' to explain-"

"That you're getting married so the two of you can still have sex if Aydan goes to prison," Kane said. His voice was flat but his eyes were pure pain.

My heart cracked, and so did my voice. "I'm so sorry. I hope you'll listen to my reasons."

"I'll listen." His reply was as cold and remote as the dark sky above us.

I sucked in a deep breath. "John... I love you."

"You've got a damn funny way of showing it." His words snapped out like a whip.

I flinched. "I know this seems totally selfish, but I'm thinking of you, too. John..." I gripped his hands tighter, trying to bridge the chasm between us. "What kind of marriage could we have if I was in prison? You'd have to drive six hours if you wanted to see me, with only occasional phone calls in between. How would you explain to Daniel that he has a new stepmother but she's in jail for life? And

Alicia would claim that since you're married to a criminal, you're a bad influence on Daniel. Are you willing to risk losing access to Daniel, for a shitty long-distance relationship with a woman who will never be able to give you more? If I go to prison, John, I'm not getting out. Ever."

He opened his mouth to speak, but I kept talking. "And think about this: I know you take marriage seriously, but a lifetime alone is too much for anybody. What happens when you meet someone else? Someone who's warm and loving and great with Daniel, and she's *present* in your life for all those little daily conversations and spur-of-the-moment coffee dates and late-night phone calls? When do you tell her, 'Oh, by the way, I'm married to a convicted criminal'?"

Kane's voice was very quiet. "And what if you pass your interview? What if you don't go to prison?"

"Then Arnie and I fly back to Vegas and get a divorce. Couple of weeks, tops, and everything's back to normal."

"Divorce?" Kane frowned. "Marriage means so little to you that you wouldn't even try to make it work?"

"Cap..." Hellhound laid a hand on his shoulder. "It doesn't mean a damn thing to either of us. We don't wanna be married."

"It's just a means to an end," I agreed. "Arnie will never want commitment with anybody, so being married to me won't mess up any future relationship for him. He won't even try to be faithful, and that suits me fine. We've never wanted that from each other. So being 'married'..." I made air quotes around the word. "...won't change anything except in the eyes of the law. And..." My throat was tightening again. "I'm a coward. So I'm willing to go through a legal process that's completely meaningless to both of us, just... just... for the sake of..."

I couldn't say it out loud.

Kane's face softened. "Human contact," he finished my sentence gently. "A few short hours of comfort every now and then, to ease a life sentence."

I searched his face. "Can you... are you going to be... okay... with this?"

He blew out a breath, rolling his shoulders as though settling a heavy load. "It hurts to know I'm not the person you need for this." His fist clenched, his jaw hardening. "No, to hell with pretending to be calm and rational! I've loved you all this time, and I've always made it clear that I want to marry you. It's *my* place beside you!"

My stomach twisted.

Kane's voice softened. "That's my knee-jerk reaction. But when I stop and think about the reality you've described..." He squeezed his eyes shut before meeting my gaze again. "You're right, it would be sheer misery to be married to you with no hope of ever having a life together. I could bear that; but... if I lost Daniel, too..." He shook his head. "I'm angry and hurt, but I'm also..." A sigh escaped him as his shoulders sagged. "Ashamed. Because I'm relieved that you've already decided, and I don't have to choose."

"There's nothing shameful about that," I said softly. "Never feel guilty for putting Daniel first."

Kane gave us a bittersweet smile. "Well, I never thought I'd be saying this to the two of you, but... I guess you have my blessing. For what it's worth."

"Thank you." I flung my arms around him. "I'm sorry," I mumbled into his shoulder.

His arms closed around me in turn. "I'm sorry, too. For everything that brought us to this point."

He lowered his lips to mine. Our kiss was tender, but the undertow of sorrow left me breathless.

At last we resurfaced, blinking.

"I won't say goodbye," Kane whispered fiercely. "Just... au revoir." He caressed my cheek, then turned and strode rapidly away.

Arnie and I stood in silence.

"How ya doin', darlin'?" he asked at last.

"I'm..." I sucked in some air as if learning to breathe again. "I'm... okay. That went better than I thought it might. Thank you for making me do it." I turned and slid my arms around him. "What would I do without you?"

"Prob'ly die from lack of orgasms."

We both chuckled ruefully at our old joke, and turned together toward the terminal.

"Better haul ass," Hellhound added. "It's a quarter to five." As we picked up the pace, he went on, "I'll grab the first flight I can get to Vegas an' get everythin' organized there. If your interview's at two, ya oughta be able to get to Vegas with enough time left to do the deed in the evenin', an' then we can grab a red-eye home. Book your ticket an' let me know when you're comin' in, an' I'll meet ya at the Vegas airport."

I tugged him to a halt and turned to look him in the face. "Arnie, are you sure? You're not going to prison, I promise. You don't have to be saddled with this marriage."

He took my face between his palms and gazed down at me with a smile that transformed his battered features into the face of an angel.

"Darlin', I'm sure. Let's do it."

I cleared the special security screening for armed agents with time to spare. Holt was already in the boarding lounge, chin sunk on chest and eyes closed. I copied his posture and shrank into myself, grateful for some quiet time to process the last few tumultuous hours.

By the time the boarding announcement came over the loudspeaker, I had second, third, and fourth-guessed myself, and returned to my original decision.

What could it hurt to marry Arnie? If I didn't end up in prison, I wouldn't be trapped. The divorce would be quick and simple...

"Step it up, would you? They're almost finished boarding." Holt's gruff voice broke into my thoughts. He gave me a closer look. "You look like shit."

I flipped him a weary middle finger and mumbled, "I didn't get much sleep last night."

"Too much information," he said with a leer, but he moved out of reach before I could smack him.

On the plane, I dozed most of the way, rousing only to trudge between connecting flights. By the time we arrived in Kansas City my nerves vibrated on a knife-edge of suppressed panic.

The forty-minute drive from the Kansas City airport felt all too short. When the forbidding skyline of USDB Leavenworth loomed up in the windshield of our rental car, it took every ounce of my courage to keep from flinging myself out of the vehicle and running in the opposite direction.

As we neared the entrance, the sight of the armed guards stationed outside made my heart hurl itself against my ribs in a rapid-fire attempt to escape. I was so immersed in fear that Holt's words didn't register the first time he spoke.

"Wh-What did you say?" I quavered.

"I said, something's wrong." He pulled to a halt at a respectful distance and one of the guards approached, weapon at the ready.

Holt laid his ID open on the dashboard and replaced both hands on the steering wheel. I copied him, flipping my ID onto the dashboard and laying my hands on my thighs, palms up. My fingers quivered, and I clasped my hands together instead.

"Holt and Kelly, CSIS," Holt said as the guard came up to his open window. "We're here to interview one of the inmates."

The guard gave our IDs a cursory glance. "Sorry, we're in lockdown."

"Shit." Holt blew out a breath. "We should have called before we left the airport. Is it likely to be a long one?"

"Don't know yet."

"How long have you been locked down?" Holt asked.

"Half an hour."

"So we wouldn't have known even if we had called from the airport." Holt gave a resigned shrug. "Okay. We'll call later today, see how things are going and whether we can set it up for tomorrow."

The guard looked relieved, as though he'd expected us to kick up a big stink. "Sorry for the inconvenience."

Holt offered him an understanding grimace. "Shit happens."

As the terrifying building receded in the rearview mirror, I eased out a long breath, hoping Holt wouldn't notice.

He glanced over. "Guess we'll be using those hotel

vouchers. Even if the lockdown ends in an hour, there still won't be enough time to go back there, interview Grandin, drive back to the airport, clear security, and make it onto that five o'clock flight. We might as well go and check in." He shot a disgusted look at our surroundings. "Welcome to Kansas Fucking City."

"It can't be that bad," I ventured.

"Sure it can. It's only half the size of Edmonton. And Edmonton is only two-thirds the size of Calgary-"

"Yeah, I know; I've heard this song before," I interrupted. "And Calgary is not even a quarter the size of Toronto, which is the standard to which all cities should aspire."

"Too fucking right."

"But they must have something here. Art galleries, some kind of tourist district. Shopping centres. A museum, or zoo, or *something*."

Holt blew out a martyred sigh. "Yeah, I've always wanted to go to a shitty little zoo in a shitty little city on a shitty cold day in January."

"You're such a whiner."

He shot me a glare. "So what do *you* want to do, Little Miss Sunshine?"

I didn't bother to stifle the yawn that seized me. "Check into the hotel, have a nap, and change my plane reservations. I have friends getting married in Vegas. Since we're delayed here, I'm going to grab a flight to Vegas tomorrow and help them celebrate."

"Are you nuts? That's out of your way by half the continent! And for what? A tacky ten-minute ceremony led by an Elvis impersonator?"

I shrugged and told the truth. "I don't know what the

ceremony will be like, but I'm going anyway. I just hope I can get a flight that'll get me there on time."

"This lockdown could last for days if it's a riot or something." Holt scowled. "And the U.S. government might not let you fly halfway across the country with a firearm for personal reasons. You're wasting your money. You'll get everything booked and have to cancel anyway."

"Thank you, Little Mister Sunshine," I snapped, but my heart sank. Would Spider be able to work his magic and clear me to fly home via Vegas?

Holt snorted and returned his attention to the road, and we rode in silence the rest of the way.

In the hotel lobby, cardkey in hand, he turned to me. "You want the car for anything?"

"No, I'm going up to my room."

"Okay, I'm going out. See if I can find anything interesting in this Podunk town." He shot a disparaging glance around the modest lobby. "I'll check in with the USDB and call you if their status changes, and I'll report to Stemp. Should I pick you up for supper? The Hilton should have decent food, and it's not far from here."

God, I really didn't want to have dinner with Holt. But it would be rude to refuse.

"Sounds good," I lied. "Name the time. I'll meet you here in the lobby."

"Five-thirty."

"See you later." I turned and headed for my room.

CHAPTER 6

As soon as my hotel room door closed behind me, I hit the speed dial for Arnie. My call went directly to voicemail. He must be in the air, already on his way to Vegas. I sighed, feeling guilty. Now he'd have to pay for an expensive hotel room for the night.

Although... if the lockdown at the prison ended soon and we got to interview Grandin this afternoon, I could hop an evening flight to Vegas. I'd get to skip dinner with Holt, and have a hot and sexy nightcap with Arnie instead.

Spirits rising, I fired up my laptop and surfed to the airline reservation site. I found a direct flight that only took three hours, leaving just after seven PM and arriving just after eight o'clock local time in Vegas. Thank you, Time Zone Gods.

I booked the flight, heart thumping with hope. Now for the next hurdle. Heart in my mouth, I dialled Spider's number.

Our conversation was short but reassuring. He could make the arrangements for me to clear airport security with my weapons. Thank God.

I fell onto the bed and let glorious sleep claim me.

A sharp report jerked me upright, Glock in hand and pulse pounding. A moment later I processed where I was, and identified the sharp sound as a slamming door in the hotel corridor.

Letting out a breath, I holstered my gun and checked the time. A quarter to five. Shit, I'd slept for two solid hours.

And Holt hadn't called me. I wasn't flying anywhere tonight.

Growling obscenities, I plopped down in front of my laptop again. Most of the morning flights were too early. Even if we got to see Grandin right on the dot of eight AM, I couldn't reasonably expect to catch a flight any earlier than ten. And all those flights had stopovers that amounted to a trip of five hours or more.

Shit.

I chose a flight departing at eleven-thirty AM, crossed my fingers, rebooked, and sent Spider my new flight times. Another call to Arnie netted me his voicemail again, and this time I left a message updating him on the situation.

Promptly at five-thirty, I plodded reluctantly down to the lobby. Holt was already there, dressed in a fresh shirt and expensive-looking slacks. Holt The Magnificent in his designer duds. Was there to be no end to my suffering?

Suppressing a groan as I walked over, I greeted him with, "Before you say anything: Yes, this is what I call 'dressing for dinner'. These are the only clothes I have with me."

His contemptuous gaze flicked over the yoga pants and slim-fitting fleece sweater I wore over my plain black T-shirt. "If you'd told me earlier, I could have picked up some nicer clothes for you."

"I'm sure you could have. And if you had, I'm sure they'd

look a hell of a lot better than what I'm wearing," I agreed sincerely. "But this is what I've got. We can sit at separate tables if you want."

"Forget it, I'm just yanking your chain. Come on." He turned and strode away and I followed in his wake, silently cursing.

In the restaurant, he surprised me by holding my chair to seat me before taking his own seat across the table. I momentarily considered teasing him about his good manners, but I didn't feel up to dealing with the inevitable deluge of reciprocal abuse.

We perused the menus in silence. After we had ordered and the waiter had departed, I asked, "Any news from the USDB?"

"They're still locked down, but they expect the lockdown to end before morning. I've booked our interview for eight AM."

I leaned back with a sigh of relief. "Good. I should be able to make my eleven-thirty flight, then."

Holt frowned. "You're still trying to do that? There's no guarantee we'll get to see Grandin right at eight, you know. They'll do their best, but if some kind of shit happens again, we might not get to see him at all tomorrow." He eyed our tasteful surroundings gloomily. "And then we'll be stuck here for another damn day."

The waiter arrived with Holt's single-malt scotch and my craft beer, and I took a largish gulp of crisp ice-cold comfort. Bracing myself for another litany of complaints about Kansas City, I asked, "So where did you go this afternoon?"

"I found a few decent designer boutiques, believe it or not. Check this out." He extended his arm, displaying the sophisticated charcoal-on-black watch that adorned his wrist. "Major score on this baby. Even with the U.S. exchange rate, it was still a steal."

"It's gorgeous," I agreed, wondering whether 'a steal' meant it had cost hundreds of dollars, or thousands.

"They had women's as well," Holt said with a pointed glance at the ancient watch on my wrist.

I eyed it, too. The fake-silver finish had worn away years ago, revealing the cheap brownish metal underneath. The woven nylon strap was frayed, and the face bore a patina of fine scratches.

"I like this watch," I argued. "It cost me twenty dollars at Shopper's Drug Mart fifteen years ago, so I never have to worry about damaging it. And it has nice big numbers so I can tell the time without my reading glasses."

"You're hopeless." Holt savoured a sip from the glass of scotch that had cost more than the sweater I was wearing. After a few moments of awkward silence, he added, "So did you get your nap? Or just spend the afternoon booking futile airline tickets?"

"Both." I sucked back another mouthful of beer. "Yum, this is great!"

"I thought U.S. beer was just Canadian beer warm-filtered through a kidney."

"Not their craft beer. This is really good."

Another silence fell.

Holt shifted in his chair. "So what time is your flight tomorrow?"

"I booked it for eleven-thirty. I figured that should give me lots of time."

"Huh. Good luck." He took another sip of scotch and set the glass down.

After a moment he began tapping a manicured fingernail

against the edge of the glass. The tiny percussive clinks bored through my eardrums and into my brain like parasitic worms.

I shuddered and gulped some more beer. Come on, waiter, deliver our damn food before we implode from sheer awkwardness.

Holt stopped tapping his glass and switched to rotating it in circles on the glossy tabletop instead. Then he blew out a breath and his lantern jaw firmed as if coming to a decision.

"You know Stemp's going to have your ass if you don't make it back for your requalification testing on Thursday," he said.

"Yeah, I know."

He eyed me, frowning. "What time is this wedding?"

"I don't actually know. Afternoon sometime."

I hoped. If it wasn't, I was sunk.

Holt's frown deepened. "How can you not know what time the ceremony is? And why the hell didn't you book a plane ticket weeks ago if you wanted to go that badly? You're on admin duty; it's not like you couldn't have made plans in advance."

"It was a spur-of-the-moment thing," I replied in complete honesty. "They didn't know they were going to do it. I only found out late last night. They don't expect anybody to come, but... it's important to me."

Holt grunted. "It must be. I sure as hell wouldn't take a chance like that. Skipping out on a requalification test is like going AWOL from the army."

"It's worth it." My heart warmed at the thought of what Arnie was doing for me. And what John had already done, graciously giving his blessing when he objected with all his heart. "I have some pretty awesome friends."

"Must be nice." Holt moodily sipped his scotch.

My heart suffered a pang on his behalf. "It must have been hard for you to leave all your friends behind when you got transferred. Do you get back to Toronto very often?"

"No."

It seemed that the monosyllable would be the extent of his answer, but then he added, "You know what it's like. Book a vacation, and then some shit happens in the Department and we all scramble, and the whole thing gets cancelled. After the first half-dozen times you tell your friends you're coming to see them and then cancel 'because of work'..." He made vicious air quotes around the words. "... they stop altering their plans for you. I went back and got to see a few of them, but..." He shrugged, took another drink, and changed the subject. "So have you known your Vegas friends long?"

"I've known her all my life. Him, I've only known for a couple of years, but he's a great guy. She's so lucky to be marrying him."

Holt's steel-blue eyes sharpened. "Does she know you're in love with her fiancé?"

I nearly sprayed my mouthful of beer across the table. "Give me a fucking break!" I sputtered.

"Uh-huh. Gotcha." He gave me a sardonic grin. "So that's why you're so desperate to get there. Planning to break up the wedding?"

"No! God, you're such a pig! Why do you always think the worst of everybody? Even if I..." I bit off the words 'wasn't the one getting married to him' and substituted, "...really was in love with him, I'd never break up somebody else's relationship. That's just sleazy!"

I expected him to needle me unmercifully, but instead he

gave me a sympathetic grimace. "This fucking job never gives you a chance with anybody. Guess now I know why you haven't picked one of your other boyfriends and settled down."

I couldn't manufacture a response that wouldn't drag me into shit far deeper than I was willing to wade, so I turned the tables instead.

"Spoken like a man with an unhappy past."

Holt shot me a startled glance before his expression closed down. "Do you know any agents *without* an unhappy past?"

I did a quick mental inventory. "Hmph. No, I guess not."

He gave me a 'well, duh' look, and I probed gently, "So what happened?"

"Don't want to talk about it."

"Okay."

We drank in silence until the waiter arrived with our food. "You're driving, right?" I asked Holt as I drained my beer glass. At his nod, I turned to the waiter. "Another, please."

"Certainly." The waiter turned to Holt. "Sir, would you like another scotch?"

Holt hesitated. "One more. That's my limit."

"Very good, sir; madam. Please enjoy your meals."

By the time I had finished some delicious wild mushroom ravioli and my second beer, I was feeling considerably more charitable toward the world. Even Holt.

When he looked up from the last of his steak and asked if I was having dessert, I gave him a smile. "The hazelnut chocolate mousse is calling my name."

Holt grinned. "At least you've got *some* taste. That's what I'm getting, too."

As the waiter departed with our order, Holt tipped the last drops of scotch into his mouth and leaned back. "So... you're really not going to try to break up that wedding tomorrow... are you?" His posture was casual, but his steel-blue gaze was intent.

"No, I'm really not. Promise." I leaned back, too, and added, "Somebody must have really burned you if you're that much of a cynic."

He hesitated, but he must have been mellowed by good food and booze, too.

"Yeah." He sighed. "That's how I ended up getting transferred. I had been dating this woman for a while and it was going well. Then I got assigned to a sting op. First thing I do in a case like that is get the analysts to do a complete background check on everybody involved, including anybody that's gotten close to me in the prior year. I made sure her name was on the list, and she checked out okay. So a couple of months later I was deep in the op, and some shit happened. I had to trust her with more information than I'd usually give a civilian; but I felt okay about it because I knew the analysts had cleared her."

My stomach clenched. "They screwed up."

"Fucking right they did. She double-crossed me. Blew the op, killed my partner, and damn near killed me, too. And then..." His fist clenched on his water glass. "I got transferred to Bumfuck, Nowhere; and the fucking incompetent *dipshit* that gave me the faulty intel got to stay in Toronto!"

I winced. "Oh, God, that's awful. No wonder you had

anger problems when I first met you."

"I still have anger problems." He bared his teeth. "I just hide them better now."

"I don't blame you. I'd be furious, too. I can't believe they punished you for the analyst's mistake."

"Oh, Command swore it wasn't a punishment," he said sourly. "They tried to spin it. 'We need another experienced agent in Silverside, you'll get a promotion and a raise, it'll be a great opportunity and you can settle into your new home while you recover, blah, blah'." He tossed back a mouthful of water and crunched angrily on an ice cube. "Bullshit! No promotion is worth living in a fucking backwater like Silverside. They were just getting rid of me because I wasn't mission-ready in ten minutes or less. They brought in my replacement before I was even out of the hospital."

Beneath the bluster, his pain and betrayal showed clearly.

Sympathy twisted my heart. "Shit, Greg, I'm so sorry that happened to you."

"I'm sorry for me, too." He gave me a grim smile, obviously trying to lighten the mood. "I'm working on shutting down my pity party, and hoping the anger follows it when it goes." He let out a breath as though shifting mental gears. "Anyway, Command really didn't have a choice. My cover was blown, and it took two months of physiotherapy after I got out of the hospital to get back into shape to pass the physical. And there was no way I could pass the psych evaluation. You know what I was like then; I couldn't even deal with day-to-day frustrations without losing it." He shrugged. "I did get the promotion and raise, and it's so much cheaper to live in Silverside that I'm taking home nearly twice what I did before. I got a big boost to my security clearance, and working with Webb and his team is a joy after dealing with the idiots in the Toronto office. And I'm still doing good work, even if it is in a fucking backwater."

"You do excellent work," I told him sincerely. "I've learned a lot from you."

His craggy features softened. "Thanks." He leaned confidentially over the table. "You're a good partner, too."

Just as I was savouring the hard-won compliment, he added, "So what do you say we go back to our hotel after dessert and... have dessert?"

CHAPTER 7

I gaped at Holt across the polished table of the Hilton's upscale restaurant. After a long moment, I found my voice.

"You... did *not*... just proposition me."

He grinned. "Okay, I didn't. So what do you say?"

"I say *no!* Jesus, Holt, you-"

At the last moment, I spotted the discomfort in his usually-arrogant posture. He was rebuilding his walls. Pushing me back to a safe distance.

"You're just yanking my chain again," I finished mildly. His grin widened, and I added, "You'd damn well *better* be just yanking my chain."

"I am, but you'd be surprised how often that works."

I retreated to the safety of our usual insults. "God, you're such a pig! Was any of that shit you shovelled at me actually true?"

Holt sobered. "All of it, unfortunately. I hate reliving it, so I usually try to get a bit of pleasure out of it." He hesitated, not quite meeting my eyes. "The part about you being a good partner was true, too."

I grinned. "It's far too late to butter me up now."

He returned the grin as the waiter arrived bearing our dessert plates, and we ate our mousse in companionable silence.

Six-thirty came too early the next morning, but at least I'd had a moderate amount of sleep in between nightmares about being trapped in an ever-shrinking cage. And I hadn't woken myself screaming. Yay, me.

Holt didn't show up for breakfast, but as I was leaving the restaurant he strode into the lobby. "Ready to go?"

"Just about," I replied. "I'm going to grab my backpack in case we end up tight for time. That way you can drop me at the airport on the way instead of coming back here."

"We might as well check out. I'm going straight to the airport afterward."

A few minutes later, we were on the road to Leavenworth again. As we approached the gates, my heart thumped and my hands quivered.

When the gates closed behind me I had to fight my breathing under control.

In... two... three... four. Ocean waves...

The security personnel were polite but inexorable. After reviewing our identification, one of the uniformed men held out his hand, palm up.

"Your weapon, please, Agent Kelly."

Sheer terror closed my throat.

Without my gun, I was utterly helpless. Trapped inside a building with over five hundred potentially violent male criminals and no way to defend myself.

Slowly, and completely against my will, my hand moved to my holster. My nerveless fingers extracted my little Glock and obediently handed it over while my mind ricocheted frantically around the inside of my skull.

Christ, I'd had issues with uniforms before they'd

searched me, taken my gun away, and left me helpless. Now I'd probably have a full-blown panic attack at the sight of a UPS delivery man.

The guards directed us to a pair of chairs, and we sat.

And waited.

And waited.

I glanced at the clock for approximately the hundredth time. "What the hell's taking them?" I whispered to Holt. "They said eight o'clock. It's nine-thirty!"

Holt stretched out his legs, crossing his arms over his chest. "Thanks, Kelly. I didn't know how to read that giant fucking clock all by myself."

"But my flight goes at eleven-thirty, and it's a forty-minute drive back to the airport, and I have to get through security so I need to be at the airport at least an hour before-"

Holt held up a hand to halt my babble. "You're not going to make that flight. I told you so." His face softened. "Go out to the car and rebook your flight for later. If I get in to see Grandin in the meantime, I'll stall until you get back."

Controlling the urge to jump up and dash for the door, I nodded my thanks and left.

Out in the car, I dithered over my few remaining options, then dialled Hellhound's number.

Even though I knew he couldn't do anything to help, his reassuring rasp eased the tension vibrating in my shoulders. "Hey, darlin'. Ya at the Kansas City airport?"

"No." My voice came out sounding hopeless. "We're still stuck at Leavenworth. I don't know what the delay is. They keep saying everything's fine and it'll just be a few more minutes, but they've been saying that for the last hour and a half. I'm not going to make my eleven-thirty flight."

"Shit." His breath of resignation came clearly over the line. "Okay, what are our options?"

"We don't have many if we're going to get back to Calgary in time for me to drive to Silverside tomorrow morning. The last possible flight out of Vegas today goes at nine PM, and it's a killer. Ten and a half hours for what should be a three-hour direct flight. With the time change, we'd be getting into Calgary at eight-thirty in the morning."

"Fuck, that's brutal. Is there an earlier flight?"

"The next earliest is at five-thirty. But that would mean we'd have to be in security by three-thirty at the latest because it's an international flight, and all the flights out of Kansas City after eleven-thirty have long stopovers. I can't make a connection that gets me to Vegas in time."

"Okay, no big deal," he reassured me. "We'll take the red-eye home. Ya know I'm always up half the night anyway, so ya can sleep on my shoulder an' I'll watch out for ya."

I sagged in the seat. "Thanks. There's a flight that goes out at two-twenty, arriving at five-forty. That gives us an hour and twenty minutes. Is that enough time?"

"Sure. It's only a ten-minute ride from the airport to the chapel, an' it only takes about ten minutes to get married. We'll have time to get some supper, too. I'll set everythin' up. Don't worry 'bout a thing."

I squeezed my eyes shut, my heart swelling with gratitude. "Thank you so much!"

"No problem, darlin'. See ya soon."

A quick and apologetic call to Spider revised my flight reservations yet again, and I let out a long breath and plodded across the parking lot.

Somehow I managed to go back into that terrible building. Squirming again on the uncomfortable chair in the waiting room, I tried to distract myself by counting backward from five hundred by threes. Then by sevens. Then by elevens. Then I started again from ten thousand.

Breathe. Ocean waves.

Like ocean waves, the terror surged back, over and over. Rollers of adrenaline swamped me with the almost-overwhelming urge to run, to scream, to kick and punch and claw my way out of this hellish place. The constant background noise scraped my nerves raw.

At last one of the uniforms returned at ten-fifteen. "Sorry for the delay. We're ready for you now."

As we walked toward the interview room, the emptiness of my ankle holster felt like a missing limb. When I finally faced Grandin, I had never felt so naked.

His shark-grey eyes were the same as I remembered them, his posture still arrogant despite the chains on his wrists and ankles.

I flopped gracelessly into the chair when my trembling knees abruptly refused to bear my weight.

Fortunately, Holt spoke before my voice could betray my fear.

"So, what do you want to tell us?"

Grandin began the same tale as he'd told when we had originally arrested him. In fact, it might have been the same words. The whole thing sounded memorized.

He'd received orders to abduct me and eliminate Agents Dirk and Rand. He'd been told that if anything went wrong, to cooperate with Canadian authorities and he would be safely extracted. He'd been promised a big cash bonus when he delivered me to the drop point. Yadda, yadda.

By the time he finally wound down, irritation had replaced my earlier fear. Or rather, overlaid it as usual.

"That's the same goddamn thing you said when we questioned you the first time," I snapped. "And the same goddamn thing you put in your letter asking us to come here. Are you seriously telling us that you've wasted our fucking time flying all the way down here to tell us absolutely fucking *nothing new*?"

Both Holt and the guards gave me a warning glance, and I belatedly recalled that the prison prohibited bad language.

It seemed to have a beneficial effect on Grandin, though. As I glowered at him, his arrogant body language changed. His shoulders hunched and his fingers flew to his chin in an uncertain gesture.

"Well, but... I'm telling you, I've been framed." He squirmed. "Everett Marsh gave me that order. I'm not lying, I swear it. And your fancy lie detector said I'm telling the truth."

"Okay, so why would your boss want to frame you?" I asked with my best show of patience. "Or if it wasn't Everett Marsh, you need to give us some other names. Or employment positions. Somewhere to start. Who else might have had access to your communication channel? You know we don't have any jurisdiction here."

He smoothed back his hair with an unsteady hand. "I know, but... I don't have any other name. The order came through my usual field communication, so I just assumed it was from Marsh. It had to be somebody that had access..." He shifted again, his hand clenching and releasing. "I thought it was Marsh so I didn't question it..."

After ten long unproductive minutes of Grandin's squirming and fidgeting, he had still revealed nothing new.

"Yeah, we *got* all that," I snarled after he'd repeated it for the third time. "And for the third fu-" I bit off the f-bomb with an effort. "...the third time: It was in your letter, Everett Marsh has already denied it, the CIA has already completed their internal investigation and found no evidence against him, and it's a dead end!"

Grandin straightened into his arrogant posture again, his shark-eyes cold and flat. "Well, it's up to you to figure it out now." He nodded to the guard. "I'm finished. You can take me back."

CHAPTER 8

We were halfway back to the Kansas City airport before I stopped trembling.

Holt glanced over from the driver's seat. "Feeling better now? You were shaking pretty hard earlier."

"It was just from the effort of keeping myself from throttling Grandin," I growled. "What a fucking waste of time."

"Yeah..." Holt didn't sound as annoyed as I'd expected. "He sure got twitchy for a while there, didn't he?"

I sat up straighter. "You're right, he did. Totally different body language. And then at the end he went back to the original asshole-Grandin. Just like flipping a switch." I glanced over at Holt. "I want to get the video footage of our visit. Maybe there's something we missed."

"I'll call them when we get to the airport." He hesitated. "Are you going to make your flight?"

I consulted my watch, as I'd been doing every five minutes. "No problem. I rebooked for a two-twenty flight. I'll even have time to grab some lunch before I leave."

He nodded, and we didn't speak again until we'd returned the rental car.

"Well, that's it," he said as we stood outside the building. "I'm heading to international departures. I'll have that video footage sent directly to the Department and we can look at it tomorrow. Good luck with your wedding."

His unintentionally apropos words made me smile. "Thanks. Have a safe trip home."

"You, too."

The shuttle delivered me to the terminal with time to spare, and I soothed my ravelled nerves as best I could with lunch and a cup of tea.

Finally, things were going right.

A couple of hours later, they weren't.

Despair choked me as I stared at the blinking text on the Departures screen in Salt Lake City. *Flight Delayed.*

Oh God, no. Not after all this effort and expense...

I called Arnie again.

This time his greeting didn't sound quite so cheerful. "Hey, darlin'. I just found out your connectin' flight's gonna be late."

Somehow I managed not to wail, but it was a near thing. "They're saying it won't get in until six-thirty now! That only gives us half an hour. It's not enough time! And who knows if they're accurate. If there's another delay..."

Arnie sighed. "Guess we'll just hafta fly out in the mornin'."

"But then I wouldn't get back to Silverside until mid-afternoon. I can't skip that test. Holt says it's like going AWOL. If I don't show up..."

"Well, darlin', if ya don't get here in time to make the connection, you're stuck anyway. It's the last flight out tonight. Stemp can't blame ya for the airline's fuckup."

All my fear and desperation returned in a choking wave.

Stemp *would* blame me, because I could have made it back in time if I'd flown from Kansas City as he'd ordered.

I was going to prison.

Alone and unmarried.

We might be able to get married later, but I would already be in prison. It could take months to untangle all the red tape. Maybe longer.

Another wave of panic hit me. Maybe never. What if it wasn't even possible to get married in a maximum security prison?

Maybe I should just take the next flight out of here. Somewhere that didn't have an extradition agreement with Canada...

"Aydan?" Hellhound sounded worried. "Ya okay? Sounds like you're hyperventilatin'."

"I..." Bringing my breathing under control with a supreme effort, I steadied my voice. "I was, a bit. I'm okay now."

"Don't worry, darlin'." Strong and firm and reassuring, his gravelly voice wrapped around me like a hug. "I got this under control. Whenever ya get here, I'll be waitin' for ya. I'll meet ya outside the entrance to international security."

"But, Arnie, if we-"

"Hush, now, darlin', just trust me. I got this covered."

I couldn't quite believe him, but just knowing he was there and doing his best made me feel better. My rigid muscles eased and I let out a breath. "Okay. Thanks."

"No problem, darlin'. See ya at security."

By some miracle, my flight arrived on the dot of six-thirty. Giving feverish thanks that I'd travelled with only my small backpack as a carry-on, I ran.

As I panted up to the entrance of international security at six-forty-five, my already-hammering heart picked up the pace.

Where was he?

Oh, God, what else had gone wrong?

"Aydan! Over here!" Hellhound's voice jerked my attention to the left.

No wonder I hadn't recognized him. He was wearing his full dress army uniform.

Tears rose in my eyes. He had tried so hard.

"Arnie!" I dodged around some other passengers and flung myself at him, hiding my face in his shoulder and causing a clamour of jingling from his rows of medals. "Oh, Arnie! I'm sorry, it's too late and we have to catch that flight..."

His arms came around me. "Hush, darlin', it ain't too late. It's only a quarter to seven." He tucked his finger under my chin and raised my lips to his for a light kiss. "Come on over here."

As he guided me a few steps closer to the wall, sudden comprehension flooded me, along with a hysterical urge to burst out laughing.

"You got an Elvis impersonator!" Laughter bubbled up in spite of my best efforts.

He was the worst Elvis I'd ever seen. Corpulent and middle-aged with greasy hair and pockmarked skin, he was crammed into a grubby white jumpsuit missing half its sequins. The stench of alcohol on his breath was easily perceptible even from where we stood. The two weasely men who flanked him looked as though they stole cars in their spare time.

Arnie indicated them with a wave of his hand. "Our weddin' guy, an' our witnesses." Leaning down, he whispered, "Sorry, they're pretty pathetic, but they're the only ones that'd come to the airport on short notice. I double-checked their papers, an' they're official."

I hugged his arm. "Then they're fine with me."

"Awright, darlin', we only gotta say a coupla things to make it legal. I got 'em memorized."

I smiled up at him. "Of course you do. You and your photographic memory."

He smiled back and guided me closer to Elvis, who let out a poorly concealed hiccup and mumbled, "Dearly b'loved, we're gath- *hic!* ...gath'r'd here t'day-"

"Shut up," Hellhound said.

Elvis obeyed. The two weaselly men shuffled their feet nervously.

Arnie took my hand in his. "Okay, here's the first official thing we gotta say: I solemnly declare that I do not know of any lawful impediment why I, Arnold Helmand, may not be joined in matrimony to Aydan Kelly. Now it's your turn, darlin'."

Looking up at the dear ugly face and earnest eyes of the man who had moved heaven and earth to marry me, I had to swallow a huge lump in my throat. My voice came out in a husky whisper. "I solemnly declare that I do not know of any lawful impediment why I, Aydan Kelly, may not be joined in matrimony to Arnold Helmand."

Arnie smiled at me. "That's one down. There's one more thing we both gotta say, but first..." He dipped into his pocket and brought out a gunmetal-grey ring. "This's titanium. It's the toughest metal there is. Tungsten carbide's stronger, but it'll crack an' break. Titanium never gives up." He tilted the ring so I could read the engraved inscription inside.

One word: "Always".

Arnie's hand tightened on mine. "Aydan... These are my weddin' vows. I'm never gonna be faithful to ya. I don't wanna live with ya now, an' I ain't ever gonna want to. But I'll promise ya this." He met my gaze steadily. "I promise I'll always love ya. I promise I'll always be there for ya. An' I promise I'll look out for ya, an' look after ya if ya need it. For better or worse, for richer or poorer, 'til death do us part. That's my solemn promise, married or not." He slipped the ring onto my finger and brought my hand to his lips. "Always."

I blinked back the tears prickling behind my eyes. "Oh, Arnie..." My voice wobbled, and I cleared my throat. "I probably won't be faithful and I don't want to live together either, but I'll always love you and be there for you..." Reality choked off my words. I couldn't be there for him if I was in prison.

I tried again.

"I'll be there for you as much as I can, and look out for you and take care of you as much as I can, for better or worse, for richer or poorer, 'til death do us part. Married or not." I clutched his hand. "I don't have a ring for you," I whispered around the lump in my throat. "I'm sorry."

"It's okay, darlin', I got one for myself in case ya wanted to give me one." He brought another grey ring out of his pocket and handed it to me, the cool metal surprisingly lightweight.

I slipped it onto his finger and pressed my lips to his hand. "Always."

Arnie took both my hands in his and held them to his

heart. "Awright, darlin', we got one more thing to say." He raised his voice. "I call on those present to witness that I, Arnold Helmand, take Aydan Kelly to be my lawful wedded wife." His grip on my hands warmed my entire body. "Your turn," he prompted.

Somehow I managed to hold my voice steady and clear. "I call on those present to witness that I, Aydan Kelly, take Arnold Helmand to be my lawful wedded husband."

We gazed at each other in silence.

"Th-That's it?" I quavered.

Arnie smiled. "That's it. Paperwork's all done, ya just gotta sign your name in a coupla places an' they'll witness it. I already signed."

Elvis hiccupped and let out a resounding fart. "Y'may kish th' bride."

Arnie bellowed out a laugh and swept me into his arms.

As Elvis began to sing a truly awful rendition of "I Want You, I Need You, I Love You", Arnie disengaged our lips long enough to tell him, "If ya shut up right now, I'll give ya an extra fifty bucks."

CHAPTER 9

We made it to the boarding lounge in time. Settling onto a seat beside Arnie, I pulled out our marriage certificate with trembling hands. Leaning our shoulders against each other, we studied it.

I let out a shaky breath. "We did it."

"Yeah." Hellhound's voice was as shaky as mine. "We did it."

"I can't believe we're-" Dismay flooded me as my fingertips skimmed the spot on my finger where the ring should have been. "My ring!" I stared with horror at my empty finger. "It's gone! It was a bit too big, and it's so light I didn't realize..." I sprang up. "It must have fallen off in security."

Hellhound grabbed my hand as I turned to hurry away. "Whoa, darlin', it's no big deal."

I gave him an incredulous glare. "It *is* a big deal! You bought it for me! I'm not going to just walk away without trying to-"

"Shh, it's okay." He rose and folded me into his arms. "I got more right here. I didn't know what size ya needed, so I got a few."

"You got..." I pulled away to stare at him as he withdrew a clinking handful from his pocket. My jaw dropped. "How many did you buy?"

He flushed. "Half a dozen. They were only twenty bucks. Sorry. Like I said, I didn't know what size ya took, an' I figured... even when we're divorced, ya might wanna have one for a different finger..." He hesitated. "Or it's fine if ya don't even want one. They ain't worth fuck-all. It was just a little somethin' to remind ya that I'll always keep my promises."

I could only stare at him while my heart swelled so much it blocked my voice.

His forehead creased, worry filling his eyes. "Aydan, I'm sorry, darlin'. I wanted this to be nice for ya, an' it ended up a total clusterfuck. The chapel I picked out was really nice, an' they had flowers an' ya coulda gotten a better ring-"

"Oh, Arnie!" I silenced him with a long kiss. When I could finally bear to release him for a moment, I pulled away just far enough to look into his eyes. "Don't ever apologize for this! It was the best wedding *ever!* The chapel would have been okay, but... all that formal stuff, walking down the aisle..." I shivered. "But this, what you did... I can't believe you went to so much trouble for me! It was perfect!"

"But that sorry-ass Elvis was fuckin' drunk."

"I know." A giggle escaped me. "And our witnesses looked like pickpockets. And when Elvis hiccupped and farted at the same time..." I burst out laughing, falling back into the seat and pulling Arnie down beside me. "Ohmigod, it was awesome!" Helpless laughter overtook me, and I lay back and let it wash away my tension and the frighteningly powerful emotion that had gripped me. "It couldn't... have been... more fitting!" At last I managed to get myself more or less under control, wiping away tears of mirth between feeble aftershocks of giggles. "I'm going to treasure that memory forever."

The anxiety had been fading from Hellhound's eyes while his lips turned up. "Seriously?"

"Seriously. It couldn't have fit us better if we'd planned it for years."

His laughter rolled out, warm and rich and perfect as he slid an arm around me and held me tightly. "Darlin', I hate to say it, but you're one fucked-up puppy."

I grinned. "Takes one to know one. Now, how about that ring?"

After a couple of tries we found one that fitted perfectly, and I rotated it on my finger with a smile.

Arnie fingered his, too.

"How's your wedding phobia?" I asked.

He grinned. "Gone."

"Get out of here."

"Honest," he insisted. "I was shittin' bricks in that chapel, but when we were down to the wire, I was just... gettin' the job done. No problem at all."

"And now that the emergency is over?"

Hellhound drew a deep breath and shifted his shoulders cautiously, as if assessing some invisible burden that might explode without warning. "I'm... still okay."

But he fidgeted with the ring that encircled his finger, twisting it and easing it up and down as though searching for a less constricting fit.

I laid my hand over his. "You don't have to wear that. Take it off and keep it in the drawer with the rest of your medals." I tapped the ring. "Consider it a Medal of Bravery."

He smiled and his shoulders eased as he slipped the ring off and tucked it into his breast pocket. "Thanks, darlin'. It's 'way better than a medal." He hesitated. "So... everythin' okay? Nothin' else gonna blow up in the next coupla minutes?"

I leaned back in the seat with a long breath. "I'm almost afraid to tempt fate by saying this, but... I think everything's okay."

"Awright, then. I'm gonna go change my clothes. Gonna be a long night, an' this uniform ain't the most comfortable."

"Okay." I gave him a kiss. "Thank you for wearing it, though. It really means a lot that you went to so much trouble for me."

"No problem, darlin'." He rose, smiling. "Some things are worth the trouble."

Arnie was right. It was a hell of a long night.

I couldn't sleep during the first leg of the flight. The dimmed cabin lights and steady drone of the engine should have been relaxing. Beside me, Hellhound's slow even breathing should have had its usual soothing effect.

It didn't.

I stared at the seat in front of me without seeing it. Were these my final hours of so-called freedom? Crammed into a barely-adequate seat, cooped up in a metal tube hurtling through the air in pitch darkness?

Claustrophobia swelled into my throat and my legs twitched with the urge to run.

Breathe.

Just breathe.

Think about something else.

I turned to study Arnie's sleeping profile, memorizing anew the lumpy long-ago-broken bones of his face. His hand lay loosely on my thigh, and I suppressed the urge to take it.

To kiss it and hold it to my heart, the way I would hold the memory of this day close forever.

But that would scare him. If he knew the depth of my feelings right now...

Hell, it scared me, too.

I sighed and eased a little lower in my seat, leaning over to rest my head on his shoulder.

"Hey, darlin'," he mumbled drowsily, and kissed the top of my head before relaxing into sleep again.

I still didn't sleep. But the steady rise and fall of Arnie's shoulder under my head held fear at bay. The terror was still there, glaring into my eyes and groping for me with hungry talons.

But just for these few short hours, it couldn't reach me.

In Vancouver, I plodded through Canadian Customs blinking gritty eyes.

"Six hours layover," I groaned to Hellhound when we reconvened on the other side. "We could almost drive to Calgary faster."

He laid an arm over my shoulders and turned me toward the boarding lounge. "Not quite. I've done it in less than ten, but it's a shitty drive in the dark. Flyin's better, darlin'. Come on, let's grab a snack an' find someplace to sack out for a while." He smiled. "I know ya can't sleep if somebody's watchin' ya, but I'll stay awake an' scare off anybody that looks your way."

"Thanks."

I dozed fitfully in the Vancouver Airport, and again during our flight to Calgary. By the time I stumbled off the plane, every muscle in my body ached.

"Okay, darlin'?" Hellhound asked as I wove an erratic course up the gangway to the terminal.

"I'm awake... ish..." My words were momentarily swallowed by an enormous yawn. "...but my body's not. Come on, feet, get with the program."

He chuckled. "Let's get ya some breakfast. That'll help."

I hugged my midsection. "I'm so exhausted, I feel sick. I don't know if I can eat anything." A glance at my watch increased my queasiness. "And by the time we get to the car, it'll be a quarter to nine. If everything goes exactly right, I'll get to Sirius with just enough time to run to the gym and get changed." Realization struck like a punch to the gut. "Shit! I don't have my car! And I don't have time to go back to your place-"

"Calm down, darlin', I'll drive ya. I woulda come with ya anyway. An' ya gotta eat," he added firmly. "Passin' out halfway through the test ain't gonna do ya any good."

"I know. I'll grab a breakfast sandwich from one of the kiosks and bring it with me."

By the time we hurried down the stairs to the Arrivals level, my pulse was pounding. How long would Stemp wait before he decided I had skipped out on my test?

As I half-jogged into the terminal with my attention already riveted on the exit door, a familiar deep voice jerked me to a halt.

"Aydan!"

My gaze snapped over to where Kane stood next to one of the pillars, Daniel at his side.

Shit.

CHAPTER 10

Kane and Daniel hurried over, and I forced a smile. "Hi. I wasn't expecting you to be here."

Kane smiled back, but the storm-grey of his eyes betrayed him as he glanced at the ring on my finger. "I know you're in a hurry, and I have to get Daniel to school, too. We're already late. I just wanted to see you before..." He hesitated, glancing down at Daniel's attentive face. "...before you left," he finished. "Good luck."

He folded me into his arms, pressing his lips to my cheek and whispering, "I wish I could come with you to Silverside, but I have Daniel today and I have to-"

I hugged him. "It's okay. Thanks for coming. It was good to see you." I didn't add 'one last time', but the unspoken words echoed in the silence between us.

"I love you," Kane murmured.

"I love you, too," I whispered back, but the words felt wrong in my mouth.

He felt wrong in my arms.

I was married.

I pulled back. "Sorry, I really have to go. I'm late."

"I know." Kane squeezed my hand. "Au revoir."

"Au revoir." I turned and ran.

As we pulled out of the airport, Hellhound glanced over from the driver's seat. "Ya didn't hafta run so hard," he said gently. "Ya know I can put my lead foot down an' get ya there in plenty a' time."

Still panting and shivering with clammy sweat, I wrapped my arms around myself and attempted a smile. "I know, I just... I'm just going to call Stemp and let him know I'm on my way."

I hit the speed dial.

When Stemp's cool precise, 'Yes?' came over the line, another shiver shook me.

"H-Hi, it's Aydan. I just wanted to let you know I had a problem with airline connections last night so I'm just leaving Calgary, but I'll be there on time for my physical qualification."

"Very well." He hesitated. "Was there anything else?"

Was he expecting something else?

"Um, no... that was it," I mumbled.

"Very well," he repeated, and disconnected.

Still shivering, I eyed the phone. Why had he asked that? Was I in trouble? Oh God, had Holt been whispering his suspicions about Arnie?

"What's wrong, darlin'?" Arnie eyed me worriedly.

"N-Nothing. It was just kind of a weird conversation. Like he was surprised I'd called. Or he was expecting me to say something else."

Hellhound's frown deepened as he cranked up the heat to maximum. "Well, no point in worryin' about it. You'll find out when ya get there. Now ya better eat that sandwich. You're shiverin' up a storm, but it's pretty damn warm in here."

"Y-Yeah. I g-guess you're right." I eyed the sandwich without enthusiasm, but unwrapped it anyway.

My stomach rolled, and I laid my sandwich in my lap while I unwrapped Arnie's and handed it to him. Stalling.

"Eat up, darlin'," Hellhound mumbled around a mouthful.

I nibbled a bit of the bun.

The small mouthful went down uneventfully, and I tried a slightly larger bite the second time. My stomach emitted a few protests but deigned to accept the food, and eventually I managed to eat the entire sandwich.

"Better?" Hellhound eyed me with concern.

"Yeah." I let out a breath. "My stomach feels a bit better and I'm getting warmer. I guess I'm just wound up and overtired."

He grimaced and reached over to squeeze my knee. "I wanna tell ya everythin's gonna be okay, but..." His grip tightened. "I'm just gonna tell ya I'll be here for ya no matter what."

"Thanks." I covered his hand with my own. "That makes me feel better than a comforting lie that neither of us can believe."

When we slithered to a halt in the icy parking lot of Sirius Dynamics, I gave Hellhound a smile. "A quarter to eleven, just like you promised. Thanks."

"No problem." He unbuckled his seatbelt. "I'm comin' in with ya."

"You don't need to. You won't be able to come into the secured area to watch my physical test, and I'm doing firearms right afterward. I won't be out until around noon."

"That's okay, I'll wait in the lobby. Got my guitar in the back, so I won't be bored." He swung out of the SUV and went around to get his guitar case.

I followed, grabbing my small backpack. We hadn't taken the time to stop at my farm for gym clothes, but my yoga pants and T-shirt would have to do.

"Ya gonna wear that?" Arnie asked, nodding at my ring finger.

My hand flew protectively to the ring, but I slowed the gesture to a more casual movement.

"I'll wear it on my other hand." I transferred the ring and held up my right hand to show him. "For luck."

My shaking legs carried me into the lobby and up to the security wicket, where I signed in and claimed my security fob.

"See you later," I said to Arnie, but he pulled me into his arms and kissed me lingeringly.

"For luck," he said as he gently broke the kiss.

I lowered my voice. "The physical and firearms tests are the easy part."

He shrugged. "A little luck never hurts."

When I stepped into the secured area's time-delay chamber and the heavy door swung shut behind me, my knees went weak and my breathing accelerated to rapid panting. Forcing myself to move slowly and calmly, I stepped forward for the retinal scan that would release the secondary door.

After the longest thirty seconds in all of history, it finally unlatched. The enclosed concrete stairwell was a fresh hell, and I dashed down the stairs at full speed, clutching the handrail in case my wobbling knees let go entirely.

Dodging through the door at the bottom, I plastered my

back against the wall and sucked in deep breaths.

Nice wide white-painted corridor. Glassed-in labs. Lots of space. Lots of fresh air.

Just breathe.

I glanced at my watch.

Minutes to spare.

Prying myself away from the wall, I hurried for the gym.

A few minutes later I was stepping up to the starting line, and the familiar stairs and pylons of the obstacle course comforted me. This, I could do.

When the examiner called the start, I began at my usual comfortable run, knowing I was well ahead of the pace. Up and down the stairs, over the obstacles, controlled fall. Up and down the stairs, over the obstacles...

My heart rate was too fast. Panting, I slowed, forcing my wobbly legs through all six rounds of the course.

Off pace. No time to spare.

I threw myself at the seventy-pound push-pull apparatus, sweat pouring down my face and slicking my grip. I yanked and strained at the weight. My muscles felt like wet noodles. What was wrong with me? I should be able-

The apparatus wavered in front of my eyes and the floor rushed up and smacked me.

I couldn't catch my breath. My pulse jackhammered my temples. The examiner was on his knees beside me, shouting.

At me? Or maybe at the phone...

My guts wrenched and I vomited on the nice shiny hardwood floor.

Oblivion claimed me.

Unfortunately, oblivion didn't last. As paramedics rushed in with a gurney, I became miserably conscious of my own reeking self and the foul stench of failure.

"I'm fine," I muttered as they helped me onto the stretcher and strapped me down.

'Fine' might have been a bit of an exaggeration. Long tremors rocked my body and my stomach felt as though I'd swallowed an enthusiastic troupe of miniature can-can dancers. The stretcher's sheet was already soaked with my sweat.

As we rolled through the main lobby, Hellhound charged over, worry creasing his brow.

"I'm okay," I said hurriedly. "Just low blood sugar or something."

"You can meet her at the hospital," one of the paramedics told him as they wheeled me out to the ambulance.

The Silverside Hospital was only a couple of minutes away. By the time the paramedics wheeled me into the secure wing, my favourite ER doctor was already on her way toward us.

I was reflecting on how fucked up it was to have spent enough time in Emergency to have a 'favourite ER doctor' when Dr. Roth strode up.

"What happened?" she demanded.

"I don't know." As her brow creased with concern, I hurriedly added, "I mean, I know what happened; I just don't know why. I was doing my physical qualification, and all of a sudden I felt weak and sweaty and my heart was pounding and then I kind of passed out and threw up..."

Before I had finished my recitation, she was barking orders and my stretcher was in motion. In short order I was hooked up to a heart monitor and oximeter and an IV was taped into my vein.

Linda, Spider's diminutive wife, drew several vials of my blood, her usually-smooth brow crinkled with concern.

"I'll get these down to the lab right away," she said with a pat on my shoulder. "Don't worry, you're in good hands." She hurried out just as Hellhound loomed up in the entrance to my cubicle.

"How is she?" he demanded.

"Her ECG looks normal," Dr. Roth replied, scrutinizing the squiggly black lines. "We'll know more when we get the bloodwork back. Aydan, are you having chest pain?"

"No. And I didn't have any at the gym, either." I gave her an apologetic look. "I'm pretty sure it was just low blood sugar, and I'm exhausted because I haven't really slept in two days. And I've been eating fast food. I might have food poisoning."

"Maybe, but I'll want to rule out the more serious possibilities first. Heart attacks in women often occur with symptoms like you experienced." She gave me a rueful grimace. "We don't always get the easy-to-diagnose symptoms like chest pain and pressure the way men do."

"I doubt if it was a heart attack," I said, hoping to reassure myself. "I'm in great shape. I do that obstacle course at least once a month just to stay sharp, and I don't have any trouble."

"But we were just flyin'," Hellhound put in worriedly. "We just got off a ten-hour flight."

Dr. Roth's brows snapped together. "And you said you were short of breath." She advanced on me with her stethoscope. "Take deep breaths for me. And then we'll do a chest X-ray."

A couple of hours later, I had been poked, prodded, punctured, scanned, X-rayed, and possibly anal-probed, although I fortunately had no recollection of that.

Apparently reassured that I wasn't about to drop dead, Hellhound had appropriated a chair next to my bed and was picking out a quiet melody on his guitar. My eyelids drooped, fatigue turning my limbs to lead.

The swish of cubicle curtains made my eyes pop open again.

Stemp.

Oh hell.

CHAPTER 11

My pulse bounded into rapid drumming at the sight of Stemp's reptilian features and emotionless amber eyes. Dr. Roth bustled into my cubicle right after him, her brow creasing at the too-fast blinking of the telltale heart monitor.

"Aydan, how are you feeling?" she asked. "You heart rate is elevated."

Stemp's eyes narrowed.

Oh God, he knew I was scared. He knew I was hiding something...

"Aydan!" Dr. Roth's sharpened tone jerked my attention back to her. "Tell me what's happening!"

"N-Nothing," I stammered. "I'm fine. I just... I was half asleep and Director Stemp came in and startled me."

I took a few yoga breaths, willing my pulse back to normal. It didn't quite cooperate, but at least it slowed.

Stemp regarded me in silence for a moment. "Well, Agent Kelly, this seems like a rather excessive attempt to avoid your requalification testing."

I hid my spasm of guilty conscience behind a rueful smile, hoping the uptick of my pulse hadn't been too noticeable on the heart monitor. "Sorry. I think I've got food poisoning or something."

Stemp's eyebrow rose as he transferred his gaze to Dr.

Roth. "Or something?"

"She hasn't had a heart attack or stroke," the doctor replied. "Her initial blood tests showed slightly elevated troponin levels, but that can be temporarily raised by hard physical activity. We'll do another blood test in a few hours, but considering her other test results, it's unlikely to be a concern. There's no sign of pulmonary embolism or blood clots. I'd say..." She turned a severe look on me. "...Agent Kelly has been ignoring the needs of her body as usual. Low blood sugar, inadequate sleep..."

"And food poisoning," I contributed helpfully.

"It's possible, but unlikely," she disagreed. "If that was the case you'd still be vomiting or having diarrhea or both. So likely all you need is food and sleep."

My heart sank. No reason to delay my requalification. Stemp would probably want to do my interview and psych evaluation right away, and finish up with the physical and firearms tomorrow.

And I wouldn't need to complete those if I failed the interview.

Dr. Roth was still talking and I belatedly tuned in. "...twenty-four hour Holter monitor before you attempt the physical test again."

I nodded as though I knew or cared what she was talking about.

Stemp had been eyeing me in silence while she spoke. His customary lack of expression made it impossible to know what he was feeling. Sympathy? Contempt? Indifference?

When he opened his mouth to speak, I braced myself.

"Is she well enough to attend a briefing this afternoon?"

"Assuming her next blood test doesn't show anything of concern, she should be fine for administrative duty," Dr.

Roth agreed. "We'll draw more blood around three o'clock, and the analysis will only take fifteen minutes or so. We'll hook her up to the Holter monitor before she leaves and remove it tomorrow around three. Assuming she feels better tomorrow and the Holter indicates no problems, it would be okay for her to attempt the physical test tomorrow afternoon."

Here it comes...

Stemp let out a barely-noticeable breath, the equivalent of a normal person heaving a frustrated sigh. "Very well." He turned those amber-pebble eyes on me. "Congratulations. You have successfully avoided your requalification testing until Monday."

The reprieve was so unexpected that I could only stare blankly at him. "M-Mon...?"

Reality crashed down on me. It wasn't a reprieve at all. Good God, I was going to have to live with this horrible uncertainty for *three more days*.

"B-But..." I stammered. "Why can't we just do the interview this afternoon? Dr. Roth said I was fine for admin-"

"I am aware of what Dr. Roth said. However, the lie detector was only available to me until fifteen hundred today, and it will not be available again until Monday." Stemp's gaze flicked over my face.

Probably checking to see whether I looked relieved.

Apparently my expression clearly showed my chagrin. Stemp gave me a small sympathetic grimace. "Assuming your bloodwork shows no concerns, please come to my office for a briefing after you are released. I will schedule it for fifteen-thirty, but should you feel unwell, please contact me and we can postpone it." He hesitated before adding formally, "I am glad this was not a serious health event for you." Giving us a tiny nod, he left.

Hellhound rose and stretched. "Well, darlin', I'm glad you're gonna be okay, too." He leaned down to drop a kiss on my forehead. "I gotta go take a leak, an' make a phone call." As he straightened, he mouthed 'Kane'.

I nodded with a sinking feeling. Another three days of miserable uncertainty for Kane, too. The thought of him and Arnie hovering over me while we waited for the axe to fall was almost enough to make me wish it was over and I was on my way to prison.

Almost. But not quite. I shuddered.

"Okay, darlin'?" Hellhound asked anxiously.

"Fine." I smiled. "Go make your phone call."

"Be right back."

As he strode out, Dr. Roth seated herself and leaned forward, clasping her hands on her crossed knees. "Aydan, is there anything else you'd like to talk about, now that we have some privacy?"

My paranoia reared up, gibbering. "Um, no... Why?"

"I just wondered if there's anything else going on in your life that's causing you undue stress." She gave me a rueful smile. "I do understand that stress is an unavoidable part of your job as an agent, but I am concerned that these episodes keep recurring. Most people feel headachey and irritable with low blood sugar. They don't lose consciousness. Not unless there's some underlying condition like hypoglycemia or diabetes."

"I didn't pass out, not really. My legs just went so wobbly that I fell down. And you've tested me for diabetes, right?"

"Several times. I was just wondering if you were aware

of anyone else in your family who had these symptoms, or whether there might be some environmental factor."

I sighed. "No environmental factor that I know of. And I don't know if anybody else in my family had it, but I've had these weird low-blood-sugar episodes since I was a kid. If I've had lots of sleep I can get along with irregular meals; and if I have lots of food I can get along with no sleep; but together..." I gave her a grimace. "Well, here we are."

"Could this be related to your..." She hesitated with a cautious glance around us. "...other abilities?"

"Who knows? There are only a handful of other women in the world who can do what I do, and each of us has a different reaction when we do it. One of them had terrible nausea and vomiting. I get headaches, or pass out. Tammy Mellor used to get dizzy before she started working with us, but now she's fine." I shrugged. "Your guess is as good as mine."

Dr. Roth sighed and rose. "All right, I guess we'll just... keep guessing, then. I'll get Linda to bring you some lunch."

Only moments later Linda arrived with the promised food and her usual sparkling smile.

"Here you go," she chirped, handing me the tray. Her smile widened. "It's so nice to be able to look at food now without throwing up."

I eyed the tray with concern, but my stomach growled instead of churning. I let out a breath of relief and returned my attention to Linda. "Same here. I'm glad you're over the morning sickness. That must have been horrible. Any baby bump yet?"

She smoothed her pink flowered scrubs over her still-flat abdomen. "I can't do up my skinny jeans anymore, but everybody else says they can't notice anything yet. I know

I'm going to regret saying this when I'm as big as a house, but I can hardly wait to have a baby bump!"

"Everybody?" I smiled as she cradled her non-existent belly. "Does this mean you're officially telling people?"

"Yes!" The wattage of her smile could have powered the entire town. "I'm past the first trimester now so the news is out." She giggled. "It's been such a relief for Spider. We're both so excited, and it was so hard for him to keep it a secret!" She sobered, sudden worry crimping her brows. "I'm not... upsetting you, am I?"

"Of course not! How could you possibly upset me?"

"Well... some women have a hard time when they see other women pregnant. I know you never had children, and I don't want to make you sad."

A laugh barked out before I could stop it. "Hell, no! I hate ch-" I stopped myself in the nick of time and rapidly revised my words. "...hate to admit it because I know how excited you are about your baby, but I never wanted children. I'm always happy to see other people excited about becoming parents, though. You and Spider are going be a great mom and dad."

"Thanks." She beamed at me. "Well, I'd better get back to work. I'll be back to take another blood sample in a little while."

She hurried out, and a few minutes later Hellhound returned, peeking cautiously through the curtains before coming into the cubicle.

He lowered his voice. "I passed on the news. So... I guess now we wait."

I blew out a sigh. "Yeah. I wish it was over."

"Be careful what ya wish for, darlin'."

Promptly at three o'clock, Linda returned to do her mini-vampire act. Fifteen minutes later my blood test had come back clear and I was wired up to a pocket-sized heart monitor, given strict instructions to note any activities that might affect my heart rate, and pronounced free to go.

As we went out the hospital doors, I sucked in a deep breath of fresh cold air. The sun was already mellowing to gold in the ice-blue sky, reflecting bright sparks off the undisturbed snow in the field beyond the parking lot.

I slowed, breathing deeply and drinking in the flawless arch of blue above and sparkling white below.

"Okay, darlin'?" Arnie asked.

"Fine. Just... looking."

He put an arm around my shoulders and we stood in silence for a moment.

How many more chances would I get to enjoy a view like that?

I let out a breath. "Well, back to Sirius, I guess. Sorry, you're stuck with chauffeur duty until I can get home and get my truck."

"No problem. I'll just hang out in the lobby an' piss off the security guard playin' my guitar."

I frowned. "Leo doesn't like your music?"

"Nah, Leo's okay, but he's goin' off-shift at four. Some a' the other guys don't like it much."

Indignant on his behalf, I snapped, "Well, they can just suck it up."

Hellhound grinned. "Or just suck it. I don't care which."

A few minutes later I was climbing the stairs to the

second floor offices at Sirius, my heart thumping harder than necessary. The itch of sticky electrodes on my skin reminded me of the small Holter monitor busily recording my fear for all to see.

At the top of the stairs I pulled out the sheet of paper Linda had given me for a diary and scrawled, "15:30 – Climbing stairs". If my tattletale pulse kept speeding up I'd have to fabricate some other activities to explain its antics, but that would do for now.

Taking a deep breath, I headed for the meeting room.

Stemp and Holt were already there, and I muttered, "Sorry I'm late" as I took a seat facing the door.

Holt's steel-blue gaze flicked over me, his brows drawing together. "You look like shit."

I flipped him the finger. "Flattery will get you nowhere."

Stemp gave us a quelling look and cleared his throat. "Let's begin. Holt?"

Holt gave me a smug grin. "I figured out who's pulling Grandin's strings. It's Volslav."

The blood drained from my face, leaving my lips cold and numb.

CHAPTER 12

"V-Volslav?" I stammered. "What... how did you come up with that?" I couldn't help darting a glance at Stemp. His habitual expressionless mask was in place, but his pupils had dilated. I wasn't the only one with an instinctive reaction to that name.

"Grandin told us himself," Holt said smugly. "I got the video of our interview this morning. I watched it a few times and it wasn't hard to figure out. You know how he got all twitchy for a while there?"

I nodded.

"He was using American Sign Language. The squirming was just to make it less obvious. But whenever he touched his face or hair, or moved his hands while he was crossing his legs or whatever, he was signing letters. Same thing, three times in a row. V-O-L-S-L-A-V." Holt signed the letters as he said them.

Leaning back in my chair, I let out a breath. "And when he was done, he quit the twitching and ended the interview. He wanted to make sure we spotted the difference so we'd pay attention."

"He must think Volslav has ears in the USDB," Holt said.

"But why?" I demanded. "Volslav is an arms dealer. As far as we know, his primary operations are overseas. Why would he bother getting his hooks into the U.S. government and... oh. Never mind, forget I said that. He's still trying to get a foothold in North America. We shut him down in Canada and took a chunk out of him in Europe a few months ago, so now he's going for the States."

Stemp nodded. "Possibly. Although, keep in mind that we still don't know whether Volslav is a person or an organization. And I suspect that in this case, political power is merely a means to an end. I believe Volslav's primary goal is still to acquire and control the ultrasound weapon prototype that Arlene Widdenback..." He inclined his chin in my direction. "...stole. Arlene Widdenback is known to use Aydan Kelly as an alias, so if Grandin's orders to abduct you originated from Volslav..."

He didn't need to finish the sentence.

I slumped in my chair as all the connections played out in my mind. "Shit. They figured if they had me, they'd have the ultrasound weapon. But now that there's another weapon out there-"

"*What?*" Holt jerked forward in his chair, scowling. "When the hell did you find that out, and why wasn't I told? Who-"

Stemp stemmed his barrage of questions with a raised palm. "On Monday, Kelly discovered a few words of conversation that had been recorded by Frankfurt airport's security system seven days ago. The weapon was not specifically mentioned, but the speaker said 'have to get within twenty-five feet' and 'never guess what the bottle is'. Coincidentally..." Stemp's mouth twisted as he said the word, "...the otherwise-healthy presidents of three African nations died of unexpected vascular events within the next three days."

My blood went cold and my voice came out in a croak. "They used the weapon already."

"Yes. The three nations in question were in the throes of civil unrest. Coups are now under way by unusually well-armed guerrilla factions."

"Hell of an opportunity for an arms dealer," Holt said lightly, but his jaw was clenched, his face grim.

"Yes," Stemp agreed. "Webb and his team are working on tracking the speaker."

I massaged my forehead, trying to ease the ache that originated in my chest. "The speaker that I discovered too late. The presidents were already dead by then."

Holt frowned and corrected, "We never would have known at all, if not for you. In all the data in the whole damn world, how the hell did you find a few words of conversation that didn't even specifically mention anything dangerous?"

"I..." I gave him a resigned shrug. "I don't know. When I'm inside the internet, I'm just zipping around in the data streams with all the information in the world. It's like being in a huge crowd of people all talking at once. You know how you can be sitting in a restaurant or someplace crowded and you don't really hear any of the conversations, but if somebody says something that attracts your attention, you home in on it?"

Holt nodded slowly, still frowning.

"It's like that." I grimaced. "Kind of. But it's more than hearing, it's like tasting, smelling, feeling... all the senses at once. And if I get a sniff of something that seems relevant, I follow it. I guess maybe the conversation was easier to catch because it was in English among all the German, but if I hadn't known about the ultrasound weapon in the first place, I would have missed it."

"I'd bet any money it's Volslav's weapon," Holt said. "I bet they got to the lab that originally built the prototype before we shut them down. They either got the plans or grabbed one of the developers."

All the pieces fell into place, and I sat up. "That's got to be it. Yana Orlov was trying to steal the prototype to give to Volslav a year ago, but Kane and I killed her and sneaked it off the airplane. That was Volslav's first attempt to get control of the weapon. Then when Dawn White tried to get the prototype from Kane, Volslav must have found out about the lab that had built it, probably from that expert they consulted." Another thought hit me. "We need to see if that expert is still around. If they turned him to their side..."

"That'd give them a leg up on the weapon development," Holt agreed.

"So then we shut down the lab and Dawn White got killed," I went on. "Strike two. Then two months ago, Volslav convinced Frederick Labelle to double-cross me and sell the prototype to them instead. They must have figured that without the prototype, Arlene Widdenback wouldn't be able to compete in the market."

"And then Labelle ended up dead, too," Holt said. "Grandin must have been Volslav's latest recruit."

"Or dupe," Stemp pointed out. "It wouldn't be easy to turn a CIA agent. Better to simply manipulate him. Particularly if he believed he was doing his job, he would be a much more formidable opponent than the people Volslav had deployed against Arlene Widdenback previously."

"And now that Grandin realizes he's been played, he's pissed," Holt finished. "So he's siccing us on Volslav."

I tugged thoughtfully at a lock of hair. "But I don't understand how Volslav plays into this. My m-" The word 'mother' still wouldn't come. I sighed. "Nora was the one who bribed Grandin to abduct me."

"Yes, she did," Stemp agreed dispassionately. "But if you will recall, she said she was not the one who set Grandin up. And the lie detector confirmed it."

Squeezing my eyes shut, I forced my shuddering mind to revisit the horrible memory. My mother's flushed cheeks, the sign of her skyrocketing blood pressure as she incriminated herself. The flat meaty thud of her lifeless body hitting the floor...

"Kelly?" Stemp prompted.

I shuddered and opened my eyes. "I can't remember all the details of what she said. I'd have to watch the video footage again." Just as soon as hell froze over. "I'll take your word for it," I added.

"So if we know Nora didn't personally give the order to Grandin, but she benefited from it..." Stemp let the sentence hang.

Comprehension and nausea arrived in a rush, and I blurted, "Nora was working with Volslav! For shit's sake, the more I find out about her, the worse it gets. Next I'm going to find out she ate kittens for breakfast."

"If she was working for Volslav, that's another reason why she'd want Agent Rand dead," Holt contributed. "MI6 has been trying to nail Volslav overseas, and Rand would be part of that."

"As if she needed another reason, besides trying to cover up the two murders she committed," I said sourly. "But sure, that makes sense. So why would Volslav do her a favour? Or was Nora the head of Volslav, too? Hell, at this point I wouldn't be surprised to find out she was Satan in drag."

Neither man offered an opinion, and I blew out a breath.

"I always assumed Agent Dirk was just collateral damage, but maybe they needed to eliminate him for some reason, too. And I want another look at Everett Marsh, Grandin's boss. Maybe there was no evidence to show he gave the order, but there might be some other connection with the other players. I'll tell Spider to get his team looking for it."

Another thought popped into my mind, and I added, "So here's a question: Does Grandin really believe I'm an agent, or does he think I'm an arms dealer pretending to be an agent? If he went to this much trouble to tell me in person that Volslav made him do it, is he hoping Aydan Kelly the agent will somehow get him out of prison, or is he just hoping Arlene Widdenback the arms dealer destroys Volslav for revenge?"

After a moment's thought, Stemp replied, "Irrelevant, at least for now. What matters is that Volslav's primary goal is likely to acquire the weapon prototype and eliminate the competition. It would make no difference to Volslav whether the competition were Aydan Kelly the agent, or Arlene Widdenback the arms dealer. Either would be a difficult and risky target..." His voice faded to background noise in my mind.

I was the target of an international criminal mastermind. Again.

Fan-fucking-tastic. Maybe I should start a betting pool on whether the Department could send me to prison before Volslav managed to kill me. Or better yet, abduct and torture me to find out where I was keeping that goddamn weapon...

"Kelly?" Stemp's question made me blink my attention back to my surroundings.

"Sorry, what?"

"I asked if you were able to take adequate precautions on

your own, or whether I should assign Holt as protection until you're able to requalify for active duty." His tone gave away nothing, but the tilt of his eyebrow suggested he was wondering whether I was even capable of navigating out of the meeting room on my own, let alone protecting myself from Volslav.

The potential consequences of his question filtered into my tired brain a moment later.

Holt living at my house. Eating at my table. In my face 24/7.

"No, I'm fine," I said hurriedly. "I always take precautions. Plus, with Spider's high-tech surveillance system at my farm, nobody's going to sneak up on me there. I'll just be extra-careful."

Stemp's expressionless countenance made it impossible to tell whether he was reassured, so I added, "And anyway, Hellhound is with me this weekend so I won't be alone out there. And Kane might come up, too." I ignored the sardonic glint in Holt's eyes.

"Very well," Stemp allowed. "Holt, you'll be on call for backup. And I want you both to collaborate with Webb on an analysis and risk assessment. Now that we've identified our enemy, we may be able to predict their next move. I'll contact Interpol to see whether Volslav has been active overseas lately. Kelly, if you feel well enough in the morning, I want you to look for connections to Volslav in the internet." He gave me a severe look. "But only if you've gotten adequate rest. I don't want you losing control inside virtual reality again."

I nodded. I didn't want to lose control in virtual reality, either. So far I'd only come close to killing myself; but if I really screwed up, I could accidentally kill my friends in there, too.

"What about your George Harrison cover?" I asked.

"There may be repercussions," he replied in his usual dispassionate tone. "I will inform Interpol and my contacts overseas."

I read between the lines with a new wave of worry. His secret wife and daughter might be at risk.

Stemp glanced around the table. "Is there anything else?"

Holt and I both shook our heads, and Stemp added, "Dismissed." He got up and strode out.

Holt rose, too. "Come on, let's see if Webb's available now. I want him and his team on this ASAP."

I stifled a yawn as I dragged myself to my feet. "I'm so glad Spider's here to do all that analysis. Frankly, I'd rather be shot at than wade through all that crap."

Holt grunted agreement. "Never mind shot *at*, I'd rather be shot." As we stepped into the corridor, he glanced at my right hand. "New ring. Were you the one secretly getting married in Vegas?"

CHAPTER 13

Hiding my surge of adrenaline in a derisive snort, I raised my right hand and waggled the ring finger at Holt. "Ooh, with deductive powers like that, you should make janitor in no time. Wrong hand, buddy."

He waggled a different finger at me. His middle one. "I can see it's your right hand, idiot. But the ring is new. You weren't wearing it yesterday, and I've never seen you wear a ring before."

Dammit, he was far too observant.

"You're right," I said as casually as I could fake. "I did make it to the wedding yesterday, and I stood up as a witness." Which was technically true; I had witnessed the whole thing. I spun out my next line of bullshit. "The bride and groom bought me this as a thank-you. It's just a cheap mass-produced ring and I probably won't wear it much, but I'll treasure it as a keepsake."

That part was true, too. I kept my expression bland, and the subject dropped as we arrived at Spider's office.

I tapped on the open door. "Hey, Spider, are you busy?"

He glanced up from his computer, his face lighting in a smile. "Hi, Aydan. I'm never too busy for you."

"Good," Holt said, shouldering past me into the room. "We've got an urgent analysis for you and your team."

By five o'clock we had finished our brain-dump of information, and Spider, Holt, and I had batted several possible scenarios back and forth. At last I leaned back in my chair, hiding another cavernous yawn behind my hand.

Holt shot me a look. "Christ, Kelly, go home and get some sleep, would you? If you yawn any wider we'll be able to see clear down to your asshole, and that's not something I ever want to see."

I couldn't summon enough energy for a snappy retort. Instead I nodded groggily and hauled myself to my feet.

"And stay alert," Holt added sharply. "It's been enough of a pain in the ass getting used to you; I don't want to have to break in another partner."

Behind his gruff words I recognized genuine concern, but I knew he wouldn't want me to acknowledge it.

"I'll be alert," I confirmed. "Because the world needs more lerts."

The resulting barrage of abuse followed me down the hallway.

I was still grinning when I emerged into the lobby, and Hellhound rose with an answering smile.

"All done, darlin'?"

"Yep, done like dinner. Let's get out of here. I've got a bed calling my name."

He grinned. "Thought you'd never ask."

I leaned in for a kiss. "You've got a one-track mind. I like it."

I surrendered my fob at the security wicket and turned for the doors, adrenaline trickling into my veins despite my exhaustion. Funny how being a target could do that.

Was death lurking outside?

Squaring my shoulders, I settled into combat mode. I'd

been doing the firing range sims regularly for over a year and I hadn't died yet. And I hadn't failed to kill any hostiles, either. I could do this.

I went outside, making my usual quick sidestep. Left today. I always kept it random.

No bullets greeted us.

I hurried for Hellhound's Forester in the parking lot, cataloguing the threat level of each pedestrian. There seemed to be a lot more people around than usual, and my pulse picked up as I scanned the unfamiliar faces.

The sun was sinking toward the horizon, and my gaze automatically flicked over the long shadows and the rooflines of the surrounding buildings.

We buckled in without incident, and as Hellhound pulled out of the parking lot I relaxed in the passenger seat with a sigh.

"Everythin' okay?" he asked.

"Yeah. I just found out that somebody might be gunning for me, but..." I waved a hand. "Same old, same old." Sudden fear gripped me. "But you'll be in the crossfire. You should drop me off at the farm and then go home tonight."

His response didn't surprise me in the least. "Fuck that. Who's gunnin' for ya?"

"The name I have is Volslav, but I can't tell you anything more. Classified."

Hellhound shrugged. "Doesn't matter. I got your back, darlin'."

I reached over to squeeze his thigh, knowing there was no point in arguing. "Thanks." I hesitated as a thought struck me. "Hey, Arnie... I need your professional opinion."

"Sure. What d'ya wanna know?"

"If you were going to kill me, how would you do it?"

"Take ya to bed. An' when ya were lyin' there all limp an' smilin' after comin' your brains out, I'd put my hands around your head while I was kissin' ya, an' snap your neck."

I gaped at him.

Clearing my throat, I squeaked, "That was a disturbingly quick and detailed answer."

He glanced over, his eyes widening. "Shit, no, darlin', I'd never do that to ya! I was just... I thought ya were askin' the best way to kill somebody if you're close to 'em. Ya said 'kill me', so I..." His mouth flattened into a hard line. "Now you're wonderin' if I ever did that."

"No, I-"

"I didn't. An' I never will." He stared out the windshield, his profile like iron. "I don't kill women or kids. If they want somethin' like that done, they send somebody else."

"Arnie..." I laid a cautious hand on his shoulder. "I was just kidding."

"No, ya weren't." His voice was hard. The Killer's voice. "Ya were scared a' me."

"I'll never be sc-" I bit off the lie. "Okay, you have scared me sometimes, but I've never been afraid you'll hurt me. It's kind of like..." I hesitated, trying to find the right words. "...like when you see a big explosion from a distance. It's that sudden gut-fear when you realize how dangerous something is, but at the same time you know you're perfectly safe."

His posture eased as he glanced over again. "No lies?"

"No lies. You must've had that feeling, haven't you?"

He relaxed into a smile. "Hell, yeah. Two weeks ago when ya yanked open the bathroom door an' pulled your gun on me."

Relief made my laughter a little higher-pitched than

usual. "Holt was scarred for life by the sight of your junk."

Hellhound gave me a smug smile. "Some guys just can't handle bein' in the same room with greatness." He sobered. "So... sorry, darlin', I guess I didn't help ya. What were ya tryin' to figure out?"

"I was just wondering, if you didn't know me but you got assigned to kill me, how would you do it?"

"Do I know you're armed an' dangerous?"

"Yeah."

He shrugged. "Long-range rifle. Or artillery from a coupla miles away, or get air support to drop a bomb on ya. I wouldn't get anywhere near ya unless I didn't have any other choice."

Obscurely comforted, I sat up a little straighter. "You really think I'm that dangerous?"

"Fuck, yeah." He gave me a quick sidelong smile. "But even if I didn't, I wouldn't fuck around. The farther away I am, the easier it is to bug out afterwards. Killin' people's easy. Gettin' away with it's the hard part."

He turned off the road and stopped at my gate, and I reached for the door handle.

"Stay put, darlin'. I got it." He got out and unlocked the gate, drove through, and relocked it behind us.

As he got back in the vehicle, I said, "Just wait here for a second. Have a look at the layout. Where would you set up your rifle if you were going to shoot me?"

Ignoring my instructions, Hellhound drove down the lane. "Don't need to look around. I scoped out the sightlines long ago." He glanced over. "An' before ya freak out, I do that everywhere I go." He sighed. "After thirty damn years, I can't stop myself. Anyhow..." He jerked his chin behind us. "Best shot is when you're comin' through the gate. Ya gotta get outta your car, always in the same place, ya got no cover, an' you're movin' in a predictable line when ya open the gate." He indicated the trees around the creek to the south. "I'd park on the other road east a' here an' hike in along the creek. Set up in the woods an' wait for ya to show up." His eyes narrowed, calculating. "I'd do it after dark with a night-vision scope. You'd never spot me unless ya were scannin' with infrared. An' Rossburn ain't gonna bother checkin' out one gunshot in the dark in the middle a' winter. But even if he did, it'd take him a while to find your body an' call the cops. By the time they got here, I'd be long gone."

Hiding the chill around my heart in a matter-of-fact tone, I said, "Okay, I'll have to figure out a way to avoid the gate, then. Second choice?"

He shrugged. "The hill up there has good sightlines but no cover for me. Prob'ly not a big deal out here in the middle a' nowhere, but it ain't as good as the trees. I'd still be aimin' for the gate from there. There's no clear shot if you're around your garage an' house."

I let out a breath. "Guess I'll be leaving my gate open from now on. So if I don't stop at the gate anymore, then how would you do it?"

He frowned as we pulled up in front of my house. "Hafta think about that. You'd be damn hard to hit at Sirius. You're too careful comin' an' goin', an' ya don't keep regular hours. There's no shot from the hotel or the second floor a' Eddy's. None a' the other buildin's near Sirius are over two storeys, an' anyway, it'd be too hard to get down off a roof without gettin' spotted. Could do a driveby, but it'd be really fuckin' hard to get away with it. Too many nosy people in a small town, not enough strangers. Plus there's no place to run where the cops wouldn't spot my truck from the air, an' ya can bet if there's an active shooter they'd have a bird up fast. Even if they hadta come from Calgary, they'd be here before I could get far on the highway. I'd have to stash the truck an' lie low, an' that's a risk. The whole point is to get in, do the job, an' get out."

"Well, that's good to know, I guess," I said as we got out of the vehicle and climbed the steps to my front door. "So if you-" The words died in my throat as I swung the door open and adrenaline seared my veins.

CHAPTER 14

My Glock was already in my hand.

"Get in the truck!" I snapped at Arnie.

"No," he snapped back, eyeing the devastation inside my house. "I'll cover your six while ya clear it."

"Are you armed?"

"Nah. We'll go back-to-back. I'll yell an' drop if I see anythin'."

No time to argue; and he wouldn't listen anyway.

I gave him a nod and stepped forward, Glock at the ready. He glued himself to my back and we moved cautiously inside.

In the murky twilight of sunset, I could see that my unauthorized visitors had been thorough. The kitchen cabinets, fridge, and chest freezer had been completely emptied. The floor was littered with debris and rotting food. Broken glass crunched under our boots.

I was vaguely aware of my heart hammering and my breath whistling through my nostrils but I ignored the sensations, concentrating on holding my gun steady and scanning for movement or traps.

We moved quietly from room to devastated room. Each corner and door induced an extra spurt of adrenaline until I was panting audibly, my arms aching with strain. But my

Glock rested lightly in my grip. If I had to take a shot, I wouldn't miss.

At last we finished the final corner of the disaster zone that used to be my basement. Even my secret room had been discovered. Holes had been kicked in the drywall, and its supposedly-concealed door panel hung open.

I lowered my weapon with a grunt. "Guess that room wasn't as secret as I thought."

"Shoulda been," Hellhound replied, eyeing it. "They musta had time to measure up the walls an' figure it out. Why didn't your monitors catch 'em?"

"Good question." I pulled out my bug detector and checked it. Green light. At least we had no listeners. I sighed and plodded up the stairs. "Would you close all the blinds, please, so we can turn on some lights? And do a bug scan through the rest of the house, too." I handed the bug detector to him.

"Sure." Hellhound hesitated. "Ya okay, darlin'?"

Eyeing the chaos, I swallowed hard. "Yeah. I stopped caring so much after the second time my house got trashed." I gave him a grimace. "Everything I really cared about got destroyed the first time around, and I couldn't replace it so I didn't try. After the second time, there was nothing left. This is all just..." I waved a hand at the mangled heaps. "Disposable. But my garage, and my c-cars..." My throat closed.

Arnie's face softened and he pulled me into a hug.

"I can't go out there just yet," I mumbled into his shoulder.

"I'll do it," he promised.

"Not without a weapon. And I'm not giving you mine, so... later." I pulled away. "Let's see what's going on with my system. It should have vibrated and showed me a live camera feed as soon as anybody got near my house."

I toggled the view on my specialized wrist monitor. About half of the cameras were dark. I toggled through all of them, swearing softly. "How the hell did they do it? They knocked out the ones that cover the garage, shed, and back door, but all the rest are still active. Nobody should have been able to get close enough to disable the cameras without setting off the motion sensors; and then my monitor would have gone off."

Hellhound peered over my shoulder. "Shouldn't the analysts have noticed when the feeds went down?"

"They discontinued monitoring when I got this portable monitor." I waved at my wrist. "Cost savings."

"Fuckin' bean counters," Hellhound growled.

"No, I'm the one that suggested it. Long story, but it seemed like a good idea at the time." I sighed. "I'm going to call in now."

"I'll get the blinds." He headed for the kitchen, holding the bug detector at arm's length so I could see its reassuring green glow.

Pulling a secured phone out of my waist pouch, I sagged against the wall and hit the speed dial.

"Yes?" Stemp's crisp voice answered on the first ring as usual.

"It's Aydan. Somebody disabled half my security cameras and searched my house. Looks like they knew they had lots of time. So they must have had access to the airline reservation system if they knew I was going to be gone. I didn't even know that I'd be leaving, until a few hours before I left."

"Or perhaps they saw you leave carrying baggage and

when you didn't return within a few hours, they surmised you wouldn't be back for a while."

"I hope it's that," I agreed. "Anyhow, I'm going to need a tech out here to replace the cameras, and to figure out how they disabled them in the first place."

"Expect a tech within half an hour."

Hellhound had returned from his tour of the blinds while I talked, and he waved to attract my attention.

"Hang on," I said into the phone, and raised my eyebrows at Hellhound.

"Tell 'em to bring me a rifle an' sidearm from Stores when they come," he said.

I relayed the request to Stemp, who agreed and disconnected.

"Better check the perimeter," I said, and headed for the tangled heap that had once been the contents of my front closet. Rooting through the mess, I let out a grunt of satisfaction. "They dumped out my grab-and-go bag but didn't take my gear. Good." I extracted a set of combination night-vision and infrared goggles, as well as a pair of binoculars with the same setup. "Which do you want?"

"Gimme the binocs." Hellhound extended a hand. "So what the hell were they lookin' for if they passed these up?" he added, hefting the binoculars. "This's some pretty nice tech."

I grimaced. "They were probably looking for that ultrasound weapon we took to the Five Eyes conference." I leaned into him for a quick hug. "And I'm really glad you're a weapons specialist and you've got the security clearance for me to tell you that."

He smiled and dropped a kiss on my lips. "Awright, darlin', let's do this together. You scan close range an' I'll do far." We headed for the kitchen window, shuffling cautiously through debris in the near-darkness.

Leaning across the kitchen sink side by side, we parted the blinds and scanned the twilight. After a moment, I said, "Nothing. But I can't see the spot where you said you'd set up your rifle. Like you said, there's no sightline from the house. Do you see anything?"

"Nah. Next."

We were just turning away from the window when the sound of a distant vehicle made me stiffen. "Somebody's coming. And it's too early for the tech."

I peeked through the blind again, switching my goggles to night vision just as Hellhound said, "It's prob'ly Kane. When I called him from the hospital he said he'd come up."

I couldn't keep the dismay out of my voice. "But he has Daniel today!" I shot a desperate glance around the chaos. "Shit!"

"It's okay, Dan's with Lish now. Kane just hadta drop him off at school this mornin'. Come on, let's make sure nobody's hidin' on the hill, before he gets to the gate."

Sudden fear seized me and I bounded through the debris to the next window. Hellhound joined me with the binoculars and we studied what we could see of the hillside.

"See anything?" I asked.

"Nah. But this's a bad angle, too. Nobody can shoot ya, but ya can't see 'em, either."

We hurried to the next window to check the partial view of the trees surrounding the creek. The sound of the SUV's engine swelled, and I scanned frantically.

"Anything?" I demanded.

"Nah, but just gimme another sec..."

By the time the squeak of tires on snow announced

Kane's arrival, I was fairly sure he wouldn't get shot on his way to the door. Still, when I heard the thump of his boots on the front porch, I pulled open the door and yanked him inside.

"Wha-" he began, then took in the shambles a single glance. "Status!" he snapped as he dropped into a combat-ready stance, his gaze raking the room.

"Clear," I assured him. "Sorry about the cloak-and-dagger stuff. We were just checking the perimeter with our night vision and infrared when you drove up. It's safe to turn on the lights now."

He reached over and flipped the switch, wincing at the sudden brightness. Or maybe at the mess.

"What happened?" he asked.

I made an airy gesture at our disordered surroundings. "I decided to redecorate. Tidiness is so passé."

"Which decorator did you use?" Kane asked grimly.

"Volslav."

"Dammit." He hesitated, his gaze searching my face. "Are you all right?"

"Fine. They were gone long before we got here." I sniffed the air. "I'd say that milk's been spoiling for at least a day. And seeping into my damn hardwood, too. I'd barely gotten the smell out from last time. Assholes."

"And... the garage?" Kane's voice held the same dread I was feeling. He understood. Probably loved my cars as much as I did.

"Haven't looked yet," I said shortly, wrapping my arms around myself in an attempt to ward off the coming blow.

His face softened. His arm came up as if to draw me into a hug, but he hesitated. Instead he gave my shoulder a soft reassuring squeeze. "I'll go and check it for you."

"No. Not until the tech gets here with some weapons. I don't want you going in there unarmed."

"Tech? Weapons?" Kane's gaze bounced between Hellhound and me. "What's happening?"

"Volslav somehow managed to knock out half my surveillance cameras. That's how they got in without alerting me. A tech is coming to look at them. While I was on the phone with Stemp, Arnie asked for a rifle and sidearm from Stores."

Kane's face pinched for a bare instant before smoothing into his impassive cop face. "Good. I'm sorry I can't bring firepower to the game anymore."

My heart smote me, and I forced a grin. "Except that your entire body is a lethal weapon."

He shrugged. "Not much good against bullets." His gaze swept the room again as he processed the implications with his usual keenness. "So I assume they were looking for the ultrasound weapon they tried to get from us in November?"

"That's what I'm guessing. They didn't take anything, as far as I can tell. And they didn't vandalize unnecessarily; just tore apart everything that could have hidden a bottle-sized weapon."

"Professionals."

I sighed. "'Fraid so."

"Well." Kane squared his shoulders and headed for the kitchen. "I assume your garbage bags are somewhere in the vicinity of where they used to be under the kitchen sink?"

"Probably. But I was thinking of just setting the house on fire and claiming the insurance money." When he shot me an uncertain look over his shoulder, I added, "Kidding. Kind of."

"Want us to do the same as the last coupla times,

darlin'?" Arnie inquired as he went over to help Kane search. "Chuck the busted stuff an' lay out what's left so ya can take stock?"

"Sure, you know the drill. Thanks."

Kane looked up, frowning. "The last couple of times? How many times has this happened?" His frown deepened. "And where was I while you were dealing with it?"

"You were working. And this is the third time." I aimed a not-too-vicious kick at a milk carton lying in a crusty pool of its former contents. "And every time it was because of that same damn weapon. I'm getting really fucking sick of this."

The sound of an approaching engine picked up my pulse. "Stay down," I commanded, drawing my Glock.

Kane and Hellhound exchanged a glance that made it clear neither of them was pleased with the order, but they stayed hunkered behind the kitchen cabinets anyway.

I crouched at the corner by the front door, gun at the ready.

The squeak-clang of my gate sounded, followed by a brief engine rumble and a second squeak-clang as the gate closed behind the vehicle. A few moments later, tires crunched outside.

"Prob'ly the tech," Hellhound muttered. "Ain't tryin' to sneak up."

I nodded, but none of us relaxed.

The vibration of my phone made me twitch. I pulled it out and studied the text message: 'Tech outside. Clear to enter?'

I texted back, 'Come in', and dropped the phone back into my pocket to keep both hands free for my gun. Trust was just a little beyond my abilities at the moment.

There was a timid tap at the door. After a momentary

pause, the door eased open and a slight towheaded figure advanced cautiously into the entry.

At the sight of my gun he blanched and flung both hands in the air. "I'm your tech!" His eyes widened with inspiration behind thick glasses. "Wait, I'll show you my ID!" He plunged his hand into his parka pocket and jerked out a Sirius fob, thrusting it at me.

"Thanks," I said, holstering my Glock as I stood. "Just a word of advice: If you come into a room where somebody's holding a gun, don't dive into your pocket like you're going for a weapon. You might not live long enough to pull out your ID."

He went even paler. "S-sorry, I d-didn't... sorry."

"It's okay. Listen..." I consulted the fob still trembling in his outstretched hand. "Christopher... If something like this ever happens again, just have your ID in your hand when you go in. Or if you forget to do that, say you're a tech, keep your hands in the air, and tell them your ID's in your pocket. Let them get it, or if they tell you to show it to them, just move slowly and tell them what you're doing every step of the way."

He nodded vigorously. "Okay. Th-Thanks. I will." His fair complexion turned crimson and his gaze dropped to his boots. "I thought I was being so smart leaving the guns in the car so you wouldn't think I was a threat."

Hellhound and Kane had risen, and Hellhound came over, towering over the young man. "Car unlocked?" he rasped.

Christopher gulped. "Y-yes."

Hellhound strode out without another word.

"I *so* screwed up," Christopher mumbled miserably.

My heart went out to him. "It's okay. It was smart not to

bring the weapons in with you, especially if you're not used to handling them."

"I'm not," he said shyly, still studying his boots. "Director Stemp had to give me a special one-time clearance. I don't think he wanted to because I'm so new, but I was the only one available."

Hellhound returned bearing a rifle case and a handgun carry-bag, and Christopher glanced up at him fearfully before lowering his gaze again. "I'm sorry, Mr. Helmand. If I ever do this again, I'll make sure I lock the car, I promise."

"See that ya do," Hellhound growled. "Mistake like that coulda killed us all."

"I'm s-sorry." Poor Christopher looked absolutely wretched, his face flaming.

Hellhound relented immediately. "It's okay. Nothin' bad happened, an' you'll know for next time." He thumped the young man gently on the shoulder and made for the table, where he laid down the rifle case and extracted a Sig and shoulder holster from the carry-bag.

As he strapped on the holster, Christopher edged closer. "I got you a Sig Sauer P226R," he said diffidently. "I asked the Stores clerk which was your favourite weapon but he said he didn't know."

If I hadn't happened to glance over at Kane, I would have missed the instant he stiffened. An eye-blink later he was back to picking up garbage as though he hadn't heard the exchange.

My heart hurt for him. The P226R had been his weapon of choice before he quit the Department. If he were still an agent, he'd have taken charge of this situation as soon as he came in the door. He would be clearing my garage with his Sig, not scraping rotten lunch meat off my kitchen floor.

Everything about this must feel wrong to him.

Back at the table, Hellhound shrugged. "My favourite weapon is any weapon that works." He slapped the magazine into the gun, jacking the slide before he tucked the weapon into the holster.

"The clerk said you've fired every gun that's ever been made." Christopher gazed up at him with shining eyes.

Hellhound grunted amusement. "He's full a' shit."

"Oh." The young man looked crestfallen. "So... that story about how you killed a gunrunner with a blowgun disguised as a cigar..." Colour rose in his cheeks again. "Never mind. He was just making fun of me."

"Nah, that one's true." Hellhound glanced over at me. "Let's go clear that garage, darlin'. Doubt if anybody's in there by now, but..." He shrugged.

I nodded and followed him to the back door, my stomach knotting with dread.

CHAPTER 15

The few steps between my house and garage seemed to take forever. At the garage door, Hellhound and I exchanged a glance, weapons at the ready.

I laid my hand on the knob, and he gave me a jerk of his chin.

Heart pounding, I flung the door open and lunged sideways into a crouch behind my truck. The overhead lights flared on courtesy of Hellhound.

Silence greeted us.

From behind my big tool chest, Hellhound nodded, covering me as I popped my head up to peek into the truck cab.

Empty.

I did the same for the box topper.

Also empty.

My half-rebuilt '53 Chevy was easy to clear, since I'd removed the seats and the interior was open from dashboard to trunk. At last I let out a breath of abject relief when I discovered my 1966 Corvette unscathed.

"All clear, darlin'." Hellhound came up behind me, slipping his arms around my waist as I laid trembling hands on the 'Vette's undamaged convertible top.

"They didn't hurt your babies," Hellhound murmured.

"Thank God I leave the doors unlocked so they didn't have to slash the top to get in." I leaned into his warm strength, finally allowing myself to assess the extent of the destruction.

The contents of my carefully-organized shelves had been swept off onto the floor. All the cabinets had vomited their contents. The beer fridge...

"Aw, darlin'." Hellhound's voice was heavy with emotion as he regarded the smashed bottles and sticky residue that marked the final resting place of some delicious craft beer. "Now that's just fuckin' tragic."

"I know." I swallowed hard. "And I could really use a beer right now. Or ten."

"Tell ya what." Arnie turned me to face him, linking his arms lightly around my waist. "Let's blow this joint. You're bagged, ya gotta be starvin' by now, an' there's nothin' we gotta do here that ain't gonna keep for tomorrow. Let's go get some supper an' drinks at Eddy's an' then go to the hotel for the night."

I hesitated. "That sounds great, but... should I really be going anywhere public? If Volslav is serious about getting rid of me, an awful lot of people could get caught in the crossfire."

Hellhound frowned. "Doubt it. When I'm on a job, I stay away from people whenever I can, 'less it's a crowd big enough to hide in. Remember, it ain't just about gettin' the job done, it's about not gettin' caught. As long's they don't know where you're goin' or when, they can't set up in advance."

"And I'm guessing Volslav works with professionals." I sighed. "I never thought I'd be grateful to be stalked by a professional assassin. Okay, let's go."

When we came in through the back door, Kane's shoulders relaxed as he surveyed my face. "All clear?"

"Yeah. Same mess as in here, but they didn't hurt my cars."

Kane's smile mirrored mine. "That's good. Anything else can be replaced." He nodded at the young tech hovering near the front door. "Christopher needs to access the cameras but I wouldn't let him go outside until someone was available to cover him."

"Oh, good. Thanks." I wearily drew my Glock again. The G26 was a tiny lightweight gun, but it seemed to be getting heavier and heavier.

"Stay here, darlin', I'll do it." Hellhound strode over to the table and appropriated the night vision and infrared goggles. He shot a look at Christopher as he headed for the door. "Stay inside 'til I tell ya it's clear."

He slipped outside and I took up a position beside the door, gun in hand. I was pretty sure nobody was out there, but if bullets started flying I could at least provide some covering fire so Arnie could get back inside.

My blood chilled. If a professional sniper was out there, Arnie would be dead in a single shot.

When the door opened and he stuck his head inside, it was all I could do not to fling arms around him.

"All clear," he said to the tech. "Come an' do your camera thing."

As they went out, Kane came over to lay a hand on my shoulder. "Come and sit down," he said gently. "You're white as a sheet." He took my hand, gauging its tremor. "And you need food. I've found an unbroken bowl, and I'll heat up some canned soup for you."

"It's okay, don't bother," I objected. "As soon as

Christopher is done, we're all going to Eddy's for supper. I'll buy."

"Eddy's sounds fine, but it'll be a while." Kane guided me over to the kitchen table and righted a chair for me. "Sit. The soup can be your appetizer."

Too exhausted and wrung out to argue, I dropped into the chair and sagged back in it, closing my eyes.

It seemed only seconds later when Kane spoke again. "Aydan, your soup is ready."

I dragged my eyes open to see a steaming bowl of cream of mushroom soup on the table in front of me. "Thanks," I mumbled, then managed a smile. "You found crackers."

He smiled back. "Some of them are even intact."

"Won't matter, where they're going." I started spooning soup.

A few minutes later Hellhound and Christopher returned. Laying out four cameras on the kitchen counter, the young tech went to work with his diagnostic equipment.

After probing the cameras' innards to the accompaniment of small electronic beeps, Christopher looked up. "I want to take them back to Sirius and check them better, but it looks as though they got fried with some kind of electromagnetic pulse. Are any of your other electronics dead?"

I waved a hand at the mess around us. "How would I know?"

He flushed. "I guess. But a pulse big enough to knock out all these cameras at once should have fried pretty well everything in the house. Are your phones okay?" He appropriated a handset from the floor and pressed the button. "Seems fine. Do you have a computer?"

"I had my laptop with me, but my desktop is in the back

bedroom."

He hurried down the hall only to return a few moments later, looking puzzled. "It's fine. And one of the cameras that got knocked out was in the eaves right outside where your computer was. Anything that fried the camera should have fried your computer, too."

I spooned the last of the soup from my bowl and shrugged. "No idea. I leave that stuff to you guys."

His brow furrowed. "Hm. Well, I'll take these back to the lab. And I'd like to come back here in daylight and have a look around outside. In the meantime, I have some replacement cameras in the car, but..." He trailed off.

"But what?" I asked with a sense of impending doom.

"Um, nothing, really. They'll work fine. It's just that if it really was an EMP that took out these cameras, it'll take out the new ones, too. I think we should put Faraday cages around-"

I held up a hand to silence him before he could overload my tired brain with tech-talk. "Whatever you think is best. We're not staying here tonight, so I'm not worried about it."

He brightened. "Okay, good. That gives me more time to figure this out. I'll touch base with you tomorrow at Sirius." As he headed for the door, Hellhound put out a restraining hand.

"Hang on. Lemme check outside again, an' then I'll ride with ya to the gate an' let ya out." He turned to Kane and me. "We might as well all go together." He tossed me his keys. "Bring the Forester an' I'll get in at the gate."

As I moved automatically to the sink to rinse my bowl, Kane took it out of my hand. "It can wait. Come on. You drive out ahead and I'll follow you in my vehicle."

A few minutes later I idled slowly down my lane at the

wheel of Hellhound's Forester, scanning the hillside and the trees by the creek with my infrared goggles. I didn't spot any threatening glows, but the Forester drifted perilously close to the deep snowbanks beside my lane until I jerked my attention back to where I was steering the vehicle.

When I halted at the gate, Hellhound opened the driver's door, grinning. "Damn, darlin', thought ya were gonna plant my truck."

Slipping out of the driver's seat, I took off the goggles and gave him a kiss. "I was a bit distracted." I hefted the goggles. "All clear, though."

"Good." He laid a casual arm over my shoulders and guided me around to the passenger's side.

I wasn't fooled. His body was between me and the shooter's potential location at all times. With the door shut safely behind me, he hurried back to the driver's seat and had the vehicle in gear almost before his own door closed.

When we pulled into the parking lot at Blue Eddy's, I glanced around with chagrin. "Shit, I forgot it's Thursday. I've never seen it so busy this early before."

Hellhound frowned. "That's weird. It's only seven. Jam doesn't start 'til eight; an' the joint doesn't usually start jumpin' 'til nine."

"I thought there seemed to be a lot more pedestrians around than usual, too." My heart sank. "Shit, maybe there's a hockey tournament or something this weekend. I hope the hotel isn't full."

"Guess we'll find out." Hellhound unbuckled his seatbelt and got out casually, but I had noticed his sharp gaze evaluating the parking lot and surrounding buildings for potential threats.

Letting out a small breath of gratitude, I followed. Between him and Kane, who had pulled in right behind us, I couldn't be safer.

Which didn't mean I was safe. Only that I was as safe as I could be under the circumstances.

I set that unpleasant thought aside and followed Hellhound's bulky figure toward the entrance while Kane brought up the rear.

Stepping into the light and warmth and noise of the bar was like entering a different world. The tables were full, and the roar of conversation almost overpowered the blues music playing over the speakers.

Behind the bar, Eddy glanced up from filling a tray of glasses. His face split in a smile of welcome, and he flashed us a quick 'hold on' signal before passing the full tray to one of the waitresses.

Ducking out from the behind the bar, Eddy made a beeline for my favourite table in the corner.

"Oh, shit, he's going to ask those guys to move." I hurried forward in an attempt to stop my friend from evicting his paying customers.

I was too late. By the time I pushed through the crowd to the table, its occupants were already rising with their drinks, and Eddy was thanking them profusely.

"Here you go," he said, looking up with a smile as the four young men departed. "I'll just send Darlene over to clean up, and you'll be all set."

"Eddy," I admonished. "Did you just offer to cover their tab if they'd move?"

He shrugged, his eyes twinkling. "I own the place. If the owner wants to move people, people move."

"With a healthy bribe." I gave his arm a quick squeeze. "Thanks, Eddy. I feel guilty, but I still appreciate it."

"Anything for my bookkeeper," he replied with a smile. "You're worth your weight in gold." Hellhound and Kane came up behind me, and Eddy glanced around our group. "Beer?" he asked me and I nodded with a grin. "Beer," he said confidently to Hellhound, who also grinned and nodded. "And..." Eddy hesitated at Kane. "Lime and soda?"

Kane smiled. "I'm not working tonight."

"Ah! I have some of that dark draft you like. Or..." Eddy gave him a conspiratorial wink. "I have a brand-new Islay single-malt behind the bar. The bottle hasn't even been opened yet."

"Perfect. Thank you." Kane gestured me toward the chairs as Eddy hurried away, and I slid into the middle one, my back to the corner.

"Snuggle in, you guys," I told them. "There's room for all of us to have our backs to a wall."

They took chairs on either side of me, and we settled in to scan the crowd.

They seemed unusually animated.

Voices rose sharply at some tables on the other side of the bar, and I revised my opinion. Not just animated. Rowdy.

I had been expecting to see mostly the young men who usually descended on the town for hockey tournaments, but this crowd seemed oddly varied. About an even mix of male and female, a wide range of ages, and some very strange outfits.

"What's going on here?" I muttered to my companions. "This isn't the regular Thursday crowd. Or the regular hockey crowd."

They both shook their heads, looking as puzzled as I felt.

After a longer-than-usual wait, the waitress wove between the crowded tables bearing our drinks. She had to stop several times as other patrons accosted her with orders, and I could imagine the complex list of food and drink accumulating in her brain as she made her way toward us.

At last she arrived, looking slightly frazzled. "Here you go," Darlene said as she rapidly unloaded our drinks. "Sorry for the wait."

"No problem," I assured her.

"Hey, Darlene," Hellhound said. "What's with the crowd? Got somebody famous playin' the jam tonight?"

She shook her head. "I wish. No, they're all the alien people. Are you eating tonight?"

We each gave her our food orders and she departed with her usual smile.

"Dunno how she does it," Hellhound said as we watched her wend her way back to the bar, collecting more orders from random tables on the way. "She never screws up."

"She must have a memory like yours," I said.

He chuckled. "Prob'ly does. But she's a helluva lot nicer'n me. I wouldn't even make it halfway back to the bar before I slapped some asshole upside the head. Look at that fucker!" He surged to his feet as a man snagged Darlene's apron and reeled her toward him.

She gave the man her professional smile and extricated herself with aplomb, nodding at his order. As she hurried back to the bar to enter the order into the computer, Hellhound threaded his way over to the man's table.

Kane and I tensed, but Hellhound only leaned down to speak quietly. The man paled and nodded, and Hellhound straightened and returned to our table.

"He won't do that again," he said with satisfaction as he took his seat.

I grinned. "Nice." The noise level ratcheted up higher, and I eyed the boisterous patrons. "I wonder what she meant by 'the alien people'. I didn't like to keep asking her questions when she was so busy."

"Well, they *could* be aliens," Kane pointed out, cocking a humorous eyebrow in the direction of a noisy group wearing outfits that appeared to be made entirely from tinfoil, hats and all.

"Maybe it's some kind of sci-fi conv-" I began, but I was interrupted by shouts from across the bar. People lunged to their feet and the yelling got louder.

My "Uh-oh" was lost in the commotion as two groups launched themselves at each other with bloodthirsty cries.

CHAPTER 16

The saloon quickly polarized into Tinfoil versus Non-Tinfoil. Only a handful of people were actually fighting, but that could change fast.

Kane and Hellhound were already in motion, converging on Eddy as he whisked a baseball bat out from under the bar. At Eddy's shout and gesture, Darlene and the other two waitresses retreated behind the shelter of the bar.

I hovered indecisively, on my feet but unwilling to blow my cover by drawing my Glock.

As the three men waded into the fracas, I was relieved to see Eddy tapping knees, not bashing heads. Yelps from the crowd and a general withdrawal marked his progress toward the fighters.

Kane and Hellhound moved purposefully into the centre of the fight, pulling combatants apart and shoving them back. A few misguided idiots tried to team up on them, only to be dropped in groaning heaps with a few lightning-fast blows.

In short order an uneasy truce descended, with the two groups snarling on opposite sides of the barrier formed by Kane, Hellhound, and Eddy's bat.

Eddy raised his voice. "You're all on video." He glared around at the crowd with an authority I rarely saw from my easy-going friend. "The police are on the way. If you settle your tabs, in cash, and get out of here and don't come back, I won't show them the video. Make four lines, one at each corner of the bar, and don't bother asking for change. If even *one* more person throws a punch, all your tabs are doubled. Now *MOVE IT!*"

Despite some grumbling, the crowd obeyed with alacrity. Eddy and the three waitresses were soon raking in handfuls of cash while Kane and Hellhound patrolled the perimeter to make sure the people fidgeting anxiously at the ends of the lines didn't get too pushy.

Fifteen minutes later the room had been deserted by everyone but the regulars. We straightened tables and picked up tipped-over chairs while the waitresses scurried around wiping spills and collecting wayward food, and soon Blue Eddy's looked like itself again.

As we finished up, Eddy came over to Kane and Hellhound. "Thanks for your help. Without you, things could have ended up a lot uglier tonight." As the RCMP officers came through the door, Eddy turned to Kane. "Do you want to coordinate with the police?"

Kane shook his head. "Sorry, it's up to you. I retired from the RCMP five months ago."

Eddy's face split into a grin. "Wow, that's great! Congratulations!" He offered Kane a handshake.

"Thank you." Kane's lips turned up as he shook Eddy's hand, but his eyes weren't smiling.

As Eddy strode over to talk to the police, the three of us took our seats again. I leaned back in my chair, willing my hand not to tremble as I took a deep swallow of beer. Beside me, Hellhound did the same with a groan.

"Are you okay?" I studied him worriedly.

"Fine. Just bagged. Long fuckin' day." He gulped some more beer.

I turned to Kane. "What about you? When those guys ganged up on you-"

"I'm still capable of defending myself against a few pathetic drunks," Kane snapped. He took a larger-than-normal swallow of scotch.

I couldn't hide my instinctive flinch. "I'm sorry, I didn't mean-"

"No, don't apologize," he interrupted again in a gentler tone, and squeezed my hand. "I'm sorry I was short with you. I'm just..."

He didn't finish the sentence, but I nodded and said, "It's okay."

Poor guy. He was worrying about me going to prison or getting killed, dealing with the knowledge that Arnie and I were married, and grieving the end of the career he'd loved. Throw in a bunch of combative morons and the adrenaline of a fight, and it was no wonder he was a little snappish.

We sat in silence, drinking and watching the waitresses finish the last of the cleanup while the blues played on in the background.

A few minutes later Darlene arrived with our food. After handing over Kane's steak sandwich and Hellhound's burger, she set my Caesar salad in front of me, accompanied by a brimming basket of hot wings. "I thought you might like a few extra," she said. "The kitchen's full of food that was ordered and paid for, and now there's nobody to eat it all." She eyed Hellhound with a smile. "I've got an extra burger set aside for you, if you want it."

He grinned back at her. "Darlin' Darlene. Have I told ya lately that I love ya?"

Kane stiffened beside me, but when I glanced over he had hidden his reaction behind a pleasant expression as he sliced into his steak sandwich.

"So is that a 'yes'?" Darlene teased Hellhound.

"That ain't just a 'yes', that's a '*hell* yes'," Hellhound informed her.

Darlene turned to Kane. "I'm pretty sure I saw another steak in there, too. Would you like it?"

He turned a smile on her that made her blush as her gaze swept over his broad shoulders and powerful chest.

"That's very kind of you, Darlene," he said. "Thank you, but no. I'm afraid I'm fighting the battle of the bulge these days." He patted his iron-hard midsection and her gaze followed the gesture downward as her cheeks went even pinker.

"I don't think you've got anything to worry about," she said, sounding a bit breathless.

"Thank you." His smile was genuine this time.

"I'll go and get that burger," Darlene squeaked, and hurried away.

Hellhound chuckled and leaned over to punch Kane in the shoulder. "Ladykiller."

Kane shot him a look. "Just like you."

Hellhound either missed the subtext or chose to ignore it. He took a gulp of beer. "Hell, when you an' I are together, the ladies don't even see me. I'm just the furniture." He let out a satisfied belch, grinning. "Ugly furniture."

I patted his leg. "But oh-so-comfortable."

He smiled and we fell silent again, concentrating on our food and watching while Eddy finished up with the police. Darlene came back with Hellhound's extra burger, as well as two large takeout bags which she bestowed on the police officers. They headed for the door, looking happy, and Eddy turned back toward our table.

"Everybody okay here?" he asked.

"We're fine," I assured him. "Thanks for the extra food."

He grinned. "You can thank those alien people the next time you see them." His expression darkened. "As long as it isn't in here."

"What's going on, anyway?" I asked. "I go out of town for two days, and all of a sudden we've got bar brawls in Blue Eddy's. Who are these 'alien people'?"

Eddy's gaze flicked over the room, apparently reassuring himself that everything was under control before he sank into the remaining chair at our table with a sigh. "Somehow word got around that somebody saw space aliens in Silverside. Less than a day later, all these wackos started showing up. Half of them want to welcome the aliens, and the other half are trying to drive the aliens away with their tinfoil getups and crystals and chanting."

I fell back in my chair and massaged my forehead. "Space aliens. You've got to be kidding."

"I wish I was. These people have been nothing but trouble, and more of them are arriving every day. The hotel's full, the campground's full even though it's supposed to be closed for the winter, and still more people keep showing up. Now they're taking up all the parking lots in town with their campers. Don't get me wrong, it's nice to have some extra business; but I can do without crap like this." Eddy waved. "Darlene!"

She halted on her way to another table. "Yes?"

"I'm going to put out the 'cover charge' sign tonight. Let the others know, please."

She nodded and hurried away.

"Cover charge?" Hellhound asked. "Ain't that gonna cut into your business for the open jam?"

Eddy gave him a grin and rose. "Not really. If we know you, we let you in for free, and all the locals know that. The sign's just for strangers."

"Ya need a bouncer?" Hellhound offered.

"No, thanks. I've never wanted to run the kind of bar that needs bouncers." Eddy's face twisted into a rueful grimace. "Even though I needed them tonight. Thanks again, guys. Your food and drinks are on the house."

Both men protested, but Eddy silenced them with a headshake and a smile. "Don't worry, I can afford it. There might have been a little extra premium on those tabs that got settled in cash." He winked. "Funny how generous people get when they're covering their butts."

"That seems fair," I said. "You deserve some hazard pay. Oh, I was going to ask you... is it okay if I come by tomorrow morning at eleven to do your books?"

"Perfect. See you then." He gave me a smile and headed back to the bar.

I drained my beer mug. "Aliens. Jeez. I'm constantly amazed by people. And not in a good way. If the hotel's full, I guess we'll be going back to my place tonight after all."

Kane swallowed his last bite of steak sandwich and pushed his plate away. "I guess there's no point in postponing the inevitable. The sooner we start digging beds out of that mess, the better." He glanced over at Hellhound, who was just biting into his second burger. "Arnie, do you want to stay for the jam? I can take Aydan back and you can come when you're ready."

"Nah, I ain't in the mood for jammin' tonight." Arnie hesitated with a quick glance between Kane and me. "Unless the two a' ya want some time to talk... or... whatever. I can hang out here for a while if ya like. How long d'ya want?"

Kane shot me an uncomfortable glance. "No, I don't have anything to say that can't be said in front of you. And I don't do..." He raised an eyebrow. "...'whatever'... with married women."

Arnie flushed, but didn't retort. Instead, he turned to me. "Aydan, d'ya want a bit a' space? I don't mind."

"No, that's fine," I said hurriedly. "I was just thinking that if I have to face that mess again tonight, I'm going to need another beer."

And if I had to deal with both of them and the unacknowledged tension between us...

"Two more beers," I amended. "I'll keep you company while you finish eating."

"Okay," he agreed, and I signalled Darlene.

An hour later I slumped in the passenger seat of Hellhound's Forester, staring dully at the darkness beyond our headlights.

"Okay, darlin'?" he asked as he accelerated onto the highway from Silverside. "Three beers is a lot when you're wiped out to start with."

"Fine." My tongue felt too big for my mouth. "Needed it."

I sensed his concerned gaze on the side of my face, but couldn't summon the energy to turn my head.

"Well, just relax, then," he said gently. "Grab a quick nap."

"Can't," I mumbled. "Rigor mortis has set in. My eyelids won't close."

He chuckled and reached over. "Go to sleep." His cupped palm brushed lightly over my forehead and down my face.

My eyes fell shut.

"Time to wake up, darlin'." Hellhound's soft rasp roused me.

I groaned. "Jus' gonna sleep inna truck t'night."

"Bad idea. It's twenty below." A gentle hand patted my face. "C'mon, Aydan, wake up. We're comin' up to your place, an' I wanna scan with the night vision an' infrared before we go closer."

"Knock yourself out," I mumbled.

"Surveillance gear's on the floor by your feet," he replied patiently. "C'mon, wake up. Nobody's gettin' shot on my watch."

Shot.

As in, snipers trying to kill me. Or worse, one of the men I loved.

I shook my head vigorously and pulled myself up out of my slouch. "Sorry. I'm awake." I put on the goggles and handed him the binoculars.

Blinking groggily, I scanned the creek, yard, and surrounding area until my eyes crossed. "I don't see anything. Do you?"

"Nah. Let's swap." He handed me the binoculars and I relinquished the goggles.

"Clear," he said a minute later. "You?"

"Clear," I agreed as he pulled into my driveway. "I'll get the gate."

Stepping out into the icy darkness felt like a brisk slap in the face. By the time Hellhound and Kane had driven through and I'd relocked the gate and scurried back to the Forester, I was wide awake.

I blew out a shivery breath. "Well, that did it. I'm all sobered up now."

Hellhound grimaced as he pulled to a stop in front of my house. "You're gonna wish ya were drunk again in a few minutes."

"Yeah," I agreed as I headed for the front door, bracing myself for what lay inside.

I had just closed the door behind us when my cell phone vibrated. I pulled it out of my waist pouch and glanced at the call display. "Oh, for shit's sake!"

"What's wrong?" Kane asked.

"Nothing. Sorry, I have to take this." I pressed the answer button. "Hi, Margaret."

"Hi, Aydan, are you okay?" Her earnest voice made me wince. "I saw them taking you out of Sirius Dynamics on a stretcher. I called Linda right away and she said you were okay, but I've been worried about you."

God, she was like the mother I'd never had. And never wanted.

"I'm sorry you were worried, and thanks for your concern," I said warmly. "It was nothing serious. I'd missed a meal and I got a bit shaky. They just took me in as a precaution."

"Oh, Aydan, that must have been so scary for you! I was expecting you to call me as soon as you got back like you promised, but I can see why you didn't feel like it if you were that sick. I wouldn't have bothered you tonight but I saw you coming out of Blue Eddy's a little while ago, so I thought I'd give you a quick call and make sure you're okay."

Nice guilt trip.

"Thanks for calling," I said through my teeth. "So, what's the verdict on your get-together?"

"Well, everyone else can make it for Saturday evening at seven. Does that work for you?"

"I'll do my best. I may have to work on the weekend because of all the time I've missed, but even if I can't make it to your place on the dot of seven, I'll get there sometime in the evening."

"We could do it a different night," she began, but I overrode her with my best attempt at politeness.

"No, of course not. You've gone to so much trouble to get everybody together. Just go ahead and start the movie without me if I'm late, and I'll catch up when I get there." I faked an exclamation of surprise. "Oh! Sorry, I've got a call coming in from the office that I have to take. I'll see you Saturday, and thanks again!" I disconnected. "Argh! That woman!"

"Friend of yours?" Kane inquired with a lift of his eyebrow.

"She wants to be. Ever since she moved to Silverside she's latched onto me like a second... shadow..." I trailed off as horrible certainty overwhelmed me. "*Shit!*"

Whisking out my bug detector, I took an instant to confirm that its light was green before I punched in Eddy's number.

When he answered, I raised my voice so he could hear me over the music in the bar. "Hi, Eddy, it's Aydan. I've got a quick question for you."

"Sure, what's up?"

"I'm just wondering, did you happen to mention to anyone that I was going to be out of town this week?"

"No." His voice took on a worried note. "Why?"

"Somebody broke into my house, and I'm trying to figure out if it was just a random thing or whether somebody actually knew I'd be gone."

"Hang up and call 911!" he said urgently. "Get in your car and wait for the police to get there!"

"No, Eddie, it's okay," I reassured him. "Sorry, I didn't mean to worry you. I found it hours ago." I crossed my fingers to dilute my upcoming lies. "The police have already been here."

"You already knew about it before you came to the bar?"

"Yeah. It wasn't a big deal," I lied again.

"Oh, good." I could hear the relief in his voice. "So nothing was taken?"

"No, it doesn't look like it." I glanced around the chaos with a mental shrug. "Like I said, Eddy, I'm sorry to have worried you. I was pretty sure you wouldn't have mentioned it to anybody, but I had to ask."

"For the police report," he said understandingly. "Of course. Well, I'm glad you're okay. If you need anything, or if I can help in any way, just let me know."

"Thanks, Eddy, you're the best."

I said my goodbyes and hung up, then dialled Lola and had almost exactly the same conversation. As soon as I disconnected from Lola, I hit the speed dial on my secured phone.

When Stemp's crisp 'yes' came over the line, I blurted, "I know how Volslav knew I'd be gone!"

CHAPTER 17

"The woman's name is Margaret Young," I told Stemp. "She moved here nine months ago and she's been trying to get close to me ever since. She's the only one besides Lola and Eddy who knew I was going out of town, and the other two didn't mention it to anyone. I'll talk to the analyst-on-call and get them to investigate her right away, but I wanted to let you know first."

"What is your status? Do you need backup?"

"I'm at home, and Kane and Hellhound are here. Hellhound and I are armed. We should be fine unless Volslav starts shelling us with long-range artillery or something."

"Knowing Volslav's reputation, that is not beyond the realm of possibility. Come back to Silverside and spend the night in the secondary bunker. Until we know more, I'm not willing to risk your safety."

My heart sank. "Is it okay if Kane and Hellhound stay there, too? The hotel is full and they don't have any other place to go."

Stemp hesitated.

I braced myself for his refusal. After all, John was a civilian now. And Arnie was an asset, not an agent. Dammit, how could I convince Stemp-

"Very well, bring them."

I barely prevented myself from blurting, 'Really?'

"Thanks," I said instead.

"No thanks necessary. They can help you move your business into the vacant office space with Spider's Webb Design."

"Uh...what?"

"The office space Kane used to use for his petroleum consultant cover. It's optimal to have it occupied by an agent with your security clearance, and it will aid your cover as a bookkeeper. I'll have the exterior signage updated as soon as possible. What name would you like on the sign?"

"Um... I don't really have a business name. I guess it could just say 'Aydan's Bookkeeping' or something."

"Very well. The door keys will be ready for you to pick up at the Sirius security wicket in ten minutes. I'll expect your office equipment to be substantially moved in by morning. Is there anything else?"

My jaw opened and closed a couple of times, but my beer-blurred brain refused to supply anything useful. "Um, no, that's it, I guess. I'll call the analyst now."

"I'll transfer you."

The line clicked in my ear, and a moment later the analyst-on-call's crisp voice spoke in my ear. "Belling."

Still trying to recover from Stemp's breakneck thought process, I mumbled, "Hi, Trish, it's Aydan."

"What can I do for you?"

I shook my mind into gear. "I need you to dig deep on a woman who's been trying to get close to me. I think she's working with Volslav. The name she's using is Margaret Young. She moved to Silverside about nine months ago and she lives over on Elm Street. I don't remember the house number, but it's a little yellow bungalow with green trim, on the west side of the street in the middle of the block between Walnut and Willow Avenue."

"I'll find it. What else?"

"She claims to be a widowed housewife, so she probably won't have any work records. She sells kitchen and household products from her home for one of those pyramid-type organizations, but I can't remember the name of it. She's fiftyish, but I don't know her exact age. Since she moved here, she's been joining some of the local organizations and making friends with my friends and clients. She joined the Chamber of Commerce and CRAPS."

"Craps? What's that?"

"Citizen's Reconnaissance And Protection Services. CRAPS. Lola Ives runs it, with her merry band of geriatric snoops."

"Lola Ives." I could hear the chuckle in Trish's voice. "I should have known. Anything else?"

"I think Margaret is a professional. She didn't just zoom in on me as soon as she got here, she came at me obliquely through her friendships with Lola and Linda. Shit, and she's been at Tom's place a few times that I know of, maybe more. That's the farm directly south of mine. Tom Rossburn. He's a bachelor and I figured she was making a play for him, but maybe it was an excuse to get close to my place." I hesitated. "That's about all I know, I guess. I've been avoiding her because..." I trailed off, not wanting to admit that I was an antisocial hag.

"Gut feeling," Trish finished for me.

"Yeah." I agreed gratefully. "Oh, and she drives a silver Honda Civic."

"I'll have a preliminary report for you by tomorrow

morning. Deeper dive will take longer, but I've flagged it for priority."

"Thanks, Trish. Have a good night."

"You, too."

I disconnected and mumbled, "Not bloody likely."

Kane and Hellhound had been listening intently during my recital, and Kane said, "Good catch, Aydan."

"Not really," I growled. "I should have checked her as soon as she started getting pushy. And I probably wouldn't have thought of it at all if it hadn't been for something Holt said a couple of days ago."

At least I'd been luckier than Holt. So far.

"So, we goin' somewhere tonight?" Hellhound inquired.

With a sigh, I shoved aside the nearest pile of debris with my foot. "Yep. The bunker under John's old office. And in exchange for letting both of you stay there tonight, Stemp expects us to move all my office equipment in there by tomorrow morning." I applied an ungentle foot to the next heap. "Might as well clear a path. We're going to be making a few trips."

An hour later, the last fizzy bubbles of my earlier inebriation floated sadly away into the icy darkness.

I leaned on the tailgate of my truck, willing my eyes to stay open. "That's good enough for tonight."

"Are you sure?" Kane asked. "We could bring your filing cabinet."

"No; the last time I was at Spider's office, your old office furniture was still there. I'll use that filing cabinet. And it's going to take me a while to sort through that mess..." I jerked my chin in the direction of my house. "...and pull together my paper files anyway. Some of them are business and some are personal, so I'll still need a filing cabinet at home. I'll use Spider's printer, so mine can stay here."

I straightened with a groan and slammed the tailgate. "Stemp left the keys for me at the Sirius security desk. I'll meet you there."

Hellhound raised an eyebrow at Kane. "Ya wanna take point, or six?"

"Six," Kane replied. "Lead the way."

Our little convoy moved out with Hellhound in the lead, then me in my truck, then Kane bringing up the rear in his Expedition. Somehow I managed to stay awake for the fifteen-minute drive back to Silverside.

Kane, Hellhound, and I made short work of transferring my business paraphernalia out of the back of my truck and into the small converted house that had just become the office for my cover identity. Propping my tired self against the doorframe, I eyed my new domain.

"Well, this is probably going to be a big pain in the ass, but at least it's done." I turned to the other two. "Let's leave our vehicles in the Sirius lot tonight. I don't want to attract any more attention here than necessary."

"Good plan," Kane agreed. "We can go in through Sirius and come back here via the tunnels."

Hooray. Nothing like a nice three-block walk through subterranean catacombs, ending with a night in a crypt. I didn't actually groan out loud, but my face must have betrayed my feelings.

Hellhound slipped an arm around my shoulders. "Hang in there, darlin'. Just a few more minutes an' ya can go to sleep. You're so bagged, ya won't even know you're underground."

"I hope you're right." I plodded toward the door.

I knew I was underground.

My heart started hammering as soon as the door to the time-delay chamber closed behind us. The chamber felt too damn small even when I was alone. The two big men took up all the available breathing space.

I made it down the stairs and into the corridor below without screaming, but barely.

"Okay, darlin'?" Hellhound asked worriedly as we strode along.

"Okay."

I was pretty sure both he and Kane knew that my breathlessness wasn't due to exertion, but neither of them commented.

After following the twists and turns of the tunnel for what seemed like far longer than three blocks, we were confronted by a featureless door.

Even though I knew we weren't trapped, the walls of the dead end seemed to be closing inward. I took a jerky step forward and bent for the retinal scan. The door swung open, and I hesitated on the threshold.

Another thirty-second time delay chamber.

It looked like a prison cell.

"Aydan." Kane's quiet voice made me jump. "You can do this. You know where all the exits are. You aren't trapped."

I tried to swallow, but my mouth was too dry. "I know." My voice came out in a papery whisper. "I'm fine."

Summoning all my courage, I stepped into the chamber.

"D'ya want us to wait 'til ya clear it?" Hellhound asked.

"You can't," I croaked. "Your fobs will work for the regular doors, but your retinal scans won't work on the time delays."

"Mine will," Hellhound countered. "Whenever I'm on a job I get full clearance down here, to get to the Weapons Lab an' the armory. Guy at the wicket told me Stemp cleared me for tonight."

I let out a breath. "Okay, good."

The door swung shut on their worried expressions, and I hurried across the few feet to activate the second scan.

A too-long thirty seconds later, the latch released and I sprang forward. As I emerged into a nearly-dark corridor, the motion-activated lights flickered on. The air smelled flat and stale even though I could hear the reassuring hum of the HVAC system.

Conscious of the surveillance cameras watching my every move, I managed to contain the panicky urge to flail my arms. Instead I hurried down the corridor, emerging with a breath of relief into the large open work area at the end.

A minute later Kane and Hellhound rounded the corner and stopped at the entrance to the room.

"Okay, darlin'?" Hellhound asked.

Sinking into a chair at the big worktable, I managed a smile. "I promise I'm not going to freak out. It's safe to come near me."

"How about a cup of chamomile tea?" Kane asked, heading for the tiny kitchenette. "Webb probably still has some here."

"That sounds good, thanks."

"Coffee, Arnie?" Kane asked as he disappeared inside.

"Sure. Thanks." Hellhound ambled over and sat beside me. He lowered his voice. "He's better now that he's got somethin' to do."

"Yeah," I agreed softly. "He feels at home here. I wonder how many hours he's spent down here over the course of his career? This must really suck for him. All the things he's used to doing without a second thought, he can't. No weapons, no security clearances..."

Arnie's brow furrowed. "I dunno if he's gonna be able to do this Dad thing. I mean, he'd walk through fire for his kid, but fuck. What's he gonna do all day? 'Specially now that he only has Dan every second day."

Kane emerged from the kitchenette bearing two mugs in one hand and a third in the other, and I raised my voice to normal levels. "Arnie was just saying you've got Daniel every second day now. How's it working out?"

"All right so far." Kane placed the mugs in front of us. "On school days one of us picks Daniel up at school and takes care of dinner and homework and whatever activities he might have, and he stays the night. The next morning he gets dropped off at school, and the other parent takes over to pick him up that night. On weekends he's scheduled to move between our houses around ten AM, but we live close enough that he usually runs back and forth a few times a day. Alicia and I alternate so we each get half of his regularly scheduled activities on a two-week rotation. This week my days are Monday, Wednesday, Friday, and Sunday; and next week I'll have him on Tuesday, Thursday, and Saturday."

I took a warm, soothing sip of chamomile. "Are you still volunteering at Daniel's school?"

"Yes, that keeps me... busy."

Noting his hesitation, I asked, "Does it? Have you thought of doing anything else?"

Kane grimaced. "For the past five months I've been

struggling with that." He hesitated again. "I... this can't go any farther than the three of us, but... I..." His fist clenched on the handle of his coffee mug. "Don't get me wrong, being a father is a dream come true, but..." His knuckles whitened. "I... need more."

As if the admission had broken the floodgates, his words poured out. "I can't do this. I can't just sit there! When I have Daniel I'm busy and involved, but... and I do want to be an involved parent... but to be completely wrapped up in your child to the extent that it's your entire identity..." He shook his head. "It's not healthy. Not for me or for Daniel. I have to *do* something! I had everything unpacked and the whole house organized in the first week. What do I do now?"

My heart clenched at the desperation in his voice. "How about that book you were working on?"

"Finished," he said flatly. "Writing and illustrating a children's book was really just a substitute for having a child of my own. Now that I have Daniel..." He shrugged. "I self-published the book. I'm proud of it, but I never really wanted to be an author. And anyway, I already spend too much time sitting around. I'm out of shape. Getting soft."

"No, you're not," I disagreed. "You're more ripped than I've ever seen you. You're taking out your frustration at the gym, aren't you?"

Kane let out a breath and slumped in the chair. "Yes. But I still feel as though... it's all slipping away. I'm losing my edge. In another few months, I won't even be able to pass requalification testing."

"Bullshit," Hellhound growled. "Ya could pass that in your fuckin' sleep."

"Are you... thinking of requalifying?" I asked cautiously.

"Y... No..." Kane blew out a forceful breath. "I always

swore I would quit active duty if I ever had a family. It's not fair to Daniel to have a father who vanishes with no warning and no indication of when he might be back. It wouldn't be fair to expect Alicia to pick up the burden of fulltime childcare again on a moment's notice. And it wouldn't be fair to the job. I don't have the focus anymore." He grimaced. "I have too much to lose now."

"So you're stuck." Hellhound's blunt words landed in the silence with a metaphorical thud.

Kane gave him a humorless smile. "I'm stuck. Daniel comes first, full stop. And that means my career as an agent is over."

We sat in glum silence.

"Well." Kane rose. "Thank you for listening. I knew from the start that this would be a difficult adjustment, and I'll figure it out. Both of you look exhausted. Why don't you head for the bunkroom?"

I drained my mug. "Are you sure? We're here for you. Let's talk this out."

"Thank you, but not tonight," he said firmly. "Go to bed."

Rising, I hid a gaping yawn behind my hand. "At least we can all sleep instead of rotating one of us on guard duty through the night."

"Yes," Kane agreed. He hesitated and glanced around at the cameras silently recording us. "Stemp never does anything without some underlying strategy. I wonder when we'll discover his true motive."

CHAPTER 18

I was dragged awake by the irritating beeping of my cell phone's alarm.

In the bunk below me, Hellhound let out an aborted snore. "Wha...? S'mornin' awready?"

"Go back to sleep," I murmured. "I have to go to work, but you don't."

He grunted and resettled, his breathing slowing and deepening.

A glance across the room showed that Kane had already vacated his bunk. It had been remade with military precision, with no sign it had ever been occupied.

I twisted and slithered over the edge of the bunk. As my feet touched the floor, a warm hand traced up the contours of my bare leg.

"Nice legs, darlin'," Hellhound mumbled.

Tugging down the hem of the T-shirt I'd worn as a makeshift nightgown, I leaned down to drop a kiss on his lips. "Hold that thought."

"Damn, darlin', I been holdin' that thought for a day an' a half," he teased, grinning. "I dunno about this. We used to get it on a lot more before we got married."

I chuckled. "Welcome to married life. Nothing to hold but good thoughts." I nodded toward his crotch. "Or yourself."

"Ya could hold it for me." Mischief glinted in his heavy-lidded eyes. "Maybe even rub it a bit."

"I'd love to, but..."

I trailed off as he shifted in the bed, widening his legs. My gaze snagged on the rise of his erection under the thin blanket, and desire punched me low in the belly. Before I could stop it, my hand traced down over his chest and abs...

"Shit," I croaked, and pulled my hand back before I could start something both of us wanted to finish. "I'd really, *really* love to, but there's this international arms dealer who's probably trying to kill me..."

"It's okay, darlin', I'm just teasin' ya." Arnie took my hand and brushed a kiss over my knuckles. "Go do what ya gotta do." He nodded downward. "This'll be ready for ya whenever ya want it."

"I want it now."

"Music to my ears." He turned me gently toward the door and patted my ass. "Hit the shower."

I sighed and obeyed.

When I emerged into the workroom showered and dressed, Kane was sitting at the table with a coffee mug in front of him.

It was strange to see him doing nothing. No screens alight on the computers that lined the walls. No documents spread across the large table. No sense of controlled urgency.

Even though I knew he'd longed for and welcomed fatherhood, my pulse ticked up in panic-by-proxy at the thought of being trapped in that life sentence. I ducked into the kitchenette to hide my reaction. When I emerged a few minutes later munching on a not-quite-stale granola bar,

Kane gave me a twisted smile.

"Not much of a honeymoon."

I shrugged. "Not a big deal, since it wasn't a real wedding."

His gaze sharpened. "What do you mean? Aren't you legally married?"

"Yes, just not... emotionally married."

His expression went grim.

"Besides," I went on hurriedly, trying to lighten the mood. "I'm under surveillance." I tapped the small pouch around my neck containing the Holter monitor, which was presumably still recording my heart function. "I have to write down anything that raises my heart rate. A honeymoon is far more information than I want to share with Dr. Roth."

Kane's lips jerked up into a wooden smile, not-too-effectively concealing his grimace.

Shit, the last thing he needed right now was to be thinking about Arnie and me raising our heart rates as husband and wife.

"Are you okay?" The stupid question fell from my lips before I could stop it.

"Of course," Kane said firmly. "I have a son who means the world to me, good friends who are always ready to offer a listening ear, a father who is still in good health and is delighted to visit as often as he can, my own home, and financial independence thanks to my pension and savings. I'm lucky to be in a position where I can take as much time as I need to decide what I want to do with the rest of my life. It doesn't get much better than that."

The speech sounded as though he'd memorized it while sitting there drinking his coffee alone. His smile might have looked genuine to someone who didn't know him, but it didn't warm the troubled grey of his eyes. His gaze was raw with longing as it swept the familiar surroundings that would be forever off-limits to him.

In a desperate attempt to distract him, I blurted out the first thought that came into my mind. "Would you teach me martial arts?"

Kane blinked, obviously caught off-guard by the non sequitur. Then his brows drew together in a puzzled frown. "Are you flirting with me?"

"Wha...? *No!*"

The indignation in my denial took me by surprise. Ordinarily I would have been thinking about how much I'd enjoy getting sweaty with him, but it hadn't crossed my mind this time.

Apparently Kane was surprised, too. His eyebrows rose.

"All right," he said cautiously. "Then why are you asking me this? I know hand-to-hand combat isn't included in your requalification testing because of your deep cover, but I've seen you in action. We both know you don't need self-defence training. And the one time we did do a short session..."

He didn't complete the sentence. He didn't need to. I could already feel the blush spreading up my face.

"Okay, I know things got, um..." I racked my brain for a polite way to admit I had humped his arm like a chihuahua in heat. "A little, um... heated... that time. But that wasn't what I was thinking. They took my gun away in Leavenworth, and I realized how helpless I am without it..."

Kane waited, arms crossed, skeptical eyebrow raised.

Fuck.

"Look," I burst out. "I know you think I can handle myself, but..."

His expression was closing down. He wouldn't believe me if I insisted on telling him the truth yet again: That my only martial arts training consisted of a few muay thai videos I'd watched on the internet.

Inspiration arrived at last.

"I need to develop my cover," I said. "Aydan Kelly the bookkeeper is going to take up martial arts. She doesn't know a thing about it, but it needs to be plausible if she busts out some ninja move she shouldn't know. So I need official martial arts training."

"If you're looking for official training, I can give you the names of a couple of good dojos in Calgary."

I gave up. "Forget it, it was a stupid idea. I don't get down to Calgary often enough to train at a dojo, or to practice with you." I turned and headed for the corridor, adding over my shoulder, "I have to get to work. See you later."

"Of course it's not stupid, I didn't mean... Aydan, wait."

The walls were closing in.

I turned, walking backward as I gave him a fake smile. "Sorry, I'm late and I really have to go. Give me a call at Sirius when you and Arnie decide on your plans for the day."

I tossed off a jaunty salute and fled.

This time the delay chamber felt like a sanctuary. As the door closed behind me with a muffled thud, I let out a slow breath and eased my shoulders down from around my ears.

The long corridor back to Sirius was pleasantly unpopulated. I found myself dawdling, reluctant to trade this serene white place for the threats of the world above. And the complications of the bunker behind me.

Maybe I could just stay here...

My claustrophobia returned full-force. Nope, not

happening.

I hurried for the stairs.

When I strode into my office a few minutes later, Spider was already sitting in the armchair next to my small sofa.

"I'm sorry I'm late," I told him. "I was..." I trailed off with a helpless shrug. "Everything's a bit complicated right now."

Spider glanced warily at the open doorway and lowered his voice. "You mean... Dermott?"

My stomach clenched. "What about Dermott?"

"You haven't heard?" Spider's face pinched with misery. "Stemp flew overseas this morning to coordinate with Interpol. Dermott's back in charge."

"Oh God." I fell onto the sofa, clutching my head. "Spider, my gun's in my ankle holster. Please take it out and put a bullet in my brain. No; two, for good measure. Right away, before this day can get any worse."

"Aydan, *no!*"

I glanced up to see his anguished hazel eyes burning in a chalk-white face.

"It's okay," I reassured him hastily. "I was only kidding."

His colour came back in a flood. "Thank goodness. Please don't ever joke about that."

"I'm sorry." Leaning over, I took his bony hand and squeezed it. It was ice-cold, and I folded my other hand over top, trying to warm him. "I didn't mean to upset you. Is there... is something else bothering you?"

"No, I just..." He hesitated. "I guess, with the baby coming, it's just that... life means a bit more to me now. I know you risk your life all the time, and I hate that you have to do it, but the thought that you'd intentionally..." He trailed off and shuddered.

"I'm sorry," I repeated penitently. "I really was only joking. Just my twisted sense of humour."

"It's okay." He squeezed my hand before releasing it to reach for his laptop. "I guess we'd better get started. Holt was here earlier, and he said to message him when we were ready." Spider's fingers were flying over the keyboard while he spoke. "There," he added a moment later. "He should be here in a few minutes. What do you want me to use for an internet search to call you back if you get lost?"

"I don't know. You pick. I'm too tired to think."

He frowned. "If you're that tired, we shouldn't be doing this. Especially since you haven't been cleared for duty yet." He nodded at the heart monitor's small pouch suspended from my neck.

"I'm not that tired. I got a solid eight hours of sleep last night; it's just that I'm recovering from the two nights before that. I'll be fine. And I really want to know what Volslav's up to." I grimaced. "And who else is going to get killed by their new ultrasound weapon. Has your team unearthed any more information?"

"Some. The good news is, no more African presidents have died of heart attacks or strokes recently. We got the surveillance footage from the airport and we're narrowing down who the speaker might have been. We'll probably have facial recognition pretty soon."

"If the speaker is even in the database," I said gloomily. "And even if we find out who it was, that's just the start of the investigation to figure out who sent them, who their next target is, and when they're planning to kill him or her."

Holt strode in as I spoke the last sentence. "Brock and Mellor have been watching for more conversations or fragments like the one you found, too. Nothing yet." He dropped into the other armchair. "So I hear you've got a new *friend*." He gave sarcastic emphasis to the word.

I grimaced. "Yeah. Thanks to you, I realized what Margaret was before she could do anything worse than ratting out my movements to Volslav." I hesitated. "Or whoever it was who trashed my house. I'm assuming it's Volslav. I sure as hell hope it isn't somebody else."

Holt frowned. "What do you mean 'thanks to me'? I wasn't even there."

"Something you said the other day made me think of it." Assuming he wouldn't want me to blab his story, I didn't elaborate.

His face cleared. "Oh. Okay."

I turned to Spider. "Ready?"

"Yes, but that reminds me... have you looked at your email yet this morning?"

Tension squeezed my belly. "No, should I have?"

"Well, yeah, probably. I mean, you should always check your email first thing." He flushed. "I'm not trying to tell you how to do your job. I was just asking because Trish and the night team found some more information on Ms. Young and I wondered if you'd seen it yet."

"No. Sorry," I mumbled, feeling like an idiot. "I should probably look at that right away."

"It's okay, I can give you a summary," Spider reassured me. "Margaret Young is a private investigator."

I blinked. "That's... interesting. She didn't mention that to me. Did you find any connection with Volslav?"

"No." Spider grimaced. "As far as we can see, she's squeaky-clean. She was a police officer for ten years before she retired from the force, and then she switched to private investigation. She's been a licensed private investigator for fourteen years. She joined the Alberta Association of Private Investigators, that's their professional association, when she opened her business; and she's been a member in good standing ever since. No complaints from clients, no suspensions or complaints from the professional association, nothing. She's even served on their board."

"Oh." My heart sank.

Former police officer. I didn't want to believe she could have gone bad. But maybe something had happened to make her desperate.

"Any money problems?" I asked. "Debts? Kids or lovers with debts? Gambling or drug habits?"

"No sign of anything like that. She has healthy savings, a comfortable RSP, and no mortgage, plus she has her police pension. Her husband was a police officer, too, and her kids are in their thirties, married with kids of their own, and apparently doing fine."

"Kids in their thirties? How old is she?"

"Fifty-four. She and her husband had their first child a couple of months after they both graduated Grade 12. They got their university degrees while working and bringing up their two children. Her husband joined the police force at twenty-six and Margaret joined at thirty, when their kids were pre-teens. When her husband was killed in the line of duty, Margaret quit the police force at age forty." Spider gave a frustrated shrug. "We got a warrant to hack into her computer, but there's only personal stuff on it, plus the bookkeeping from her PI business. The bookkeeping tallies with her income tax records. She's been making regular bank deposits so she must be working, but there are no client records on her computer. She must keep paper records."

I sat up straighter. "Regular deposits with no records.

So who's paying her? There isn't much call for private investigators in Silverside."

"We'll keep digging," he assured me. "Would you like me to send an RCMP officer over to question her? We can get a warrant for a physical search of her house, too."

"Um..." I considered. "No, I don't think so. I don't want her to know she's on our radar yet. I'll read the whole report as soon as we're finished with the network stuff here, and wait to see if you get any more information on her."

"Great." He smiled. "If we lose you in the internet, I'll search for 'rubber baby buggy bumpers'." He handed me the tiny network key.

Closing my hand carefully around it, I teased, "I bet you can't say that five times fast." I was leaning back and closing my eyes when my desk phone rang.

"I'm expecting a call. I'd better get that." I jumped up and hurried over to pick up the receiver. "Kelly."

"I need to talk to you and Clyde Webb right away!"

Not the call I'd been expecting from John or Arnie. Frowning at the unfamiliar voice, I replied, "Who is this?"

"Neil Christopher?" The uncertain timbre of the previous evening replaced his earlier urgent tone. "Your tech? From last night?"

"Oh, right." My heart gave a thump. This didn't sound good. "Spider and I are in my office right now."

"I'll be there in two minutes."

Christopher was good as his word. In less than two minutes, he hurtled around the corner into my office, clamping a hand on the door frame to pivot inside.

"It's a focused EMP rifle!" he blurted. "They don't exist!"

CHAPTER 19

Holt, Spider, and I stared at the breathless young tech panting in the doorway of my office.

"Slow down," I advised, at the same time as Spider said, "Of course EMP rifles exist."

"I know, but not like this! I went to Agent Kelly's farm this morning at first light-"

"Alone?" I interrupted.

"No, I went with him and cleared the area first," Holt said.

"Good." I turned back to Christopher. "Sorry, go ahead."

"...and I found footprints and a .22 cartridge in the snow," he went on without acknowledging our interruptions. "It looked like they'd stood at places that would have a clear shot at Agent Kelly's cameras from about a hundred metres away. But it had to be a super-focused electromagnetic pulse, because it didn't knock out her computer even though it was only a couple of metres away from the camera on the other side of a wall. And get this..." He sucked in a much-needed breath, cheeks glowing and eyes alight. "They must have had some kind of brand-new targeting system, too, because there's no way to spot the cameras from that distance and there were no tracks in the snow that got close enough to see them."

"They might have used a quad-copter drone..." Spider began.

"No, they couldn't have," Christopher countered. "A drone would have activated the motion sensors. They couldn't get close enough without it being seen on camera. They must have something that senses electromagnetic fields. It should be possible, but I've never heard of-"

"We have to talk to Reggie right away," I interrupted. I sprang to my feet and headed for my desk phone.

I caught Christopher's puzzled frown as I picked up the phone. I elaborated, "Dr. Chow. Head of Weapons Research", and dialled.

"Chow." Somehow Reggie managed to infuse the one-word greeting with caustic irritation.

"Hi, it's Aydan." Before he could bite my head off, I added the magic words capable of improving even his most cantankerous mood. "I think we've discovered a new weapon."

"Bring it!" I could hear the grin in his voice.

"Sorry, it's not bringable. We don't even know if it exists, but we think it does."

"Damn." I imagined his scowl on the other end of the line. "Who's 'we', and when can you get down here?"

"Spider, Christopher, Holt, and me. Now."

"Who's Chris-" He bit off the question. "Never mind. See you in a few." The click of his disconnect sounded before I had time to lower the receiver from my ear.

"Come on," I told the others. "Christopher, do you have a clearance for the secured area?"

"Yes."

His eyes sparkled as though this was the greatest

adventure he'd ever experienced. Hell, maybe it was. He looked about fifteen. Although, like Spider, I knew he had to be older than he looked. Maybe geekery was the new fountain of youth.

"I only have access to the main areas, though," Christopher added. "Not the Weapons Lab."

"I don't have clearance for the Weapons Lab, either," Holt admitted reluctantly.

"Me, neither," Spider confirmed.

They all looked at me.

"What makes you so fucking special?" Holt demanded.

Shit, Holt was friends with Dermott. If he happened to mention this, Dermott would take savage joy in stripping me of my clearances. And he'd probably accuse Stemp of favouritism, too, in another bid to take over as full-time Director.

I shrugged and kept my voice casual. "I've tested a bunch of prototypes for Reggie. I guess he keeps me cleared for access to the lab just to make it more convenient for himself. Come on, let's go."

Holt snorted as we went out the door and hurried down the corridor. "It'd have to be for his own convenience. He wouldn't give a shit about anybody else. That guy has the personality of a rabid wolverine with sore balls."

"I like him," I protested.

"You're the only one."

"I like him, too," Spider said loyally. "And so does Dr. Travers." He blushed.

Holt shook his head. "I still can't believe she's shacked up with him. What a waste of gorgeousness. Her, not him. Obviously."

"There's really no need to keep proving you're a pig," I

admonished as we clattered down the stairs into the lobby. "We already know."

After a tense trip through the claustrophobia-inducing time-delay chamber, I led the way through the subterranean corridors to the Weapons Lab.

When I waved my fob at the prox reader and opened the door, Reggie was already standing in the hallway to the right, prosthetic legs braced apart and arms crossed as if guarding the entrance to his lab.

Christopher blanched at the sight of Reggie's disfigured face.

Reggie's good eye narrowed, but Christopher managed a smile. "Dr. Chow? I'm Neil Christopher...? The new tech...?" His tentative tone made his words sound like questions.

"Are you, or aren't you?" Reggie snapped.

Christopher flushed. "S-Sorry, I... I don't understand the question...?"

"The new tech," Reggie growled. "Are you, or aren't you?"

"Y-Yessir. I am. The new tech, I mean."

"Then don't say it like a question. If *you* don't know, I sure as hell don't."

That was a lie, since Reggie wouldn't allow anyone into his domain without checking them first. But Christopher didn't know that; just like I hadn't, the unnerving first time I'd met Reggie.

"Sorry, sir. Doctor. Sir." Christopher ducked his head, his face flaming.

"Be nice, Reggie," I chided. "Christopher is the one who figured out the new weapon."

Reggie brightened. "Come on, we'll use the meeting

room." He jerked his chin to our left.

A short walk down a featureless corridor brought us to a small meeting room without glimpsing the lab. We all took seats, and Reggie pinned Christopher with his one-eyed gaze.

"What have you got?"

Christopher spilled out the information while Reggie listened intently.

"A .22 brass, eh?" he inquired. "You sure?"

"It's definitely .22; I measured it," Christopher assured him. "And I had it tested for residue. It's standard gunpowder." He withdrew a brass from his pocket and handed it over.

Reggie gave it a single glance. "It's not from a rifle, it's from a Hilti gun. It's short, and see the edge?" He pointed at the scalloped open end of the brass.

"What kind of gun is Hilti?" Christopher gazed at him as though consulting a divine oracle.

"Ramset, Hilti, DeWalt, whatever," Reggie qualified. "Just a brand name. Powder-actuated tool of some sort."

"Wha...?" Christopher looked lost.

I took pity on him. "It's a super-duper nail gun. It uses explosive cartridges to shoot special steel fasteners into hard stuff like concrete."

Christopher's face fell. "It's just a construction tool?" Pink rose in his cheeks. "Sorry," he mumbled. "I thought I'd really found something."

Reggie gave him a scar-distorted grin. "You did. This actually tells me more than if it'd been a standard .22 rifle brass."

"Really?" Hope bloomed on Christopher's face.

"Yeah. If it'd been a rifle brass, it could have just been some yokel pissing around with a .22, but I'd be willing to bet

this wasn't a projectile propellant. It's a power source."
Reggie's grin widened. "And since you only found one brass,
it means they were being careful about picking them up. I'm
assuming there were no fingerprints?"

"No, I checked before I handled it," Christopher assured
him.

"Hm, too bad. But I think you're spot-on with your guess
about a tightly-focused electromagnetic pulse rifle." Reggie
hesitated with a glance around the table. "This is classified,
by the way."

We all nodded, and Reggie grabbed a piece of paper and
a pencil from the credenza behind him. "So, we've got the
big EMP guns on military ships and vehicles, but the only
man-carried EMP rifle currently available uses a blank
NATO round with a ferro-electric generator, and a horn
antenna to distribute the pulse. The whole thing weighs over
thirty pounds, it's loud, and it's designed to knock out
everything electronic in a fairly wide area. But if you wanted
a handheld tactical unit for shorter range with more
accuracy..." His pencil flew over the paper. "Standard .22
gunstock with an optical sight; here's your chamber for the
Hilti cartridges; skip the ferro-electric generator to cut the
weight; instead the charge goes through the barrel to a
piezoelectric crystal here; use a parabolic dish to focus it
down to a beam instead of the horn to disperse it..."

He turned the paper around to Christopher and Spider,
who had been nodding eagerly while he sketched.

The drawing looked like a ray gun from a 1950s sci-fi
comic.

"I want this!" Reggie's eye was alight with the joy of new
weaponry. "The parabolic dish could even be collapsible like
an umbrella, so it'd be easy to carry and conceal..." He

trailed off as though visualizing the possibilities. A moment later his one-eyed gaze snapped back to Christopher. "You're right, they had to have some kind of scanning technology to find the cameras in the first place. Those motion-sensor cameras sleep unless they're activated, so it would have to scan for the electromagnetic radiation emitted by their wiring. You'd need a receiving unit running an algorithm to isolate a single-point linear scan, then map the point signal onto a realtime display with historical tracking so the wires would show up as lines..."

The three men launched into another round of incomprehensible techno-babble. Holt and I exchanged a glance.

"So, how about that hockey game the other night?" he inquired.

"Which one?"

"Who cares?"

"Good point," I agreed.

Holt leaned forward in his chair, pitching his voice below the level of the discussion on the other side of the table. "I was going to brief you later, but since they're busy geeking out over there, we might as well talk now. While Christopher was doing his thing out at your farm, I walked the perimeter. Looks like somebody parked on the road that runs a mile east of your place and skied along the creek to get within range."

"Arnie nailed it!" I blurted.

Holt smirked. "Too much information, Kelly."

"Pig," I retorted without heat. "What I meant was, that's how he said he'd do it if he was going to kill me."

"Why would he go to all that trouble? He could just snap your neck in bed."

"I'm never going to sleep with a man again," I muttered, then added at normal volume, "No, I asked for his professional opinion on a scenario where he didn't know me but he got assigned to kill me. And that's exactly what he said he'd do."

Holt's eyes glinted with evil amusement. "Kill you in bed?"

I sank my head into my hands. "I give up."

Holt snickered, but when he spoke again the teasing was gone from his voice. "So it looked as though the tracks by the creek were fresher than the ones in your yard. I'm no tracker, but there was a chinook on Tuesday and the tracks in your yard were melted a bit and rounded at the edges. The ones up by the creek were still crisp, so I'd say Wednesday or Thursday."

My blood chilled. "He could have even been waiting when I got home on Thursday evening. But he couldn't get a clear shot because Arnie was driving and I didn't get out to open the gate."

"Probably saved your life," Holt said soberly. "So what was Hellhound's second choice? Because now that we've spotted the ski tracks and made tracks of our own out there, this guy knows we're onto him. If they're serious about offing you, he'll go to Plan B."

"A bomb? Long-range artillery?" I shrugged, hoping to hide my quaking fear. "I don't know. We walked into my house right then and found it trashed, and we didn't finish the conversation. I'll ask Arnie again."

"You should." Holt glanced over at the three tech wizards still in animated discussion and added, "We might as well get back to work. They'll go on all day."

I raised my voice to get their attention. "Holt and I are

going back to work now."

"Oh." Spider looked up, disappointment in his expression. "I guess you need me, too."

"Sorry," I told him sincerely. "I know you'd love to stay here and play."

He shrugged and rose. "It was tough to decide between being an analyst or a tech, but at least as an analyst I get to do a bit of both." He grinned. "So much cool technology; so little time!"

I glanced at my wristwatch. "Shit, you're right about 'so little time'. Never mind, you might as well stay here. I'm due at Blue Eddy's at eleven. I have to go."

Holt scowled. "Blow it off. It's just a cover. Volslav is more important."

"It's a good cover because I show up and do the work," I countered. "I'm going to Blue Eddy's at eleven, Up & Coming at one, then I have to drop this off at the hospital." I tapped the heart monitor's small pouch. "I'll be back by about three-thirty and we can start digging then."

"Fine," Holt grumbled. "I'll check in with Brock again and see whether they've unearthed anything more on Volslav. And I'll take Christopher back out to your farm after lunch. He'll install shielded cameras, and while he's doing that I'll scout the sightlines from those ski tracks. We might install some additional cameras to monitor those access points."

My heart sank at the thought of more surveillance on my farm. When the original cameras had been installed I had intentionally kept their field of view tight to the buildings so I could have some privacy in my yard and garden.

No more.

Stifling a sigh, I nodded, and we climbed the stairs to the

time delay chamber in silence. We parted ways in the lobby, and I hurried up to my office to grab my parka. The blinking voicemail light caught my eye, and when I punched the button Kane's voice informed me that they'd meet me at Blue Eddy's when it opened at eleven-thirty for lunch.

I sighed. Good thing Eddy didn't care when I did his books. He wouldn't get his full two hours today.

Trying to look in all directions at once, I hurried out to my truck and headed for Blue Eddy's.

When I arrived, the saloon's parking lot was empty except for Darlene's rust-pocked car and an older-model half-ton truck with a camper on the back. Eddy must have evicted the rest of the alien people and their vehicles. I smiled as I turned into the lot. Eddy's easy-going manner hid considerable steel.

My smile vanished as I drove closer and spotted an RCMP cruiser parked behind the camper.

Police tape on the camper. Police tape on the door to the saloon.

Oh, shit.

As I pulled to a stop, Darlene emerged from her car. I sprang out of my truck and hurried over to her.

"What's wrong?" I demanded, taking in the tear tracks on her pale cheeks and the way she steadied herself with a trembling hand on her car roof.

"Oh, Aydan, everything's wrong!" She sucked in a shaky breath. "Eddy's been arrested for murder!"

CHAPTER 20

"*What?*" I stared at Darlene. "That's insane! Eddy wouldn't kill anybody."

"I know, he's the sweetest, nicest guy..." Her voice broke. "But they... the police... said he beat one of the alien people to death with his bat. The b-body was..." She pointed a shaking finger behind her.

My heart sank. "In the bar?"

"No..." Darlene gulped. "In the alley. B-By the garbage cans. Eddy found it and called the police. And they *arrested* him."

"Who was the victim?"

"I d-don't know." Fresh tears trickled down her cheeks. "I g-got here just when they were taking Eddy away and he s-said..." She swiped ineffectually at her tears, which continued to flow. "H-He said to keep the bar open while he was gone, b-but..." Her voice rose in anguish. "What will we do without Eddy?"

"Calm down, Darlene." I nudged her back to her driver's seat and lowered her into it, crouching beside the car to meet her eyes. "It'll be okay. It's all a mistake, don't worry."

She buried her face in her apron and gave way to sobs.

My heart went out to the struggling single mother. The extra expenses of her son's learning disability strained her meagre budget to its limits, and Eddy always found ways to make sure there was enough in her paycheque to support them. He treated all of his staff like family, but Eddy *was* Darlene's family.

I patted her knee. "Darlene. Try to stop crying for a minute and just look at me. Come on..." I pulled a tissue out of my pocket and passed it over. "Here. I know this is awful for you, but just listen for a second."

She dabbed her eyes, sniffling.

I held her tear-reddened gaze. "Remember, Eddy is innocent. The police might have thought they had enough evidence to charge him, but they can't throw him in jail without a trial. They'll take him to the police station for a while, but they'll release him soon..." I secretly crossed my fingers for that. "...and they'll keep digging until they figure out what really happened. It'll be okay."

"You th-" Her breath hitched in a suppressed sob. "-think so?"

"Well, I'm not a cop..." I crossed my fingers harder. "...but I'm pretty sure they have to let him go. He's innocent until proven guilty. They only hold people if they're a danger to society, and everybody knows Eddy isn't. He gives police officers free meals every time they come in, for shi-" I bit off the incipient obscenity. "For crying out loud."

Darlene sat up a little straighter. "You're right, Eddy is the best person I know." Her chin went up. "And after all he's done for me, the least I can do is keep the bar running until he gets back." She mopped her face and blew her nose. "Thanks, Aydan. I'm sorry I was such a m-mess." Her voice wobbled, but the tears didn't return.

"It's okay, I know this was a huge shock for you. Did the police say how long it might be before you could open the bar?"

"They said we might be able to reopen tomorrow, but it'll depend on what they find." She drew a tremulous breath. "I was just waiting for you to get here because I don't have your phone number and I didn't want you to get here and not know what had happened." She gulped. "Plus, I was too upset to drive."

"I don't blame you. Can I help with anything tomorrow?"

"No, it's okay. Eddy's usually h-here..." Her voice caught, then firmed. "But I've opened and closed for him before. I know what to do, and everybody else will pitch in. We'll keep everything running smoothly until he gets back."

"That's great. He's lucky to have you."

"We're lucky to have him." She hesitated. "I... I guess I'll just... go home, then." She gave me a helpless look. "I don't know what to do."

I squeezed her shoulder. "Just go home and take it easy. Eddy will probably be back tomorrow, but if he's not you'll have a busy day. Do you want my cell phone number? You can call me if you want to talk, and if I hear anything I'll call you."

"Oh, yes. Thanks, Aydan."

We texted each other our phone numbers and I urged, "Think good thoughts. Everything will be better tomorrow."

She nodded and attempted a smile.

As she drove off I trailed back to my truck, where I slouched in the driver's seat staring blindly at the empty parking lot.

I had only seen Eddy pull that bat out from under the bar one other time in the past couple of years. So either somebody had known it was there, or else they saw it for the first time last night and seized the opportunity to sneak inside, steal the bat, and carry it outside to kill the victim.

That wasn't an impulsive act. Someone was framing Eddy.

Why?

Pulling out my cell phone, I hit the speed dial for Kane.

His deep voice answered after the first ring. "Aydan?"

"Hi. Things are getting complicated. Somebody's trying to frame Eddy for murder."

"*Murder?*" Kane's word barked out on an incredulous laugh. "That's crazy."

"Apparently the victim was beaten to death with Eddy's bat behind the saloon. Eddy found the body this morning, called the police, and promptly got arrested."

"Dammit. Who was the victim?"

"I don't know. Darlene was too upset to tell me much, and I didn't want to push her. Do you think Constable Peters would tell you anything?"

"I doubt it, since I'm a civilian now," Kane said. "And I don't want to put her in a difficult position by asking. But you don't need me. Get Webb to call the detachment. If there's a possibility that this might be related to one of your cases, they'll share the information with you."

I thumped my forehead. Not only had I zoomed past the obvious solution, I'd also made John feel even worse about not being involved in law enforcement.

"Sorry," I muttered. "I wasn't thinking."

His sigh carried over the line. "It's all right. We all have to get used to the 'new normal'. I presume Eddy's is closed while they process the scene?"

"Yeah. At least the body was out in the alley instead of inside the building. They might be able to reopen tomorrow."

"Do you want to meet at the Melted Spoon for lunch instead? I have to pick Daniel up in Calgary at two-thirty, so I'll have to be on the road before twelve-thirty."

"Okay, see you soon."

After disconnecting from John, I hit the speed-dial for Spider.

When he answered, I blurted, "Eddy's been arrested for murder, and I need to know the details." I paused, then added virtuously, "It might have something to do with our case."

"Eddy?" Spider's voice rose. "*Murder?* That's crazy, Aydan! Eddy would never kill anybody."

"Everybody knows it's crazy." I sighed. "Except the police, apparently."

"Well, you're right," Spider said in a tone of great seriousness. "This could definitely be connected to Volslav." He hesitated. "Um, somehow. I'll call the Drumheller RCMP detachment right away."

"Thanks, Spider, you're the best." I hung up, trying not to think of how much trouble I'd be in if Dermott found out.

Hell, who was I kidding? *When* Dermott found out.

But it didn't really matter. If Stemp wasn't back to do my requalification interview on Monday, Dermott would railroad me regardless. Might as well try to help Eddy in the meantime.

And I knew exactly where to start digging for clues. I dialled Lola's number.

She greeted me with a gloomy, "Aydan, did you hear the bad news about Eddy?"

"Yeah. We need to help him, Lola. Have your super-snoops heard anything?"

"I was so shocked, I didn't even think to ask." Renewed energy infused her voice. "But that's a great idea! I'll call the team right away!"

"Um, okay," I agreed, trying not to let my sudden misgivings colour my voice. "So I'll see you around one?"

"Yes, and I bet we'll have information by then. CRAPS is on the job, and if there's anything to dig up, we'll dig it! See you at one, Aydan." She hung up.

I sagged in my seat. Dammit, I should have thought this through. Lola was like a tiny terrier. Once she got her teeth into something, she'd never let go. And if somebody was willing to commit murder to frame Eddy, they wouldn't hesitate to eliminate a few senior citizens who got too close to the truth.

Oh, Lord...

I was already hitting the speed dial. My call went straight to Lola's voicemail, and her larger-than-life voice cheerily advised me to leave a message.

"Lola," I said urgently after the beep. "It's Aydan. Don't get CRAPS involved in this, okay? It's too dangerous. Murder is a job for the police. Just call everything off for now and we'll talk about it at one." I hesitated, but there was nothing more to say.

And I was pretty sure my advice would fall on deaf ears anyway. Selectively deaf.

My phone vibrated a few minutes later as I was parking in Sirius's lot. The call display showed a blocked number.

"Hello?" I answered cautiously.

"It's Spider. I've got information." He didn't sound happy. "The victim was a twenty-four-year-old male named Herman Lopez, and he was one of the alien people. The alien-welcoming committee, not the tinfoil-hat group. His wallet and phone and cash were still in his pocket so robbery wasn't a motive. We'll have to wait for the autopsy to be sure, but the preliminary cause of death looks like multiple blows to the head with Eddy's bat." He paused, then added, "If it hasn't been wiped clean, Eddy's fingerprints will be all over it. I hope there are others."

"Any guesses on the time of death?"

"Sometime between one-thirty and six AM. They're betting closer to one-thirty, though. When the responding officers got there at nine-thirty, the body had rigor and the toes and fingertips were frozen."

"And Eddy lives alone, so I suppose he doesn't have an alibi."

"That's right. The bar closed at one AM last night as usual and Darlene and Eddy were the last to leave through the door to the parking lot at one-thirty, also as usual. Eddy always walks the female staff to their cars after dark, so he walked Darlene outside. Both Eddy and Darlene told the police that there was a camper parked illegally in the bar's parking lot when they came out of the bar. Eddy banged on the door of it, but nobody answered."

The sound of Spider's swallow carried clearly over the line. "At least, nobody answered while Darlene was there to witness it. She said Eddy seemed annoyed, but he wasn't raving mad or anything. Darlene went home, and that's the last anybody knows until Eddy called the police this morning. The camper belongs to Lopez. It doesn't have any running water or bathroom facilities, and the police think Lopez went into the alley to, um..." I imagined Spider's boyish features reddening as he hesitated. "Poop. In a garbage can. They think Eddy caught him and went crazy and beat him to death."

"That's insane. Eddy's the most even-tempered guy I know. He might have been annoyed, but he wouldn't kill a guy just for taking a dump in his garbage can. And anyway, are they sure Lopez was even killed in the alley? Somebody could have killed him somewhere else and dumped the body."

"Either he was killed there, or somebody went to a lot of trouble to make it look like he was. Garbage cans were knocked over and there was blood spatter on the walls."

"That's pretty circumstantial," I pointed out.

"It gets worse. Apparently there was a fight at Eddy's last night-"

"I know, I was there," I interrupted, my heart sinking. "I hope you're not going to tell me Lopez was one of the guys Eddy tangled with."

"Witnesses said Eddy hit Lopez in the knee with the bat. And Aydan..." Spider sounded thoroughly miserable. "We don't know Eddy as well as we think. This isn't the first time he's been charged with murder."

Shock made me blurt the first word that came to mind. "Bullshit!"

"No, it's true. It was nineteen years ago, a big sensational trial in Calgary. Eddy used to tour with a band. Not a super-famous one, but they had gigs all over the country. He was married then, and he and his wife had a ten-month-old baby girl. And..." Spider's voice trembled. "One day while he was on tour, his daughter got really sick. His wife was taking her to the hospital when their car was hit by an impaired driver in a cement truck." He gulped. "Eddy's wife and baby were killed instantly."

The horror hit me like a punch to the chest. "Oh my God!" I wrapped my arms around myself, half in empathy for Eddy and half in reaction to my own terrible memories caused by a drunk driver. "Oh my God," I repeated. "Poor Eddy! I can't even imagine..." My throat closed while I imagined it anyway.

"Eddy came home right away," Spider went on. "But of course there was nothing he could do but bury his wife and baby. The drunk driver wasn't even hurt in the crash. But four days later, he was found bludgeoned to death behind the bar where the wake for Eddy's wife and baby was being held." Spider sighed. "The murder weapon was a baseball bat that belonged to Eddy."

"S-So..." My voice didn't seem to be working right. "What happened?"

"Eddy didn't have an alibi," Spider said miserably. "He'd been drinking heavily. Around ten PM he left the wake alone, then came back a couple of hours later, showered and wearing fresh clothes."

My heart sank into my belly. "Don't tell me, let me guess. The victim was killed during that time."

"Yes." Spider heaved another sigh that sounded like it came all the way up from his toes. "The bat had been wiped, but they found a partial print that matched Eddy's. Eddy swore he'd only gone for a walk to clear his head, and that he'd gotten cold and wet in the rain and had walked home to shower and change, and that's why he was gone for so long. But he was alone all that time so nobody could corroborate, and he'd been really angry and upset before he left the bar."

"Well, duh!" I said indignantly. "He was at a wake for his dead wife and baby!"

"I know, right?" Spider agreed. "They didn't find any blood residue on Eddy or on his clothes or shoes when they searched his house. But the drunk was killed with a single blow so there wouldn't likely have been blood spatter. And Eddy used to hit home runs regularly. He was... still is, I guess... a heck of a batter."

Another unhappy sigh drifted over the line. "Eddy's brother Lionel had driven them to the bar, and their baseball gear was in the back seat of Lionel's car, left from the last game they'd played. Police found blood residue in the parking lot, indicating that the body had been dragged from near Lionel's car over to the garbage cans in the alley. Lionel testified that he'd gone outside with Eddy and offered to drive him home, but Eddy insisted he wanted to walk. The car was unlocked when the police arrived. The bat was the only thing missing, Eddy and Lionel were the only ones who had keys to the car, and witnesses confirmed that Lionel never left the bar for more than a minute or two. Lionel testified that he watched Eddy walk out of the parking lot and down the street, but Lionel was hosting the wake so he went back inside right away. The circumstantial evidence against Eddy was pretty damning."

"Did he get convicted?"

"No. Lionel swore he'd forgotten to lock the car after trying to get Eddy into it, so Eddy's lawyer argued that anybody could have passed by and taken the bat. The victim had been convicted of impaired driving several times in the past and there was a lot of public outrage, so Eddy's lawyer argued that the killer could have been some vigilante. Eddy got acquitted on reasonable doubt, but it was probably only because the jury felt so sorry for him."

I imagined my friend confronting the killer of his wife and baby with bat in hand. Had he regretted that single home-run swing ever since?

Or did he believe justice had been served?

Shaking off the dark thoughts, I argued, "But even if Eddy did kill that guy then, he's got no reason to kill Lopez now. If he killed everybody who ever did something obnoxious, he'd have run out of places to hide the bodies years ago. This just reeks of a setup. Somebody knew his history and went to a lot of trouble to recreate it."

"I know, but who? And why?"

"That's what we're going to find out."

CHAPTER 21

Spider let out a whoosh of breath. "I was hoping you'd say that. But how can we help Eddy? We're supposed to be concentrating on Volslav, and that has to be our top priority until we find out whether he..." He hesitated. "Or she, or they... are planning to kill you."

I let out an irritable grunt. "Somebody's always planning to kill me." But my bravado didn't keep me from scanning for snipers again, even though I'd been eyeing my surroundings constantly while we talked.

"Anyway," Spider went on, "There's not much we can do to help Eddy right now. They'll likely release him, although we don't know yet what the conditions will be. I'll ask the RCMP to forward us copies of their interview reports with Eddy and the witnesses, but there's no point in duplicating their work. I trust Constables Peters and Birch; and the Ident Officer who's on the way to process the crime scene is really good. She won't miss anything. But even after they've got everything from the scene, you know how backed up the NFLS is. It'll be weeks before there are any results."

I sighed. The National Forensic Lab Service did the best they could, but a garden-variety bludgeoning would have to wait its turn. And I couldn't shove it through the Department's specialized lab unless it was clearly

Department business.

"I know you're right, Spider," I said with resignation. "But I'm going to try anyway. Thanks for your help."

"You're welcome. Just... be careful, okay?"

The concern in his voice warmed me. "I will."

I disconnected with a smile. No matter how shitty the rest of my life might be, Spider was always a bright spot.

I was about to get out of the truck when my phone vibrated again. A glance at the call display showed Kane's number, and I accepted the call with a quiver of worry.

"Is everything okay?" I asked.

"Fine, but the Melted Spoon is packed with locals gossiping about Eddy, and the alien people are overrunning the town. There's no place to sit, and Hellhound and I both think you'd be safer in Sirius Dynamics anyway. We'll buy sandwiches and meet you in the Sirius lobby."

"Oh." My shoulders relaxed at the thought of retreating to the safety of my office. "That would be great. Thanks."

"What would you like?"

My brain didn't want to grapple with any more decisions. "Surprise me."

I could hear the smile in his voice. "All right. See you soon."

Fifteen minutes later they strode into the lobby, and I signed Kane in at the security wicket so we could all go up to my office.

When we got there, I flopped onto the sofa while the other two appropriated the armchairs.

Kane handed me a takeout box. "I hope you're in the mood for grilled chicken and brie with fresh apple, arugula and fig jam."

I mimed wiping drool off my chin. "Oh, *hell* yes."

Hellhound chuckled. "Lucky Kane bought your lunch. I woulda just got ya ham an' cheese."

"That would have been fine, too," I assured him. "You know I like everything." I delved into my waist pouch for a twenty and held it out. "Thanks."

Kane shook his head. "My treat."

I thanked him and we ate in silence for a few moments before he added, "Did you find out anything about Eddy's situation?"

"Yeah." I launched into the story.

By the time I had finished, Hellhound was frowning. "Fuck, I figured Eddy'd been through some bad shit, but I didn't know how bad. No wonder that bar's his whole life."

"Does he still play baseball?" I asked. "After being accused of murder with a bat once, I can't imagine why he'd keep one at the saloon."

"He's been in a baseball league long's I've known him." Hellhound shrugged. "That's only five years or so, since I started comin' up for the jams; but he's mentioned it a few times. An' when the closest cops can take twenty minutes to get here, ya gotta have somethin' under the bar just in case. A baseball bat ain't technically a weapon. He keeps a ball an' glove under there, too, to make it look good."

"That didn't help him this time," Kane pointed out.

We lapsed into gloomy silence.

Dammit, I considered Eddy a friend, but I hadn't known he played baseball. I'd never asked him about his past, or his personal life. His warm smile, his amazing musical talent, his kindness and generosity... I had taken him completely for granted.

Time to fix that.

Kane's voice interrupted my thoughts. "Any progress on

Volslav?"

"Not yet. I might find something later in the day." I didn't elaborate on my method of data-gathering. Even though Kane knew all about it, he was a civilian now; and Hellhound knew nothing about my cyber-abilities. If I dropped even the slightest hint to either of them, it would be treason.

One more way to end up in prison. As if I needed more.

"I saw Dermott earlier," Kane said as though reading my mind.

I slumped back on the cushions and lowered my voice with a cautious glance at the doorway. "Don't remind me."

Kane lowered his voice, too. "Surely he can't still be carrying a grudge. You didn't do anything wrong. It was his own carelessness that earned him that reprimand."

"But I was the reason Upper Command found out he'd been careless," I countered. "He doesn't want to take responsibility for his own shit, so he'll just keep blaming me." I grimaced. "And I didn't help by losing my temper and telling him to suck up his whiny-baby attitude."

Kane winced. "You really need to-"

"I know, I know," I interrupted. "Count to ten before I lose my temper. Great advice, but it's easier said than done."

He gave me a wry smile. "I know you get instantly angry when you feel threatened. You can't control that, but maybe you could just try counting to ten before you react."

I shot him a dangerous look and raised one finger, then the next, in a parody of counting.

Kane chuckled ruefully and shook his head. "On second thought, I'd rather deal with the explosion. The suspense is worse."

We all laughed, and Kane rose. "I have to go." He

stooped to drop a kiss on my forehead and gripped both my hands in his. "Keep in touch. Let me know how things are going. I'll have Daniel until tomorrow morning around ten, but call me if you need help before then. I'll..." He broke off and let out a breath as his shoulders bowed under the weight of his priorities. "I'll do my best to help, if I can do it without endangering Daniel."

I smiled and squeezed his hands. "That's what I want to hear." I stood, too. "I have to walk you downstairs and sign you out."

He gave me a wistful smile as the gulf between our lives opened wider.

"I'm gonna stay here an' finish this," Hellhound said, hefting the remains of his sandwich.

"Back in a bit," I promised.

As we strode down the hall, Kane lowered his voice. "Is there some reason why Arnie wants you and me to talk in private?"

"If there is, he hasn't told me." I gave him a sidelong glance. "Is there anything you want to talk about in private?"

"No," Kane said hurriedly. After a moment, he added, "And given our... history... I don't think it's appropriate for us to be alone together now that you're married." He flung up a palm as I began to speak. "I know marriage doesn't mean anything to you, but it does to me."

"I wasn't going to say that," I protested. "I was just... I'm disappointed that you think I'd..." I threw up my hands in frustration as I struggled for words. "We're friends! I'd never *molest* you, for chrissake! Or try to convince you to do something you don't feel right about. I know how you feel about marriage, and honestly, it never occurred to me to do anything inappropriate."

"And that's the problem," Kane said softly as we went down the stairs. "Because I've been having nothing but inappropriate urges."

I halted, staring at him. "Oh." My voice came out faint and breathless.

Heat crackled from his body and darkened his eyes, but he slowly stepped back a couple of paces. "Which is why I can't be alone with you. I trust you; I just don't trust myself." He turned and strode to the security wicket.

After a long moment I pulled myself together and attempted a casual walk over to add my signature to his on the sign-out sheet.

"See you later," Kane said. "Be safe." He left without touching me again.

Still flustered, I trailed upstairs.

Hellhound looked up as I came into my office. "Everythin' okay with you an' Kane?"

"Um... yeah. I guess. A bit... weird. But okay, I think." I shook off my bemusement as I flopped down on the couch. "Hey, can we pick up that conversation we were having when we found out my house was trashed? Holt found ski tracks right where you said you'd go if you were planning to kill me. Whoever was up there will see the overlapping tracks if they go back, so they'll know they're busted. Holt figures if they're planning to kill me they'll switch to Plan B. So if it was your job, how would you do it?"

Hellhound swallowed the last bite of his sandwich and leaned over to brush the crumbs out of his beard before slouching back in the chair with a frown. "Fuck, I hate thinkin' about killin' ya."

"Better you than somebody who actually intends to."

"Huh. Yeah. Okay, darlin'..." He stared into space, still

frowning. "So, ya figure this's a high-budget operation, right?"

"If it really is Volslav, then yes."

"Ya figure they're in a hurry to knock ya off?"

"I don't know." It was my turn to frown. "I'm a threat, but I don't think they have any particular reason to eliminate me right this minute."

I pondered for a moment. If Volslav had a weapon of their own, would that make them more or less anxious to get rid of me?

"Why?" I added.

"'Cause if they ain't in a hurry, their guy'll play it safe. Take his time an' make sure he ain't gonna get caught. If that's the situation, I pretty much know how he's gonna think. But if they're gettin' desperate..." Hellhound didn't finish the sentence.

I sighed. "If they're desperate enough to not worry about getting caught, then I'm going to get dead no matter what. Let's concentrate on what we can control."

"'Kay. So, lucky for us it's winter an' ya found their tracks, an' they're gonna know ya found 'em. Our guy won't try anythin' from there now. That's good, 'cause that was his best option. Next option..." Hellhound hesitated. "If they ain't in a hurry, a remote-controlled bomb'd be their best bet. You're checkin' your vehicles before ya drive 'em, right?"

I tensed. "Um, not recently." I drew in a shaky breath, my heart thumping. "But my truck's in the Sirius lot under video surveillance, so Security would tell me if anybody tampered with it. I haven't left it anywhere else since we came from my farm. And I always check my vehicles with my bug detector before I drive them, so that should identify any radio-frequency connection to a remote control, right?"

"Maybe. It'd depend on what kinda bomb they're usin'. Keep doin' what you're doin'. An' if ya need to go anywhere ya gotta leave your vehicle for a while, I'll drive ya. What about your farm? Ya got full video coverage out there yet?"

"I should have by this afternoon."

"Good, 'cause it'd be easy to hide an IED under the snow on your driveway."

My spine turned to ice. "Holt and Christopher just went out there!" I lunged for the phone, punching the speed dial with a shaking finger.

"Stop where you are!" I barked the instant Holt picked up. A muffled oath on the other end of the line told me he was complying. "It's Aydan," I added, realizing the number would be blocked on his call display.

"I figured. What the hell?" Holt demanded.

"Where are you?"

"Just turning into your lane."

"Don't move!"

Tension tightened his voice. "We're not. Why?"

"Arnie says he'd put an IED in my lane."

Holt's voice rose to a shout. "*What the FUCK?* He could have blown us to hell! That fucking moron!"

"No, no! I didn't say 'he did'. That's what he *would* do if he were the assassin."

"Fuck." The word blew out on a released breath. When Holt spoke again, it was with his usual decisive tone. "Okay, hang on." His volume decreased as though he'd lowered the phone to speak to his companion. "Do you have anything to sweep for IEDs?" A moment later he spoke to me again. "Christopher doesn't have anything like that with him. We'll wait for a field crew and get everything checked over before we go in."

"Okay, good." I hesitated, then said what was on my mind anyway. "I'm glad you're okay."

"Thanks," Holt replied awkwardly. His tone went taunting. "Your boyfriend come up with any other great ways to kill you?"

I didn't rise to his bait. "I'm sure he's got lots of ideas. I'll keep you posted." I hung up without a goodbye, knowing Holt wouldn't expect one.

Shuffling over to the sofa on shaky legs, I flopped down to face Arnie again. "Thanks. Okay, what's Plan C?"

He blew out a breath. "Fuck, I dunno if it's B or C or Z, I'm just spitballin' here. I'd-"

He broke off as we both glanced toward the movement in my doorway.

My heart leaped into my mouth.

Dermott.

CHAPTER 22

To my surprise, Dermott's florid face wore a neutral expression as he stood framed in my office door. Then again, maybe it wasn't that much of a surprise. He usually saved his vitriol for when we had no witnesses.

"Helmand," he snapped. "What are you doing here?"

Hellhound gave him a level look. "Consultin' on the Volslav thing."

"Consulting." Dermott's voice dripped with sarcasm. "What the hell for? It's an investigation, not an assassination."

"Keep your voice down," I hissed.

Dermott's face twisted with rage, but an instant later he controlled the expression as one of the civilian researchers walked past in the hallway.

Dermott's eyes glittered with hatred, but his voice was level. "Helmand, get out. Your clearances are rescinded as of right fucking now. Turn in your weapons on your way out."

Hellhound rose unhurriedly and took a couple of slow steps toward Dermott. When he spoke, his face and voice were The Killer's.

"Who's gonna protect Aydan?"

"From what?" Dermott snapped. "There's no evidence

that anybody's trying to kill her, she's armed, she's got a shitload of gear at her fingertips if she wants it, and she's a fucking trained agent. She's supposed to be able to protect *herself.*"

Hellhound advanced another step, looming over Dermott, who suddenly looked much smaller.

"She ain't cleared for active duty," Hellhound said. "Stemp wants her protected."

Dermott flushed burgundy. "Stemp's gone. I'm DCO now. So get the hell out before I call security to throw you out." His eyes narrowed. "Unless you want to get written up for insubordination."

The corner of Hellhound's mouth curled in a sardonic half-smile, but his gaze was as cold as death as he paced toward Dermott.

Dermott blanched, but held his ground.

"Arnie, don't..." I began.

Hellhound gazed down at Dermott from inches away.

"Just keep wavin' your dick around, little man," Hellhound rasped quietly, and brushed by without touching Dermott or completing the implied threat.

Heart hammering, I let out a breath as his bulky figure disappeared down the hallway.

Dermott swallowed audibly, but a moment later he hid his reaction in a truculent expression. "What the hell do you think you're doing?" he demanded.

I held my voice steady and jerked my chin at the empty takeout containers on the coffee table. "Eating lunch."

"No shit! I meant, what the hell are you doing interfering in an RCMP investigation?"

"I'm not interfering, I just asked the RCMP for updates."

Dermott's lip curled. "You wasted Department resources

and the valuable time of an analyst to snoop on a completely unrelated civilian case. That's a violation of Departmental regulations, as well as a breach of federal privacy laws."

Fear clenched my guts, and my temper surged. "It's not an unrelated case," I lied. "It's part of the Volslav thing."

Dermott let out a bark of sarcastic laughter. "Fuck off. We both know you're misusing Department resources to help your friends, just like you always do. Only this time..." His brows drew down, his eyes as hard as granite. "...I'm going to make sure you don't get away with it."

My hands twitched with the need to wrap around his neck and squeeze until all my troubles went away. When I managed to force out words, they were a half-strangled growl. "Do you really want to try making those charges stick again?" With a tremendous effort of will, I managed not to add 'dickhead'. "Because you might remember it didn't work out so well for you last time."

He bared his teeth. "Fucking pansy-ass chain of command isn't going to be involved this time. This time, it's just going to be you and me. I hope you like prison, bitch!"

He spun and stomped off down the hall.

I was glaring at the air with my hands crooked in the shape of a throat when Spider stuck his head in the door and recoiled.

"Is, um... everything okay?" he asked cautiously.

"Fine," I muttered instead of spitting out the other four-letter F-word that was on my mind. "I'm just getting really fucking sick and tired of getting called a bitch."

Oops. Said the F-word after all.

Spider frowned. "Who called you a...?" He flushed and didn't repeat the insult.

"Dermott. Again. He's such an asshole."

Spider glanced over his shoulder before coming into my office and swinging the door shut behind him. He lowered his voice. "Aydan, that's really inappropriate."

I sighed. "Sorry. I take it back. I'm just-"

"No, no!" he interrupted. "I didn't mean you, I meant him! It's completely against Department policy to use abusive language, particularly to someone who's lower in the hierarchy. And he used a gender-based slur against you, too. You should report him. Especially if this isn't the first time it's happened."

I snorted. "That would just make everything worse. Besides, it'd be pretty hypocritical for me to report him after all the times I've called Stemp a dickhead. I'm the one that should be getting written up."

Spider's frown deepened. "I only ever heard you call Stemp a name once, and that was a long time ago, and you had a pretty good reason..." He trailed off uncertainly at my rueful headshake.

"Thanks, Spider, but it's been a lot more than once. Um... actually, I called him that only a couple of days ago." Heat rose in my cheeks. "And I said some inappropriate stuff to Dermott a couple of weeks ago, too, after the last time he called me a bitch. I've really got to start counting to ten."

"But you're never mean for no reason," Spider protested. "Everybody knows redheads are hot-tempered, and nobody holds it against you."

I grimaced. "They probably should. It's just as inappropriate for me to talk that way as it is for Dermott. Anyway, he's always had a potty-mouth, and it doesn't bother me. We speak the same language." I patted Spider on the shoulder and faked confidence. "Dermott and I will work it out. Thanks for being concerned, though."

"Okay. If you're sure." He eyed me anxiously. "I just don't think it's right for him to be stressing you out even more. You've already got so much on your plate."

"I'm fine. Don't worry. But speaking of worrying... I'm afraid Lola's going to try to investigate Eddy's case, and I don't want her anywhere near a murder. Is Linda working at the hospital this afternoon, or can she spare some time to ride herd on Lola and CRAPS?"

Spider's face scrunched with anxiety. "No, Linda's on day shifts all this week."

"Shit. Well, I'm due over at Up & Coming at one, so I'll try to talk Lola out of it then."

"Is there anything I can do?"

I sighed. "Not unless you can make Lola... not Lola."

He shook his head with a rueful grimace. "Good luck."

He disappeared down the hallway, and I tossed the takeout boxes into the garbage, my mind circling back to Holt and Christopher.

Was the bomb squad there yet?

And how pissed off would Dermott be when he discovered Holt had called them out based only on my boyfriend's speculation?

My brain screeched to a halt.

My *husband's* speculation.

Warmth expanded in my chest and my tense shoulders eased. Even if Dermott managed to send me to prison, he couldn't take Arnie's love away. Or John's. I was so lucky to have so many people who cared for me.

My guts clenched as that thought led to the next.

Tom.

Shit, if he saw activity over at my place, he'd go and

check it out like the good neighbour he was. And if he decided to ride his horse across the creek instead of coming around by the road where Holt could stop him before he stepped on a bomb...

I was snatching up the phone before the thought was complete.

The phone rang a couple of times before Tom's pleasant voice answered, sounding cautious. "Hello?"

Hiding my sigh of relief, I kept my voice casual. "Hi, Tom, it's Aydan. Sorry about the blocked number. I'm calling from one of my clients' offices."

His voice warmed. "Oh, hi. How's everything over at your place?"

"Actually, that's what I'm calling about. I've got some guys over there today doing..." Shit, why hadn't I figured out a cover story before I dialled? "...um, a bit of work on my lane and around my yard. So don't be surprised if you notice some activity."

Christ, how lame was that? What kind of 'work' would I be getting done in the middle of winter when the ground was frozen eight feet down?

"Okay..." Tom said slowly, as if wondering the same thing. "You know you can call me anytime, don't you? I thought I'd cleared your lane almost down to the gravel after the last snow, but I'd be happy to-"

"Oh, no, it's nothing like that," I interrupted hurriedly, cursing my lack of forethought. "You always do a great job with the snow and I really appreciate it, but this is..." The bullshit factory between my ears spun up to speed at last, thank goodness. "...a drilling company just looking around. Something about an old natural gas pipeline that wasn't marked. They promised me that if it's actually there, it's not in use anymore, but I'd like to know."

"Of course." Tom sounded relieved. "I wouldn't be surprised if there were a bunch of pipelines they'd forgotten to mark. I'll never forget the first time I saw a pipeline map of Alberta. The lines are so close together it looks like a solid block of colour."

Somehow I managed to keep my chuckle casual. "Crazy province." Inspiration struck. I could kill two birds with one stone. "Hey, speaking of crazy... have you heard any gunfire in the past couple of days?"

Tension knifed into his voice. "Yes, I heard a few shots on Monday evening. Why, what's wrong?"

"Nothing. I found some footprints in the snow and some .22 brasses, but it was probably just somebody popping at jackrabbits. There's no damage to my buildings or anything. How many shots did you hear? And did you happen to notice any strange vehicles around?"

"There might have been half a dozen shots or so, maybe more. I wasn't really paying attention. I had company that evening, and the shots sounded like your .22 so I didn't think much of it. Although now that I think of it, I should have called you. It was maybe around..." Tom hesitated as though calculating the time. "...nine-thirty or ten o'clock. Long after dark. And I didn't notice any vehicles. I'm sorry. I'll pay more attention from now on."

"It's okay, no big deal. I was out of town anyway, so it wasn't like there was any danger. But do you think your company might have spotted anything as they came or went from your place?"

"I'll ask Margaret, but..." Discomfort crept into his voice. "She stayed a little late that night. She didn't leave until long after the shots, so she probably didn't see anything."

A needle of jealousy jabbed me. Damn Margaret Young. If I hadn't been swept into this unwanted clandestine life, I could have been the one taking my handsome neighbour for a test-drive.

Shaking off the green monster, I faced the facts. I already had two extraordinary men. And even though Tom was a great guy, I didn't really want him for himself. I only wanted the safe peaceful life he represented.

The one I could never have.

With a silent sigh, I relinquished the last of my dreams and kept my voice light. "That's okay, don't bother Margaret with it. You wouldn't want to upset her with the thought that somebody was shooting near your place in the dark. You know how some city people are about guns."

"Well, she used to be a police officer so she's probably okay with guns."

Interesting. She'd told him about her past. But wouldn't a former police officer have paid attention to gunshots in the night? If Tom had heard them, she should have, too.

So she must have been expecting the shots.

Dammit.

Tom was still talking. "...but you're right; it might bring back bad memories for her, so I won't mention it. I'll just ride out this afternoon and have a look around."

"Oh, don't worry about it," I said hastily. "I mentioned it to the pipeline guys so if there's anything else to find, they'll find it. And they got a bit twitchy when I mentioned guns, so it might be kinder not to sneak up on them."

Tom chuckled. "City boys. Well, thanks for letting me know they're over there. And give me a call if you want me to have a look around. I'm happy to do it."

"Thanks, Tom. You're too good to me."

His voice softened. "It's my pleasure. 'Bye for now."

I said goodbye and hung up, then hurried out.

As I emerged into the lobby, Arnie rose from one of the chairs with a smile. "Where ya headed, darlin'?"

"Over to Lola's."

"I'll drive ya."

My heart warmed. He really was extraordinary.

Somehow I managed not to fling myself at him and kiss him senseless. Lowering my voice, I shot him a sultry look from under my lashes instead. "Promises, promises."

He grinned and pulled me close. "Ya know I always keep my promises."

"I'm counting on it." Slipping out of his embrace before I could put on an X-rated show for the security guard, I headed for the wicket to sign out.

On the street outside Up & Coming, I eyed the rows of parked cars occupying both sides of the street. "Shit, the damn alien people are everywhere. You'd think that a murder would take the shine off the whole thing for them."

Hellhound shrugged. "These're True Believers." I could hear the capital letters in his voice. "Nothin's gonna stop 'em. Lopez was just a martyr to the cause."

"That's really scary." I unbuckled my seatbelt. "Are you coming?"

He grinned. "Not even breathin' hard yet, but I got high hopes for later."

I shivered at the heat in his eyes. "Mmmm. Me, too."

His fingertips traced an unhurried path from my cheekbone to my jaw and I leaned in. Our lips touched and my eyes drifted closed. His fingers threaded through my hair and a brush of his tongue made me moan and open for him, heat blazing through my body.

The kiss ended far too soon. Drawing back, Arnie murmured, "Ya better get goin', darlin'. Can't afford to get distracted out here." He gave me the lazy smile that always preceded mind-melting pleasure. "I'll plan our honeymoon while you're doin' your thing with Lola."

"I could skip the bookkeeping and we could go straight to the honeymoon," I suggested. "Lola would approve."

He snickered. "She'd sell tickets."

I grinned. "Too right." Reality cooled my desire, and I sighed. "I need to get in there and make sure she's not doing anything that's going to get her killed. I'll be done around three. Thanks for looking out for me."

"No problem, darlin'." He winked. "What're husbands for?"

I was still smiling when I opened the door to Up & Coming, only to stop short. The small store was so packed with people that the only merchandise still visible was a row of rainbow-coloured dildos above where elderly Bud Weems perched on the seat of a walker. A sparkly blue penis appeared to be sprouting from the top of his head, and I hurriedly looked away.

My heart sank as I surveyed the rest of the geriatric crowd. CRAPS was out in full force.

A familiar chime jerked my attention across the room, and I managed not to tense. Shit, not all the CRAPS members were geriatric. Margaret silenced her ever-present phone and returned it to her purse, giving me a cheery smile and wave.

"Aydan!" Lola hurried over, grinning. "CRAPS is on the job! We'll have Eddy cleared and find the real murderer in no time!"

"Didn't you get my message?" I demanded. "This is too

dangerous. If you start asking questions in the wrong places, you might end up dead, too. Just let it go. Let the police do their job."

"No offense, Miss Kelly..." Bud Weems stopped to take a breath before continuing, "I'm just speaking for myself here..." He sucked in another breath and went on, his voice weak and wheezy with gasps for breath between phrases. "I've got nothing to lose... but a few more years... of slow suffocation. Eddy's a good man. If I can help him... I'm willing to take the risk."

CHAPTER 23

My heart clenched at Bud's bravery, his frail back held military-straight and his emaciated shoulders squared. Only a couple of weeks ago he'd been hospitalized with pneumonia, and he still didn't look well enough to have been released.

"These colours don't run," I said softly, quoting the slogan he'd told me from his army days with the Princess Patricia's Canadian Light Infantry.

Fierce pride illuminated his paper-white features. "That's right, Miss Kelly."

"It's just Aydan, remember," I reminded him gently. "And even though I know you're willing to lay down your life, I'm sure Eddy would rather you didn't." I raised my voice to include the rest of the group. "And I really don't think you should interfere in police business. Eddy will likely be released soon, and the police lab will probably find evidence that shows Eddy couldn't have done it. We all know he's innocent." I mentally crossed my fingers in the hope that was true. "We just have to trust the system."

"Miss Kelly." A slender woman with her white hair coiled into an elegant chignon stepped forward. Her wrinkled face was impeccably made up, and her fashionable outfit was only slightly marred by the walking cast on her foot. "With all due respect," she went on in a prim and precise voice, "That's bullshit. When you've lived as long as I have, you'll know that you can't just sit back and trust the system. You have to grab it by the balls and squeeze."

Somehow I managed to squelch my laughter. "You must be Pearl."

Her chin came up. "How did you know that?"

I let my grin leak out. "Lola might have mentioned her ninety-three-year-old friend from the erotic literature club who broke her ankle a few weeks ago. I also seem to recall a story about you deterring an intruder with a load of rock salt from Bessie, your shotgun."

Wicked amusement glinted in Pearl's faded blue eyes. "I don't remember anything about that. I'm old, you know, and my memory is very poor."

"Yeah, right," I agreed, still grinning.

"Come on, Aydan," Lola cajoled. "We're going to do this no matter what, so you might as well help us. We'll be careful. And anyway, like Pearl says, we're old. Nobody pays attention to old people. That's why we're perfect for investigating."

"You're not old." I eyed her diminutive figure fondly, from her spiked magenta hair down over the wrinkled cleavage displayed by her hot pink leather bustier, to the tiniest biker boots I'd ever seen, liberally festooned with chrome chain. "You'll never be old. And you'll sure as hell never be ignored."

She hooted with laughter. "Honey, I'm seventy-four. I don't think I'm old, but everybody else does."

"Not I," Pearl said. "You've barely reached the prime of life."

Lola turned a grin on me. "And that's why we're

friends."

I shook my head, realizing that the only way to protect them was to join them. "Okay, I'm in. What have you got?"

"The aliens done it!" A thready voice from the back of the store was followed by a witch-like cackle.

"Oh, for heaven's sake, Martha!" Pearl turned to glare in that direction. "Everyone knows there's no such thing as aliens."

"Sure there is," Martha persisted from behind a shelving unit. When I bent to look between the open shelves, I spotted a pair of beady eyes peering out between an anal plug and a bottle of flavoured lube. "Everybody knows there's aliens. Bud even saw 'em."

I straightened, eyeing Bud with a smile and waiting for him to spin the yarn.

"Well, now, Martha... I don't rightly know... that it was aliens," Bud wheezed thoughtfully. "But I saw something."

My smile dwindled. Bud might be in poor physical health, but there was nothing wrong with his mind. Or his eyes.

"What did you see?" I asked. "And when?"

"Monday night around two AM. I was in my recliner. I cough if I lie flat. Had the curtains open." Bud spoke in short sentences with wheezy gasps in between, but his smile was as bright as ever. "I like to look at the stars."

"So what did you see?" I prompted.

"It's what I *didn't* see. Bright moon that night. Sky was clear. Beautiful." His brow furrowed. "And then the stars vanished."

"Vanished? What do you mean?"

"Something blacked 'em out. Wasn't a cloud. This was black. And moving."

Despite my skepticism about aliens, a chill shivered down my spine. "How big was it?"

"Maybe fifteen, twenty feet across." His frown deepened. "Flying slow. Moonlight caught the edges... as it went up and over... the Sirius Dynamics building. Big triangular wing. Like one of those hang gliders."

"But it was black?"

"Flat black."

Suspicion niggled at the edges of my mind. Monday night, when my house got trashed. That was 'way too fucking coincidental.

"How long did it stay up?" I asked. "And where did it fly?"

"Back and forth over downtown. Low." His troubled gaze met mine. "Like it was flying recon."

My stomach clenched.

"It was up for half an hour," Bud went on. "I poked my head out the door. Couldn't hear anything... except a hum when it climbed. It'd climb and then glide low. Silent gliding in a grid pattern. I called the police." A faint flush rose on his bloodless cheeks. "They were polite. Figured I was just an old crank." His indomitable smile flashed out. "And I am, but..."

He trailed off into a coughing fit. It didn't last long, but he was gasping for breath by the time he got the paroxysm under control.

Lola glanced at Bud and received a shaky 'take over' gesture. She turned to me. "The police did come but it took them half an hour to get there, and by then the flying thing was gone. Bud didn't see it again, and nobody else has seen it, either. But somebody must have been listening on a police scanner, because the very next day it was all over the internet about how aliens were flying over Silverside, and then the alien people started pouring in."

"Anyway, it doesn't matter," Bud wheezed. "I don't know... what that thing was... but it didn't beat a man... to death with a baseball bat."

"Quite right," Pearl agreed. "So let's put aliens aside for now." She shot a quelling look at the anal plug. A disdainful sniff came from behind it, but Martha said nothing else.

Limping over to the sales counter, Pearl set up a small whiteboard on a tripod and uncapped a felt pen. "What are the facts surrounding the murder at Eddy's?" she inquired. "We know the murder weapon was a baseball bat." She wrote 'baseball bat' in perfect penmanship at the top of the board. "Do we know who the victim was?"

"I heard it was one of the alien-lovers," an elderly woman contributed. "Hector something. Or maybe Hector was his last name."

"Herman," another woman corrected. "I remember, because it made me think of Herman Munster." Giggles and chuckles rippled through the group.

Pearl wrote 'Victim: Alien-lover, Herman", then eyed the group. "Last name?"

"Gomez," someone shouted.

"It wasn't Gomez," a short man in the front snapped. "You and your damn TV shows. You're thinking of Gomez Addams. It was some other Hispanic name."

A barrage of possibilities issued from the group, and I tuned them out and switched to worrying over Bud's 'alien spacecraft'. It sure as hell sounded like a high-tech drone to me. And if it was mapping the town, concentrating on the area around Sirius Dynamics...

My blood chilled. Volslav would have the resources to do

that. And it was no secret that Arlene Widdenback and/or Aydan Kelly spent a lot of time at Sirius Dynamics.

I needed to report to Dermott, and talk to Reggie. Pronto.

But did I dare leave the CRAPS meeting? God only knew what they might decide to do. And if the murder of Herman Lopez turned out to be somehow related to Volslav, the situation could be far more dangerous than I'd realized.

And there was Margaret in the thick of the discussion, eyes alight with interest. Was she Volslav's spy, pretending to be an ally while secretly cataloguing any potential threats that might need to be eliminated?

A glance around the animated elderly faces made me suppress a shudder. So vulnerable.

Lola's bigger-than-life laugh rose above the chatter, and my heart twisted. Vulnerable, and so damn important to me.

The Department would have to wait.

By the time I returned my attention to Pearl's whiteboard, the group had correctly identified the victim and dredged up most of the facts I'd gotten from Spider. Score one for the small-town grapevine.

Nobody had mentioned Eddy's history, but it likely wouldn't be long before some nosy CRAPS member discovered it. I kept my mouth shut, hoping the revelation of his past wouldn't hurt Eddy or his business.

"Just wait'll the police start spraying Luminol around in that saloon," the short man in the front was saying with relish. "Whee-oo! When they find all that blood, Eddy's goose'll be cooked!"

Pearl delivered a smart rap to his bald head with her marker. "We're supposed to be *helping* Eddy!"

The man rubbed his head sulkily. "Don't shoot the

messenger. It's not my fault there's blood all over the place in there."

"What blood?" I inquired with trepidation.

"The whole saloon's full of blood," the man informed me with ghoulish delight.

"Anthony, *really!*" Pearl gave him a frosty look and turned to me with a long-suffering sigh. "Despite his tastelessness..." She shot Anthony another disapproving look. "...Anthony unfortunately does have a point. Blue Eddy's Saloon occupies one of the original buildings from when Silverside was founded in 1915. It was a saloon when it was built, and it has been a saloon for most of its existence. Over the decades it's seen a great many brawls and at least two murders." Pearl paused. "Two that I know of, in any case. It's quite possible there were more. The early days of this town were certainly..." Her lips turned up as if enjoying some juicy memories. "...colourful. Especially during Prohibition. I was only a toddler at the time, but my elder siblings told tales of bootleggers smuggling their merchandise underground, just like the famous tunnels in Moose Jaw, Saskatchewan."

"That's fascinating!" Lola exclaimed. "Are there any tunnels left in Silverside?"

"Oh, heavens, I doubt they ever existed." Pearl smiled. "But there might be a grain of truth in the old legends. Maybe that can be our next CRAPS investigation."

Shit, that would be bad. Those tunnels had probably become Sirius's secret infrastructure.

"So," I said loudly. "What you're saying is that there's a lot of old blood in Eddy's."

"Oh, yes," Pearl assured me. "And when Eddy bought the building and renovated it, he removed the newer flooring to expose the original hand-hewn wood floor. It would be very surprising indeed if there wasn't a considerable amount of blood. Luminol will reveal blood residue decades after it was spilled, you know."

I didn't ask how she knew that; but she was right, dammit.

"I'm sure the police know that," I said instead, making a mental note to tell them about the saloon's bloody history.

Pearl turned back to the group. "So let's concentrate on what we can do to help Eddy. Did anybody see or hear anything unusual last night? Anybody live near Eddy?"

Silence prevailed.

A frail-looking woman offered timidly, "I could ask Marilla Newton."

Pearl smiled. "An excellent idea, Connie. Please do." She turned to me. "Marilla Newton is the biggest busybody in town, although she won't admit it. And she's an insomniac. She lives at the corner of Eddy's street, so she might have seen Eddy coming home last night if she was still up."

"And maybe she can confirm that he didn't leave again," Lola put in eagerly.

Shit, Volslav just acquired a potential target.

"That would be great," I agreed, trying to sound enthusiastic while making Margaret realize that poor Marilla Newton wasn't a threat. "But I doubt if she watched out her window all night long without a minute's break. The police would argue that Eddy could have slipped by when she wasn't looking."

Lola slumped. "I guess you're right."

Feeling as though I'd just kicked a puppy, I added, "But it could still help if she saw him coming home."

Lola perked up again. "What about the alley behind the saloon? What if somebody went through the alley sometime in the night and there was no body yet? That would help narrow down the time of the murder."

Pearl nodded. "Yes, and we should also ask if anyone saw any strangers lurking around the area, or entering or leaving the alley." She brightened as though an idea had struck her. "Or entering or leaving Eddy's after hours. Someone sneaked into that building and stole Eddy's bat."

Lola straightened and eyed her troops like a tiny general. "All right, everyone, we know what we're looking for. Let's go out and find it! Eddy's freedom is at stake, and we owe him for letting us hold our meetings there."

"And for the free appetizers he gives us," Anthony seconded.

"Right," Lola agreed. "Good hunting, everyone. Get on the telephone chain right away if you find anything."

The group rose, chattering eagerly among themselves, and shuffled out the door.

As the last of the stragglers departed, Lola turned to me. "Well, I guess you can get started on the books-" She broke off, hope lighting up her eyes. "You just thought of something. I can see it on your face."

I smiled. "You're right, I did. Somebody stole Eddy's bat from under the bar, but Eddy has video surveillance. I bet the police already know who took that bat. They've probably already got a suspect. Maybe they've even arrested somebody."

"Oh." Lola looked disappointed for an instant before rallying. "Well, that would be great. But we'll keep investigating. Just in case we can dig up more evidence."

I briefly considered warning her of the dangers again,

but it would be futile. I went for a distraction instead. "I see Margaret has joined CRAPS."

Lola's smile lit up her face. "Yes, isn't it great? It's so nice to have some younger members. She and Tom make a lovely couple, don't they?"

Somehow I managed not to wince. "I didn't know they were a couple, but yeah, that's nice. Tom couldn't make it today?"

"No, this was a last-minute meeting, so he couldn't get away." She returned to the topic that interested her more. "He's so handsome and nice, I'm surprised he's stayed single all this time." She nudged me with a sly smile. "Margaret's a lucky woman."

"I'm sure she is," I agreed. "And it's great that she's interested in CRAPS. Has she been helpful?"

"Well..." Lola's smile dimmed. "Not as much as I'd hoped. She's an honest-to-goodness private investigator, you know. I thought she'd be a big help, but when I asked her to lead this investigation, she said she didn't want to step on any toes." Lola shrugged, her usual sunny expression returning. "But I get it. We've all lived here forever, and Pearl likes to take charge. Margaret's probably just figuring out where she fits in."

I faked surprise. "A private investigator? Surely there can't be much business for her here in Silverside."

"I don't know." Lola's face wrinkled into an impish grin. "As soon as I found out what she did for a living, I asked who she was investigating here, but she just laughed. All of a private investigator's records are completely confidential, you know. Even if she wanted to tell me, she couldn't. But she's getting out of the business. She said she was getting rid of her last client and retiring at the end of this month."

My heart gave a thump. "Getting *rid* of her client? That's kind of a weird way to put it, isn't it?"

"Oh, honey, that's just me talking. I can't remember exactly what she said. But we'll all get to know her better tomorrow night. It's going to be such fun!"

I infused as much enthusiasm into my voice as possible. "Right, it'll be great! Well, I'd better get to work. Your books aren't going to do themselves."

Lola winked and gestured at the shelf of X-rated literature and videos. "If any books were ever going to do themselves, these ones would."

"You're incorrigible." I headed for her small office, grinning.

Then I spent the next hour and a half correcting my absent-minded bookkeeping mistakes while I worried over how to protect Lola and her friends from a cold-blooded killer.

CHAPTER 24

Shortly after three o'clock I emerged from Lola's office, trying to rub away my tension headache.

"See you tomorrow at Margaret's," she chirped as I went out, and I managed to suppress my groan.

Hellhound was still waiting across the street in his SUV. Shooting a wary glance up and down the street, I hurried over to slide into the passenger's seat. "Sorry for keeping you waiting all this time."

"No problem, darlin', that's why I'm here. So how did it-" He broke off, his brows snapping together at the sight of my expression. "What's wrong?"

I poured out the story of the 'alien spacecraft', Margaret's presence, and the seniors' determination to solve the murder. "I didn't know whether to run straight to Sirius and report the drone, or hang onto my cover and stay at Lola's," I finished. "But I decided the drone wasn't really an emergency. Nobody's seen it since Monday. If it had been back, somebody would have spotted it now that everybody's watching the sky."

Hellhound shook his head. "What a clusterfuck. I s'pose ya couldn't talk Lola outta investigatin'."

"Of course not. Hey," I added as a thought struck me. "You're a member of the private investigators association, aren't you?"

"Yeah, but I never heard a' Margaret Young."

I sucked in a breath. "She's not really a member?"

He shrugged. "I wouldn't know. I don't go to any more a' those damn meetin's than I hafta, an' I've never read the full membership list. I keep in touch with a coupla other members so we can cover for each other if we get backlogged on cases, but about all I ever do with the AAPI is pay 'em my membership dues."

"Oh." I slumped in the seat. "Okay. Well, I guess if you're still up for playing chauffeur, it's time to head back to the hospital." I fingered the edge of one of the sticky heart monitor pads that had been driving me slowly nuts. "I can hardly wait to get these damn things off me." As he put the vehicle in gear, I added, "Oh, do you mind stopping at the post office on the way? I haven't picked up my mail since Monday."

"Sure."

When we pulled up in front of the tiny building a few minutes later, I unbuckled my seat belt. "Sorry about this, I'll just be minute."

Arnie frowned. "Why are ya apologizin'?"

Hand on the door handle, I gave him a puzzled frown of my own. "Um... because it's an extra stop and you'll have to wait for me."

"That's why I'm here." His frown deepened. "To take ya wherever ya need to go an' wait there 'til you're done, no matter how long it takes."

"And I really appreciate it," I assured him. "I just don't want to waste your time."

He shook his head. "Think about what ya just said, darlin'."

When I gave him a 'what-are-you-talking-about' look, he sighed and reached over to take my hand. "Ya basically just said thirty seconds a' my time is more important than you stayin' alive. Aydan, did your ex-husband give ya shit for wastin' his time whenever ya wanted to do somethin' that wasn't his idea?"

I gaped at him. "What? Of course n…" My denial trailed off as the old bad memories replayed.

"Yeah," Arnie said softly. "Ya hadta apologize for every little thing, didn't ya, just to keep the peace?" When I didn't reply, he turned to face me fully, taking my other hand and holding my gaze with his. "Listen, darlin'. Your time's just as important as mine. Do what ya wanna do. I'll wait, an' I'll be fine with it. An' if somethin' changes an' I ain't fine with it, I'll let ya know an' we'll figure out somethin' else. I won't get mad at ya." He touched my cheek. "An' I won't freeze ya out. No mind games. Okay?"

My heart warmed at his concern, and at the way he instinctively understood the hangups I didn't even know I had. I leaned forward to drop a kiss on his lips. "Okay. Thanks. But you're making a bigger deal out of this than it really is."

"Don't think so, darlin'." He gave me a troubled look. "I never noticed it 'til Kath moved in, but now I can't stop noticin' it. She's always apologizin'. Fuck, the other night I farted, an' she apologized for puttin' too many beans in the burritos."

I would have laughed, but his expression was dead serious.

"Think about that," he went on. "She busts her ass to make this great supper, an' I'm always tellin' her she doesn't owe me an' she sure as hell doesn't hafta cook for me, but she does anyway. An' then she fuckin' apologizes for it. An' you do that, too. So did my mom. Apologizin' for shit that wasn't even her fault, 'cause the fuckin' ol' man'd beat the hell outta her if she didn't." He let out an unhappy breath. "An' even when she did."

I squeezed his hand, wishing I could somehow take away his horrible childhood. "I'm sorry, I didn't mean to bring up those awful memories for you. I'll try not to..."

My words trailed off and we stared at each other.

"Did I really just apologize for apologizing?" I asked.

He sighed. "Yep. Listen, darlin', I ain't sayin' ya oughta change. I just want ya to know you're as important as everybody else. Ya don't hafta apologize to anybody, least of all your fuckin' husband."

Leaning over the shifter console, I threw my arms around him. "Thanks."

"No problem." He drew back and planted a kiss on my forehead. "Now, no more mushy stuff, 'cause I'm startin' to freak out here."

Relieved at the change of topic, I laughed. "Code Red! Give this man some hot meaningless sex, STAT!"

Hellhound chuckled, then pulled a long face. "If we ever get a chance."

"Anticipation makes the heart grow fonder," I misquoted as I slid out of the SUV.

"An' the wood get harder," he growled with a sizzling look that carried me across the street and into the post office without even noticing the winter cold.

My mailbox contained a bundle of envelopes and a parcel card, and I stepped up to the wicket and passed the card over to the postmistress.

"Hi, Aydan. Nice day, isn't it?" she said over her

shoulder as she scanned the rack of parcels.

I glanced out the window, realizing for the first time that the sun had been shining all day. "Um, yeah." I shifted mental gears to small talk. "Nice to see the sun. How have you been?"

"Fine, thanks. Enjoying a breather after the Christmas rush." She returned to the counter bearing a medium-sized box wrapped in brown paper. "Here you go."

Sudden realization struck me. I wasn't expecting a parcel.

And Arnie had told me to watch out for bombs.

"Oh, that's a bit bigger than I was expecting," I blurted, backing up a few steps. "I might not be able to take it with me today."

The postmistress gave me an odd look. She'd obviously seen me getting out of a full-sized SUV across the street. Cargo space wasn't an issue.

"Who's it from?" I asked. "I might leave it for now and come back and get it later."

She turned the box around to study the return address. "Bill Harks."

"*What?*" I recoiled another step.

"That's strange," she said, still frowning at the label. "It was mailed from Calgary. I wonder why he didn't just give it to you personally?"

"Because he's in prison?" My voice came out a little shriller than I'd intended while my mind rocketed through scenarios and options.

What if it was a bomb? What should I do?

It must be stable if it had travelled safely through Canada Post's mail trucks to get here. But if someone was outside watching, waiting for me to take possession before activating the detonator...

The postmistress glanced up. "I'm sorry to be the bearer of bad news, but Bill Harks is out on parole." She grimaced. "I wish they'd kept him in jail. He's horrible."

If someone was outside waiting to hit the trigger, did they care about collateral damage? Or would they blow up the postmistress just to get me?

Dammit. The sooner I left, the safer she'd be.

"And he can keep his damn parcel," I agreed, retreating another step. "I can't imagine what he'd be sending me, but I don't want it."

"No problem, I'll mark it 'Return to Sender'." She shrugged. "Or if he comes in before the next pickup, I'll just give it back to him."

"Thanks." I edged toward the door. "And you might want to handle it carefully just in case there's something awful in there."

Her hands flew away from the package. "Ooh, do you think...?" She straightened with indignation. "He'd better not have sent something awful through my post office!"

"Well, we'll never know, because it's going straight back to him," I comforted. "Thanks again, and have a good day."

I scurried out, leaving her glaring at the offending parcel as though it had defiled her pristine counter.

When I got back in the SUV, I whisked out a secured phone and hit the speed dial. The analyst on call answered immediately, but Dermott took his time picking up after the call was transferred.

"There might be a bomb at the post office," I blurted when he finally answered. "We need to get the bomb squad over there and grab it. It's a package addressed to me, about a foot square."

"How do you know it's a bomb?"

"I don't. I just... it's from a person who would never send me a parcel. And if somebody's trying to kill me..." I trailed off. Damn, now I felt like a paranoid idiot.

Dermott's contemptuous tone didn't help. "So now you're seeing bombs in every fucking parcel." He gave a martyred sigh. "Fine. I'll send the bomb squad over after the post office closes."

"But what if it blows up before then?"

"If it didn't explode while Canada Post was kicking it around their mail trucks, it'll be fine sitting on a shelf for another two hours. We can't barge in and confiscate property all over the place just because poor little Agent Kelly is feeling nervous."

I was opening my mouth, unsure whether my next words would be another request for the bomb squad or a deluge of profanity, when Dermott added, "And you'd better not be wasting the Department's resources. *Again.*" He hung up.

"What's goin' on?" Hellhound demanded as I glared sightlessly through the windshield, mentally shoving bomb-disposal tools up Dermott's ass.

"Bill Harks is out on parole." My voice came out in a growl. "And he sent me a parcel."

"Who's Bill Harks?"

"Oh. I guess I never told you his name. He's one of the guys that beat me up a year and a half ago. When John... when we thought John had been killed."

"An' now I know his name." The Killer's wolfish smile sent an involuntary chill down my spine.

I knew I should try to protect Harks, but I just wasn't that nice. "Yeah," I said instead. "My testimony sent him to prison. I've really got to remember to register with the

parole board for notifications when somebody gets released."
I hesitated. "Although, come to think of it, Harks is the only
one who's still alive. My enemies tend to die before they
make it to prison."

Hellhound's evil smile widened. "Just the way it oughta
be."

"Hmph." I shifted my shoulders under the
uncomfortable weight of guilt. "It feels kind of wrong to be
glad they're all dead, but it was them or me..." Before he
could point out that I was feeling guilty for not dying like a
good little victim, I changed the subject. "Anyway, I'm sure
the parcel from Harks is just a thoughtful gift. You know, to
show there are no hard feelings."

Hellhound snorted. "Yeah, no doubt."

"I can't believe he thought I'd open it."

"Most people would. Curiosity."

"Hm." I considered. "You're right. I am morbidly
curious about what's in there, but I guess I'll find out when
the bomb squad opens it." Sighing, I eyed the post office.
"What if it explodes in there? I'd never forgive myself if the
postmistress got hurt. Maybe I should go in and get it."

"Nope," Hellhound said with certainty. "If it didn't blow
when they were shippin' it, it'll be safe sittin' on the shelf 'til
the bomb squad gets there."

"You're probably right. That's what I thought, and that's
what Dermott said, too. But I just..." I sighed again.

Hellhound put the SUV in gear. "I know, darlin', but this
is the safest way for everybody. Try not to worry. Let's get
ya to the hospital."

Dropping off the Holter monitor only took a few
minutes. As I hopped back into Hellhound's SUV, I glanced
at my watch. "Damn, it's nearly three-thirty, and I forgot

Reggie leaves early these days to pick up the kids. I hope he's still there. I really want to talk to him about that drone."

Hellhound accelerated. "We're only a coupla minutes away. I'll drop ya right in front a' Sirius."

Two minutes later I hurried into the lobby, only to come face to face with Reggie and the gorgeous Dr. Honey Jacqueline Travers.

"Shit, you're leaving," I blurted.

"I am; Jack's not," Reggie pointed out. He frowned, eyeing my expression, and lowered his voice. "Something happening?"

"'Fraid so."

"I'll pick up the kids and come right back," he began, but Jack laid her hand on his arm.

"It's all right," she said. "I'll just give Penny a quick call and ask her to take Brendan and Ivy home along with her kids. Aydan, how long do you think this will take?"

"It's not an emergency," I assured them. "Go ahead and pick up the kids, Reggie. We can talk tomorrow. It's about something that happened on Monday, so it's not-"

"So it's something I should have known five days ago," Reggie interrupted.

Jack was already dialling her phone. While she made arrangements with her friend, Reggie turned to me.

"You okay going down to the secured area, or do you want to stay above-ground?"

"I think we need the secured area."

His face hardened. "Yeah, I figured. Don't bullshit me again, Kelly. If it's important, say so. Picking up the kids is a high priority for me, but it's okay if we have to make other arrangements sometimes."

"Sor-" I bit off the reflexive apology. "Okay," I said

instead. "Now that I know that, I will."

As Jack disconnected from her call, Reggie said, "Come on, let's go."

Focused on my other worries, I managed to navigate the time-delay chamber without getting too claustrophobic. Seconds after my butt landed in the chair in Reggie's office, I blurted, "There was a drone doing aerial mapping in downtown Silverside on Monday night."

"Details!" Reggie snapped.

As I reported Bud's observations, Reggie's face grew grim. "You're damn right it was a drone. Mapping with ground-penetrating radar, or I'll eat my shorts. And that configuration, with the flat black finish... it was designed to avoid radar." He scowled. "And it did. Our radar-detection system didn't even squeak." He grabbed the phone and punched in a number. After waiting a moment for the connection, he said, "Leo? Yeah, it's Chow. Who was on security Monday night, between one-thirty and three AM? ...Okay, thanks."

He hung up, his scowl deepening. "Those assholes better hope they didn't miss anything. Come on, let's go into VR and check the security camera records."

Reggie and Jack immediately accessed the brainwave-driven network, their bodies slumping in their chairs and faces going slack. I was cringing at the thought of the headache coming my way, when glorious realization struck me. My decryption abilities wouldn't be needed. I didn't have to endure the pain of the specialized network key.

Letting out a sigh of relief, I fingered my security fob and closed my eyes, mentally stepping into the white void.

"What took you?" Reggie demanded as my avatar joined his and Jack's. As we strode down the virtual corridor looking for an unoccupied sim room, Jack asked, "Did you have difficulty accessing the network?"

"No."

I glanced over to see her avatar's forehead furrowed. Recognizing the expression as scientific concern, I elaborated, "Nothing to worry about. I'm just not used to accessing the network with a standard fob anymore."

Her frown deepened. "It caused a delay in access time. We should run some tests-"

"No, there was no delay," I interrupted before she could get going. "I just didn't go in right away."

Jack's brow cleared, her blue eyes softening. "Aydan, are you having an aversive reaction to accessing the network because of the pain you experience every time?"

I grinned, trying to lighten the mood. "If that's science-speak for 'I hate pain', then, yeah." I went on before she could dig deeper. "Seriously, though, it was more a habitual thing. I'm so used to having to wait for Spider to give me the network key, it just took a few seconds before I realized I could use my Sirius fob this time."

There, no need to pry into my psyche. Dr. Rawling would be doing that soon enough.

It worked. Jack dropped the subject as we all stepped into a blank white sim room, and Reggie commanded, "Run sim, 'Chow Basic'."

A desk, computer terminal, and chair popped into existence. Reggie waved a hand and two more chairs appeared. "Might as well get comfortable," he said as he dropped into the desk chair and commenced rapid two-finger typing.

Jack and I sat, and a few seconds later Reggie spoke again. "Run all feeds in simultaneous 3-D."

The walls and ceiling of the sim dissolved into a bubble of night sky overhead, with streets, buildings, and parking lot surrounding us.

"Nice," I said with admiration as I gazed around. "It's like being right in the centre of the building, if the building was completely transparent."

"Yeah, this is actually a mod of our defence sim," Reggie replied absently. "The target acquisition is fully computer-controlled, but if we were under attack we'd have a tactical team inside this sim bubble controlling the shooting."

I hid a gulp. One more thing I hadn't known about Sirius Dynamics. If I ended up owning the building, would they tell me all this stuff?

"What kind of weapons have we got?" I ventured. "And where are they mounted?"

"Mainly roof, but there are a few mid-building..." Reggie trailed off, concentrating on his computer screen. "Okay, here we go. I'm going to start the footage at two AM. If we don't spot anything, I'll start earlier."

Our surroundings came to life. Bare tree branches scraped the star-studded velvet sky and wisps of snow chased each other down the empty street. The air chilled, and I shivered.

"Whoever's making it cold in here, cut it out," Reggie complained, his gaze glued to the sky.

"Sorry," Jack and I said simultaneously, and the temperature warmed.

"It's so realistic," Jack murmured. "It's hard not to let my mind fulfill my expectation of cold. I can see why these sims can be so effective as weapons against someone who doesn't know about them."

I shivered again. Not due to cold this time.

Controlling my thoughts with all my might, I did *not* think about all the times I'd seen people tortured in sims.

"There!" Reggie's exclamation interrupted my mental efforts, and I focused gratefully on his finger jabbing toward the virtual sky.

A barely-perceptible ripple of darkness disturbed the stars, momentarily blacking them out before they reappeared. The ripple passed overhead, then vanished on the horizon.

"Damn," Reggie said softly. "Let's look at that again." He returned his attention briefly to his keyboard before training his gaze on the virtual sky again. "Okay, watch for it..."

Holding my breath, I stared at the stars.

The ripple reappeared, moving toward us from the east, then passing overhead and disappearing in the west.

"Fuck, no wonder the guards didn't catch it," Reggie muttered.

We all fell silent again, watching the virtual sky.

After watching the ripple make a few more passes, Reggie slumped back in his chair. "They planned their approach angles perfectly. Your witness; Weems, you said...?" I nodded and Reggie went on, "His house was far enough away that he got an oblique look at it, not the optimum stealth angle they used to approach Sirius. So the wing area was larger from his angle, and easier to see when it blotted out the stars. But even then, he probably wouldn't have been able to see its shape if not for the moon."

"Yeah," I agreed. "He said the moonlight caught the edges."

Reggie let out a long sigh. "Well, let's sling the shit into the fan." He punched a few more keys before leaning back in his chair. "Dermott should be here in a few minutes."

Somehow I managed not to flinch.

CHAPTER 25

Several minutes later, Dermott's avatar marched into our sim. "This better be good," he snapped. "I just ditched a phone conference with Upper Command."

"Will you settle for 'really fucking bad'?" Reggie inquired sarcastically.

Dermott tensed. "What's wrong?" He snapped a glance around the dark winter scene and the temperature plummeted. "What am I looking at?"

"A 3-D replay of all the exterior camera feeds on Monday night at two AM," Reggie replied. "And if you can stop expecting it to be cold, we'll all be a lot more comfortable."

Dermott flushed and scowled.

"Reggie," Jack said with gentle tact. "Why don't you set the temperature as an external parameter? I've been struggling to keep myself from making it cold, too."

It would have been polite to second her. But if I did, Dermott would think I was trying to suck up to him. He detested suck-ups no matter who they were, and since he hated me already...

I stayed silent.

"Good thinking." Reggie tapped at his keyboard.

"So what's this big problem?" Dermott demanded as the temperature warmed again.

"Watch," Reggie instructed. "Right... there." His pointing finger followed the ripple of blackness across the virtual sky.

Dermott's question snapped out like a whip. "*What the hell is that?*"

"Stealth drone," Reggie replied. "We're guessing, but it's probably mapping the area with ground-penetrating radar."

"And this was *Monday* night?" Dermott's voice rose dangerously. "Why the fuck am I only hearing about this now? Why didn't Security spot it? And why didn't our fucking state-of-the-art radar system scream like a scalded cat?"

"It's a *stealth* drone," Reggie repeated impatiently. "Judging by Kelly's intel, I'd say it's a delta-wing glider with a radar-absorbing coating and a small top-mounted electric motor. Barely a hum when it climbs, silent as an owl when it glides. The GPR unit was probably top-mounted, too, to minimize the radar profile. And they were really careful about their approach angles."

"*Kelly's* intel?" Dermott turned his glare on me. "And you waited until fucking *now* to report this?"

Fighting the urge to let my reflexive anger erupt in profanity, I held my voice level. "I just found out." A more tactful person would have stopped there. I didn't. "It was intel I gathered as part of that case I've been coordinating with the RCMP," I added. I tried very hard to prevent '*So there, asshole*' from creeping into my tone, but apparently Dermott heard it anyway.

"Don't give me that bullshit!" he barked.

My temper bubbled up and over. "If I hadn't been asking questions about Eddy's case, we'd never have found out about this!" Clamping my teeth on my tongue, I managed not to add 'So don't give me any of your damn bullshit!'

I could hear Dermott's teeth grinding from several feet away. Pretty good simulation, considering our avatars had no actual physical form.

Apparently constrained by the presence of witnesses, Dermott refrained from any more verbal attacks. He jerked his gaze back to Reggie. "How many times did this thing fly over?"

"Don't know yet. I've sent a request to the analysts, top-priority," Reggie replied. "They'll run a computer analysis of the video feeds. You saw how hard it was to spot that thing even in a full-resolution sim like this, so I don't want to count on human eyes. The security guards couldn't possibly have seen it in realtime on their small screens."

I sent warm thoughts Reggie's way. His famously abrasive personality hid a wide streak of empathy and scrupulous fairness. The security guards wouldn't have to face Dermott's ire today.

"So what was it looking for?" Dermott demanded.

Reggie shrugged. "No idea. I'm only guessing about the ground-penetrating radar, but if that's what it was, they were probably mapping our underground infrastructure."

Dermott paled. "Shit. What kind of detail can they get?"

"Piss-poor," Reggie said reassuringly. "GPR is hard to interpret even when it's done with a high-resolution scanner inches from the ground surface. From that altitude, they'd be able to figure out that there are tunnels underground, but that'd be about it."

"But they'd know where the tunnels are."

Reggie grimaced. "Probably."

"Damn." Dermott squared his shoulders. "Well, I'll break the news to Command. They're going to shit." His scowl snapped to me. "Hospital called. You're fine. The examiner's waiting for you in the gym, and Rawling will see you right afterward. If you pass fitness, firearms, and psych, you're back on active duty."

"What about the lie detector interview?" I asked.

"Command agreed to reinstate you without it until we can get it done on Monday." Dermott's scowl deepened. "Holt's got better things to do than fucking babysit you. And anyway, the interview is just a formality." His lip curled as he uttered his final word with taunting sarcasm. "Right?"

"Right," I snapped.

A thoroughly unpleasant smile spread over his face as he strode out. Somehow I managed not to mutter 'Asshole' at his receding back.

"Guess I'll go and do my requalification," I said to Reggie and Jack instead.

"Are you sure that's wise?" Jack asked, her flawless forehead creasing in concern.

"Hospital said I'm fine," I said lightly, and folded simspace to get to the portal before they could respond.

Sucking in my usual hard breath and clenching my teeth, I stepped through.

Into... normalcy.

Blinking, I straightened cautiously. No pain.

I let out a whimper of sheer gratitude and slumped in relief just as Reggie and Jack blinked and sat up in their real-world chairs beside me.

"Aydan, what's wrong?" Jack demanded.

"Nothing." I gave her a smile. "Just appreciating my pain-free exit from the network."

Her eyes darkened. "Oh, Aydan, I'm sorry you have to suffer so much with your daily work. That must be awful!"

Embarrassed, I waved off her sympathy as I sprang up and made for the door. "No big deal. See you later."

Hurrying out of the Weapons lab, I headed for the gym.

Typical Dermott, springing this on me at the last minute. I had no gym clothes with me, but my stretchy jeans and T-shirt were easy enough to move in. And after all, it was supposed to be a fair evaluation of my fitness for duty. If I had to run or fight, the bad guys wouldn't wait around while I changed into gym clothes.

Stepping up to the starting line a few minutes later, I swallowed my nerves.

I could do this. I did it at least once a month.

I *could*.

When the examiner gave the signal, I ran.

A few minutes later, bent over panting with my elbows propped on my knees, I grinned at the floor.

I *could*. So suck that, Dermott.

"Good job, Kelly," the examiner said. "Let's do your weapons qualification."

Confidence restored, I breezed through the weapons testing. Even the psych interview didn't faze me. Dr. Rawling asked his usual prying questions, I responded with my usual evasions and half-truths, and all was well.

Relieved, I was walking out of Dr. Rawling's office when a heavy impact buffeted the building.

Snatching my Glock from its holster, I flung a wild glance around us. The building alarms hadn't gone off, but the windows had rattled...

"Get under your desk!" I barked at Rawling as I lunged across the room.

As he scrambled to obey, I slapped my back to the wall beside the window, heart hammering and Glock at the ready.

A peek out the window made my stomach clench. The streetlights across from the post office revealed mangled wreckage. Scattered pedestrians. Some fleeing, some doubled over. Two on the ground, terrifyingly still. Oh, God, no...

"Stay down until Security gives the all-clear!" I stuffed my gun back into its holster and ran for the door.

The hallway was clogged with wide-eyed civilian researchers.

"Stay in your offices!" I shouted as I made for the stairs. "Under your desks, away from the windows! Go, go! *Move it!* NOW!"

My final bellow seemed to wake them from their stupor. By the time I reached the top of the stairs, the only person remaining in the hallway was Dermott barrelling toward me.

"What the hell?" he demanded as we pounded down the stairs.

"Bomb. Post office." My words jerked out between gasps of fear and exertion.

Dermott let out harsh breath as though he'd been punched in the gut. "Fuck!"

The public-address speakers came to life with a calm, firm male voice. "Everyone stay calm. The building is secure. Stay in your offices, away from the windows, until further notice. I repeat, stay calm, stay in your offices, stay away from the windows."

Black-clad tactical personnel already ringed the lobby by the time we skidded to a halt in front of the security wicket. The air crackled with tension.

"Status!" Dermott snapped.

Leo didn't look up from his multiple video monitors, his hands flying over the controls. "One explosion near the post office. Nothing else on the-"

The lobby door burst open and all weapons snapped around to point at Hellhound as he lunged inside. "Status!" he demanded, ignoring the firepower that could have shredded him to ribbons.

"One explosion near the post office. Nothing else on the perimeter," Leo repeated loudly. "No visible threat to the building. Still scanning."

"I'll get to the scene." Hellhound spun, snatching a walkie-talkie off the belt of the guard nearest to him as he dove out the door again. "Radio check, over." His gravelly voice came through the remaining walkie-talkies, and one of the other guards responded.

A tense silence fell.

A frantic voice shrieked in my brain. *God, Arnie, why did you run back out there? You're not even armed!*

Every muscle in my body clenched tight with the effort of willing him to be safe.

His voice came over the walkie-talkie again a moment later. "Base, this's Helmand. Looks like a car bomb, driver's dead, non-life-threatenin' injuries to pedestrians. Police an' ambulance on the way. Can't see any other threats."

The creak of tactical gear betrayed the easing of the taut muscles in the room.

Hellhound went on, "Aydan still there, over?"

The nearest man handed me his walkie-talkie, and I responded, "Aydan here." A second later I remembered to add "Over" and release the button.

"Witnesses say the casualty is Bill Harks, over."

"Shi-" I bit off the useless expletive and pressed the button again. "I'll be right there. Aydan out."

As I handed the radio back to its owner, Dermott stepped

between me and the door. "Not so fast. We don't know if it's secure out there, and you can't help the dead guy." For once, his tone wasn't unkind.

"The dead guy sent the bomb to me. And I need to talk to the witnesses before the RCMP get here." I shouldered past him.

"Report as soon as you're done," he snapped as I went by.

"Will do." I sidestepped out the door ready to dive for cover, but no bullets whistled past. The ambulance had already arrived, and I hurried toward the flashing lights and clusters of people holding each other.

As I neared the scene, Arnie stepped out from behind the ambulance. "Ya don't need to see this, darlin'." He turned me gently away.

I had already glimpsed a torn and blood-spattered arm. I nodded and let Arnie lead me around the side of the ambulance, blocking the view.

The arm had been lying several feet away from the wreckage. Not attached to its former owner. There had been a lot of less-identifiable chunks lying around, too. Someone was vomiting behind us, and I gulped down my own surge of nausea.

"Looks like Volslav got the wrong truck," Arnie said grimly. "Red half-ton, like yours."

"No, I think-" I began, but a frantic cry interrupted me.

"Aydan! Ohmigod, Aydan!" The postmistress flung herself at me, wrapping me in a suffocating embrace. "Omigod, omigod!"

I held her in return, or, more accurately, held her up. She was trembling so violently that most of her weight was suspended from my neck.

"Omigod," she whimpered into my shoulder. "Omigod..."

"Shhh," I soothed, rocking her. "It's okay. Shhh. It's okay, you're okay."

"It blew up!" Her clutching arms tightened, nearly throttling me. "It blew *up!* He said he didn't send it and he didn't want it but I made him take it and it b-blew up! I k-killed him! *I... k-killed... h-him!*"

CHAPTER 26

The postmistress's sobs turned into wordless wails half-strangled by too-rapid gasps for breath. My shushing and back-rubbing only seemed to make things worse.

Arnie hurried back to the ambulance and returned moments later with a paramedic, and together they peeled the hysterical woman off me.

As the paramedic helped her away, I turned to Arnie. "Thanks. I need to talk to the witnesses before the police..." The distant wail of a siren caught my ear. "...dammit, they must have been on patrol near here." I hurried over to the nearest white-faced group of people. "Did you see what happened?"

One of the women made a feeble gesture toward the chaos behind us. "The truck blew up."

Biting back the urge to snap 'No shit!', I kept my voice gentle and unhurried. "Did you see what happened?"

"N-No. But Angie did." The woman pointed to another group of people surrounding a woman slumped on the sidewalk. A paramedic dabbed at the blood on her face, but she was sitting up by herself so her injuries were probably superficial.

Shit, I couldn't question her without blowing my cover. And the first RCMP cruiser was already turning onto the street.

Gripping Arnie's parka sleeve, I turned us away from the scene so nobody could read our lips. "Did you find out anything?" I asked.

"Nothin' to find out. I saw the whole thing."

I sagged with relief and wrapped my arms around myself, aware for the first time of the frigid wind biting through my sweater. "What happened? And why were you outside? I thought you'd be waiting for me in the lobby."

"Chow came through on his way to pick up Jack's kids, an' he said ya were doin' your fitness an' firearms requalification an' you'd be a while. I figured you'd be ready to fall over after your fitness test, so I went over to the Melted Spoon to grab ya a snack."

I hugged his arm to me, my heart warming. "Thanks."

He gave me a wry smile. "Don't thank me too soon, darlin'. I dropped your tea an' muffin when the truck blew."

The wind gusted and my teeth began to chatter. "It's the thought that c-counts." I reached up to kiss his cheek. "So wh-what did you see?"

He frowned and unzipped his parka. "Here, take my parka. You're freezin' your ass off."

Tightening my hug around my body, I did my best to control my shivers. "N-No, it's okay, I'm g-going back into the building in a minute. You'll need your p-parka. You'll have to stay out here and talk to the p-police."

"'Kay, but c'mere." He folded me into his arms, wrapping the parka and his arms around my back. I burrowed into the blissful warmth and tucked my head under his beard as he went on, "I was walkin' along the sidewalk, comin' this way 'bout fifty yards the other side a' Sirius. Big guy came outta the post office, 'bout six-six, three-fifty pounds, shaved head. Couldn't make out his face in the streetlights, but one a' the witnesses said it was Harks."

"Yeah, the postmistress confirmed it. Go on."

"He was carryin' a box maybe a foot square. Got into an old red Dodge half-ton but didn't drive away. I couldn't see what he was doin' in there, but I wasn't really payin' attention. Coupla seconds later, boom. I thought it was a car bomb, but it musta been the box he sent ya."

"He opened it," I said with sick certainty. "Shit. He didn't send it. He didn't know what was in it, and he was curious. That poor bastard."

"Poor bastard, my ass," Hellhound snapped. "That fucker beat the hell outta ya. Him an' his friend, right? I remember ya sayin' there were two a' them. He deserved to get blown to hell."

I sighed. "Yeah, and he assaulted and raped a bunch of other women, too, but they never came forward to testify so he got off easy. He probably did deserve to get blown up, but..." Shrugging, I let it go. "Anyway, you have to give your statement to the police, and I have to go and report to Dermott. Let's meet in the lobby whenever we're both done."

"Okay." Arnie lowered his lips to mine.

Letting out a sigh, I kissed him back, releasing my pent-up fear and giving in to the sheer glorious relief of having him safely in my arms again.

He deepened the kiss and I pressed closer, running my hands under his parka to grip the hard muscles of his back. Time stalled while our tongues made sensual promises that heated the layers of fabric between us to combustion temperature.

"Sir. Excuse me, sir."

A firm and unwelcome voice intruded, and I drew back far enough to see an RCMP constable beside us. He looked impatient, as though he might have been standing there for a while. "Sir, witnesses say you were on the scene. Will you answer some questions for us?"

I sighed and turned Arnie loose. "I'll see you later."

"Ma'am, before you go, did you see anything?" the constable asked.

"No, I was inside the building when I heard the explosion." I indicated Sirius Dynamics with a jerk of my chin. "By the time I looked out the window it was all over."

"See ya later, darlin'," Hellhound said as he turned to follow the constable back to his cruiser.

Bereft of his body heat, I hurried back into Sirius Dynamics, shivering uncontrollably.

The lobby was back to its usual peaceful hush. The armed men had vanished, and the only sign of life was Leo behind the bulletproof glass of the security wicket.

I headed in that direction before realizing I didn't need to sign for my fob. I was still wearing it.

Shit. Dermott was going to have my ass.

"I guess I set off all the alarms," I said sheepishly to Leo as I fingered my fob.

He grinned. "Yep."

I hung my head. "Sorry."

"No big deal. The alarms were in silent mode so I could make announcements over the PA system. I reset the alarm as soon as you went out." His eyes crinkled in good-natured teasing. "I figured you weren't much of a security risk. I knew you'd be back fast, since you went out without your coat." He sobered. "Plus I wanted the alarm reset in case we had a real breach."

"Thanks," I said gratefully. "I owe you."

He waved a dismissing hand. "Like I said, no big deal." Leaning closer, he added, "But if you really want to repay me... what happened out there?"

I grinned. "So this is how you always know everything before everybody else. You extort information in exchange for favours."

He drew back in mock affront. "I would never."

"Never pass up juicy gossip," I agreed, and propped my elbows on the counter as I lowered my voice. "Bill Harks got blown up by a bomb in a parcel he picked up at the post office."

Leo raised an eyebrow. "And it serves him right, but I already knew that." He corrected himself hurriedly. "Well, I didn't know it was a parcel from the post office, but I overheard Hellhound say on the radio that Harks was the victim. So why do you think the bomb was meant for you?"

I shook my head. "Damn, you don't miss anything, do you? I have to report to Dermott first or I'll catch holy hell, but I promise I'll talk to you next."

"I'll know more than you by then," Leo teased.

"I don't doubt it." Tossing him a salute, I turned my reluctant feet toward the stairs.

Dermott looked up with his usual scowl when I tapped on the open door of his office. He jerked his chin to summon me inside, then added, "Close the door."

I obeyed, bracing myself for another fight to the death. Or at the least, another round of insults and temper tantrums.

"Spill it," was all he said.

I began with the eyewitness account from Bud Weems and finished with the parcel from Bill Harks. "So I only just found out about the drone," I concluded. "And I'm guessing Harks wasn't the one who mailed me the bomb. He wasn't the sharpest knife in the drawer, but he wasn't dumb enough to blow himself up."

Dermott shook his head. "I've seen some really fucking stupid shit in my life, but you're probably right. So who sent it?"

"No idea. I didn't look at the parcel that closely, but it had a computer-printed label. Even if the wrapper wasn't in a million tiny shreds right now, we probably wouldn't be able to get anything off it." I slouched lower in my chair, frowning. "What I don't get... why would anybody pretend the parcel was from Bill Harks? Anybody from around here would know I wouldn't open anything that came from him. But there's no way somebody just randomly chose Bill Harks for a fake name on the address label."

"Maybe they thought you wouldn't check the label?" Dermott looked as puzzled as I felt. "But that's pretty fucking lame. If they were smart enough to mail a bomb that wouldn't explode while it was being shipped through Canada Post, they should be smart enough to figure out that a fucking arms dealer isn't going to just rip open a parcel she didn't order."

"So maybe somebody was trying to frame Harks?" I speculated. "Keep attention away from themselves? If I got killed, Harks would be a plausible fall-guy for the murder. He hated my guts."

"Yeah... but that seems iffy. If they were serious about killing you, they would have put one of your friends' names on it."

My blood chilled. If Nichele's name had been on the return-address label, I would have ripped the parcel open eagerly. And those would be my body parts scattered across hell's half-acre right now.

"Maybe somebody was trying to get rid of Harks," I suggested. "Somebody who didn't mind killing me if it accidentally happened; but they figured the parcel would end up being returned to Harks and he'd be curious enough to open it. But that seems like a really complicated and unreliable way to kill a guy."

Dermott drummed his fingers thoughtfully on the desk, frowning into space. Then his brows snapped together, his face twisting in fury. "You sneaky bitch!"

CHAPTER 27

Taken completely by surprise, I gaped at Dermott's suddenly-infuriated face. "Wh-What?"

"You fucking sneaky *bitch!*" he repeated. "You had this all figured out, didn't you? Now Harks is permanently out of your hair, you look like an innocent victim, and the fucking chain of command falls all over itself to make sure their special, precious *Agent Kelly...*" He said my name with a vicious snarl. "...gets extra protection."

"What the fuck? I didn't-"

"You were in Calgary Monday night," Dermott growled. "The package was mailed from Calgary."

"A million people live in Calgary," I retorted. "And where and when do you think I had a chance to build a fucking bomb?"

"Chow probably built it for you. He could build something like that in his sleep. And everybody knows you two are buddy-buddy." Dermott's lips twisted in an ugly grin. "You just fuck your way into everybody's hearts, don't you? Well, news flash, honey, it won't work with me."

I rocketed to my feet, fists clenched. "Too goddamn right it won't! Because I wouldn't fuck you if you had the last dick on earth, you disgusting sack of shit!"

As I stomped toward the door, he spoke with quiet

menace behind me. "Just wait 'til Monday."

Without turning, I jabbed my middle finger skyward and kept going.

As I forged into the hallway I nearly plowed into Dr. Rawling. Slamming on the brakes, I did my best to smooth my face into an apologetic expression. "Oh, sorry, I didn't see you."

"It's quite all right, no harm done." He smiled his mild little smile, but his eyes were far too sharp behind those innocuous wire-rimmed glasses. "You seem upset, Aydan. Is everything all right?"

It was the last straw.

After my psych interview with him earlier, I had absolutely no deception left in my body; and even if I could have summoned some convincing bullshit, I didn't have any patience left to apply it.

"Dermott just accused me of *blowing that guy up!*" My voice rose to a full-throated shout. *"THAT IS NOT ALL RIGHT!"*

Rawling twitched.

It was only a tiny movement, but it was enough to shake me back to reason. This man could incarcerate me just as quickly and surely as Dermott. One failed psych exam could be all it took.

"Sorry," I added hurriedly. "I'm afraid tempers got a little hot in there." I jerked my chin in the direction of Dermott's door. "We'll work it out. As soon as the lie detector is available, he can question me and it'll show I didn't do it."

Rawling gave me his patented accepting smile. "But it must be quite upsetting to be wrongly accused in the meantime."

Somehow I managed a rueful grin. "Apparently. I'm sorry for yelling at you."

"Try not to be too hard on yourself," he said gently. "You and Director Dermott have just experienced an extremely stressful situation. I heard that you went to the scene of the explosion and that you knew the victim. And Director Dermott takes his responsibility to protect everyone in this building very seriously. It's not surprising that you're both ruffled just now."

Dumbfounded, I could only stare at him.

Support. Understanding.

Not condemnation.

Had I been misjudging his motives all along?

"Th-Thanks," I stammered after a moment. "That makes me feel better."

"I'm glad." He smiled.

Was that a genuine smile?

"I was just on my way to turn in your psych report," he added. "I'm clearing you for active duty." His smile widened. "Even if our earlier interview hadn't convinced me, I would certainly have been convinced after the way you responded when the bomb exploded. Instant action, immediately protecting others with no thought for your own safety. You're a good agent."

I gulped down the sudden, foolish lump in my throat. "Thanks," I croaked.

"You're welcome." Rawling patted my arm and went into Dermott's office, leaving me completely rattled.

After a moment of hesitation, I trudged down the hall toward my office. The corridor was deserted and all the other office doors stood open. Apparently even the most dedicated of the researchers had abandoned ship.

The silence was pleasant, and my shoulders relaxed. As I drew nearer to my own office, the rapid tapping of computer keys drifted to my ears. Poking my head into Spider's office, I smiled. Of course he was still hard at work.

"Hey, Spider," I said.

He started violently. "Oh." He let out a breath and slumped back in his chair. "Hi, Aydan. I was deep in..." He gestured at his laptop and his voice faded as his gaze drifted back to the screen.

"Sorry. I'll leave you to it."

I drew back, but he blurted, "No, wait." He flushed. "If you don't mind waiting? I just need another minute to finish up..." He trailed off again as his gaze snagged on his screen.

Smiling, I came in and sat watching him while his fingers flew over the keyboard. His concentration was absolute, and I studied his intent features with a pang.

My favourite man-child had grown up. His limbs were still lanky, his face unlined; but there was a firmness to his jaw and a confidence in his voice that hadn't been there two years ago. And the innocence was gone from those clear hazel eyes, replaced by resolute optimism.

I stifled a sigh. Another casualty of the Aydan Kelly Shit-Show.

"There." Spider hit a few final keys and sat back, his brows drawing together as he studied me. "You look really down. Do you want to talk about it?"

How do you apologize to a kid for destroying his innocence?

I sighed. "I'm okay. Just tired. Did you want me for something?"

"I was just wondering if you still want to go into the network and look for Volslav this afternoon, but if you're tired, you'd better not."

"Actually, that's what I was going to ask you, too." I dragged myself out of my slouch. "I'm not that tired. Not physically, anyway. Just..."

Disillusioned and sad and desperately sick of blood and violent death.

I waved a vague hand. "You know."

Spider gave me a sympathetic grimace. "Yeah. It's really scary about that bomb. But at least Dermott took over the investigation from the RCMP. We'll be processing the evidence through our lab."

A small spurt of hope straightened my spine, but a moment later reality intruded. Dermott was only analyzing the bomb because he hoped he'd find evidence that I'd built it.

I suppressed another sigh. "That's good. So, do you mind anchoring me in the network? With everything I've found out today, I'd really like to snoop around a bit and see if I can find some more information."

Spider rose. "Okay, but only a short session. An hour, max. You've been through a lot today, and I don't think you should push it."

"An hour's fine." I gave him a smile as I stood, too. "I'm getting hungry anyway, and Arnie will probably be waiting for me by then."

"Great. I'll go and get your network key from the secured area and meet you in your office." Spider hurried out, and I plodded to my office and dropped onto my sofa.

Fatigue turned my limbs and eyelids to lead. I had been tired this morning. Now, after the physical and emotional demands of my requalification and the explosion, I just wanted to curl into a ball and sleep for a week.

"Aydan?"

Every muscle in my body convulsed. I was on my feet and grabbing for my Glock before my half-asleep brain registered Spider's presence.

"Oh. Sorry." I collapsed back onto the sofa. "I guess I dropped off for a few seconds."

Spider eyed me worriedly. "You're too tired to be doing this. It's not safe."

I stretched out my hand, wiggling my fingers in a 'give' gesture. "My whole *life* is not safe. If I was ever actually completely safe, I'd probably drop dead from the shock of it." When he hesitated, clutching the tiny piece of circuitry, I added, "It's only for an hour. I'll be fine."

"But if you're too tired to control your thoughts, you could die in the sim," he argued. "Or what if you have a data collision with another mage again? It takes hours to separate yourself, and you use every ounce of energy you've got."

Great, just what I needed. More panic-inducing thoughts.

"I know what I'm doing," I lied. "I'll be fine. Come on, Spider, hand it over and let's get this done. An hour, tops, I promise."

"But Holt isn't here to anchor you..." he began.

"Holt probably won't be available for a while. I think Dermott assigned him somewhere else." I didn't elaborate on that unpleasant conversation. "You can anchor me externally. Let's just do this."

"But it's not as safe as when Holt anchors you." Spider reluctantly handed me the network key, his brow furrowed with worry. "Couldn't you just tell Brock what you're looking for, and let him and Tammy look for it? It's so much safer in the network for them."

"I thought they had been looking for stuff all day. Did they find anything?"

Spider sighed. "No."

"So we're doing this." I closed my hand around the tiny cube of circuitry. "Rubber baby buggy bumpers?"

He sighed again. "Okay."

As I closed my eyes, my last glimpse of him showed furrows on his forehead and his eyes dark with worry.

Trying to ignore the guilt, I stepped into virtual reality and vanished. Letting the data tunnels carry me where they would, I extended virtual feelers in all directions.

Smelling, tasting, sensing...

Alert for the slightest tingle of anything that felt relevant...

I stretched farther, then farther still. The attenuated bits of my consciousness wavered in the data flow like hairs tethered in a fast-flowing stream.

Wait.

I knew that flavour.

Snapping all but one of my tentacles back into a compact bullet of consciousness, I rocketed down the data tunnel following the filament that had sensed my quarry.

Their server was aggressively protected.

Bobbing in the churning data outside it, I would have smiled if I'd been capable of it in my current form. Earlier in my career I would have been quaking in terror at the knowledge that the server's defences could shred my consciousness like a tissue in a spin-washer.

But not now.

I extended gossamer-thin tentacles, gauging the flow of data around me.

There.

In the turbulence of data packets flinging themselves at the server and being violently rejected, one small tranquil stream trickled out.

My way in.

An eyeblink later, I was riding the current of data into the CIA's internal network, straight to Everett Marsh's files.

In only a second, I digested the snippets of new information. No answers. Only more damn questions.

Spreading myself through their network, I searched for more.

Nothing.

Dammit. Reach farther...

A nagging sensation interrupted my concentration. Spider must be signalling me to return.

Easing invisibly out of the server, I slipped back into the internet and followed the faint tugging back to Sirius Dynamics.

When I reassembled myself behind the Sirius firewall, I let out an airless sigh of relief. Made it back safely, one more time.

Popping my avatar into visibility, I headed for the portal.

A few minutes later the pain of my exit subsided enough for me to release my hold on my throbbing real-world temples. I straightened slowly.

"How did it go?" Spider asked.

"I found something interesting." My voice came out in a croak, and I cleared my throat and rolled my shoulders. "Everett Marsh, the guy Grandin swore gave the order to kidnap me?"

Spider nodded, wide-eyed.

"Marsh knew Nora." I spat the distasteful words out. "My so-called mother."

"How?" Spider demanded. "You mean, like, Marsh knew Nora personally?"

"No. Marsh was her handler. She was selling intel to the CIA."

CHAPTER 28

"Oh." Spider's voice was small. He reached over and squeezed my hand. "Sorry," he said awkwardly. "It must be pretty awful to find that out. But... I don't see how that connects to Volslav. And Grandin was definitely signing 'Volslav', not 'Nora'."

I blew out a breath. "I don't see it yet, either. But hell, at this point I wouldn't be surprised to find out Nora *was* Volslav. If Nora was selling intel to the CIA, that means she already had a way to harvest it..." I trailed off, staring at Spider.

"What?" he asked. "What are you thinking?"

"Did you or Jack ever have time to analyze the extra network keys we seized from the UK branch of Sirius Dynamics when Rebecca got trapped in the internet? Remember how there were two extra pairs and we thought there was another secret mage besides Rebecca?"

Comprehension dawned on his face. "Oh. No, we haven't had a chance to look at them yet."

"Well, I'll bet you any money that the extra pairs of keys weren't for another mage. They were for Nora to use with Rebecca. So she could secretly push Rebecca into the internet and use her to steal data."

The enormity of that thought hit me like a punch to the

gut. "Shit, Spider, we've been wrong from the start. Nora wasn't trying to save me from extradition so she could recruit me to steal data. She was already using Rebecca for that."

He looked dubious, and I added, "Think about it. Nora moved to the UK thirty years ago. Volslav has been a player in the overseas arms market for a long time. In the past couple of years Volslav has been trying to get a foothold in Canada. Sam, Nora's..." I couldn't keep the sarcasm out of my voice. "...*devoted husband*, moved back to Canada a couple of years ago."

Spider was still frowning, and I leaned forward, trying to get him to understand. "Spider, don't you see? Nora was Volslav. She'd been trying to get her people to get that weapon from me for months, with no results. So she came here to get it herself, and that's why she specifically asked for me to be at that Five Eyes seminar." Bitterness filled my throat. "She wanted Grandin to abduct me so she could get the weapon from me and then kill me."

"Oh, no, Aydan!" Distress darkened Spider's eyes. "That can't be right! Remember what Nora said? She said she loved you, and the lie detector showed she was telling the truth!"

"Yeah." I could feel my lips curl in disgust. "Loved. Past tense. And remember, the lie detector also indicated she was telling the truth when she denied coming back here to recruit me. We never thought to ask if she came back to kill me."

"No," Spider said firmly. "It seems like it fits, but it doesn't. Nora died right before Christmas. Somebody just searched your house on Monday, and it wasn't Nora's ghost who told them to do it."

"Right..." I drew a breath of cautious hope. "And there was the drone on Monday, too."

"*Drone?*" Spider's question came out in a yelp. "What drone?"

"Oh, sorry, I guess I haven't talked to you since this afternoon." I filled him in on Bud's observations and Reggie's educated guesses. "So if Volslav is behind this week's stuff, either Nora wasn't the head of Volslav, or somebody else has already taken over from her," I finished. "But she's definitely mixed up in this somehow."

"She wasn't trying to kill you," Spider said with certainty. "A mother would never kill her child. She loved you."

"Thanks, Spider," I said gently.

I didn't bother to point out that sometimes mothers did kill their children. And my mother had murdered two other people in cold blood.

"I need to dig into Everett Marsh some more," I said instead.

"Not tonight," Spider said. "You're too tired."

"But-"

"No." His tone was decisive, and he rose. "I'm going to take your network key back down to the secured area now. You're done for the day."

All grown up.

I couldn't help smiling. "Okay," I agreed. "I'll just file a quick report about this, and then I'm out of here."

"Only the report," he said sternly. "Nothing else. You need a rest."

"Yes, Dad."

Spider blushed. "Did I really sound like a dad?" His eager hazel gaze searched my face.

"You really did," I assured him.

His smile flashed out like the sun. "Oh, that's so cool! Wait 'til I tell Linda you said so." His smile widened. "I'm going to be a *dad!* Oh, Aydan, I can hardly wait!"

My gloomy cynicism melted away in the brightness of his joy, and I got up and gave him a hug. "You're going to be the best dad ever."

"Thanks!" He beamed at me for another moment before hurrying out with the key. He wasn't quite skipping, but the bounce in his step lightened my heart despite the weight of my worries.

My scant store of information only took a few minutes to report. I scanned my emails, ignoring the routine ones. I skimmed the dossier on Margaret, and let out a sigh of relief at Christopher's reassurance that my farm was once again under full surveillance from shielded cameras. After replying with a thank-you, I stood up from the computer with a sigh and stretched the stiffness out of my neck and back. My belly felt hollow, hunger combined with the emptiness left by the destruction of yet more illusions about my mother.

I plodded down the hall feeling a hundred years old.

When I emerged into the lobby, Hellhound rose from one of the chairs with a smile.

My heart squeezed. My mother might have betrayed me, but Arnie never would.

"Hey, darlin'," he murmured, welcoming me into his arms.

I clung to him. My husband, the man I could count on no matter what.

A cold wash of terror turned me rigid.

"What, darlin'?" Arnie pulled back, holding my shoulders and studying my face anxiously. "What's wrong?"

"I..." Staring up into his concerned eyes, I swallowed hard. Just Arnie. My husband in name only.

Safe. I was safe with him.

The release of tension left me trembling all over.

"Aydan?" Arnie's voice was tight with worry. "Talk to me, darlin'. Should I call the ambulance?"

I let out a breath and fell back into his arms. "No. I'm okay. Sorry. I was just... I had a moment."

"What kinda moment?" He frowned down at me. "Were ya dizzy? Did ya-"

"No, it's okay," I interrupted. "It wasn't a health thing. I was hugging you and all of a sudden I thought 'husband' and I had..."

A warm rush of love and trust and happiness.

He didn't need to hear that. No point in terrifying us both.

"...a moment," I repeated.

"Ya mean a panic attack," he corrected gently.

"Well, yeah, kind of. But then I looked at you, and I realized you were *you*, and I was okay again. I *am* okay."

Arnie cupped my cheek in a gentle palm. "Don't worry, darlin'. Divorce papers are already drawn up. All ya gotta do is sign 'em, an' you're single again. You're never gonna be trapped with me, I promise."

"Thanks." I reached up and kissed him. "I'm fine now." My stomach let out an audible growl. "Hungry," I admitted. "But fine. Let's go get something to..."

I trailed off as the weight of the world crashed down on me again. Blue Eddy's was closed. The few remaining restaurants in the small town would be packed with alien people. Every scrap of food in my house was rotting on the floor.

"No wonder you're starvin', it's a quarter to seven," Hellhound said. "Come on, let's head back to your place."

My heart plummeted even lower. "Oh, God, I can't face that right now. Maybe Fiorenza's can squeeze us in."

"On a Friday night, with Eddy's closed an' all the alien people in town? Doubt it." He laid a warm arm across my shoulders and turned me toward the security wicket. "Don't worry, darlin', Kane an' I cleaned up a bit at your place this mornin' an' got some groceries, an' Kane made a big lasagna an' left it in your fridge. Your place ain't back to normal, but it ain't a total disaster anymore."

The love and happiness was back.

I flung my arms around him. "Thank you," I whispered, squeezing him tightly.

"You're welcome." He pressed a kiss to my temple. "Come on, let's go get that lasagna. I'm starvin', too."

Out in the parking lot, I circled my truck warily. Its box was empty. Nothing on the snow-caked undercarriage appeared to have been disturbed. My bug detector showed a reassuring green light.

Despite the knowledge that it had been under video surveillance all day, my eyes squeezed shut involuntarily when I opened the driver's door.

No explosion obliterated me, and I let out a shaky breath. A careful survey of the interior showed nothing out of place.

"All clear?" Hellhound asked, looking up from his study of my truck from the opposite side.

"Looks like it. You?"

"Looks okay to me," he agreed.

"I'm just going to pop the hood." I grasped the hood-release lever and hesitated, heart thumping.

Sucking in a breath, I yanked it.

The muffled bang of the latch release made me twitch

even though I'd been expecting it.

"Breathe, breathe," I muttered as I circled around to the front of the hood and eased it open.

The streetlights cast heavy shadows in the engine compartment, and I extracted my small flashlight from my waist pouch. After probing every nook and cranny with the beam of light, I let out a long breath.

"Okay. Let's get out of here," I told Hellhound.

Driving up to my farm and finding the gate wide open gave me a moment of instinctive fear before I remembered that my gate would be staying open from now on. A quick survey of the woods and hillside with infrared goggles revealed no telltale heat signatures, and I toggled through the views from my surveillance cameras without spotting anything untoward.

When the garage door finally rolled down behind the truck, I slumped in my seat with a shaky exhalation.

Home free.

Sort of.

Unless Stemp hadn't been joking about Volslav's access to long-range artillery.

Straightening, I pasted a smile on my face and headed for the house.

Hellhound met me on the front porch. "All clear on your cameras, darlin'?"

"Yeah, they're all working and everything looks fine." I unlocked the door and let us in, hesitating before I reluctantly flipped the light switch to face the destruction.

I was greeted by a clean floor, clean table and chairs, and a clean kitchen counter, with one side of it occupied by my surviving glassware. The fridge and freezer hummed quietly, and the smell of sour milk and rotten meat was only a memory.

"Oh..." The syllable escaped me on a breath of relief. "Oh, this is so much better. Thank you!"

"No problem." Hellhound kicked off his boots and headed for the kitchen. "D'ya wanna nuke pieces a' the lasagna, or put the whole pan in the oven?"

"Let's just nuke pieces. If there's enough for another meal-" I broke off, a smile splitting my face as Hellhound reached into the fridge and brought out my biggest pan filled to the brim. I hurried over to admire the feast from close range. "Omigod, that looks amazing! Um... should this be getting me hot?"

Hellhound chuckled. "Hell, why not? Works for me." He turned back to the fridge. "He made a salad, too, an' some dressin'. Raspberry vinaigrette." He emerged with a bowl of crisp greens and a small tub of pink liquid.

"Yum!" I hurried over to extract a couple of plates from the unbroken stack. "Dare I hope for dessert, too?"

"I picked up some brownies from the Melted Spoon," Hellhound replied. "Figured you'd need some chocolate."

"I've died and gone to heaven."

He grinned. "Heaven sounds good, but how 'bout ya skip the dyin' part?"

"I like that plan." I loaded a juicy slab onto my plate and headed for the microwave. "I'm going to call John and thank him, while this heats."

After an evening spent tidying the house, I went downstairs to find Hellhound at ten PM. "Okay, I'm officially done and wiped. I'm just going to check my email, and then I'm heading to bed."

He straightened from his task of sweeping up drywall rubble from my formerly-hidden room in the basement. "Bed. Best word I've heard all day."

"Go on up and get comfortable," I urged, slipping my arms around him. "I really appreciate all the work you've done, but I don't expect you to do it."

"Hell, darlin', it's easy work, an' I don't mind." He dropped a kiss on my lips before turning me toward the stairs. "Let's go. I'm right behind ya."

"Mm. That sounds promising." I stepped backward, shimmying my ass against the fly of his jeans.

"Mm." His voice lowered to a gravelly rumble as he gripped my hips and pulled me tight against him. "That feels promisin'."

"It's supposed to." I turned in his arms and pressed my body against his, linking my arms around his neck.

Our kisses were light at first, deepening unhurriedly to teasing tongues and playful nibbles.

Hellhound let out a growl that sent tingles to all my nerve endings as his hands coasted down my back to fondle my ass. "Better stop now if ya still wanna get to that computer tonight," he mumbled against my lips.

"Mm." Dizzy with lust, I did a little fondling of my own. "Computer? What computer?"

He chuckled and pulled away. "If ya keep doin' that, we ain't even gonna get upstairs."

"You say that like it's a bad thing." I stole another kiss, then sighed and returned reluctantly to reality. "Unfortunately, I do actually have to check my email, and I'm sure as hell not going to feel like it after you work your magic on me. Meet you in the bedroom as soon as I can get there."

"Deal."

We turned for the stairs.

Plopping down in my desk chair, I skimmed the last five days of email and responded to the most urgent ones. I had closed the application and was rising from my chair when I spotted a tiny blinking white square in the corner of the screen.

Stemp's emergency communication system, unknown to everyone but him and me.

My guts clenched.

CHAPTER 29

Frozen halfway between sitting and standing, I stared at the tiny blinking square on my screen.

Then I blew out a tense breath and dropped back into my chair.

Alt-Shift-Click.

The text window bloomed on my screen. "Compromised. Going off-grid approx. 24 hrs."

My heart sank. Over the next twenty-four hours Stemp would be moving his wife and daughter to some new secret location and setting them up with new identities.

And when he suddenly severed communications with the Department, Dermott would seize the opportunity to cast suspicion on him.

Again, dammit.

Some quick mental math increased my worries. Twenty-four hours off-grid would make it tough for Stemp to get back here by Monday morning for my lie-detector interview.

Oh, God, Dermott was going to crucify me.

Without much hope, I typed "ETA?"

"Mon AM." The blinking cursor hesitated as though Stemp had heard my groan. "Will attempt earlier," it added.

I straightened my spine. Nothing I could do but hope for the best. After all, this was Stemp. The man was practically superhuman. If it was even remotely possible, he'd do it.

"Safe travels," I typed, and the text window closed without acknowledgement.

Hauling myself wearily up from the chair again, I stretched my back and grimaced at the resulting pops and crackles.

When I trudged down the hall, my bedroom door was closed.

I hesitated. Awkward.

Did Arnie want privacy for something? We'd never stood on ceremony with each other before, but we *were* in a bit of a weird situation.

But surely he didn't expect me to stay out of my own bedroom. Things might be weird between us, but they weren't that weird.

I tapped on the door. "Arnie?"

"Oh, sorry, darlin'." The rustle of bed linens was followed by his footsteps. He opened the door and smiled down at me. "Didn't mean for ya to think ya shouldn't come in." He glanced at the hall light. "Gonna turn out the lights?"

"Right." I trekked down the hall and flipped the switch, then returned.

As he stepped aside to let me into the room, I stopped, staring.

He'd found my stash of emergency candles, and the motley assortment of sizes and colours burned in their makeshift tin-can holders on the dresser and bedside tables. A bouquet of supermarket flowers, still in their plastic, occupied a quart sealer half-filled with water. My side of the bed had been turned down, and a cellophane-wrapped box of chocolates rested on the pillow.

Arnie gestured self-consciously at the room. "Hope ya like it."

My heart melted. Such a sweet thing for him to do.

And so damn terrifying.

"Uh," I croaked. "Wow. This is, um... thank you." I reached up to kiss him.

Our lips bumped together with none of his usual finesse.

"It's too fuckin' weird, ain't it?" he mumbled, his shoulders stiff under my palms.

I swallowed. "Of course not, it's..."

"No lies, darlin'," he reminded me.

"Oh, Arnie." I hugged him hard. "You're so sweet to do all this. And... yeah, it feels a bit weird."

His shoulders slumped.

My heart smote me and I hastened to add, "But only because, even though it's really nice, I don't need stuff like this from you. And I feel like you're uncomfortable with it."

He let out a breath, and I realized that what I had interpreted as a dejected slump was actually his shoulders relaxing as a rueful smile softened his face.

"Yeah, it ain't my thing," he admitted. "I mean, I wanted to do it for ya 'cause I promised ya a honeymoon an' I thought ya might like it, but..." He hesitated, the tension returning to his posture. "A real husband would do stuff like this for ya. Kane would do stuff like this for ya."

"Probably, but it would scare the shit out of me." I reached up to touch his cheek. "That's why I married you instead."

Arnie straightened, his smile widening. "So can we blow out these candles? I feel like I'm in the fuckin' bowels a' hell."

I laughed. "Not to mention the fire hazard."

"I brought the extinguisher in from the garage just in case." He pointed to the large red cylinder in the corner. "It was too fuckin' scary otherwise."

Still smiling, I started blowing out candles. Arnie began at the other side of the room and we met in the middle, our arms sliding around each other.

"That's better," he rasped. "Now, where were we?"

"Hmm. Right about here, I think..."

As I linked my arms around his neck, the bedroom smoke alarm shrieked. A moment later the one in the hallway joined in a deafening duet.

We sprang apart, grabbing pillows to fan the smoke away from the ceiling. The acrid haze caught in my throat, making me cough. The blaring of the smoke alarms went on and on.

Giggling between coughing fits, I fanned harder, waving my pillow ineffectually one-handed while jamming my shoulder against one ear with a finger stuffed in my other ear.

The sight of Arnie's naked tattooed bulk rushing around flapping his pillow made me laugh until I doubled over.

At last the smoke alarms fell blessedly silent, and my gasping and giggling were the only remaining sounds.

Arnie tossed his pillow back on the bed and turned to me with a wry smile. "Well, nothin' says 'romance' like smoke inhalation."

"And tears and snot," I croaked around a final giggle, mopping my eyes and nose.

He sobered. "Sorry, darlin'."

"Don't apologize." Stepping close, I wrapped my arms around him. "I don't need romance. But this?" I waved a hand at the defunct candles and contorted pillows. "This is so... us."

The corner of his mouth quirked. "Fuckups?"

I laughed. "Well, yeah, that, too. But what I meant was, we're not the 'sappy-love-scene-with-violins-playing' types. We belch and fart and..." I leaned back to cast a mischievous gaze over him from head to toe. "...jump around naked, waving pillows."

His arms tightened around me. "Hell, darlin', if I'd known that was all it took, I'd'a got out the pillows the first time I met ya."

"You can make up for lost time now." I reached up to kiss him, and this time his lips joined mine like they belonged there.

And they did.

Oh, Lord, the man could kiss. Leaning into the warmth of his powerful body, I savoured the heat of his lips and the tantalizing friction of his beard and moustache. He gathered me closer and the tip of his tongue brushed mine, reminding me of all the wonderful things that tongue could do.

Trailing kisses across my jaw, he nibbled his way down the side of my neck, waking every nerve along the way. His fingertip traced a light teasing path along the neck of my sweater.

"Ya got too many clothes on, darlin'," he growled against my throat.

"Mmhm." I pressed against him as his hands slid down my back and up under my sweater.

Clutching the hard muscles of his naked back, I gave myself to the feel of his hands on my skin.

Deft fingers unhooked my bra, then followed the band of elastic around to the front of my body. His palm lightly cupped the underside of my breast, a whisper of heat and sensation that made me moan with the need for more.

"Higher," I whispered against his hungry mouth.

He responded with a deep chuckle, his hand teasingly testing the weight of my breast without touching the nipple that strained toward him.

I yanked my sweater over my head, bra and all. Locking my hands on his hard-muscled ass, I pressed against his erection and leaned forward to trace my nipples across his chest. The erotic prickle of his chest hair set the sensitive nerves on fire and I sucked in a breath.

Arnie let out a gravelly half-groan, half-purr, sliding his hand down to support the small of my back as he kissed his way across my collarbone, then lower.

A flick of that dexterous tongue followed by an exquisite whisker-tickle tore a whimper of hunger from my lips. "Arnie..."

"Darlin'," he said against my breast a moment before his hot mouth closed around my nipple. Need scorched a blazing path down between my legs, and I fumbled at the button on my jeans with lust-clumsy hands.

"Lemme help ya with that." Arnie sank to his knees, undoing my pants with the adeptness of long practice.

Easing the denim down to my thighs, he stopped, his voice rough with arousal. "Damn, darlin', is that underwear or gift wrap?" His fingertip traced a satin ribbon, the lightness of his touch making me shiver with hunger.

"Gift wrap," I assured him, my voice almost as hoarse as his. "For you. Belated Merry Chr-" A flick of his tongue across the ribbon made me lose my words in a moan.

"That's too pretty to unwrap," he growled as he pulled my jeans down to my ankles. "Step out, darlin'."

"I have to take my holsters off... *oh!*" I gasped as he nuzzled the ribbon again. His whiskers prickled through the sheer scrap of fabric, an electric-bright shock of pleasure.

"Nah." The upturn of his lips against an extremely sensitive spot made my vision blur. "I'm likin' this look. Hot chick in nothin' but a thong an' guns."

He lowered me to the bed and crouched to work my jeans off over the holsters I wore on each ankle, devouring me with his hungry gaze.

"Sit at the edge, darlin'," he prompted. "Open those long legs for me."

Tossing back my hair, I complied, spreading my legs wide and arching my back to present my breasts.

"Hot *damn*." He nibbled whiskery kisses along each of my thighs, stopping just short of Ground Zero. His hot breath laved me from close range and I shuddered, pressing my hips toward him in heated anticipation.

Barely touching me, he slipped a finger into my thong and eased it aside, baring me to him. Lifting my knees over his shoulders, he smiled, watching me as he eased closer and closer to his goal.

"Arnie..." My voice was thick with hunger.

"Mmhm," he replied, using his tongue for a far more important task than speech.

I fell back on the bed, dissolving under the heat of his mouth. His hands reached up to find my breasts, gently squeezing and fondling. Arms and legs spread wide, I opened myself to the deluge of sensation.

Hot mouth licking and sucking. Incredible musician's hands stimulating my nipples with soft tugs that struck cymbal-crashes of bliss through my body.

Magic tongue.

Ohmigod...

Magic...

The room faded as my world contracted to nothing but the ever-rising need tightening my body.

Hot sweet pressure building...

An inarticulate cry ripped from my throat.

"Yes-ohGod*Arnie...!*"

I bucked helplessly under his hands and mouth, wave after wave of orgasm crashing through me.

As the storm slowly subsided, I floated back to the shore of semi-coherence.

"Arnie..." I dragged my eyes open to see his smile. "Need you *now*..."

The condom was already in his hand. "Shift up a bit, darlin'."

Arms and legs still quivering with aftershocks of pleasure, I squirmed up to make room for him.

Poised between my legs, he smiled down at me.

"*Now.*" I clamped my hands on his ass and pulled him in, driving my hips up to meet him. "*Yes!*"

Rocking into the perfect rhythm, he nibbled kisses across my collarbone. When his whiskers and teeth found the spot at the base of my neck, I arched under him.

"Harder..." The word came out strangled, my body already sizzling with overheated nerves. "God-*harderYes!*"

My world melted into the savage rhythm of carnal bliss, the slick of sweat and exultant cries without words. Ecstasy seized me, flashing lightning through my limbs.

Mindless, I rode his hunger higher and higher. His final hard thrusts and deep-throated groan catapulted me to a place beyond heaven, my body writhing with powerful contractions beyond my control.

Slowly awareness returned, leaving me limp and sated as the last ripples of sensation ebbed.

Arnie held me tightly, his face buried in the hollow of my neck, our bodies still joined. Our panting filled the room.

"Damn, darlin'," he croaked at last.

"Damn," I agreed breathlessly.

He rolled off me and disposed of the spent condom with expert speed before reaching out to cuddle me to him.

Laying my head on his chest, I lazily traced the lines of his tattoos with one fingertip, my eyes half-closed as he caressed my back and shoulders with gentle strokes.

Long contented minutes blurred, until the crinkle of cellophane roused me from my lassitude.

"Want some a' these chocolates?" Arnie wafted the box next to my nose. "Wouldn't wanna waste 'em."

The mouthwatering scent popped my eyes open. "Yum! How did you know cherry chocolates are my favourite?"

He chuckled. "I didn't. But I do now."

"Mmmm." I bit into one, rapidly shifting position when the liquid inside overflowed.

Arnie's eyes darkened as I licked the sticky sweetness off my fingers. "Well, darlin', now cherry chocolates are my favourite, too."

I grinned. "Bet I can make you like them even more."

His voice coasted down into a sexy growl. "Oh, yeah?"

"Oh, yeah." Nibbling a small hole in another chocolate, I reached down to let the glistening syrup trickle along a rapidly-stiffening appendage. "Oh, damn. Look at that mess. I'll just have to lick that off."

As I went into action, he let out a raspy groan. "Hot *damn...*"

The ring of the phone slammed me awake.

A glance at the clock sent my already-pounding heart into overdrive. Two-fifteen AM.

Grabbing the handset, I hit the talk button and barked, "Kelly."

"Aydan?" Lola's usually throaty voice was high-pitched and tight. "Big John's a police officer, right?"

CHAPTER 30

"What's wrong?" I demanded.

"Big John *is* a police officer, isn't he?" Lola asked again instead of answering my question.

"Not anymore. *What's wrong?*" I repeated.

"Oh," she said uncertainly. "Well... Do you think maybe... we could ask him for some advice?"

She sounded so small and lost.

So un-Lola.

"He's not here, but I can call him for you." I made my voice as firm as it could be with my heart vibrating in my throat. "Lola, tell me what's going on."

She attempted a light laugh that rang so false it made me wince. "Oh, honey, never mind, it's nothing. I'm sorry for calling you in the middle of the night-"

"Arnie's with me, and we're coming to help," I interrupted, glancing over at Hellhound, who was sitting bolt upright and following my end of the conversation with a worried frown.

"No, honey, don't bother," Lola said hurriedly. "We're fine-"

"Who's 'we'?" I demanded. "If you don't tell me what's happening right this instant, I'm going to call 911 and send the police, firefighters, and ambulance to your house with all their sirens screaming."

"For God's sake, don't do that!"

"Lola," I said slowly and loudly, hoping to calm both of us. *"What's... happening?"*

Her breath of surrender came clearly over the line. "I'm at Pearl's. Her house is at the other end of my street. It's number 126, the cream-coloured bungalow that backs onto the park. Come to the front door, and be quiet."

"We'll be there in ten minutes," I snapped, and sprang out of bed.

Hellhound was already pulling on his jeans. "What's happenin'?" he demanded.

"No idea." I swore as I hopped from one foot to the other, yanking on socks. "But Lola and Pearl are in trouble. As in, *don't-call-the-cops* trouble."

"Fuck."

Two minutes later, we were in his SUV and barrelling down my lane. We made the fifteen-minute trip to Silverside in about eight.

Too late.

As we turned down Maple Street, the red-and-blue strobing of police lights lit up the snow like a disco nightmare.

"Fuck," Hellhound muttered again.

Straining forward in my seat as though it could get me to Lola faster, I surveyed the scene. "One cruiser in front, two in back, and an ambulance. It's bad."

Arnie pulled over to the curb. "What d'ya wanna do?"

"I can't blow my cover. I'll have to run over playing the worried friend and see what I can find out."

"Awright, I'll watch from here." He leaned over to kiss me lightly. "Call me on your cell now, an' keep the line open." As I obeyed and reached for the door handle, he added, "An' watch yourself. If this's somethin' to do with Volslav..."

He didn't finish the sentence, but my spine turned to ice anyway.

Margaret had been all ears at the CRAPS meeting. Now something bad was happening to Pearl and Lola.

If she had hurt either of them, I'd kill the bitch.

I ran.

An RCMP officer intercepted me before I got to Pearl's sidewalk. "Ma'am, please stay back," he instructed.

"Pearl and Lola are my friends," I pleaded. "Lola called and said she was here and they needed help. Are they okay? What happened?"

"I'm sorry, I can't give you any details." He must have seen the desperation in my face. He added, "But I can tell you that they're both unhurt."

My knees went weak with relief. "Oh, thank God." Renewed worry struck. "But there's an ambulance in back. Why-"

"I'm sorry, I can't give you any details," he repeated. "Your friends can call you when we're finished, but it will likely be quite a while. You might as well go home."

"But Lola said she needed help!" My voice was rising even though I knew he was only doing his job.

"Your friend is unhurt. There's nothing you can do here right now. Please go home," he repeated firmly.

Fortunately my phone chimed its call-waiting tone before I could lose my temper. I snatched the phone out of my pocket and sucked in a breath at the sight of Lola's cellular number.

Hurrying away so the police officer couldn't hear, I

muttered, "Lola's calling me, I'm putting you on hold" for Hellhound's benefit, and transferred to the incoming call.

"Aydan?" Lola's voice was a tremulous whisper, but she was still doing her best to sound casual. "Don't bother coming over. Everything's under control here. I'm sorry I woke you, just go back to bed."

"Bullshit," I growled. "I'm standing in front of Pearl's house right now, and *nothing* is under control. What's happening?"

"Oh, Aydan." The words came out on a sob that wrenched my heart. "I'm sorry, honey, I didn't want to dump on you, but... it looks as though Pearl shot somebody."

"With rock salt?" I asked, clinging to faint hope.

"No. With bullets." Lola sighed. "Well, with her shotgun. I guess that's not really bullets, but..." Her voice trembled. "He might be dead."

"Tell me what happened."

"I don't know how long I'll be able to talk. I'm in the bathroom and the police are going to get suspicious if I stay in here too long."

"That's okay." I tried to sound calm and patient and encouraging. Judging by my deathgrip on my phone, I probably hadn't succeeded. "Just tell me what you can."

"Pearl didn't do it," Lola said fiercely. "The gunshot woke her up. Somebody sneaked into her house and got her shotgun and loaded it and shot somebody else out the window, and then the guy who shot the other guy sneaked out of Pearl's house and ran away."

"The guy? Who? Did Pearl see him?"

"N-No... Pearl didn't see or hear anybody. But that had to be what happened. Pearl would never shoot anybody with real bullets! And anyway, she was asleep when the gun went off and- *they're coming!*" Her last words came out in a barely-audible hiss, drowned out by a toilet flush. The call disconnected.

I barely stopped myself from shouting, "Lola!" into the phone.

Don't panic. She's fine. 'They' would be the police coming to check on an elderly lady who had been in the bathroom too long.

"I'm coming back," I said to Hellhound, and disconnected.

When I slid into the passenger's seat, he eyed me worriedly. "What's happenin'?"

His frown deepened while I relayed Lola's story.

"Think Pearl really shot the guy, an' now she's coverin' up?" he asked when I was finished.

I shook my head. "That doesn't feel right to me. I think if she intentionally shot somebody, she'd have a better story." I grimaced. "Or she'd just own it, like she did when she fired that load of rock salt at the intruder at Spider and Linda's place. But there's a hell of a difference between putting a scare into somebody with rock salt and ripping them apart with buckshot. Pearl doesn't strike me as the buckshot type."

"Pretty far-fetched that somebody sneaked into her place just to shoot a guy with her gun, though."

"Yeah," I agreed thoughtfully. "Just as far-fetched as somebody sneaking into Eddy's to get his baseball bat and beat somebody to death."

"Huh." Hellhound frowned out the windshield. "How many people d'ya think knew about Pearl an' the rock salt?"

"A lot more than knew about Eddy's murder charge."

"Somebody's fuckin' around," Hellhound said with certainty. "Diggin' up dirt. Buncha people in town knew

Harks had bad blood with you, too."

I slumped with a sigh. "Shit. I wonder how many other people in Silverside have potentially murderous skeletons in their closets?"

"Dunno, darlin', but I got a bad feelin' we're gonna find out." He put the vehicle into gear. "Guess we might as well go home. Cops're gonna be hours here, an' Lola'll call ya as soon's she can."

After a nightmare-ridden sleep, it was almost a relief when the phone jerked me from a fitful doze at seven-thirty AM.

Checking the call display, I told Helllhound, "It's Lola", and pressed the Talk button. "Hello?"

"Hi." Lola sounded exhausted. "I hope I didn't wake you."

"No, this is my normal wake-up time," I assured her. "Are you okay? Where are you?"

"I'm home." Her dejected tone tightened my throat with worry.

"What about Pearl?" I demanded. "What happened last night?"

A long sigh carried over the line, and I imagined Lola sinking wearily into her favourite chair by the window.

"Pearl was fast asleep last night at two AM," Lola began. "Which is pretty darn rare when you get to be her age."

I grasped at the first available straw. "Was she drugged?"

"No, she doesn't take sleeping pills."

"No, I meant, could someone have given her something? Sabotaged her food or drink or something?"

"Oh." Lola's voice lifted with momentary hope before subsiding into its former minor key. "No, I don't think so. She was wide awake when I got there."

"I'm sorry I interrupted," I said. "So Pearl was asleep. Then what happened?"

"There was a godawful bang. She woke up, but didn't know what had happened. She lay there for a few seconds, you know how you do when you're startled out of a dead sleep and trying to figure out what woke you."

"Right," I prompted.

"Then she realized it had been a gunshot, so she jumped out of bed and ran to get her shotgun."

I bit the side of my cheek to prevent an involuntary smile. Most nonagenarians would have called the police. Pearl went for her shotgun.

"That's when she felt a cold draft coming from her spare bedroom," Lola went on. "She only uses it for storage so the door's always closed, but it was open. She was scared, so she turned to go back to her bedroom and call the police, and that's when she spotted her shotgun lying on the floor by the window. She was so relieved to have a weapon, she ran in and grabbed it, and that's when she realized there was a body lying out at the edge of her yard where it joins to the park. The bedroom window was open just enough for the shotgun, and the screen was blown to ribbons."

"So she called the police," I surmised.

"No, she called me. She knew it was going to look like she'd shot somebody, and she didn't know what to do." Lola sighed. "I went over right away, and that's when I called you. But the neighbours had already called the police. As soon as we heard the sirens, Pearl called 911 to let them know that the shot had come from her house and it was safe for the police to come in."

"I bet that went over well."

Lola sighed. "It could have been worse, I guess. At least nobody else got shot. They searched in case the shooter was still in the area and had another weapon, but they didn't find anybody. The man who was shot is in the hospital but they expect him to survive, so maybe they'll be able to figure out who'd want to shoot him after they talk to him."

"So they didn't charge Pearl?" I ventured.

"They arrested her and charged her with attempted murder." Lola sounded even more depressed. "And a bunch of other firearms charges. She's down at the RCMP station in Drumheller. They confiscated all her guns, too. Oh, Aydan." A sniffle carried over the line. "She looked so little and old when they took her away. So... helpless." Lola's voice wavered, and she gulped and fell silent.

"But can't they see she's being framed?" I demanded. "She's ninety-three years old and she's had guns all her life, for chrissake! If she was going to start shooting random strangers from her window, she would have shown some sign of instability a hell of a long time before now."

"No," Lola said in a small voice. "She's old. The first thing they said was 'dementia'. That she was confused, and she got up and purposely shot that guy."

"Could that have happened?" I asked cautiously. "Has she ever had any episodes of confusion?"

"Never. Sure, she forgets things every now and then, just like everybody. But as soon as you get old, people use any little thing to make it look like you're senile." Lola sighed. "Sorry, honey, I didn't mean to sound bitter. It's just... this is really hitting home for me, you know?"

"I know," I agreed.

It was hitting home for me, too. What if Lola was next to be framed?

CHAPTER 31

After I had extracted a promise from Lola to call me as soon as she had any news about Pearl, I disconnected and fell back on my pillow with a groan.

Arnie rolled over, tucking an arm around me. "That sounded bad."

I sighed and snuggled into his embrace. "It was. Is. Pearl got arrested, and they're saying she shot the victim because she has dementia and she was confused."

"Hm." He hesitated. "Well, I guess it could be worse. If they're goin' with dementia, she likely won't serve any time."

I bolted upright to glare down at him. "Are you kidding? If they decide she's got dementia, she'll be locked up for the rest of her life! She'll lose her house, get shoved into some institution... she'll die in there!"

Arnie's brow furrowed. "Shit. Didn't think a' that. But... the cops can't decide that. A doctor'd hafta check her out. Prob'ly more'n one." He shuddered. "That'd suck, tryin' to convince some asshole ya still got all your marbles. Hope somebody offs me before I get old."

I glared harder. "Not helping!"

"Sorry, darlin'." He sat up, planting a contrite kiss on my forehead. "My brain ain't workin' yet this mornin'. So... you're sure Pearl didn't do it?"

"Lola's sure," I said stiffly. "That's good enough for me."

"Then it's good enough for me, too. So how are we gonna fix it?"

All my misdirected annoyance drained away. After only a few hours of sleep he'd been confronted by the problems of near-strangers, and he was still ready to help just on my say-so.

I leaned in to kiss him. "Thanks. I don't know what to do yet. And I'm sorry I snapped at you."

"No big deal, darlin'. I know this's buggin' the hell outta ya."

"You can say that again." Sighing, I got out of bed and headed for the bathroom. "I'm going to go to the office. I want to see if there's anything new on Eddy's case, and I'll ask for updates on Pearl's as well. But I can't see any reason why Volslav would target Eddy and Pearl." I sighed. "We need to figure out what Pearl and Eddy have in common."

"Uh, darlin'..." Something in Arnie's voice sent a chill of foreboding down my spine.

I turned slowly, afraid to ask. "What?"

"*You're* what they got in common."

The chill turned into an ugly shiver. "I don't even know Pearl," I protested. "I only met her for the first time yesterday."

"But Lola's your friend an' client, an' Pearl's Lola's best friend. Ya hit Pearl, you're hittin' Lola."

"I guess..." I shook off the creeping paranoia. "But nobody would try to hurt me by going after a friend of my friend. That's 'way too obscure."

"Yeah, but maybe they ain't tryin' to hurt ya." Arnie frowned. "Maybe they're just tryin' to distract ya. An' it's workin'."

I hissed out a breath. "True, but what else can I do? I won't sit here and watch my friends get railroaded."

"Listen, darlin'." Arnie rolled off the bed and came over to hold me. "The worst is over for Eddy an' Pearl, at least for a little while. Gettin' arrested an' charged sucks, but they prob'ly ain't gonna get held; an' the legal stuff takes for-fuckin'-ever to sort out. Nothin's gonna change for them for a while. Go as hard as ya can after Volslav. If Volslav's behind this, the sooner ya nail 'em, the faster this shit goes away for Pearl an' Eddy."

"You're right," I agreed, trying not to think about the fact that I only had two days left before my confrontation with Dermott removed me from all my cases permanently.

As usual, Sirius Dynamics was deserted early on a Saturday morning, but as I approached my office I heard the rapid-fire clicking of computer keys in Spider's office.

Poking my head through his open door, I tapped lightly at the doorframe.

He started and glanced up from his laptop. "Oh. Hi, Aydan."

I eyed him with concern. "You look tired. And worried. What's wrong?"

"Nothing, really... at least, not for me personally." His frown deepened. "But there's something weird going on in this town. Look at this." He turned the laptop so I could read the headline splashed across the screen: *'Alien Mind-Control Murders in Rural Alberta'*.

I groaned. "God, really?"

"Really," Spider confirmed. "They're saying the aliens are putting murderous suggestions in people's minds and they're acting on them. They've reported on the murder at Eddy's and the bomb on Main Street, and they even covered the shooting at Pearl's last night."

"You knew about that already?" I demanded.

He grimaced. "Small town. Everybody knows about it by now. But that's not all that's worrying me. I just found something else. Come and take a look."

He spun the laptop back to face himself and I came around the desk to watch over his shoulder as he clicked to a site.

"There." He jabbed a bony finger at a video titled, *'Alien Death Ray in Silverside, Alberta'*.

My guts clenched. "Tell me that isn't what I think it is."

"It's what you think it is," he said grimly. "Watch."

He hit the Play button on the video, and a man's eager whisper came from the speaker as the camera view jiggled across a night-dark landscape. "The alien ship is back. Look, there are their lights!"

A beam of light flared from the black sky, its puddle moving slowly across a snowy pasture.

"This is it! They're coming in!" The man's voice shook. The camera shook, too, making me queasy. "Those are landing lights!" The narrator's whisper went squeaky with excitement. "This will be *first contact!*"

The puddle of light lazily crisscrossed the field as though searching for an optimum landing zone. Straining my eyes at the poor-quality video, I could barely make out a shadowy triangle of dark wing.

The light skimmed over a cow, then halted and backtracked.

Accompanied by agitated panting and the noisy crunch of snow, the camera jiggled even more violently as the narrator bounded toward the field.

"Oh, no!" he half-wailed, half-whispered. "They can't make first contact with a *cow!* That's just *wrong!*"

The light stabilized over the cow's head, and the animal stared upward as if wondering what the hell was going on.

Then its legs buckled. The cow collapsed without a sound and lay motionless in the snow.

The narrator let out a stifled shriek and the video oscillated wildly before going black.

My knuckles cracked, and I realized I'd been gripping the back of Spider's chair and chanting, "Shit, shit, shit, shit..." Stifling my flow of obscenities, I added, "Did the guy survive?"

"Yes," Spider replied shakily. "He ran, and the drone didn't follow him. But the farmer found the dead cow and called the vet, and the vet said its brain had been pulverized without leaving a mark on its skin or skull."

"Shit!" A thought struck me, and I added, "Hang on. Could that video have been faked?"

"Yes, and the video editing technology is so good these days that it's really hard to spot a fake." Spider grimaced. "But I'm pretty sure it was real. The dead cow definitely was."

"Right..." I said slowly. "So... Volslav wanted to be seen." At Spider's frown, I elaborated, "If they hadn't wanted to be seen, they wouldn't have used the light. Or if they had to use the light, and they realized they'd been seen, they'd have just killed the guy. Or knocked him out and destroyed his camera."

"But they might not have known he was there," Spider pointed out.

"The guy was talking out loud and barging through the

snow like a bulldozer. On a quiet night in the country, you could probably hear him for half a mile."

"I guess," Spider agreed hesitantly. "But the drone will be remote-controlled. The control unit could have been miles away. They'd have video onboard, but probably not audio."

"Hm." I rounded his desk again and slumped in the chair across from him. "I guess you're right, but the whole thing just seems... careless. And I don't think Volslav is careless. You don't kill a cow with a classified weapon and leave the body there to be found unless you're trying to get noticed."

"But why?" Spider asked.

A gush of adrenaline made my voice shake. "Shit! They have a buyer. They're demonstrating the weapon. And the whole 'alien' thing is just to cover up what they're doing." Fear and anger tightened my fists. "They're probably posting the damn 'alien' headlines on the internet themselves."

"But why here?" Spider persisted. "And why now? And killing a cow as a demo is one thing, but if Volslav is behind the murders in Silverside, what does that gain them? Surely they're not trying to convince the buyer that they have..." His words slowed as the blood drained from his cheeks. "...mind control?"

My jaw was so tense I could barely open my mouth to speak. "That's... not possible." My voice came out in a croak. "Is it?"

"N-No..." He didn't sound certain. "We need to talk to Reggie and Jack. And we'll have to notify Dermott." His fingers trembled as he dialled the phone.

After a couple of terse conversations, he laid the receiver back in its cradle. "They're on their way."

We fell silent.

My thoughts circled frantically. Volslav couldn't have discovered a way to control people's minds. They just *couldn't* have.

But if they had...

My mind shied away from the thought of good-natured Eddy, transformed into an unwitting killing machine. Of elderly Pearl sleeping innocently in her bed, unaware of the darkness about to seize her. Of Bill Harks...

Okay, no. Bill Harks had gotten what he deserved.

But who might be next?

CHAPTER 32

Desperate to shut out the terrifying speculations, I asked the first question that came to mind. "Hey, Spider, is there anything new from the RCMP on Eddy's case?"

"Oh." Spider looked relieved, as though he appreciated the distraction, too. "Yes. They released him on the condition that he stays in Silverside and has no contact with any of the alien people. And he's not allowed to have any more baseball bats."

"But don't they have another suspect yet? They must have caught somebody on video, taking Eddy's bat from under the bar."

"Video?" Spider frowned. "There wasn't any video."

"Of course there's video. The night of the fight, Eddy told everybody they were on video."

Spider shook his head. "There's no video surveillance. Eddy was just fibbing to the troublemakers to get them out of his bar."

"Shit." I slouched lower in my chair. "I wondered about that. I'd never noticed any cameras in Eddy's, but I figured I just hadn't been paying attention."

"Bars aren't allowed to film patrons without their knowledge," Spider said. "It's a privacy thing."

"Yeah, but... damn. Are there any other developments?"

I asked without much hope.

"I haven't looked at the latest," he admitted. "I was focused on this death ray thing. I've got the file right here, hang on..." He clicked and scrolled a few times, scanning his screen. "Okay, here we are. ...Oh." The corners of his mouth drooped, his brow furrowing. "Oh, crap."

I sank my head into my hands. "I really didn't want to hear 'oh crap'. What is it?"

"When they processed the scene, they found out that the murder actually took place behind the bar, right next to where Eddy kept his bat. Then the body was dragged outside and the murder scene in the alley was staged."

"No, that's wrong!" I thumped my forehead. "I meant to tell the police, but I forgot. The old-timers say there's blood all over the inside of that building, from decades ago. It'll still show up with Luminol, but..."

I trailed off at the sight of Spider's palm-out 'stop' gesture. "It wasn't old blood," he said unhappily. "And they didn't find it with Luminol. There were actual streaks of it on the floor. Drag marks. And some glassware had been broken, but everything was cleaned up and the broken glass was in the garbage bin behind the bar. When the police asked about it, Eddy and the waitresses all said none of them had put broken glass in that bin while the bar was open that night."

"Shit." Slumping in my chair again, I stared at my boots.

"But there is a bit of good news," Spider added. "Darlene and a couple of the other witnesses described the clothes Eddy was wearing at the bar that night, and the police retrieved them from his laundry basket. There wasn't a speck of blood on his clothes or shoes, or anything else he owned. Only on his bat."

"Just like last time," I muttered.

"Eddy didn't kill anybody," Spider said firmly. "I don't believe he did nineteen years ago, and I don't believe he did this time, either."

"Same here, but there's too much circumstantial evidence against him. We have to prove somebody else did it." I slouched lower in my chair. "And if it happened right in the bar, that's even worse. As far as I know, the only people who have keys to the bar are Eddy and Darlene and their kitchen manager. And me."

"They've already interviewed Darlene and the kitchen manager. They both have alibis. And you were on a plane when it happened, so I passed your alibi on to the RCMP."

"So we're back to Eddy."

Spider grimaced. "I'm afraid so."

"But anybody could get in that place," I protested. "It's such an old building. I've seen Holt open a lock like Eddy's with a bump key, and it didn't take him any longer than it would have if he'd had the real key." I frowned. "And Pearl's house is pretty old, too. I bet her locks aren't any better."

Spider sat up a bit straighter. "Would a bump key leave any marks that the police could analyze?"

I sighed. "No."

"Crap."

Our dejected silence was broken by the sound of feet on the stairs, and a few moments later Jack and Reggie hurried into Spider's office.

"What's happening?" Reggie demanded.

"Let's wait until Director Dermott arrives," Jack objected. "And we should move to a meeting room."

Spider agreed, rising to fold up his laptop. As we trooped down the hallway, Dermott emerged from the stairwell and joined us, scowling as usual.

As soon as we were all seated around the table with the door closed, Spider turned his laptop toward us without speaking. As the video ran again, we all watched in tense silence. Reggie's fist clenched, and Jack's ivory complexion paled to dead-white.

"Fuck!" Dermott exploded. "Pretty damn ballsy, using that thing out in the open like that! What the hell are they trying to prove?"

"Aydan thinks they were demonstrating for a buyer," Spider said. "And that they're using the furor over aliens as a way to cover their tracks. And... look at this." He toggled to the 'Mind Control' headline and hesitated, his fingers trembling over his laptop keys. "Jack... is this... possible? Could they have figured out how to control people's minds?"

"No!" Jack snapped, too quickly.

We all eyed her pale face and quivering lips.

"Why am I not feeling reassured?" Dermott ground out.

Spots of colour rose on Jack's cheeks, and she straightened her spine. "I apologize," she said evenly. "That was a knee-jerk reaction. In my professional scientific opinion, I repeat: No. There is no current way, nor can I conceive of any possible way, that human minds can be controlled at any distance via any technology. The only way to alter human behaviour that profoundly is via mental programming, which is typically a lengthy process requiring frequent contact with the subject."

The air pressure in the room lightened by several tons.

Easing back in my chair, I let out a breath. "Okay, good. That's a relief. So, next question, why the light? The weapon doesn't need light to work. I was guessing they were putting on a show for a potential buyer, but could there be another reason?"

"Well, it'd be hard to spot a black cow in the dark otherwise," Reggie pointed out.

I blinked at him, embarrassment heating my cheeks. "Oh. Duh."

"Not 'duh'," Reggie countered with surprising tact. "Spotting the cow likely wasn't the primary reason for the visible light. They could have just as easily used night vision for their targeting system. I'd guess that the main reason would be to make sure the cow looked up."

Dermott snorted. "Why? For the drama?"

"No, because the weapon might not have worked otherwise."

We all gaped at Reggie.

I found my voice first. "You mean there's a way to defend against that thing? I thought it was an unstoppable death ray."

"It is," he replied, destroying my moment of hope. "But remember, it's ultrasound. It can't penetrate hard surfaces like bone. It's easy to kill a human with it because we have so many access points. Big orbital cavities in the skull let it get to the brain; spaces between the ribs allow access to the heart; the whole abdominal area is unprotected so they can explode the abdominal aorta and pulp the liver and spleen..." He eyed the greenish tinge rising on Spider's cheeks and moved on. "But a cow's head is just a big chunk of bone, and the eyes are set toward the sides of the skull. They needed the cow to look up so they had a straight shot to the brain through some soft tissue." He frowned thoughtfully. "I'm not too familiar with bovine anatomy, but with those big shoulderblades and wide ribs... if the cow hadn't looked up, they might not have been able to hit anything vital from above at all."

Hope rose again as I processed that. "So you're saying that if they shot a person in the back of the head with it, it wouldn't be lethal?"

Reggie shot a questioning glance at Jack.

She frowned. "As long as the neck was in sufficient flexion that the vertebrae protected the spinal cord, and as long as the beam didn't hit the carotid or jugular or come low enough to pass between the clavicles or ribs..." Her frown deepened. "To answer the exact wording of your question, no, it wouldn't be lethal if the beam was confined only to the back of the skull." She hesitated. "Unless the ultrasound had been re-tuned to fracture hard structures, similar to the ultrasound technology currently used to break up gallstones."

"Never mind the theoretical bullshit," Dermott snapped. "It's a death ray and we're not going to fuck with it." He turned his scowl toward Reggie. "Is our weapon still secure? Who had access to the Weapons Lab last night?"

Reggie scowled back, but answered without rancour. "Our weapon hasn't left the lab since we took it down to Calgary for that Five Eyes conference."

"Are you sure?" Dermott demanded. "Did you check it this morning?"

"No." Reggie pinned him with the cold one-eyed gaze that had cowed braver men than Dermott. "But the weapon is in a secure lockup that's keyed to my retinal scan, and mine alone."

"Your real eye, or your fake?" Dermott asked tactlessly.

"My prosthetic eye doesn't have a retina." The word 'idiot' hovered unspoken at the end of Reggie's reply.

Dermott flushed and lunged to his feet. "We're going

down there right now to check."

"I can just bring up the security records on my laptop," Spider offered. "There will be a complete record of everyone who went into the lab-"

"And we still won't fucking know whether the weapon is actually there, will we?" Dermott interrupted. "Come on, move it. All of you."

We rose without comment and followed him out.

Inside the crowded time-delay chamber, Dermott stood well within my personal space, his gaze an arrogant challenge.

Using all my self-control, I managed not to let my breathing accelerate.

Don't freak out.

Don't draw your Glock and threaten to shove it up Dermott's nose.

And especially don't shriek obscenities at the top of your lungs while ripping Dermott limb from limb with your bare hands.

Just... don't.

Breathe...

When the dreaded concrete stairwell disgorged us into the bright white subterranean corridor at last, Dermott looked disappointed.

I had fooled him, thank God.

Breathe...

Inside the Weapons Lab, Reggie ushered us into one of the secured labs and bent for the retinal scan to open the locked cabinet.

As the lock released, Dermott commented, "Pretty risky, using only your retinal scan for security, isn't it? What if something happens to your real eye?"

Reggie straightened slowly, and I braced myself for the deluge of invective that would flay Dermott where he stood.

But apparently Dermott was beneath contempt. Reggie only grunted. "If I lose my remaining eye, the last thing on my mind is going to be 'How shitty of me to inconvenience the Department'." He swung the cabinet open and indicated the bottle-shaped ultrasound weapon inside. "Ta-da."

"Is that the working model?" Dermott demanded. "Or the fake that Kane built?"

Okay, this time Reggie was going to blow.

Reggie smiled, the scar tissue distorting his expression into something far more frightening than a scowl. "Good question," he said. "We'd better test it." His smile grew a few more teeth as he whisked the bottle out of the cabinet and swung it toward Dermott.

Dermott dodged behind me.

"Oh, nice," Reggie drawled. "Really fucking brave."

"You crazy fuck!" Dermott's face was crimson. "I'll have your ass for threatening the Director!"

Reggie gave him a single chilling look. "You can try. But everybody else knew I was aiming at that." He jerked his chin at the body-shaped composite target behind where Dermott had stood. As Reggie depressed the trigger mechanism in a short burst, he added, "If this is the real ultrasound weapon, the gel in that dummy will turn to liquid."

At the words 'that dummy', his eye contact with Dermott sharpened, but apparently Dermott wasn't about to start anything with a pissed-off guy holding a death ray.

"Check it," Dermott growled instead, and we all stood in silence while Reggie crossed the room and opened a small port on the dummy's side.

Blue liquid oozed out, and Reggie said unemotionally, "Yep, it's the real ultrasound weapon."

"Webb!" Dermott snapped.

Spider twitched. "Uh, yes?"

"Check the lab security records. Give me everybody who went in and out of here in the last twenty-four hours."

"Why?" Reggie challenged. "That's a waste of time. My staff and I are in and out of here all day long. Just check the access logs for this cabinet." He replaced the weapon in the cabinet and relocked it.

"Um..." Spider's gaze bounced between Dermott and Reggie, clearly trying to decide which of them would be more dangerous to antagonize. Reggie and Dermott were locked in a glaring contest, so after a moment of hesitation Spider swivelled to place his laptop on the nearest counter and started clicking keys.

"Well?" Dermott demanded, still glaring at Reggie.

"There were forty-three accesses to the Weapons Lab in the last twenty-four hours," Spider said bravely. "The logs only show one access to this cabinet, just a few minutes ago when Reggie opened it."

A flush rose on Dermott's neck. "How many accesses to this cabinet in the last month?"

"Um..." More key-clicking. "Just this one."

"Bullshit!" Dermott rounded on him, scowling. "Somebody's fucked with those records. The weapon was transported to Calgary for that conference, so somebody sure as hell opened the cabinet then."

"Um, no..." Spider flinched under Dermott's glower and clicked some more keys, his fingers trembling. "That was more than a month ago. If I go back another week, it shows the access for the conference." He turned the laptop to display the records.

A short uncomfortable silence filled the room.

"Fine," Dermott grunted. "So there's no way they could have used our weapon. Now we know for sure that they've got one of their own. You sure about that veterinary report?"

"Yes," Spider replied. "I checked with the vet right away. The damage was definitely the same as what our ultrasound weapon would cause."

Dermott blew out a breath. "Shit. Okay, I'll brief Upper Command, and put Holt on the case." He turned to Spider. "Have you found the guy who recorded the video yet?"

"Not yet, but I've got a team working on it."

"Okay. Coordinate with Holt, and get Brock and Mellor digging for anything they can find in the internet." Dermott's gaze swung to me, his brows drawing down. "You, too." Turning to Reggie, he added, "Get your geeks working on a way to detect that drone and the ultrasound weapon."

"Already started yesterday," Reggie replied. "We're working on a couple of possibilities, but we don't have anything practical yet. We've beefed up our detection systems around the building so we won't miss the drone if it comes back, but catching it out in the middle of nowhere in some farmer's field?" He grimaced. "Not likely. And the weapon is mostly ceramic and composite materials, so any kind of wide-area search for it will be pretty damn tricky."

"That's what we're paying you for. Get on it." Dermott turned and strode out.

CHAPTER 33

Reggie eyed the doorway where Dermott had departed and muttered something under his breath before speaking aloud to us. "All right, folks, this show's over. Everybody out."

As we trooped out of the Weapons Lab, Spider turned to me. "I'll grab your network key and meet you in your office."

"Okay, thanks." I headed for the stairs along with Reggie and Jack.

"Do you need us for anything else?" Jack inquired as we climbed.

"I don't think so." I grimaced. "But then again, I haven't expected anything that's been happening lately, so who knows? Are you staying to work on the detection systems, Reggie?"

"No, we promised to take the kids tobogganing today. My team's been on this since yesterday, and Murray and Melinda are the experts. I can't imagine them needing me, but if they do, they'll call." He fixed me with his gimlet gaze. "Jack and I will both have our cell phones with us. Call if anything else comes up. And I mean *anything*."

"Yes," Jack agreed. "We can be back here in twenty minutes if necessary."

As we stepped into the time-delay chamber, the warm

glance that passed between the two of them brought a smile to my lips.

"Fingers crossed that we won't need you," I said. "Have fun tobogganing."

Back in my office, I dialled Hellhound's number.

At his gruff "Helmand", I replied, "Hi, it's me."

"Hey, darlin'. How's it goin'?"

"Looks like it's going to be a long day. There's no point in you waiting around for me here, so you might as well do your own thing until lunch. Or head back to Calgary if you want. I can get Spider to give me a ride-"

"Ain't happenin'," Hellhound interrupted. "Call me whenever you're ready to get picked up. Meantime I'm gonna dig around a bit. Talk to Lola, see if I can find out more about last night. Kane's comin' up, too. He oughta be here by noon."

My heart sank. As much as I appreciated their concern, it was getting uncomfortable. A twitchy shiver of claustrophobia shook me.

"Okay, sounds good," I lied. "We can get together for lunch. Or if anything comes up before that, I'll give you a call."

As I said goodbye to Hellhound, Spider arrived. Handing me the network key, he sank into his usual chair and opened his laptop.

He studied me with a troubled expression. "You look tired." He flushed. "I mean, you look great, you always do, but-"

"It's okay," I interrupted. "I look tired because I *am* tired. I feel like I've aged twenty years this week."

"You should go home and rest."

I snorted. "Wouldn't Dermott love that."

Spider's jaw stiffened. "It's Saturday. You've been working crazy hours all week, you collapsed two days ago, and it's super-dangerous for you to be in the network when you're tired. Dermott can hate it all he wants, but he'll be in really deep doo-doo with Upper Command if anything happens to you."

"Nothing's going to happen to me. I've been fine in the network when I'm a lot more tired than this." I raised the tiny network key in a parody of a toast and closed my eyes. "Wish me luck."

"*Wait!*"

His cry popped my eyes open again. "What?" I demanded.

"Just hang on," he instructed, fingers flying over his laptop keys. "I have to throttle Tammy's connection before you go in. Usually I do it when I pick up your network key, but I was distracted today... okay, there. It's safe for you to go in now."

I sagged back against the sofa cushions. "Thanks, Spider. I'd hate to have to dig all of Tammy's memories out of my brain again."

"Yes, and there's a good chance you might collide," he replied. "After you reported finding Nora mixed up with Everett Marsh yesterday, I asked Brock to push Tammy into the CIA's system and see what else they could find."

"And did they find anything?"

"No." He grimaced. "Brock said he couldn't find any mention of Nora. He said he went through the whole system, but there was nothing."

"How is that possible?" I demanded.

Spider frowned. "I don't know. If you found it, Brock and Tammy should have been able to. Tammy has the same access capabilities as you, and Brock should be able to push her consciousness right into the same file systems you saw. Maybe the data has been deleted."

Worry clenched my gut. "Shit, I wonder what else Marsh is deleting. I've got to go. If you lose me, search for, um, I don't know... mushrooms. Oyster mushrooms."

"Okay. Good luck."

I closed my eyes and dove into virtual reality.

It took me a long time to find the CIA's server. The ever-shifting internet connections flung me off into cyberspace again and again, but at last I sniffed out the scent.

Completely focused on my goal, I rocketed down the data corridor only to slam into a chaotic storm of data.

Panic rocked me.

Tammy.

Thank God Spider had throttled her connection. Instead of an uncontrollable deluge, her lifetime of memories writhed and slithered around me, clinging like strands of sticky hair.

Visualizing an impenetrable shell around myself, I shoved through her consciousness and emerged in the data tunnel on the other side. There I paused and reached back with a single cautious tentacle, riffling through her thoughts.

None of mine left in there. Good.

Behind her consciousness, I sensed the ghost of Tyler Brock's mind. Thank God that creepy little bastard could only see what Tammy saw, which had been nothing. The thought of him snooping into my mind made my data bits squirm.

Turning, I sped to the server with my nonexistent heart hammering.

That collision could have been deadly. If it had been a

different mage than Tammy; if her connection hadn't been throttled...

Wrenching my mind away from terrifying thoughts of what might have been, I sought out the server's tranquil stream of outgoing data and followed it to my goal.

Inside the file system, I visualized my consciousness easing outward in thousands of sensitive filaments. Smelling/tasting/feeling for Volslav, Nora Taylor, Arlene Widdenback, Aydan Kelly, Grandin, arms deals, ultrasound, bottles...

My first hit came almost immediately. Nora Taylor.

I would have frowned if my formless state had permitted it. The data was there, same as yesterday. Why hadn't Brock been able to find it?

I scoured the network for more information. Nora had been delivering her ill-gotten intel on USB thumb drives sent via the U.S. Embassy's diplomatic pouches. Tracing the records, I found entries itemizing each piece of information, organized by the dates the diplomatic pouches had been delivered.

I couldn't spot any pattern, but the most recent date from a month and a half ago didn't have a corresponding intel entry. Either Nora hadn't delivered anything useful, or Marsh hadn't updated the record yet.

That avenue exhausted, I searched back through Marsh's operational records for any mention of Grandin.

Had Grandin somehow antagonized Marsh enough for Marsh to set him up? Maybe they had the same kind of conflict as Dermott and me. Dermott would love to screw me over the way Marsh had screwed Grandin.

In fact, he was about to.

Don't think about that.

Jerking my attention back to the files, I found no evidence that Grandin and Marsh had ever clashed. No disciplinary reports, no poor performance reviews, no mediations by HR, no subtle unpleasantries exchanged via email.

I hesitated over a document. Marsh had redacted part of one of Grandin's reports. No red flags there; our Department usually did the same before issuing documents.

But there was no master copy containing the full text. I sent feelers throughout the file system.

Nothing. Not at any level of access.

That was weird.

I absorbed the abridged contents of Grandin's report. Interesting. Grandin's department had been tracking Volslav, too. This report detailed movements of arms overseas, and my attention sharpened when I discovered that some of the action had been in Africa. Was this about the arms supply for the insurgents?

I puzzled over the missing pieces of the document. The context suggested that the report had originally outlined some connections between the alleged arms recipients. That information shouldn't have been sensitive; at least no more so than the rest of the document's contents.

But if the original had been deleted, maybe Marsh was hiding something.

Deleted files. A pulse of excitement vibrated my data bits.

Whisking through the network connections, I checked each server's Recycle Bin.

Nothing.

But sometimes, if the drive sectors hadn't been overwritten yet, an image might remain...

I burrowed deeper, sifting through the tattered ghosts of deleted documents.

There.

Triumph blazed through me as I gently teased the data free.

A moment of speed-reading later, I would have slumped with disappointment if I'd been capable of it.

The redacted portions weren't sensitive at all. Just some comparisons between the countries in question, noting that their economies revolved around gold mining.

So-fucking-what? Half the African nations were gold producers.

Disgusted by the waste of time, I whisked back to the central server to resume my search. If Grandin and his team had been chasing Volslav, had they found anything I didn't already know?

Time slowed while I dug through document after document, report after report.

'George Harrison' caught my attention, and I skimmed details that I already knew. As an agent, Stemp had been part of a joint operation with Five Eyes overseas in his George Harrison cover; he'd been suspicious of Yana Orlov; he'd been ambushed in an attack that left him seriously injured and his partner dead. Then Kane had taken over the covert mission, establishing a romantic liaison with Yana only to have her supposedly die in a bombing that ended his line of investigation. I'd known that, too.

I read on.

Grandin's team had also flagged Dawn White; no surprise there.

A third woman, Tanya Rumley, was news to me; but she was only noted because she'd had drinks with Yana and

Dawn once in the Denver airport, nearly three years ago. She'd seemed friendly with them, but there was no record of any further contact.

Still, it was the only information I hadn't already known. I studied the photograph. It had obviously been taken from long range, and I tried to push the pixels into a crisper image. My efforts were futile, and Tanya Rumley remained an unremarkable woman with brown hair and blue eyes. Something about her seemed vaguely familiar, but it was probably only because she looked like a thousand other ordinary brown-haired blue-eyed women.

She and Dawn and Yana were smiling, leaning toward the centre of their table with cocktail glasses raised in a toast. There was distance between them though, making their body language ambiguous. Business associates? Friends? Or simply strangers who'd met on a trip and shared a drink?

Abandoning the photo, I sniffed around the CIA server for any more mentions of Tanya Rumley, but found none.

Did that mean there *were* none? Or had I overlooked them, the way Brock had overlooked the information about Nora?

If I had been capable of it, I would have heaved a sigh of frustration. Screw it. Time to widen the net for Tanya Rumley.

Trickling out through the data stream, I rejoined the busy traffic of the internet.

My usual tactic of sending feelers down infinite passageways netted far too many results. God, it would take me forever to check all those.

But maybe there was an easier way.

Buoyed by optimism, I stopped looking for Tanya Rumley and started looking for tax records.

The Internal Revenue servers were well-protected, but I hovered outside their fortifications with confidence. Now, where was that tranquil little stream...?

There.

A moment later, I was inside their firewall and heading for the main database.

There were several Tanya Rumleys, but the ages didn't fit the woman I'd seen in the photo. She definitely wasn't thirteen or eighty-nine. She might have been a cosmetically enhanced sixty-two; but somehow I doubted it. The photo hadn't been particularly clear, but cosmetic surgery of that magnitude would be hard to hide.

Swallowing my disappointment, I abandoned the IRS and headed for Canada Revenue Agency.

When I breached their servers, my virtual heart leaped. There was thirty-seven-year-old Tanya Rumley, along with many years of her tax returns. Except...

No returns for the past three years.

And it had been three years since she'd been spotted with Dawn and Yana. Had she died? That would explain the lack of follow-up information in the CIA file, and the missing tax records.

I extended my tentacles into Vital Statistics. No death record.

Maybe she'd gotten married and changed her name. I shuttled back into the CRA's records.

The name I found sent a shock of electric adrenaline through my data bits. No wonder she'd looked familiar.

Tanya had become Tawny.

Tawny had bleached her hair, inflated her lips and boobs enough to serve as personal flotation devices, and married Lawrence Harchman.

And Lawrence Harchman was a filthy-rich, slimy asshole who'd sell his own mother just to make a nickel.

CHAPTER 34

I rocketed back through the convoluted data connections, only to slow, disoriented. I had been so absorbed in my search, I had forgotten to leave my usual trail of markers. And Spider's anchoring presence had vanished.

I was lost.

Quelling my instinctive panic with an effort of will, I flung out feelers in all directions.

I'd be fine.

Spider would be sending out searches for oyster mushrooms. All I had to do was find that stream of data.

Easy-peasy. No different than searching out the CRA servers.

Just stay calm.

Fine. I was fine.

Oh, God, what if the internet connection to Sirius had gone down? My portal would be lost. No way to return to my physical body. I'd be trapped forever in cyberspace...

I fought the panic down again. Just keep searching for Sirius and oyster mushrooms.

A tickle of data at the end of one of my tentacles washed glorious relief over me. Snapping my consciousness back along the path, I followed the oyster mushrooms.

But it was only one instance.

Quivering in the data stream, I studied the unfamiliar server with despair. Someone else had been searching the internet for oyster mushrooms. Now I was even farther from home.

Or maybe I was closer. Who knew? Infinite loops of connections whirled around me. I could be right next door to Sirius or halfway around the globe.

Holding onto control with all my might, I fought the urge to flee, to wildly fire my consciousness out in all directions.

That would only thin me out. And if I lost cohesion...

A shudder vibrated my data bits.

Stay calm.

Send out feelers.

Smell/listen/taste...

The data flow that had felt like a buoyant stream earlier now felt like a dangerous undertow, threatening to rip me apart and banish me to eternal electronic hell.

Long, terrifying minutes crept by while I travelled the interminable data tunnels, clinging to my consciousness with all my might.

Or maybe it had been hours.

Days, even. I had lost all sense of time.

Stay.

Calm.

At last, the scent of oyster mushrooms snapped my attention down one of the tunnels. Afraid to hope, I moved cautiously in that direction, anchoring a tendril of consciousness at the junction in case I had to retrace my path again.

But the data packets were flowing by in a beautiful, continuous stream.

Oyster mushrooms.   Oyster mushrooms.   Oyster

mushrooms.

Thank God.

I gathered my trembling data bits and plunged toward Spider's homing beacon.

Coalescing into my avatar, I shot into Sirius's file repository so fast that I tumbled head over heels to lie gasping on the floor.

"*Aydan, are you okay?*" Spider sounded frantic.

"Y-Yeah." I resisted the urge to fling my arms wide and kiss the virtual floor. Dragging myself to my feet, I held my voice steady and added, "I'm fine. Just got lost. Thanks for calling me home. I'm coming out now."

When I stepped out the portal and back into my physical body, pain struck my temples like a sledgehammer. But another kind of pain nearly doubled me over.

"*Shit!*" I hissed, creeping gingerly to my feet and scurrying for the door with my knees locked together. "Gotta-pee-be-right-back!"

Thank God there was nobody else in the ladies' room. I was already yanking down my pants before I was even fully inside the cubicle. Whimpering with desperate relief, I held the door shut with one hand, unable to reach the lock from where I sat and incapable of halting the cataract.

The flow went on for so long I began to wonder whether there would be anything left of me by the time I was done. A mental image of my desiccated carcass fluttering to the floor like a sheet of dry paper made me snuffle, trying to suppress my slightly frantic giggles.

When I returned to my office at last, Spider blushed. "Sorry," he said. "I should have asked how long a session you wanted."

"Not your fault," I assured him. "You had no way of

knowing I'd forgotten to use the bathroom before we got started." My stomach growled, and I clapped a hand over it. "'Scuse me. I'm starving."

"No wonder, it's nearly one o'clock," he said worriedly. "I started signalling you an hour ago."

"Sorry, I was completely absorbed, and I didn't realize I'd lost your anchor." I reeled off my findings, ending with, "So we're back to the damn Harchmans. Lawrence Harchman has been mixed up in nearly everything we've done for the last two years. And I don't believe in coincidences."

Spider grimaced. "Neither do I, but other than that bombing hoax he pulled in November, we haven't been able to find anything to pin on him."

"And that was small potatoes," I agreed gloomily. "Is he out of prison yet?"

"He was only held for a few hours." At my look of outrage, Spider added, "I know; what he did was really awful, but it wasn't really a crime. He's being sued by the news networks that he hijacked with his fake news, but he didn't actually hurt anybody. He didn't steal money or commit fraud, he just..."

"Just faked the murder of hundreds of people," I snapped. "And he conspired with that programmer to fake a death threat against himself..." I trailed off at Spider's sigh.

"But nobody was actually hurt. In the end it was only a public mischief charge, and it was a gray area because he never tried to mislead the police into thinking there had been a crime, and that's the legal definition of 'public mischief'. By the time his high-priced lawyers finished poking holes in the case, the police realized they probably couldn't get a conviction, so they dropped the charges." Spider's face twisted in disgust. "So now he's suing the police for false arrest."

"Argh! I *hate* that smarmy little ass-pimple!" My phone rang, cutting off what probably would have turned into a tirade featuring some of my very finest insults. Feeling short-changed by the lost opportunity, I hurried over to my desk to pick up the receiver. "Kelly."

"Hey, darlin'. Guess ya ain't checked your messages lately."

I reflexively glanced down at the cell phone in the top pocket of my waist pouch. "No, I haven't been outside the jamming zone. Sorry I missed your call. What's up?"

A seductive chuckle caressed my ear. "Ya know what comes up every time I'm around ya, darlin'."

Warmth trickled into my belly and I pitched my voice a little lower. "Mmhmm. Anything I can handle for you?"

"Whole lotta things, but one stands out more'n most."

I grinned. "It certainly does."

He dropped the tease, but I could still hear the smile in his voice. "Anyhow, later for that, darlin'. I was just callin' to see if you're ready for lunch."

My stomach growled again. "Yeah, I'm starving. Where do you want to meet?"

"Nowhere. I'm pickin' ya up. But, good news, Eddy's is open again."

My heart lifted. "That's awesome!" A grin spread across my face. "And you're driving. That means beer for me!"

"I'm in the lobby whenever you're ready."

"I'm on my way." I hung up and turned to Spider. "We're going to Eddy's for lunch. Do you want to come?"

"Oh, that sounds good." He hesitated. "But no, I'd better not. I want to talk to Brock about why he couldn't find that data you said was-" He broke off as Dermott appeared in my doorway.

"What data?" Dermott demanded.

"The information about Nora that was in my report yesterday," I explained. "Brock said he checked Marsh's files on the CIA server but he couldn't find anything about Nora. I just checked again, and the information is still there."

Spider offered, "It might be because of the way Aydan accesses the data directly instead of being guided unconsciously by someone else-"

Dermott scowled and interrupted, "Or Kelly's just making shit up because she has mommy issues. We're supposed to be investigating Volslav." He glared from me to Spider and back to me again. "Does *anybody* fucking remember we're supposed to be investigating Volslav? Not Mommy-Nora, not some fucking homicidal bartender, and especially not some trigger-happy little old lady! What the hell, Webb?"

Spider flinched under Dermott's wrath, but his voice only trembled slightly as he replied, "Aydan and I think that Pearl's and Eddy's cases are related to what's going on with Volslav. That's why I asked the RCMP to keep us in the loop on both cases. And Nora is definitely tied into this somewhere."

"You'd better hope so," Dermott growled. "Because if I find out you've been misusing Department time and resources, I'll shit-can you and blackball you so bad you won't even be able to get a job flipping burgers."

"Lay off," I snapped. "Spider's the best analyst we've got, and you damn well know it. And you'll look like a total moron if you fire him again and Upper Command has to crawl back begging to rehire him. *Again.*"

Dermott's face turned purple.

"Oh, there you are." A voice from the corridor made us all twitch.

Dermott spun and roared, "Don't sneak up on me like that, asshole!"

Holt's brows snapped together as his jaw thrust out pugnaciously.

Spider's gaze flicked to my desk as though he was thinking about diving underneath it.

Poor kid. Surrounded by heavily-armed people with anger issues. Come to think of it, I was actually pretty impressed that Dermott hadn't pulled his gun on me. Yet.

"Sorry," I said loudly before Holt could jump into the fray. "I was out of line."

"Too fucking right," Dermott barked, and strode out, grabbing Holt's sleeve as he headed down the hall.

Holt jerked his arm free and shot me a warning glare before following Dermott.

I turned to Spider. "Sorry about that."

He was trembling, but his eyes blazed. "You've got nothing to apologize for. And you didn't need to apologize to Dermott, either. He was just as out of line as you were."

"I wasn't really apologizing to him. I could just see that things were getting out of hand and it was time to call a halt." I flashed Spider a wicked grin. "And, unlike Dermott, I don't need to compensate for a tiny dick."

Spider went crimson and a guffaw exploded out of him. "Ohmigod, Aydan, *burn!*"

I shrugged. "I calls 'em as I sees 'em."

Spider snickered. "I hope you didn't see *that*."

"If I had, I'd be blind from clawing out my own eyes. And, on that note, I'm going for lunch before things get any worse around here." I made for the door.

In the lobby, Hellhound met me with a smile and a kiss. "Come on," he urged. "Eddy's is hoppin', but Kane's got our usual table."

"Perfect." I signed out at the security wicket and emerged cautiously from Sirius with my usual sidestep.

"It's clear. Scoped it out on my way in," Hellhound assured me, but his gaze scanned our surroundings just as thoroughly as mine while we hurried to his SUV.

On the short drive to Eddy's, I checked my cell phone messages, discovering one from Darlene as well as the one from Hellhound. Darlene had simply said that the saloon would be opening at its usual time today, and I relaxed in my seat with a sigh. After all my assurances of support, I had completely forgotten about poor Darlene.

When we walked into the bar, Kane looked up from his pint of beer with a smile. A sweating bottle of Corona with a wedge of lime in the neck stood on the table beside a second pint, and I grinned back.

Sliding into the chair beside him, I reached for the Corona. "You must have been a Boy Scout," I teased. "Always prepared."

Kane's eyes crinkled, activating his sexy laugh lines. "I wish I could take credit. Arnie phoned me from Sirius and told me to order."

I shot Arnie a smile.

He emerged from his pint with foam dotting his moustache above a smug smile. "I sure as hell ain't a Boy Scout, but I'm always prepared when it comes to beer."

Darlene hurried over, smiling. "Hey, you made it."

"Yes, thanks for your message." I lowered my voice. "How are things going?"

"Okay. Busy." She nodded toward the full tables. "And Eddy isn't allowed to go near any of the alien people, so we're a bit short-handed."

"I won't keep you, then," I assured her. "We can talk later."

"Thanks." She leaned down, lowering her voice below the music. "Eddy's in his office. He said he couldn't stand being cooped up at his house, but I don't know if being cooped up in his office is any better. If you've got a few minutes, could you pop in and see him? You always brighten his day."

The compliment made me smile. "Thanks, Darlene. I'll do that right after we eat."

She straightened with an answering smile. "So I'll bring you some food. What would you like?"

After she departed with our orders, I leaned back in my chair and took a long blissful swallow of ice-cold beer. "Oh, thank God," I mumbled, and tilted the bottle again.

"Tough day?" Kane asked.

"You have no idea." Remembering who I was talking to, I grinned at him. "Okay, no; you probably know exactly what kind of day I'm having. One of *those* days."

He gave me a sympathetic grimace. "I'm sorry to hear that. Is there anything you can tell us?"

Reflexively, I flipped my waist pouch open to check my bug detector. It indicated all clear, and I lowered my voice below the level of the music. "Only that Lawrence Pond-Scum Harchman is involved, and that tells you all you need to know about how shitty this is getting."

Kane frowned and matched my discreet tone. "Lawrence Harchman is involved with Volslav?"

"Who knows?" I scowled at my beer bottle, then sucked

back another swallow. "You know how he's weaselled out of any criminal charges even though he's been at the edges of damn near everything for the past two years. And now he's popped up again." Compelled to accuracy, I added, "Well, not him specifically, but Tawny. And wherever Tawny is, Harchman is sure to be, too."

Kane went still. "Tawny Harchman? Involved with Volslav?"

"Nothing provable. It was only one contact three years ago..." I hesitated with a glance at Hellhound. He knew of the Harchmans, but I couldn't divulge any other names. "...with a couple of other people we strongly suspect of being involved with Volslav." I made a face. "You know how it is. Just a single contact that might not mean anything and isn't evidence, but it's just too damn coincidental."

Kane's jaw hardened. "Yes," he agreed grimly, and whisked out his phone.

"What is it?" I demanded. "What's wrong?"

When he met my gaze, Kane's eyes were dark with worry. "Tawny Harchman knows where Alicia and Daniel live."

CHAPTER 35

Kane punched a speed dial button on his phone, muscles rippling in his jaw. As he listened to it ringing, his knuckles whitened on the phone.

When a voice finally crackled at the other end, Kane's shoulders slumped with the release of tension.

"Hello, Alicia," he said formally. "John here. Something's come up, and I'd like to buy you and Daniel tickets to fly out and see your parents for a couple of days. Can you get ready to leave right away?"

Shrill indignant crackling made him jerk the phone away from his ear with a wince. "No," he said evenly. "I'm not trying to dodge my responsibilities; I'm trying to keep you and Daniel safe."

When Alicia spoke again, it was at a lower volume. Kane spent a few more minutes avoiding explanations and offering reassurances that he'd cover the costs. Finally he disconnected with a sigh.

"She'll call me back when they're through airport security." He grimaced. "At least she's still fearful enough after Daniel's kidnapping not to question me when I say it's for their safety."

"Shitty, but at least it works," Hellhound contributed from behind his beer mug. "Ya think Harchman might try somethin'?"

"Harchman himself? I doubt it," Kane admitted. "But I'm not willing to take a chance. The Harchmans both know that 'Arlene Widdenback'..." He gave me a small smile. "...and I are associates. If there's even the most tenuous social connection between the Harchmans and Volslav, there's a chance that Volslav might find out. And if Volslav wants to force me to betray Arlene Widdenback, the best way to control me is by targeting Daniel."

I scowled at my beer. "That's so shitty. What the hell is wrong with people, that they'd even think of using a child like that?"

It was clearly a rhetorical question, and neither Arnie nor John replied. We drank in silence until Darlene arrived with the food.

Conversation was sparse while we ate, but the silence was comfortable. My mind ticked over the facts I knew, turning them this way and that in an attempt to find their place in the puzzle.

"There are just too many damn pieces," I muttered.

"Pardon?" Kane inquired as he and Hellhound leaned in.

"Too damn many pieces of the puzzle," I repeated a little louder, still careful to keep my voice below the level of the background music. "Volslav does arms deals overseas. Grandin's with the CIA in the States. Somebody's murdering random people here in Silverside. Harchman sells software and operates that damn virtual reality brothel-"

I bit off my words too late.

Hellhound's eyebrows shot up as a grin spread across his face. "A VR brothel? Damn, ya been holdin' out on me, darlin'!" His smile faded as the wheels turned in that far-too-keen mind. He spoke again slowly. "Coupla years ago when we were watchin' Harchman for the first time, Wheeler said Harchman was usin' a 'new hypnosis cure'..." He made air quotes around the words. "...for guys that couldn't get it up. But that didn't line up with what ya told me later about how they were usin' mind control." His face darkened. "An' that torture they used on me sure as hell wasn't like any hypnosis or mind control I've ever seen. But brainwave-driven VR... yeah. If ya see it, you're gonna believe it, an' if ya believe it, you're gonna feel it. It all makes sense now. Finally."

His brow furrowed in concentration. "An' that explains what was goin' on when that bitch was cuttin' ya. Ya were screamin' an' bleedin' an' it looked real as hell, but at the same time I could hear ya talkin' in my ear, tellin' me it wasn't." His frown cleared as comprehension lit his eyes. "The 'you' I was lookin' at was fake. So when ya go into VR, you're 'you', but ya can make copies. An' the copies do whatever ya think they oughta 'cause they ain't got minds of their own. An' ya figured out a way to make the real 'you' invisible."

His smile widened. "An' why the hell not? It's VR. Ya can do anythin' ya want. That's why it works for guys who wanna get it up real bad..." The light went out of his eyes and his voice went flat. "An' that's why if somebody kills ya in VR, ya die in real life. Heart attack, right? Ya just believe yourself to death."

I eyed him with despair. "You're far too smart for your own good. If you'd figured that out before I knew about all your security clearances, I'd be shitting my pants. As it is..." I sighed. "You never heard of any of this, and you especially didn't hear it from me."

Hellhound grinned. "Hear what?

I returned his grin before slumping in my chair. "Back to what I was saying before... it just doesn't make sense. Grandin and his team were investigating Volslav, that's a logical connection. The Harchmans? I don't know; Lawrence Harchman is a slimeball, but we've investigated him before and couldn't find anything criminal. We thought Tawny had connections to Fuzzy Bunny, but we could never find any proof; and anyway, Fuzzy Bunny is toast now."

"Maybe she's just one of those women who cozies up to anyone who has money or influence," Kane said. "She might have been socially friendly with both Fuzzy Bunny and Volslav."

"Maybe," I agreed. "Her bimbo act doesn't fool me, but it wouldn't surprise me if she was just a smart gold-digger who latched onto Harchman for his money."

"Or maybe Harchman latched onto her," Kane pointed out. "If she has powerful social connections, Harchman might be leveraging that into something profitable. Just because we haven't found evidence of wrongdoing yet, it doesn't mean there is none."

"True," I agreed slowly. "But then what about these murders in Silverside? Eddy and Pearl don't have any connection to Volslav or Grandin or the Harchmans, so why are they being framed?"

"We don't know that they are," Kane said gently.

"Of course they are," I snapped. "You don't seriously believe that Eddy murdered somebody, do you?"

"Of course I don't want to believe that." Kane hesitated. "But... you know as well as I do that even the nicest-seeming people can commit violence if they're desperate. We really don't know Pearl or Eddy that well. If someone confronted them, maybe threatened them..." He didn't finish the sentence.

I slouched lower in my seat, following my sinking heart. "I know you're right, I just..." Straightening my spine, I firmed my voice. "No. I believe Eddy and Pearl are both innocent, and I'm going to prove it."

Kane and Hellhound exchanged a glance.

"How 'bout ya let Kane an' me handle that?" Hellhound offered. "Ya got enough on your plate right now. We can't help ya with the other stuff, but we can do this."

"Yeah, and you already think they're guilty," I protested.

Hellhound shook his head. "Nah, darlin', I'm with ya. I think they're gettin' framed, too."

We both turned to Kane, who gave us a frustrated headshake. "It doesn't matter what I believe, or want to believe; I can only follow the evidence where it takes me. This is what I *do*." He winced. "Did. Surely you don't think I've lost all my objectivity and investigative skills in less than six months."

"No, of course not," I said hurriedly. "I know how good you are, and I know I shouldn't let my feelings get in the way of the facts, but... sometimes feelings are all I've got to go on."

Kane sighed. "I know. Trust me, Aydan." He made a gesture that included Hellhound. "Trust *us*. We won't railroad anybody." He hesitated as if adjusting his worldview again. "Neither of us has the authority to railroad anybody. Whatever we find out, we'll simply pass on to you."

My heart hurt for him, but he wouldn't want my pity. I gave him my best smile. "Thanks. It makes me feel better knowing you're on the case." Gulping the last bite of my club sandwich, I drained my beer. "I need to get back to work, but I want to talk to Eddy for a few minutes first."

"I wanna talk to him, too," Hellhound agreed. "But I'll drop in on him later. He might feel better talkin' to ya alone; an' if he's cooped up in his office all day, two visits're gonna break up the time better'n one."

"Good idea." I rose, dropping a kiss on his lips, then hesitated before settling on an awkward half-nod-half-smile in Kane's direction.

He gave me a twisted smile in return, and I turned and fled down the corridor.

When I rounded the corner and peeked into the tiny office, Eddy sat oblivious to my presence, his elbows propped on his desk, head in hands. The hopeless sag of his shoulders twisted my heart.

Backing silently down the hall, I pitched my voice to a casual tone and called, "Hey, Eddy, are you in there?" as I walked toward the office again.

When I arrived for the second time, Eddy was sitting up straight and wearing his usual smile, but it did nothing to hide the bleakness in his eyes.

"Hi, Aydan," he said with his usual warmth, but uncertainty lurked beneath. "Did you... I mean, I guess by now everybody's heard what happened."

I hitched one hip up on the corner of his desk. "I heard a whole lot of bullshit. I don't believe any of it."

Eddy sank back in his chair with a sigh. "You might as well believe it. Everybody else does."

"*Nobody* else does," I corrected. "Except the police, and they've obviously gotten the wrong idea somehow."

Eddy stiffened. "So you haven't heard."

"Heard what?"

"Aydan..." His gaze fell to the floor. "I swear I didn't do it, but it's only fair to tell you... this isn't the first time I've been charged with beating someone to death with a baseball bat."

"I heard that rumour," I said gently. "But I'd rather hear your side of the story."

He sat silent, not looking at me.

"Eddy." I reached over to rub his shoulder. "You're a good person and a good friend, and I want to help. How about if I go and get us a couple of beers, and you can decide whether you want to tell me the whole story? If you don't want to talk about it, that's okay; we'll just drink our beer and everything will still be fine between us. Okay?"

Without waiting for a reply, I headed for the bar.

By the time I returned, Eddy was sitting up straight and looking resolute.

"Thanks," he said, accepting the pint I handed him. He indicated a chair he'd unearthed from its usual position under a stack of boxes. "Have a seat. It's a long story."

CHAPTER 36

As Eddy began the tale I already knew, I reached over to hold his hand. He recited the facts emotionlessly, but his eyes burned with anguish that would never fade.

"...so I got acquitted," Eddy finished at last. "There were a lot of people who thought I shouldn't have been, and I had death threats for a while afterward, but I didn't kill that man. I didn't even know he had been at the bar that night, until after the police arrested me."

"I believe you."

He stared. "You do? Just like that?"

I squeezed his hand. "Yep, just like that." I leaned back in my chair and took a drink of my beer. "So who did kill him?"

I had meant it as 'I wonder who killed him', but Eddy went still.

My heart gave a thump. "Eddy, do you know who killed him?"

After a long silence, Eddy spoke quietly. "You know, that's the one question I never had to answer under oath." Staring into the past, he went on, "They asked me if I'd killed him. They asked if I'd arranged to have him killed, or conspired with someone to kill him, or lured him there, or conspired with someone to lure him there. I truthfully answered no to all those questions. But they never asked if I knew who killed him."

I matched his quiet tone. "And you did know."

"Yes." Eddy took a deep swallow of beer and returned to the present with a sigh. "And I can tell you, now. Lionel died of cancer five years ago, so he's safe from any earthly prosecution."

I nearly dropped my beer. "*Lionel* killed him? But you said... everybody said... he never left the bar. Only for those few minutes while he walked you out."

"That's right." Eddy gulped some more beer. "He wanted to confess to the police, but I wouldn't let him. He had a wife and three young children. I had nobody. I didn't care whether I went to prison." His shoulders rose and fell in a tired shrug. "I didn't care whether I lived or died. But Lionel's family... I just couldn't bear to see more lives wrecked."

"So what happened?" I asked gently.

Eddy's knuckles whitened on his beer mug as he stared through me, facing that terrible night again. "I was drunk. Crazy with anger and grief. I needed air. Needed to walk. Lionel came outside with me and tried to get me into his car so he could drive me home. I wouldn't let him. I walked away and didn't look back. I didn't realize that just as I was walking away, the drunk driver..." He hesitated. "The victim... staggered past Lionel, following me. To apologize."

Eddy met my eyes, pain vibrating in his voice. "He wasn't a monster, Aydan. He did a monstrous thing, but he was shattered by it. He just wanted to apologize."

Eddy dropped his gaze and spoke to the floor. "Lionel grabbed his arm and wouldn't let him come after me. They struggled. The man was drunk again, absolutely plastered, and Lionel just... snapped. The car door was still open, my bat was right there. Lionel grabbed it and swung with everything he had. Just once, before he realized what he was doing." Eddy shook his head. "What he'd done. The man died on the spot. Lionel didn't remember much after that. He dragged the body over behind some garbage cans and wiped the bat and threw it away. And then he went back into the bar completely numb."

"And nobody could tell the difference," I said softly. "Because you were all numb. Blind with pain."

"Yes." Eddy squared his shoulders. "It was awful for everyone, including the drunk driver's family, but sending Lionel to prison wouldn't have fixed any of it. And Lionel suffered for the rest of his life. He never played baseball again, couldn't even watch a game. The sound of the bat made him sick. And..." Eddy sighed. "I honestly believe the cancer was caused by his feelings of guilt. It literally ate him up inside."

I shuddered. "That's horrible. Like you said, horrible for everybody. There were no winners."

"No, there weren't. But for what it's worth, I want you to know that I didn't do anything wrong. I didn't kill anybody or hide evidence or aid in a murder. I didn't lie, and I didn't even break the law by not turning Lionel in. My lawyer made sure I knew it's not illegal to just not talk to the police." Eddy sighed and reached over to touch my hand. "It feels good to get that off my chest, but I'm sorry for dumping it on you. I know you have your own trauma from a drunk driver."

"Nothing like yours. And don't apologize; I'm glad to know the whole story. But I'm so, so sorry for your loss. All your losses."

"Thanks."

We sat in silence for a few moments.

"How did you ever come to own a bar?" I asked finally. "How can you bear to serve alcohol to people? See them getting drunk?"

A sad smile twisted Eddy's lips. "Alcohol isn't the problem. Bars aren't the problem. People like you and I..." He raised his almost-empty pint. "...aren't the problem. We enjoy our drinks but never put anyone at risk by driving impaired. Most people don't. It's only a few people who are the problem. And as a bartender, I can make sure those few don't have their car keys when they leave the bar." He raised a self-deprecating eyebrow. "Besides, the only things I know how to do are tend bar and play piano. That narrowed down my career path."

I laughed. "Eddy, you can do anything you set your mind to. I know that about you just the same as I knew you were innocent."

The smile he flashed at me looked a lot more like his normal one, but it drained away fast as his brows drew together. "But this latest murder, here in my bar... Aydan, I can't figure it out. I swear I didn't kill Herman Lopez, either."

"I know you didn't," I agreed. "But it's so much like the last murder. Do you think one of those people who sent you death threats all those years ago might be trying to frame you for revenge? To give you what they think you deserve?"

He shook his head, still frowning. "I don't know. The death threats stopped years ago. If somebody hated me enough to go to the trouble of framing me, surely they wouldn't have waited this long."

"But it's weird how they matched up all the details," I

argued.

Eddy gave me a small grim smile. "There aren't too many options when you kill somebody with a baseball bat. The only place to dump the body was in the back alley by the garbage cans, and any idiot would wipe their fingerprints off the bat. They might not have even known about my past. The whole thing could have been completely random."

"Except, it couldn't," I pointed out. "Because how did they get in? And what are the chances that two random guys would somehow sneak into a random bar together, coincidentally get into an argument heated enough to want to kill each other, coincidentally find your bat under the bar in the dark, and..." I mimed swinging a bat. "And then the killer dragged the body out and faked the murder scene in the alley. That shows a lot of planning."

"Maybe they didn't sneak in," Eddy said thoughtfully. "Maybe they were already here."

"What do you mean?"

"What if the killer was hiding in that empty apartment upstairs? There's only a rope across the stairs to keep people from going up. I don't bother with anything else because there's nothing worth stealing up there."

I straightened, my pulse quickening. "Right, and the bar was so busy that night. It would have been easy for somebody to duck under the rope and go up without being noticed. I assume you didn't check upstairs before you locked up?"

Eddy gave me a sheepish look. "No. I used to check every night, but after years of never finding anybody, I stopped bothering."

"So the killer hid upstairs and then lured the victim in after you were gone. That's why there were no signs of forced entry; the killer just opened the door from the inside. Maybe offered the victim a free drink, and then *whack*."

Eddy drained his pint and sagged back in his chair. "It's a great theory, but there's no way to prove it. And the police don't want to look any farther than me."

"We'll figure it out," I promised. "John used to be a police officer, and Arnie's a private investigator. They'll help." I hesitated. "If you don't mind talking to them."

"I don't mind. But I'd rather not share the part about Lionel with anybody else."

"That's fine. It's got nothing to do with the current murder."

Eddy gave me a tired smile. "Thanks, Aydan. I don't see any way out of this, but it means a lot to have friends who are trying to help."

"John and Arnie have solved a lot of cases between them," I reassured him. "Don't give up hope." I stood up. Hesitated. Held out my arms. "Could you use a hug?"

"No, I'm fine..." He trailed off, his smile fading.

"Hug?" I repeated, arms still outstretched.

His mouth twisted as if in pain, and he rose and wrapped his arms around me in a fierce clasp.

Holding him tightly, I whispered, "We'll figure this out. It's going to be okay."

"Thanks." He let go and backed away, and I gave him a smile and headed back to the bar.

When I reported the conversation to Kane and Hellhound, a thoughtful silence fell on our table.

"Your scenario with the killer hiding upstairs seems plausible," Kane said slowly. "Except for the part where the killer lures the victim into the bar. Why? Why wouldn't he have just hidden in the alley and attacked the victim as he approached the bar? Then the murder scene would have been authentic, and the cleanup inside the bar would have been unnecessary."

"It's cold out," Hellhound contributed. "Maybe the killer didn't know when the victim was gonna get here, an' he didn't wanna freeze his ass off waitin' in the alley."

"All right..." Kane frowned. "But then why go to the trouble of dragging the victim out and staging a murder scene in the alley? Why not just flee? And how was the victim lured? Aydan, you said the RCMP report indicated there were no phone calls or texts to his number that hadn't been accounted for, right?"

"Right," I agreed. "But there were so many people; the killer might have been in the bar already. They could have made a verbal agreement to meet later. And maybe it wasn't premeditated and the killer didn't lure Lopez at all. Maybe they just intended to hide out and sneak some free drinks after the bar closed. But something went wrong, they disagreed, and Lopez got whacked in the heat of the argument."

Kane nodded. "Maybe. And if that's the case, Eddy wasn't being framed at all. It's just bad luck and coincidence. And it has nothing to do with Volslav, either."

My heart sank. "Right," I agreed glumly. "And I'm in deep shit."

"I hate to say it..." Kane began.

Hellhound shot him a scowl. "Then don't."

"...but I just don't see any way this murder could be connected to Volslav," Kane finished doggedly. "Nor Pearl's situation. I seriously doubt an international arms dealer is framing a small-town bartender and a little old lady."

Arnie threw another dirty look his way and put his arm

around my shoulders. "Don't worry, darlin', we'll keep diggin'. I don't believe in this much coincidence. There's somethin' weird goin' on here, an' we'll find it."

I leaned into him with a sigh. "Thanks." I rose. "I have to get back to the office."

"Okay." He stood and shrugged on his parka, turning to Kane. "I'll drop her at Sirius an' come back here to brainstorm." Jerking his chin at the bar with a grin, he added, "Good place to do it. Lotsa brain fuel."

Kane rose, too, holding me with his gaze. "Aydan, don't worry. Just because I can't immediately see a connection, that doesn't mean there isn't one. If there is, we'll find it."

"Thanks, I know I can count on you." I manufactured a smile and headed for the door.

Back at Sirius, I climbed wearily up the stairs and made for Spider's office. When I tapped on his open door, he looked up from his laptop with a smile. "Ready to go back into the network?"

"Not quite yet." I trudged in and sank into the chair across from his desk. "Something's been bugging me about this whole Volslav thing."

"What's that?"

"We don't have a clue what or who Volslav is. Why is that?"

A sarcastic voice spoke from the direction of the hallway. "Because that's kinda how it works when you're investigating someone. Duh."

I shot a glare at Holt, who had just appeared in the doorway. "Thanks, Einstein. That's not what I meant."

He ambled in and sat on the sofa, propping his feet on Spider's coffee table and linking his hands behind his head. "So what did you mean?"

"Are you here for a reason?" I demanded.

Holt raised a mocking eyebrow. "I work here."

"No, Spider works here. You're just crashing on his couch and wasting our time," I snapped.

Spider spoke up tactfully. "Can I help you with something, Greg?"

"You can help me piss Kelly off just a little bit more." Holt gave me a taunting grin. "I'm pretty sure she's ready to blow. One more little poke ought to do it."

Just to disappoint him, I laughed. "Asshole. But since you're here, you might as well make yourself useful. You came in on the tail end of my question, but I'm still hoping for an answer. Think about it. The Department has been chasing Volslav for what, eight years now? Stemp started it overseas; Kane had a try at it; now you and I are on it... but what do we really know? We don't even know if Volslav is a person or a group, and that's just weird."

Spider frowned. "Weird, how?"

"When Fuzzy Bunny was trying to capture me, we knew they ran a toy manufacturing and import/export business that covered up their arms deals and money laundering. They had offices and warehouses and employees. We knew the names of the owner, president, CEO; all that stuff."

"So?" Holt demanded.

"So, even the really obscure biker gangs have clubhouses," I went on. "And presidents, or some kind of leadership. They ride motorcycles. They have members. They do stuff."

Two blank expressions made me knot my fingers in my hair and tug with frustration. "Don't you get it? Every group *is* something. Or does something. You can meet them at a convention or read about them on their website or find them in their favourite bar. Volslav is just... vapour. Wouldn't you think that after investigating for eight damn years, we'd know who Volslav is and where they're headquartered? What their cover is? Or at least how to get in touch with them?"

"Well," Spider said slowly, "Stemp had contacts overseas when he was undercover as George Harrison. And Kane made contact with Yana Orlov and Dawn White."

"But we never found out who was running the show, or what their show even is," I protested. "Never found out who was next up the food chain. Seriously, two lousy names is all we've gotten in eight years? And they're both dead."

"You've got a point," Holt agreed. "And I'll tell you what else is weird. Every time we have a new development with Volslav, Stemp vanishes overseas. He just did it again. Flew over there, made some contacts with Interpol, and then dropped off the radar. And he's the Director; that's not even his job. He should be sending an agent over. Me. You. *Any* agent, for fucksakes. But he goes in person, every time. That's pretty damn suspicious." His jaw hardened. "You know, if Stemp is actually Volslav, it would explain a hell of a lot."

CHAPTER 37

"What?" I gaped at Holt.

"No, Stemp can't be crooked," Spider argued. "We've got really tight security procedures and background checks, and they're especially tight for the Director's position. Stemp passed all of them."

"Yeah, and who designed the security protocols?" Holt demanded.

Spider flushed with indignation. "I did!"

"And..." Holt prompted.

Spider blinked. Paled. "Um... Stemp and I designed them together."

"Uh-huh," Holt said knowingly. "And how many times did he suggest something and you just went along with it?"

"Never!" Spider snapped. "We each designed a different part of the security implementation to avoid conflicts of interest. He designed the crosschecks for the Head Analyst position, and I designed the ones for the Director independently, and Upper Command checked everything. There's no way Stemp could have gotten around the system."

Holt frowned. "But you've got to admit it's suspicious. He's had his hooks in every single investigation of Volslav, as an agent and then as Director. And by an amazing coincidence, we've never been able to catch Volslav or get any useful information."

My stomach clenched. God, why hadn't I just kept my mouth shut?

"And that attack on Stemp eight years ago when he was undercover," Holt went on. "The Department assumed they'd been getting too close to Volslav and that's why somebody decided to take out George Harrison, but if Stemp actually *was* Volslav, it was exactly what he needed. By the time they extracted him and got Kane over there, the trail was cold." Holt's eyes narrowed. "And it's pretty damn suspicious that Stemp's partner died, but he somehow survived close-range automatic weapon fire."

"You're wrong about Stemp," I said lamely.

"Oh, yeah? You got proof?" Holt demanded.

"No." Decided the best defence was a good offence, I scowled back at him. "Do you have proof that he's doing anything wrong?"

"Not yet." Holt got to his feet. "But if it's there, Dermott and I will find it."

"And that's not a conflict of interest at all," I pointed out sarcastically. "Dermott would love to get rid of Stemp so he could take over the Director's position."

Holt grimaced. "I won't argue that; but still. You said it yourself, it's damn suspicious."

"I didn't say I was suspicious of Stemp, I said-"

"I know what you said." Holt turned to Spider. "Anyway, what I came in here for... I tracked down the guy that posted that video. Is my fake reporter ID ready yet?"

"I just got an email from my team lead a few minutes ago. You can pick up your business cards and recording gear whenever you're ready."

"Okay, thanks." Holt headed for the door, then turned to

impale me with his blue-steel gaze. "Think about what I said. Don't let your feelings cloud the evidence." He strode out before I could retort.

I slumped in my chair with a sigh. That was what Kane had said, too. When two top agents give the same damn advice, a smart person would pay attention.

"Do you think Holt might be right?" Spider inquired timidly.

Apparently I wasn't a smart person. The words popped out of my mouth before I could audit them. "No. I see what he's saying, and it makes sense when you look at it like that, but it's wrong."

Spider eyed me. "You sound really sure."

"I'm sure. Holt doesn't have the whole picture."

"And you do?"

"Yeah."

He straightened, frowning. "Then why didn't you tell him?"

"Classified. It's above his pay grade. Dermott's, too."

Worry crept into Spider's expression. "H-How do you know? Is it something you... found? In the network?"

"No, Stemp told me." I attempted a reassuring smile. "Don't worry, I'm not snooping into anything I shouldn't. It's just a... thing that Stemp can't reveal yet. But he will as soon as he can."

Spider leaned back, letting out a breath as his brow cleared. "That's a relief. Is it something to do with..." He lowered his voice to a whisper. "Katya?"

I couldn't help shooting a glance over my shoulder, but we were unobserved. I nodded. "She was involved with him when he was George Harrison, and whenever George Harrison comes up again he goes over to make sure she's safe."

"Do you think she'd be in danger if Dermott found out?"

"I don't know. That's why I haven't said anything to anybody. If I did and something happened to her, I'd never know whether it was my fault."

Spider shivered. "I'm glad I've never said anything to anybody about her, either. But... do we really know..." He hesitated, his brow furrowed with anxiety. "Aydan, what if Katya is Volslav? What if, every time we get close, Stemp goes over there to warn her?"

An icy lump formed in my belly.

Stemp would never betray national security or the Department; I was certain of that. But what if he didn't know Katya as well as he thought? After all, they had lived apart for years.

What if, in his innocent desire to protect his daughter, he was inadvertently aiding a ruthless arms dealer?

"He wouldn't," I said aloud. "Stemp would never knowingly be involved with a criminal."

"But they're, um..." Spider blushed. "In a relationship. That might change things."

"Not for Stemp. You know what he's like. Completely detached. If he found out Katya was a criminal, he'd arrest her in an instant. Even if she was his lover."

But would he arrest the mother of his child?

I chose not to think about that. And Spider didn't know about Stemp's daughter, so our conversation had to end here.

"I'd better get back into the network," I said.

"Okay, I'll go down and get your key. Meet you in your office." Spider hurried out.

I trailed down the hallway to my office, deep in

unpleasant thought.

When Spider arrived, I accepted the network key from him and slumped on my small sofa.

"Oyster mushrooms again?" he asked.

"Sure."

"When do you want me to start signalling you to come out?"

I managed a smile. "In a couple of hours. Thanks."

He nodded, and I stepped into virtual reality.

My original plan had been to dig deeper into Everett Marsh, but instead my subconscious misgivings guided me. When I found myself hovering outside the servers of the Sofia University, I resigned myself to the inevitable.

I had to know about Katya. If Stemp was in danger, or worse, in collusion...

Don't go there.

I slipped past the university's firewalls and into their staff records, wishing my decryption abilities could also translate foreign languages. Alert for the Bulgarian form of Katya with its Cyrillic backward 'R', I sent feelers through the server.

Stemp had whisked Katya away from her university job nearly two years ago, but maybe her employment records would still be archived. I wouldn't be able to read the words, but her staff photo would do. I vaguely remembered a heart-shaped face with warm brown eyes from the first time I'd investigated her relationship with Stemp.

My heart leaped when I found her records, and I did my best to memorize her photo. Katya would have a different name now, and Stemp was far too smart to let her new identity surface in any public or law-enforcement database. Sending her photo through the Department's facial-recognition program wouldn't work even if I dared risk it.

But somewhere in the world there was probably a driver's license with Katya's face and her current name on it. I whisked back into the internet holding Katya's image in memory.

In seconds I had located hundreds of digital images of pretty heart-shaped faces with brown eyes. A moment later, there were thousands... no, more.

Hope trickled away.

Already my memory of Katya's photo was blurring. I couldn't cross-check all these photos; and anyway, Stemp was too good at disguises. Katya probably looked totally different than when she'd worked at the university.

Grudgingly admitting failure, I retracted into a compact data-blob and floated in the busy data stream to think.

Dammit, Katya couldn't be Volslav. Neither could Stemp. I just couldn't believe it.

Wouldn't believe it.

Heaving a sigh without breath, I headed for the CIA's servers.

Everett Marsh's internal communications showed that he was scheduled to question Grandin tomorrow at nine AM. Grandin was to be brought to the CIA facility for the interview.

Marsh was up to something.

My initial blaze of excitement subsided a moment later when I realized that the CIA was hardly likely to interrogate a former agent in a public interview room in a prison. So it was probably normal procedure to transfer him back to the CIA's holding facility.

But still, it would be very interesting if I could eavesdrop. My hopes rose when I checked the location noted in Marsh's calendar: A secured interview room. Those usually had video surveillance. Maybe I'd get to snoop after all.

Buoyed by that bit of possibly-good news, I returned to the server where Marsh's reports were stored. He hadn't filed anything new since the last time I'd checked, and I tethered myself in the data stream to study his report of Nora's last intel delivery again.

That missing information nagged at me. There was the date of the diplomatic pouch's arrival, six weeks ago. Within hours of receiving it, Marsh should have updated the records to show what it had contained.

Why hadn't he?

As I floated there pondering, the record disappeared. Right under my virtual nose.

What the *hell?*

Flashing along the echoes of the deletion command, I flung hungry tentacles throughout the system.

The command had been sent by Everett Marsh, or someone using his login credentials. Whoever it was, they had just removed all references to that last diplomatic pouch.

In an instant I located the local machine that had sent the command. Zipping through its connections, I hijacked its webcam.

Blackness.

No matter how I tried to force it to work, no sound or image came through. The software drivers were there, but the camera had been unplugged.

Dammit!

I whisked back to the original file.

Nothing else had been deleted. And now all the entries lined up neatly, one instalment of intel per pouch delivery.

What had that last pouch contained? Obviously,

something someone wanted to hide.

But was that 'someone' Everett Marsh?

I hovered there for a while, watching, but the user had closed the file immediately after deleting the record and nobody else opened it.

Drifting down the outgoing data stream deep in thought, I slipped back out into the internet.

Time to dig a little deeper into Everett Marsh. The Department wouldn't be able to get a warrant to examine his personal records, but I didn't need a warrant.

If I had been capable of an evil grin, I would have been wearing one. Here, Everett. Come to Mommy...

It didn't take long to locate his personal computer. After a cursory skim of the boring unprotected data, I turned eagerly to the encrypted partition.

And found nothing of interest.

Everything was organized and apparently accurate. The income reported in his tax software matched the bank statements he'd downloaded and neatly organized by year. His bank statements showed no large or unusual deposits or withdrawals, and if he had offshore accounts, he hadn't downloaded the statements. His brokerage account statements showed only modest returns over the past twenty years. He collected a healthy salary from the CIA, but his giant mortgage and maxed-out credit cards ate up most of his income.

I floated there, considering.

Marsh was solvent, but he didn't have the savings I would have expected for a man in his late fifties. He'd probably get a fat pension when he retired, so maybe he didn't need much in the way of savings.

Still, it niggled at me.

No matter how good his pension was, it wouldn't be as much as his salary. He'd probably have to downsize to get out from under that hefty mortgage.

With only a few top-earning years left, could he be getting desperate enough to consider some shadier options? Maybe an offshore account that he hadn't recorded even on his encrypted drive?

Backing out of his personal computer, I launched into the world-wide web, searching for Everett Marsh with all my senses.

When I found nothing, I headed for the offshore banks with grim resignation. I'd check as many as I could, but I was almost out of time. Any minute now Spider would signal me to return.

At least I hadn't lost our connection this time. I could still feel his faint presence like a reassuring hand between my virtual shoulderblades.

Cayman Islands, Singapore, Switzerland, or Belize? And if I didn't find anything there, how many smaller places should I try? How much time should I waste? While I was grubbing around like a repulsive little cybermole, Volslav could be selling that weapon.

How many people could be murdered in the time that it took me to dig for information that might not even exist?

Vibrating with nerves, I aimed for the Cayman Islands.

After the first eight banks, despair crept in. I could search for Marsh all I wanted, but if he was using a fake name I could look right at his bank account without spotting him.

A tiny tug at my consciousness decided me. Spider was calling me back. Best to run this by him before I wasted a bunch of-

Recognition blazed into my consciousness, followed by queasy trepidation. I recognized the name on that bank account.

Not Everett Marsh.

Arlene Widdenback.

CHAPTER 38

Hovering in the data stream, I hesitated over Arlene Widdenback's Cayman Islands bank account.

My bank account. A bank account I hadn't opened.

Steeling myself, I checked the balance.

Holy *fuck!*

If data bits were capable of hyperventilating, I would have sucked every molecule of air out of the data tunnel.

Twenty million dollars.

Twenty million. And change, of course. The 'change' was more than my life's savings.

Backing blindly away down the data stream, I attempted calm. There was an explanation; of course there was. It was probably the Department's money. Part of my cover, in case anybody checked up on Arlene Widdenback the badass arms dealer.

That was it.

That had to be it.

Dazed, I followed Spider's gentle pull back to Sirius Dynamics.

When I rejoined my physical body and finished swearing over the pain, I straightened to meet Spider's hopeful gaze.

"How did it go?" he asked. "Did you find anything else on Everett Marsh?"

"Maybe." I massaged my aching temples. "Either he's up to no good, or somebody is setting him up just like Grandin got set up."

Spider's eyes lit up. "What did you find?"

I hesitated, my brain still vibrating with the shock of seeing eight digits in that bank account. "Are you still managing the details for my Arlene Widdenback cover?"

"Um... yes." He looked puzzled by my sudden digression. "Why?"

"Did you set up all my bank accounts?"

"Yes." His brows drew together in a worried frown. "What's wrong?"

"Did you set one up in the Cayman Islands?"

"No..." Spider said slowly. "But the Caymans are usually where we set up accounts if we need them for an agent's cover. It would make sense for Arlene Widdenback to have an account there."

"Oh, good." I fell back on the cushions, closing my eyes with relief. "I just found an account for Arlene Widdenback with over twenty million dollars in it, and I was-"

"Twenty million?"

Dermott's voice made my eyes pop open to see him scowling in the doorway.

"Did I just hear you say Arlene Widdenback has over twenty million dollars stashed somewhere?" he growled.

Small hairs stood up on the back of my neck. "Yes, in the Cayman Islands. I guess the Department must have put it there to reinforce my arms dealer cover."

"No," Dermott said tightly. "We sure as hell didn't."

Trying to ignore the chill that crept down my spine, I held my voice level. "Are you sure? Maybe Stemp-"

"Maybe Stemp what?" Dermott snarled. "Paid you off

for not telling anybody he's actually Volslav?"

"What? No! Of course not!" My mouth didn't seem to be connected to my brain, and I realized I'd launched to my feet, fists clenched. "I just-"

"Just managed to save up twenty million by putting a few pennies away each month, right?" Dermott sneered. Glancing at Spider, he added, "Put that laptop down right now." As Spider complied, looking scared and confused, Dermott snapped his glare back to me. "And you, give me that key." When I hesitated, he thrust out his palm and barked, "The network key. NOW!"

Barely overcoming my urge to refuse just because he was an asshole, I stepped close enough to drop the key into his hand before retreating a couple of wary steps.

"All right, both of you come with me." He sidestepped out of my path and jerked his chin toward the door. "After you." His hand hovered near his concealed holster, and I squelched the brief and profoundly stupid impulse to grab for my gun and see if I could beat him to the draw.

I didn't try to keep the suspicion out of my tone. "Where are we going?"

"My office. Move it. Both of you."

After a glance at Spider's fearful expression, I headed for the door, moving slowly and smoothly. No need to get shot today.

I hoped.

"Stop." Dermott threw a glare at Spider. "You go ahead of her. Leave your laptop here."

"Okay..." Spider rose cautiously, still clutching his laptop. "B-But I can't leave the laptop unattended. Department security protocols-"

"Fine, give it to me," Dermott interrupted.

Spider handed it over with reluctant hands, and proceeded out the door.

"Now you," Dermott said, stepping sideways another pace as if to be sure he was out of my reach.

I didn't bother to point out that a martial arts expert could still take him with ease. It wouldn't help the situation, and my martial arts skills were practically nonexistent anyway.

As I walked down the hallway ahead of Dermott, my back tingling as though there was a target painted on it, I mentally rehearsed the movements to get him into one of the few submission holds I knew.

The thought of him on his knees with his arm twisted up behind him sustained me to his office.

"Inside," he commanded as Spider hesitated at his doorway. "Both of you, sit."

We obeyed, and I swivelled in my chair to watch Dermott, who still stood in the doorway. He pulled out one of the secured cell phones that bypassed the Sirius jamming system, and punched a button. When a blurred crackle of a greeting came through, he said, "In my office, now."

A terse crackle responded, and he responded through his clenched teeth. "*Now*. Major security breach."

Spider caught my eye, looking terrified.

"Don't worry," I murmured.

"No talking," Dermott snapped as he disconnected from his call.

Instead of taking his usual seat behind his desk, he continued to hover in the doorway. My back muscles protested my twisted position, and I sighed and half-stood so I could rotate the chair to face him.

Dermott tensed, but held his ground without speaking.

I crossed my arms over my chest and slouched lower in the chair, hoping to look relaxed while still keeping my feet under me in case I had to move fast. Letting my eyelids droop, I watched Dermott through my lashes.

What the hell was he up to? If he seriously believed I was a threat, he would have drawn his own weapon and confiscated mine. But despite that dubious vote of confidence, he didn't seem inclined to come within grabbing range.

Then again, maybe he was reading my mind. A vivid and glorious image of my hands around his throat made a smile twitch the corners of my lips.

A few tense minutes later, the thud of rapidly-approaching feet made me open my eyes and straighten just as Holt hurried up. His steely gaze flicked over Spider and me, then back to Dermott.

"What the hell's going on?" he demanded. "I was right in the middle of-"

"Inside," Dermott interrupted, herding Holt ahead of him as he entered and closed the door behind him. I rotated my chair again to keep him in view, and when he took his seat behind the desk at last, he glanced at Holt as if for reassurance before relaxing.

"Sit," he said to Holt, then ignored us all while he dialled the phone.

Holt's jaw tightened, and he shot me a 'what the hell?' look.

I returned a shrug.

Holt's frown deepened, but before he could speak, Dermott's connection apparently went through.

"Brock," he said. "It's Dermott. Go and find a bank account in the Cayman Islands, under Arlene Widdenback."

He listened for a moment, then turned to me. "Which bank?"

"I, uh..."

Shit, which one had that been?

"*Which bank?*" Dermott growled.

I made an impatient chop at the air to silence him. "Hang on, I'm trying to remember. It was the seventh or eighth one I checked..."

Dermott opened his mouth as if to make some mocking comment, but Holt caught his eye and he pressed his lips shut instead.

It was no use.

"I don't remember," I admitted at last. "I was looking for Everett Marsh and I didn't find him, and Spider signalled me right then, and I was in... maybe the bank name started with an 'A'...?"

Dermott gave me a disgusted look and turned his attention back to the phone. "Check them all, right now. Top priority. Call me as soon as you have something."

He slapped the receiver back into its cradle.

"What the hell?" Holt demanded.

"Seems Arlene Widdenback is a very rich woman," Dermott replied, but his scowl was all for me. "To the tune of twenty million in a Cayman bank."

Holt frowned. "So what? The Caymans are our standard cover accounts."

"The Department never set up that account," Dermott retorted.

Holt's frown deepened. "You sure?"

"Yes, I'm fucking sure! Webb set up her cover." He glowered at Spider. "Did you create an account in the Caymans for her?"

"N-No," Spider stammered. "But lots of other people in the Department have the authority-"

"Who?" Dermott interrupted. "Which other people?"

"Um... any of my team could have gotten instructions to do it. Stemp could have ordered it or done it himself. Anybody in Upper Command-"

"None of them did," Dermott interrupted again.

"How do you know?" I demanded. "You only found out about this account a few minutes ago, and you haven't checked with anybody else in the Department since then. We've been with you the whole time."

A flush rose on Dermott's cheeks. "I damn well know-"

"I'll just check with Accounting," Holt said calmly, reaching across Dermott's desk to appropriate the phone.

During the brief conversation with Accounting, his jaw tightened. My heart sank as he replaced the receiver, wearing a grim expression.

"Nobody from the Department authorized a transfer," Holt said.

"So Little Miss Perfect Agent stole twenty million from the Department." Dermott looked as though somebody had just handed him a birthday cake.

"No," Holt said, still frowning. "There's no record of any transfer. That money didn't come from the Department."

Dermott's grin widened as though his birthday cake had just been given an extra coat of frosting. With sprinkles. "So *somebody's* been selling intel to the highest bidder." The unholy glee in his face made me want to vomit.

"No, I haven't been selling intel," I growled. "I don't know anything about that bank account. If I did, do you really think I'd be stupid enough to mention it?"

Dermott's face fell a fraction, but he rallied fast. "Sure.

You're a tricky bitch. That's exactly what you'd do. Try to divert suspicion."

My last nerve snapped under the strain. "Listen, you fucking moron! What do you think will happen to that money now that you know about it?" I didn't wait for him to reply. "It's going to get confiscated by the Department. Because Arlene Widdenback isn't a real person; she's a cover identity. Now how the fuck do you think it would benefit me to tell you about that twenty million dollars, knowing I'd promptly lose it all?"

"Listen, *bitch*," Dermott began.

Holt overrode him. "Let's just calm down here." His words were reasonable, but his hard voice brooked no argument. "First, stop with the name-calling, both of you. Second, let's wait to hear what Brock tells us."

Holt, the voice of restraint and reason. I nearly laughed aloud in spite of the gravity of the situation.

Fortunately I managed to stifle myself, and we all sat in grim silence.

It was a long wait.

When the phone rang at last, I couldn't suppress my twitch.

Dermott snatched up the phone. "Dermott." His eyes narrowed as the voice on the other end spoke. His knuckles whitened on the receiver. "Right," he said at last. "You'll get a commendation for this."

My heart plummeted as he slapped the receiver back onto the cradle with triumph in his eyes.

"Brock found that bank account," he said, his tone almost casual. "It was just opened last week, with only one big deposit. He traced the deposit back to its source, and guess where it came from?"

Dermott looked happy.

Really happy.

My guts clenched.

"Where?" Holt demanded.

"Volslav."

In the deadly pause that followed Dermott's single damning word, I could hear nothing but my own silent mind-screams. Then Holt and Spider spoke at the same time.

"*What?*" Spider's voice came out in a high-pitched yelp.

"Whose name's on the account?" Holt demanded.

Dermott smirked. "Arlene Widdenback's. I told you."

"No," Holt said impatiently. "Volslav's account, the one that transferred the money in. The banks require ID. We should be able to get a name and address."

Dermott gave him a superior smile. "Dymt Volslav."

"Dymt? What kind of name is that?" Holt demanded.

"I can look it up." Spider reached tentatively toward the laptop that Dermott had placed on the corner of his desk. Dermott didn't try to stop him, and a moment later Spider's fingers were flying over the keys. "It's not a first name," he reported after a moment. "Not in any language. It might be an abbreviation for Dimitri. But that would be a really weird abbreviation because none of the usual spelling variations use 'y' as a second letter."

I found my voice at last, concentrating hard on the details to avoid the horrifying bigger picture. "So unless Dymt Volslav's parents couldn't spell, the account-holder probably isn't a real person."

Spider grimaced. "It looks that way. I'd have to run a detailed search through the main database to be sure, but I doubt we'll ever find a Dymt Volslav."

"We don't have to," Dermott said shortly. "Volslav will

contact Kelly when they want their next batch of intel." He turned to Holt with a vicious glint in his eyes. "Take that bitch's weapons and arrest her for treason."

CHAPTER 39

Holt and I locked eyes.

He looked confused and angry. And deep in those steely blue eyes, there was hurt. He had trusted me.

Now he didn't.

I didn't know what he was seeing in my eyes. Fear. Desperate appeal. It probably looked like guilt to him.

"Hurry up," Dermott snapped. "Take her weapons and arrest her."

"I didn't do anything," I protested, doing my best to sound confident. "I didn't even know that bank account was there until a few minutes ago. Somebody's framing me."

A glance at Dermott's gloating expression froze my heart. The Department had easy access to that bank in the Caymans. And he really wanted to burn me.

My voice came out cold and certain. "*You're* framing me."

"*What?*" Dermott's yelp sounded like honest surprise. A moment later a knowing leer creased his features. "Nice try. But where would I get twenty million dollars? If I had twenty mil, I wouldn't waste it on you. Holt, hurry up. Lock this bitch down."

"She didn't do anything!" Spider cried. "She came out of the network and asked me if I'd set up the bank account! She didn't know anything about it!"

"Bullshit!" Dermott roared. "Get out of my office!"

"No." Spider was chalk-white and his lips trembled, but his voice was steady. "Aydan is innocent, and I'm not going to turn my back on her just because you're a bully."

Dermott turned purple. "HOLT!"

Holt hesitated, his brow furrowed. "Let's just think about this for a minute," he said finally.

Dermott's lips curled contemptuously. "What, are you fucking her, too? Fine, you can go down for aiding her with treason." He yanked out his gun and levelled it at me. "Hand over your weapons. Slowly."

"Brent."

Holt's use of his first name made Dermott's gaze swivel to him.

"Slow down a second," Holt said. "If you're right and she's a traitor, I'm right there with you. Prison is too good for her, and I'll take great pleasure in making sure she gets there." His steely gaze pinned me to my chair. "Maybe she'll even trip and fall a few times on her way." He transferred his attention to Dermott. "I know how much you hate traitors. I do, too, but if you're wrong about this, you'll be in deep shit with Upper Command. Do you really want to risk your career on one flimsy piece of evidence?"

"It's not flimsy," Dermott snapped. "It's a blatant-"

"This is stupid." Spider's voice cut across Dermott's like a splash of clear water through mud. "Aydan is innocent, and she can prove it."

Dermott gaped at him. "She can?"

I barely managed not to echo, "I can?"

"Of course." Spider turned to me with confidence shining in his eyes. "We have an infallible lie detector. All you have to do is ask her."

Dermott snorted. "We won't have it until Monday. And I'm not going to let this bitch sell any more of our secrets in the meantime."

Spider stiffened. "Your language is inappropriate. Department regulations require respectful communication at all times. Aydan has served with distinction and she deserves the benefit of the doubt." He drew himself up, his shoulders square and his jaw firm. "Everyone is innocent until proven guilty. You don't have enough evidence to arrest her, and you certainly don't have enough to convict her."

Dermott's knuckled whitened on his gun. "You little-"

"Hang on," Holt interrupted loudly. He rose, rounded the desk, and took Dermott by the arm. The two of them retreated to the farthest corner of the office with Holt muttering in Dermott's ear.

With every muscle tensed, I watched their body language. Dermott, rigid and uncooperative with his gaze and gun still aimed at me. Holt leaning in, talking fast and making persuasive gestures.

Was he on my side?

Dermott's posture slowly unbent while he listened. Then an unpleasant smile creased his face as he holstered his weapon.

Shit. If he was smiling, I wasn't going to like what was coming.

The two of them returned and Dermott slid behind his desk with his usual scowl, but there was an undertone of smugness that made me nervous.

"Okay," he said. "You can thank Holt for the reprieve." He shot a look at Holt. "Bleeding-heart pussy." The epithet sounded fake, as though he was only pretending irritation. Holt didn't react to the insult, and Dermott turned back to me. "You have until Monday."

It couldn't be that easy.

I watched him, waiting for the other shoe to drop.

He made an impatient gesture toward the door. "Get out!"

We left. Holt stayed behind in Dermott's office and closed the door behind us.

Spider and I stood in the corridor, staring at each other.

"What is he up to?" Spider whispered.

"I wish I knew." I sighed. "I'm sure I'll find out, though. Whether I want to or not. I need a bathroom break, and then I want to dig deeper into-"

I broke off as Dermott's door opened and Holt came out.

"So what's your plan?" he asked casually, as though the last half-hour had never happened.

Eyeing him with suspicion, I replied, "I want to go back into the network and look at Everett Marsh some more. Is Dermott going to let me do that?"

"Sure. Here's your network key." Holt dropped it into my palm and added, "I'll meet you in your office."

"What for?" I demanded.

"I'll be your anchor." At my frown, he nudged me down the hall and lowered his voice. "I convinced Dermott that you're getting framed. I bought you time until you can do your lie-detector interview on Monday."

He looked sincere. Honest.

"You're full of shit," I growled. "What's really happening?"

He glowered at me. "I'm so glad you appreciate me putting my ass on the line for you. You're welcome."

I sighed. "Sorry. Thanks. I do appreciate that, it's just that I know there's something else going on here. Dermott is still sure he can bury me."

Holt shrugged. "He can't bury you if you're innocent." He narrowed his eyes at me. "Right?"

"He doesn't care whether I'm innocent. All he wants to do is twist around something I say in my lie-detector interview. It'll be his word against mine."

"Don't be such a fucking paranoid idiot," Holt snapped. "Sure, he can relieve you of duty if you fail the interview, maybe lock you up for a day or two while the chain of command convenes; but you're entitled to a full tribunal."

"Yeah, right. Same as when they issued a kill order for my second husband. He didn't get a tribunal. He just got dead."

Holt shook his head. "They would have held a tribunal, even if your husband didn't know about it. And they had to have iron-clad evidence. Command never issues a kill order without being absolutely sure."

"Well, they didn't ask to hear Robert's side of the story, so I guess there's quite a bit of wiggle-room in 'sure'." I cocked a cynical eyebrow at him. "And Dermott is sure I'm guilty."

"Should he be?" Holt's gaze bored into me.

I threw up my hands. "I didn't even know that bank account existed until I found it. The lie detector will prove it."

There was that flicker of hurt in his eyes again. He knew I had avoided giving a straight answer to his yes-or-no question.

"Then you've got nothing to worry about," he said curtly, and strode toward my office.

"I'll meet you there," I said to Spider, and headed for the ladies' room to beat my head against the metaphorical wall in privacy.

When I returned to my office, Spider occupied one chair, wearing a troubled expression while his fingers trembled on the laptop keys. Holt slouched in the other chair, arms crossed over his chest and impassive cop face in place.

Marvellous. I sank onto the sofa with a long sigh, wishing I could curl into a ball and pull a blanket over my head.

"Oyster mushrooms again?" Spider asked in a small voice.

"Sure." I closed my eyes and stepped into virtual reality.

Holt's avatar popped into existence beside me, and we strode down the virtual corridor.

"Where are you headed?" Holt asked.

"File repository."

He hissed out an irritated breath. "No shit. Where are you headed once you get into the internet?"

"Oh. I'm going back to the CIA's servers to see if I can hijack the surveillance camera in their interview room. I want to snoop on Marsh's meeting with Grandin tomorrow morning. And then..." I hesitated, thinking. "I'm going to keep looking at Marsh's financials. My gut tells me he's looking for a way to make some fast money before he retires. Or else he's already got some stashed somewhere and I just haven't found it yet."

Holt settled into a chair in the file repository. "Good hunting." He held out his hand.

"Thanks." I grasped it and blinked into invisibility.

After lengthy sojourn in cyberspace, I trickled tiredly back into Sirius's file repository and faded into visibility.

Holt jerked his hand out of my grip with a yelp. "Christ!"

"What?" I frowned at his expression of horror.

"Kelly?" he demanded. "Is that you?"

"Of course it's me. Who were you expecting?"

"You look like a fucking hundred-year-old zombie."

I squinted at the wisps of white hair that lay on my shoulders where my thick still-mostly-red mane should have been. When I pulled a strand closer for inspection, my hand was age-spotted and furrowed with deep wrinkles.

Letting out a hollow groan, I raised both arms in front of me and did my best zombie-shuffle toward the door.

"Really fucking funny," Holt snapped. "Change back."

Too tired to hold my arms up any longer, I let them fall to my sides.

Oops, past my sides.

One arm detached and fell to the floor with a sodden slap. The fingers twitched revoltingly.

I groaned again, sincerely this time.

"Fuck off with the zombie shit!" This time Holt sounded worried.

"I can't help it. I feel like I'm a hundred years old. The damn VR picked it up, and I'm too tired to change. And then you said 'zombie'..." One of my eyeballs dropped to the floor and rolled. "Shit."

Holt corralled my eyeball and scooped up my arm, herding the rest of my rapidly-deteriorating body out into the virtual corridor. "You're fine," he assured me. "You're only forty-eight. You're in great physical shape. You're strong and young. A walk to the portal is a piece of cake for you."

A bit of my strength returned, and my arm and eyeball reattached themselves.

"See?" Holt encouraged, still nudging me along the corridor. "No problem. We're almost there. You're completely fine. Here we are."

He pushed me through.

"*Aaagh! Cock-sucking-pig-fucking-*"

Pain overwhelmed my ability to form words, and the remainder of my obscenities emerged in a mostly-silent hiss shaped only by the movement of my lips. Hugging my splitting head, I rocked back and forth with my eyes squeezed shut.

Spider's tentative hands massaged my temples and I let out a whimper that was part gratitude and part lamentation for Kane's absence. When we had worked together, he had always known how to find the points of fiery pain and extinguish them. Now he was a civilian, and I'd never have that relief again.

"Here," Holt said roughly. Powerful fingers pushed Spider's aside and ground into the trigger points at my temples and the base of my skull. The explosion of agony-laced bliss jerked a cry from my throat.

"Stop! You're hurting her!" Spider's voice seemed very far away.

I raised a hand to reassure him, slumping as both pain and relief faded into a dull ache.

"It's okay," I mumbled. "Better now. Thanks."

Holt released my head, and I cautiously squinted my eyes open.

He was eyeing me with concern, but his lips twisted into a sardonic grin as soon as I glanced at him. "Guess I should be grateful that your subconscious decided to go with 'zombie' instead of 'fucking'."

I snorted. "I think we can all be grateful for that."

"What happened, Aydan?" Spider asked worriedly.

"Nothing. Just the usual; when I get tired it hurts more."

"You should have pulled her out when I said so," Spider accused Holt. "I told you she was too tired."

"Thanks, Spider, but it's okay," I assured him. "I needed the time."

"Did you find something?"

I leaned back with a sigh, massaging my temples. "Yes, but not what I was really looking for. Turns out Marsh isn't as broke as I thought. He made a bunch of money recently. It wasn't in an offshore account; it was in his brokerage account. I didn't think to look there because I'd checked the statements on his computer, but the most recent transactions weren't on the statements."

"So?" Holt prompted.

"So he made a few hundred grand in three days."

"Whoa!" Spider's eyes went wide. "Can you legit make that kind of money in the stock market?"

"Apparently. He shorted some stocks that crashed and made him a bundle..." I trailed off as comprehension struck. "Shit! I need to go back and look at those stocks!"

"No," Spider said, snatching the network key out of my hand. "You're too tired. You weren't controlling your thoughts at all by the time you came out."

"But I need to know." I gave him a pleading look. "I bet those stocks were for gold companies. And I bet they were gold companies that were based in the African states that are now at war."

Holt sat up straight. "With well-armed insurgents. That's got to be it. Marsh made a deal with Volslav. Volslav made a killing supplying the weapons for the coup, the stocks promptly crashed, and Marsh made a killing on the stock market."

"And that's why Marsh redacted the parts of Grandin's reports that mentioned gold production. And then he framed Grandin." I turned back to Spider. "I bet Grandin was sniffing around and Marsh was afraid he was getting too close. And I bet FBI Agent Dirk was part of that investigation, too, and that's why Marsh told Grandin to kill him. I have to go back and find out for sure."

"Not tonight," Spider said firmly. "This isn't time-sensitive. Volslav has already sold the weapons, the African presidents are already dead and their countries are at war, and Marsh has already made his money. Nothing's going to change between now and tomorrow morning. You're exhausted and you need to rest and eat."

At the mention of food, my stomach let out a ravenous growl. I glanced at my watch. "Shit! It's seven o'clock! I'm supposed to be at Margaret's stupid party!"

Holt's eyes narrowed. "Margaret Young? The woman that ratted you out to Volslav? How stupid are you? I bet Volslav knows exactly where you're going and when you're going to be there. It's a total no-brainer to set up a sniper to pick you off."

I grinned. "Yep. And it's a total no-brainer for Kane and Hellhound to grab the sniper while I act as bait."

The corner of Holt's mouth quirked up. "I'll help."

"I thought Dermott said you have better things to do than babysit me."

Holt shrugged. "Now he wants me to watch you."

He still looked completely sincere. Maybe he was even telling the truth. Or part of it.

"Okay." I heaved myself off the couch. "But first I want a bulletproof vest, and some food..." I trailed off. "Hang on. Forget the vest."

"No, Aydan! You need a vest! Don't take a chance," Spider pleaded.

I returned from my thoughts with a blink. "What? Oh, no, sorry to worry you. I wouldn't go without protection. I was just wondering if Reggie still had that bulletproof blade-proof jacket prototype. That gives me better coverage, and if there isn't a sniper at all and it's actually just a party, nobody will realize I'm wearing armour."

"Those jackets just came into production," Holt said. "Stores has a few sizes. Don't you ever read your internal memos?"

Resisting the urge to stick out my tongue at him, I replied, "Sure, in all my spare time between trying not to get killed or incarcerated."

"Go and get a damn jacket. And get the hat, too."

"There's a hat?"

Holt shook his head in disgust. "Christ, Kelly, you need a fucking nursemaid."

"No, I need a secretary. You applying for the job?"

"Fuck off."

We exchanged a few more casual insults on the way to Stores, where Holt and I each picked up a jacket and hat.

"This hat is weird." I held up the black object and peered at it. "It looks like the love child of an illicit affair between a tuque and a mushroom."

Holt let out a long-suffering sigh. "It needs the airspace between the fabric and your thick head to absorb the impact. You know how much it fucking hurts to get shot wearing a vest. Even if the bullet doesn't go through, the force still transfers. You'd end up with a fractured skull otherwise."

"Yeah, I know, but still." I donned the hat and peered at my reflection in the glass panel of the door. "This looks stupid."

"Since when do you have any fashion sense? Come on."

CHAPTER 40

When Holt and I arrived in the lobby of Sirius Dynamics, Kane and Hellhound both rose from the chairs. Hellhound's gaze flicked from me to Holt and back again.

"Everythin' okay, darlin'?" he inquired.

"Yeah, Holt's going to give us a hand. Let's grab something to eat."

"Awright." Hellhound eyed Holt suspiciously as I headed for the security wicket to turn in my fob.

The man behind the counter wasn't Leo, and I suffered a pang of guilt. I had promised to provide gossip, and I hadn't delivered before Leo went off-shift.

As I turned away from the desk, Kane stepped between me and the door. "I'll take point," he said. "Hellhound next, then Aydan, and Holt can cover our six. Aydan will ride with Hellhound. I'll lead in my vehicle and Holt can follow."

Holt's jaw tightened but he didn't argue, probably because the first person out the door would be at the most risk if there was a sniper.

I knew there was no point in arguing, so I gave Kane a smile and said, "Lead on. Let's go to the Greenhorn Café. They'll be closing in forty-five minutes, so they shouldn't be too busy."

We made it to our respective vehicles without incident,

and I took out my phone as Hellhound put his SUV in gear.

"I'm going to text Margaret and tell her I'll be arriving around eight-fifteen," I told him. "If anybody's planning to take a shot at me there, they'll be set up already because I was supposed to arrive at seven. It's not quite enough time for them to take down and set up again, so they'll likely stay put. We'll be done eating by a quarter to eight, so I'll wait at the café while you and John and Holt find the sniper. Half an hour should give you enough time."

Hellhound grinned. "An' if we need more, ya text Margaret an' tell her you'll be a bit later. An' the asshole freezes his balls off waitin' some more. The colder he is, the easier it'll be to nail him."

"Grab him and take him to an interrogation room," I corrected. "I want information."

Hellhound's grin twisted into something more feral. "Me, too." His smile faded. "Holt gonna be a problem?"

I sighed. "I don't know. He's got something going on with Dermott, and Dermott thinks Holt's on his side. I don't know whose side he's really on."

"He's gonna cover his own ass first," Hellhound said. "An' he sure as hell ain't gonna get on the wrong side a' Dermott. Don't trust him."

"I don't." I hesitated. "But... I kind of do. He's covered for me before, and I don't think he'll screw me over unless he doesn't have any other choice. We'll just have to do everything by the book."

Hellhound snorted as he parked in the Greenhorn's small parking lot. "Where's the fun in that?"

Twenty minutes later the men departed, leaving me

lingering at the café table with dessert, a cup of herbal tea, and the keys to Hellhound's SUV.

At eight o'clock I rose, wished the young proprietors 'good night' and headed for the door.

My heart thumped as I approached the exit. If we'd been watched when we arrived, my enemies would know I was alone now. And if they were getting desperate, they might meet me at the door with a burst of automatic weapon fire. My coat would stop the bullets, but that many close-range impacts would probably kill me anyway. Very painfully.

I dodged to the right, ducking low as I stepped outside.

A heavy impact bowled me over.

I tucked and rolled, snatching my Glock out of its holster as I came up into a crouch behind a leafless shrub by the door.

An instant later I recognized the sprawled figure on the sidewalk.

The restaurant owner sat up, looking around dazedly. "Ohmigod, Aydan, are you okay?"

I stuffed my Glock into my pocket as he scrambled to his feet and peered into the shrub.

"Geez, I'm so sorry!" he exclaimed, reaching in to help me up. "I was just coming out to grab our sidewalk sign. I can't believe I ran over you! Are you okay?"

I managed a chuckle, slightly strangled by the frenzied pounding of my heart. "I'm fine. I'm sorry I tripped you. I didn't realize you were right behind me, and I bent over to tie my shoelace. Are you okay?"

"I'm fine, I just..." He shook his head. "I'm so sorry. You're covered with snow and twigs. Come inside and sit down. Let me get you another cup of tea and-"

"No, it's fine, I'm okay. You hit the ground harder than I

did." This time I managed a more normal-sounding voice.

After a few more reassurances and some fake-sheepish laughter, I headed for the SUV. A surreptitious glance at my bug detector showed a green light, but with the young restauranteur still eyeing me with concern from the sidewalk I didn't dare circle the vehicle looking for bombs. Teeth clenched, I slid into the driver's seat and turned the key.

When nothing exploded, I gave a shaky wave and drove a couple of blocks to make sure I was out of sight before I pulled over. Falling back in the seat, I slumped trembling until some of the adrenaline burned out of my system.

After several long minutes, I sat up and consulted my watch, tension building in my shoulders all over again.

Ten after eight. No word from the men.

Had something gone wrong?

A horrible vision of lifeless bodies flashed into my mind, but I determinedly shoved it aside. They couldn't have all been killed. They were professionals, and there were three of them. If they had spotted a sniper or any other threat, they'd approach from different directions. At least one of them would survive to call me for backup.

But which one would survive?

Who would I lose?

My heart shuddered away from that thought.

I powered the window down a crack, shivering in the current of icy air. It was a small town. If there was gunfire, I would hear it.

All was silent.

What if...

No, dammit, they were fine. All of them. They had to be.

I put the SUV in gear and cruised slowly in the direction of Margaret's house.

I should have insisted that one of them keep a phone line open. I would go ahead unless I got a text to abort; but what if none them were able to text me?

When my phone vibrated, I nearly jumped out of my skin. Yanking the wheel of the SUV, I skidded to a halt at the curb and whisked out my phone.

The text from Holt made my bones dissolve with relief. *'Got your package. Meet you at the office.'*

I texted back *'Be right there'*, then collapsed in the seat for a bit of deep breathing. As my hands steadied, so did my mind.

I punched the speed dial for Kane.

He answered instantly. "Are you all right?"

"Fine." I hesitated, not wanting to give anything away over an unsecured line. "Did you happen to drive past Margaret's house? Does it look like the party is still on?"

Or had Margaret been 'the package'?

"It looks as though it is," he replied. "If you need to go back to the office for a while, you might want to call and let her know you'll be late."

"Good idea," I agreed. "I'll see you soon."

So, either Margaret hadn't known about Volslav's plan, or else she was angling for an alibi by tending to her guests indoors while the assassin waited outside.

Which was it?

I dialled her number.

When she answered, the chatter of happy voices in the background made my heart squeeze in sudden fear.

What if she took my friends hostage?

"Uh, hi, Margaret." My voice came out sounding more tentative than I'd intended. Firming it, I added, "I'm so sorry I'm late. I'm literally in the car on the way to your place, and

I just got a message calling me back to the office. We're in the middle of a big audit right now, and they said it's urgent."

"Oh."

I couldn't read anything in the single syllable. Was she surprised I was still alive? Furiously plotting her next move?

When she spoke again, her tone sounded exactly like a disappointed hostess trying to be polite. "That's too bad. We were waiting with the movie and hoping you could make it. Do you think you'll be stuck at the office for long?"

Don't let her form a plan.

"I don't know," I hedged. "I'm hoping it's just something quick that I can deal with and still make it over to your place, but I won't really know until I get there. I'm sorry. Go ahead and start the movie without me. I'll check in at the office and give you a call after I see what's happening there."

"All right. Thanks for calling." Her tone lightened, but her cheeriness sounded forced. "I hope it's a quick fix. Hope to see you later."

"Thanks for understanding. Talk to you soon."

I disconnected with no more certainty than when I'd called. Dammit, I couldn't read her at all. She sounded so genuine.

But nobody else could have tipped Volslav off.

Blowing out a frustrated breath, I put the SUV into gear and headed for Sirius Dynamics.

When I arrived in the lobby, Hellhound was leaning against the wall beside the security wicket. He straightened as I approached and met me with a kiss. Pulling me into his arms, he murmured into my ear.

"Holt signed Kane in an' they took the guy down into the secured area. If ya wanna sign me in, I'll come down, too."

"Good." I pulled back and gave him another quick kiss

before heading for the security wicket.

My mind was so focused on planning the interrogation that the thirty seconds in the time delay chamber barely bothered me despite Hellhound's bulky presence. When we emerged into the white corridor below, Holt and Kane were waiting.

"He's in the interrogation room," Holt said. "Blindfolded and just coming out of the trank. How do you want to play this?"

"Did he get a good look at any of you?" I asked.

"No."

"Good. Then you stay out of sight."

"That makes sense for Holt," Kane said. "But it's well-known that I'm an associate of Arlene Widdenback's. And if she was going to interview a prisoner, she'd bring some muscle."

"Except that we're trying to keep you from being involved," I pointed out. "If nobody sees you with Arlene Widdenback, they'll just assume that our on-again-off-again association is off. That will keep you safer." As he opened his mouth to protest, I added, "Which will keep Daniel and Alicia safer."

He closed his mouth again with a frown.

"I'll be the muscle," Hellhound volunteered. "I'm ugly. Just seein' me'll scare the shit outta the guy."

Holt snickered. "You got that right. Your face even scares me."

I smacked his shoulder. "Don't be an asshole. Oh, wait; I forgot. You can't help it. You *are* an asshole."

He flipped me an absent-minded middle finger, but his heart clearly wasn't in it. His brow furrowed with thought. "I don't think you should let him see either of them. You..."

He eyed me with a shrug. "You're his mark so he's going to know you anyway, and if he wakes up chained in an interrogation room it's pretty clear that you've got muscle somewhere. It might be scarier for him to wonder where, and how much."

"Good point. You guys can all sit this out." As both Kane and Hellhound scowled, I added, "But I want audio contact with all of you while I'm questioning him. I want to make sure we don't miss anything."

They looked slightly mollified, but not much.

The relief of knowing they'd be safe jarred another thought loose in my brain. "I'm thinking we should send the RCMP to pick Margaret up."

"Don't you want to talk to the shooter first?" Holt asked.

"Oh, so he was a shooter? That was going to be my next question."

"Yeah," Hellhound said. "Found him set up with a rifle in a second-floor bedroom a few houses down an' across the street from Margaret's."

"How the hell did you spot him?" I demanded. "I thought he'd be outside."

"We figured so, too. But we couldn't see anybody, an' I got thinkin' 'bout where I'd wanna set up in the middle a' winter if I knew it might be a long wait." Hellhound grinned. "Spotted an upstairs window with the lights off an' the curtains drawn, but the window was open a crack. Just about the size of a rifle barrel."

"Still, though, lots of people leave their windows open a crack in winter," I reminded him.

"Yeah, that's why it took us a bit longer to get him surrounded an' take him down. Didn't wanna bust in on some fam'ly. But he was the only one in the house."

"Did he have any ID?"

Kane nodded and handed me a wallet. "It's probably fake, but it's a decent fake. The photo is definitely him."

I studied the driver's license. "Okay. So my plan is to have the RCMP go over to Margaret's right away and detain her for questioning."

"Detain?" Holt asked. "Not arrest her for conspiracy to murder?"

"I don't care which. I just want her away from that houseful of innocent women. If she finds out her plan has gone wrong..." I shivered. "I don't want her to have access to any hostages. She might not realize yet that her gunman is gone. But the longer we wait, the more chance she'll try to contact him."

"We oughta just grab her," Hellhound said. "Stick her in another interrogation room an' see how she reacts when ya walk in."

"Maybe," I said slowly. "But what if she swears she's innocent? We don't have the lie detector so we can't know for sure, and we can't hold her without evidence. If she gets abducted, questioned, and then released unharmed, she'll easily figure out that badass Arlene Widdenback is actually an undercover agent. Then if she's crooked she'll blow my cover with Volslav, and if she's straight she'll call the RCMP and have me charged. Either way I'm screwed."

"We don't hafta let her see ya," Hellhound said, but I had spotted the warning glint in Holt's eye.

Everything by the book.

I shook my head. "No, I want the RCMP to pick her up. They can tell her they caught a gunman who said he was supposed to shoot me at her party, and they're detaining her for questioning. I'll text her and tell her I'm on my way so she'll come to the door expecting me, and they can grab her before she can pull a weapon on anybody inside."

"Unless she's expecting you to be gunned down on her front porch," Holt pointed out grimly. "We don't know what she might do when she finds out you're still alive."

"Her blinds were open an' we could see everybody inside," Hellhound said. "I'll set up my rifle in that empty house, where I got a clear shot." The Killer's flat voice added, "If she tries to grab a hostage, I'll take her out."

CHAPTER 41

A call to the Drumheller RCMP solidified our plan.

"Okay," I said to Kane, Holt, and Hellhound as I hung up. "The unmarked cruiser will be around the corner from Margaret's in about twenty minutes. I'll text Margaret to expect me at a quarter to nine."

"Awright," Hellhound said. "I gotta go get a rifle from Stores, an' I'll head over there an' set up."

"Don't contaminate the scene," Holt reminded him. "Don't touch that rifle."

Hellhound snorted. "Like I'd wanna use that piece a' shit."

We headed for the stairs.

As the time delay door closed behind us, I felt my eyes widen as a thought struck me.

"Arnie…"

He gave me a concerned glance and backed away to flatten himself against the wall. "Sorry, darlin', d'ya need more space?"

Holt and Kane moved farther away, too, as much as they could in the cramped chamber.

"Thanks, but no, I'm fine. I just had a thought. You said the sniper had a piece-of-shit rifle."

Hellhound shrugged. "Good enough to shoot across the

street, but I'm guessin' snipin' ain't his thing."

"But you said a long-range rifle is the best option if you want to get away with it."

The time-delay door opened and we moved into the lobby. Hellhound glanced around the vacant space and lowered his voice. "Yeah. So?"

I matched his quiet tone, and the three men leaned closer. "So I'm thinking, wouldn't Volslav use a professional? And wouldn't a professional use a good rifle? Why would they send an amateur with a piece of shit?"

They stared at me in silence, frowning.

Kane spoke the idea that had already twisted my gut into a slow knot. "So this might not be Volslav's doing at all."

Hellhound shrugged. "Doesn't matter right now. The main thing's gettin' everybody outta that house in one piece. I gotta get geared up at Stores. I'll signal when I'm in place." He headed for the stairs.

"Aydan, you can ride with me," Kane said. "Text Margaret. We'll wait here until eight-forty and then head over."

"I'm going to get in place behind the house," Holt said. "Kane, signal me when you're incoming."

As Holt departed I sent a mental thank-you after him, for letting Kane call a few shots without opposition.

Kane must have been thinking the same thing. He sank into one of the chairs with a sigh. "I hope you're all right with what I proposed. This is your op, not mine."

I sat down beside him. "Don't worry, if I'd had a problem, I would have said so."

"Good." He gave me a pained smile. "I'm used to giving orders, but I can take them, too."

I grinned. "But only when absolutely necessary."

At eight-forty, we slipped out to Kane's Expedition and headed for our rendezvous with the unmarked RCMP car. A few minutes later I was strolling up the sidewalk toward Margaret's, trying to look as though I hadn't a care in the world.

As I neared the house, my guts clenched.

Her blinds were drawn. Hellhound wouldn't have a shot. Shit, shit, shit!

She must have tried to contact the gunman and gotten suspicious when he didn't answer.

Were my friends being held at gunpoint behind those blinds?

Constable Noonan was already in place, silent and motionless beside the door. He wasn't one of the officers I knew from the Drumheller detachment. How would he handle a hostage situation?

What if he did something stupid and provoked Margaret into killing one of my friends? Or one of my men?

Or worse, what if I did something stupid?

My legs carried me confidently up to the door despite my frantic thoughts.

Plastering a smile on my face, I rang the doorbell.

Nothing happened.

Noonan shifted, the rustle of his parka loud in the quiet darkness.

My hand clenched around the Glock I'd transferred to my jacket pocket.

I was about to ring again when the sound of footsteps approached from the inside.

Heart hammering, I stepped back.

The door opened and Margaret beamed a happy smile. "You made it!"

As she leaned out to welcome me, the constable pushed between us. Pretending to be off balance, I stumbled backward as he said, "RCMP. Are you Margaret Young?"

"Yes," she said cautiously. "What's going on?"

"I'm detaining you for questioning about an attempted murder. You have the right to retain and instruct counsel without delay. You may call any lawyer you wish..."

While Noonan recited her rights, I sputtered feeble questions and protests and the constable ignored me, as we'd prearranged.

He finished his recitation and took Margaret by the arm.

"Just a moment, please," she said calmly. "Aydan, would you please stay here until everyone can leave, and then lock the house? There's a spare key hanging behind the front hall mirror."

"Don't bother," Noonan said shortly as the cruiser pulled up. "We'll handle it. We'll be searching the house anyway."

Margaret gave him a level look. "You'd better have a warrant. And I'll be calling an attorney."

"We have a warrant, and you can make your call as soon as we get to the station." He handed her off to his partner, who led her away.

Lola and Linda and the rest of the gang piled out of the house, chattering exclamations and protests. Noonan firmly instructed them to leave, and I milled around with them looking as clueless as possible and trying to blend in with the group.

Lola hurried over. "Aydan, are you okay? You're shaking like a leaf!"

She didn't need to know that my tremors were born of

unspent adrenaline and sheer relief.

I let my voice wobble. "I'm f-fine. It's just... I rang the doorbell and he just pushed in front of me..." I wrapped my arms around myself. "He *arrested* her! For m-murder!"

"Oh, honey." Lola hugged me. She was trembling, too. "What's happening to our town?"

I did my best scared-and-horrified act, and didn't bother to hide my relief when Kane's shiny black Expedition pulled up to the curb. He got out and hurried over to take me in his arms.

"Aydan, are you all right?" he demanded. "I came as soon as I got your text."

"I'm... okay." I huddled into him.

"I'll take you home," he comforted, then turned to Lola. "If you'll excuse us...?"

"Of course. I'm glad you're here." Lola squeezed my hand. "Don't worry, honey, everything will be okay. You'll feel better after a hot drink."

"Th-Thanks." I let Kane guide me away with his arm around my shoulders.

He opened the truck door for me and settled me in the passenger seat before hurrying around to the driver's side. I raised a hand in a wan wave to the other women as we drove away.

Safely around the corner, I straightened out of my slump. "That went well."

"Yes. I'm glad. I was worried when I saw the blinds had been drawn."

"Me, too." I let out a long breath. "She's lawyering up already."

Kane shrugged. "I'd be shocked if she didn't."

"Hmph. Well, at least if they have to wait for a lawyer

before questioning her, there's a chance that I might get finished with our prisoner and still have time to listen in on her interview. And I'll be really interested to see what they find when they search her place."

"Yes." Kane fell silent. After a few moments he added, "What if this has nothing to do with Volslav?"

Ignoring the sinking sensation in the pit of my stomach, I replied, "Even if it doesn't, I won't be in trouble. Everybody else was already at the party, the guy's rifle was aimed at Margaret's front door, and I was the only one left to arrive. It's a reasonable assumption that the assassin was waiting for me."

Kane hesitated. "Have you been able to negotiate a truce with Dermott?"

At my explosive snort, he rubbed a hand over his forehead. "Please don't tell me you've antagonized him again."

I studied my boots gloomily. "Okay, I won't tell you that."

"What happened?"

"Twenty million dollars happened. In a Cayman Islands account registered to Arlene Widdenback."

Kane braked to a halt in the Sirius parking lot and turned to stare at me. "Is that... as suspicious as it sounds?"

"Oh, hell yes. Want to take a guess whose account that twenty mil came from?"

He shook his head.

"Dymt Volslav's."

A brittle silence filled the truck.

"Did you know about this account?" Kane asked cautiously.

"Of course I didn't fucking know about it! I just found it

and didn't have time to check into it before Spider called me back to Sirius. I came out of the network and asked him if he'd set it up as a cover account, and it was just my shitty luck that Dermott overheard." I grimaced. "You can imagine what happened next."

"Why are you not imprisoned right now?"

"Holt talked to Dermott."

Kane's eyebrows shot up. "And Dermott listened?"

"Apparently." I sighed. "But I don't believe Holt really stood up for me, and I sure as hell don't believe Dermott's going to let this go."

"They're letting you run," Kane said with certainty. "Hoping you'll panic and contact Volslav, or do something incriminating that will give them solid evidence to convict you."

"Yeah, I figured. Thank God we'll have the lie detector on Monday and I can prove I didn't know anything about it."

"Right." Kane didn't sound convinced.

"What?" I demanded. "You don't really believe I've sold out to Volslav, do you?"

"Of course not. I was just thinking that the lie detector might be a double-edged sword. It'll save you on one hand, but..." Kane didn't complete the sentence.

I focused more intently on unbuckling my seatbelt than the task required, and got out of the Expedition. "Come on. Let's go question our sniper."

CHAPTER 42

Crammed into the observation room with Holt, Kane, and Hellhound, I studied the assassin on the video screen.

A blackout hood covered his head, and his wrists and ankles were chained to the table in front of him. His rigid posture telegraphed misery and fear.

I knew exactly how he felt.

I sighed and positioned the earbud in my ear. "Okay, comm check."

All three men responded. "Check."

"Check."

"Check."

"I can hear all of you just fine. If you think of any questions you want to ask him, speak up." I headed for the door.

Outside the interview room, I paused to take a few deep breaths and pull on my Arlene Widdenback persona.

God, I was tired. And scared.

And that pissed me off, dammit.

I let the anger expand, hot and heartening, stiffening my backbone and clenching my fists.

This asshole had intended to kill me. He'd pay for that.

I threw the door open with a bang, and the assassin jumped. Making my footfalls heavy, I stalked toward the table.

Around the end of it.

Behind him.

I stood still. Silent.

His hooded head swivelled blindly as he yanked at his chains. "Who's there?" he demanded, but his voice cracked. "I know you're there. What do you want?"

Resisting the temptation to slap him hard in the head, I ran a fingernail lightly across his shoulder, barely touching him.

He jerked as though I'd hit him with a cattle prod. "What's that? Who's there?" His voice rose. "What do you want? I'll tell you anything you want to know!"

I raised an eyebrow at the video camera and was rewarded by chuckles in my earbud.

A few more silent feather-light touches had my victim squirming and begging to confess.

Holt's voice spoke in my ear. "Fuck, Kelly, that's some pretty vicious torture. Might have to report you."

Hellhound laughed. "Told ya he was a fuckin' amateur."

I contemplated the sorry figure in front of me. Sweat soaked his shirt and his wrists were chafed and reddened from his struggles against the handcuffs. He was whimpering and sniffling.

Suspicion tugged at me. Okay, he was scared. Anybody would be, after being left blindfolded and chained in silence for nearly an hour. But surely a guy who killed people for a living would show a bit more bravado.

An unwanted memory of Arnie's set face under torture made my stomach twist, and I yanked my attention back to the job at hand.

Why was this man showing so much fear? Was he

messing with me, trying to convince me he wasn't a threat? Or was he really that much of an amateur?

Holt's voice pulled me out of my reverie. "For shit's sake, Kelly, ask him something before he- Fuck, too late. You get to clean that up."

I stepped back from the pool of urine widening under my captive's chair and spoke softly. "I should kill you for that."

"*No!* I'm sorry, I'm sorry! What do you want? Please, just tell me what you want!"

"What do you think I want?"

"I don't *know!*" He was sobbing now.

He had to be messing with me. Nobody could be this pathetic.

"Come on, you're smarter than that." I trailed a fingertip across the back of his neck, making him thrash against his bonds in an effort to cower farther away. "You'd *better* be smarter than that."

Holt's voice spoke again in my ear. "Just got a hit from the police database. Our contestant today is Rufus Zimm. Multiple convictions for auto theft, fraud, and drugs. A bunch of minor shit but no violent crime. This must be his first big job."

My heart sank.

"You fucking dumb shit." My words came out sounding unutterably weary. "Okay, let's start with the obvious. What's your name?"

"J-Jack. Jack Jones."

"Just like your driver's license," I agreed.

He sat up a little straighter. "Yeah."

"Well, Rufus Zimm," I said ever-so-gently, "If you lie to me again, you're going to regret it. A lot."

He cringed. "H-How did you... I'm sorry! I thought-"

"Don't think. Just talk. Who was your target?"

"Arlene Widdenback," he blurted. "Are you Arlene Widdenback? 'Cause I'm sorry, I didn't mean to-"

"Shut up. Who hired you?"

"I dunno the guy's name, but-"

"He's fucking useless," I interrupted with disgust, and made heavy footfalls toward the door. "Get rid of him."

"NO, WAIT!" The erstwhile assassin's voice was a shriek of pure terror. "I can tell you about the guy that hired me! I know where he lives!"

I froze. Kept my voice level and expressionless. "Tell me more."

"He hired me two weeks ago. It was supposed to be easy. I just had to mail a parcel."

"With a bomb in it," I prompted.

"Yeah!" His eager tone faded. "Um, sorry about that guy. The one that... got it."

"You mean, you're sorry he got blown up instead of me."

"Yeah. I mean, no! I mean, *I'm sorry!* I didn't-"

I cut him off. "How did you know what name to put on the return address?"

"It was already on the package, I just had to mail it."

Hmm. Maybe Dermott's lab analysis would turn up something useful from the fragments after all.

I returned to questioning. "So you blew up the wrong guy. Then what?"

"The guy said I screwed up, and I had to finish the job or else. He wanted his deposit back but I'd already spent it and he said he'd send his guys after me if I didn't finish the job so I had to..." His babble faded into hysterical panting.

"Describe the guy. And his house."

"His place is out Highway 22 by Priddis, you just go..."

He provided directions and a description of an estate that I already knew far too well.

"Describe the guy," I snapped.

"Short and chubby. Fancy clothes and big diamond rings-"

"I don't care about his fucking clothes! What colour hair and eyes?"

"Um... blond. I think. Kind of thin blond hair. Maybe... blue eyes?"

Lawrence Fucking Harchman. That slimy little asshole.

"How did he find you?"

"Um, I dunno. Friend of a friend told me he had a job."

"You don't know." I clenched my fists in my hair. "You took a random job from a random guy without even checking into it. God, you're too dumb to live."

"Don't kill me," he whimpered. "Please don't kill me!"

I sighed. "How did you know where to set up tonight?"

"The guy gave me the address. He said you'd be there at seven." The hitman's voice took on an aggrieved note. "You were late. I waited but I got too cold, so I had to break into that house."

"How did your guy know I was going to be there?"

"I dunno."

"How did he get in touch with you?"

"Texted me."

"We've got his phone," Holt said in my ear. "Checking the incoming numbers now."

"What about the guy you killed with the baseball bat?" I demanded. "And why did you sneak into that little old lady's house and shoot that guy?"

"I didn't kill anybody! I didn't hurt anybody at all!"

"Except for the guy you blew up."

"It wasn't my fault! All I did was mail a parcel for somebody else. I dunno about any baseball bat, and I sure didn't sneak into any old lady's house. Gross."

My silence prompted him to backpedal.

"I mean... I dunno. Do you mean the house I was in when you caught me? 'Cause I dunno who lives there, I just found an empty house and broke... I mean, let myself in. The door was unlocked. Honest."

"Don't lie to me, you fucking piece of shit," I growled.

"Sorry, sorry! I broke in, okay? But nobody was there! I didn't hurt anybody!"

I stared at him, wishing I had Xray vision so I could peer through his skull and into his mind.

Holt spoke in my ear. "No other questions here. Come back to the interview room and let him stew for a while."

I nodded and made for the door.

As I opened it, the prisoner's voice rose in a desperate appeal. "*Wait!* Don't kill me, I'll do anything you want! I'll kill the guy that hired me if you want, I promise, *I'll do anything...*"

I let the door swing shut on his cries.

Back in the interview room, I dropped into a chair and massaged my forehead. On the video screen, the captive struggled frantically, still yammering at the top of his lungs.

Holt turned the volume down and raised an eyebrow at me. "Thoughts?"

"I think he's a small-time loser in over his head; but there's always the possibility that he's a real professional and hiding it like a frigging Oscar contender."

"I'm goin' with 'loser'," Hellhound said. "Look at his rap sheet."

Kane nodded. "I'm inclined to agree. But why would

Lawrence Harchman hire him to kill you?"

I snorted. "Let me count the reasons. Harchman thinks I've tried to steal his two latest software apps. I've publicly intimidated him twice, crushed his nuts, and generally made him look like the sleazy little idiot he is. His gold-digger wife hates me because she thinks I'm putting the moves on him, and he'll want to keep her happy if she's his connection to Volslav. Plus, he probably doesn't want to split the proceeds from the Arlene Cherry porn videos anymore."

"You're still making money from your porn videos?" Holt inquired with interest.

"They're not *my* damn porn videos! I can't help it that Harchman used his VR network to make it look like I was..." I trailed off with a shudder. "God. There's not enough money in the world to make up for having people think I screwed that disgusting little sleazebag."

"How about twenty million bucks?" Holt needled. "Would that do it?"

"No, asshole!"

Kane raised his voice over our bickering. "That wasn't actually what I meant. Aydan, I realize there are many reasons why Harchman would like to be rid of you. My question was, why would he hire somebody like Zimm? He could afford a top-of-the-line assassin."

I shrugged. "Harchman's bone-deep stupid. Seriously, he invited a hired killer to his house and met with him in person. Talk about setting yourself up for blackmail. Or worse."

"That doesn't make sense," Kane said slowly. "He can't be that stupid. He's a very successful businessman."

"He started out with Daddy's money, and he's always had a smart wife to manage everything behind the scenes," I countered. "He's so rich and self-important, he thinks he can buy his way out from under anything. Look at that hoax he pulled at Remembrance Day. He didn't give a shit about what he was doing to anybody else; he just went ahead and did what he wanted. And he got away with it." The words tasted of bitter bile as the horrible memories flooded back.

Pulling myself back to the present with a shiver, I added, "But maybe we've got him this time. I'm thinking we should trank our friend there..." I nodded at the video screen, where the captive was still struggling. "And put him back in the bedroom with his rifle and invite the RCMP over. You guys didn't disturb too much evidence when you grabbed him, I hope."

"No, we just tranked him," Holt said. "I told the RCMP we'd gone into the room to detain him. Speaking of, I checked with them while you were in there..." He jerked his chin at the interview room. "...and Young's lawyer is on the way. They expect to be able to start interviewing her in an hour or so."

"Has she said anything in the meantime?"

"Not a word."

I blew out a breath. "Of course she hasn't. She's an ex-cop. She knows the ropes. Did you arrange for us to watch the interview?"

"Yep. And if we have any questions we want to add, they'll ask them." Holt raised an eyebrow. "Unless you want to confront her for the shock value."

"Not right away. We'll see how it goes first."

Holt turned to Kane and Hellhound. "You two can't observe."

Kane shrugged. "I assumed as much. We have other work to do."

"Is that so?" Holt's eyes narrowed. "What kind of work?"

"Private investigation. Confidential."

"You're not a licensed PI."

"I am," Hellhound rasped. "He's helpin' me."

"All right, you guys," I interrupted before Holt could retort. "You can have your pissing contest later. Holt, let's hand Zimm over to the RCMP and then head to Drumheller for Margaret's interview."

"You're going to blow your cover if you hand him over to the police."

I shook my head. "By the time I'm done with him, he'll probably run to the police as fast as he can, begging to be arrested."

As I headed for the door, Hellhound crossed his arms and leaned back in his chair, grinning. "This oughta be fun."

As soon as I opened the door to the interview room, the prisoner redoubled his struggles and pleas. *"Don't kill me, please don't kill me, I'll do anything you want!"*

I ghosted across the floor to lean close behind him and speak softly. "Okay."

He spun to face me as best he could with both wrists tethered to the table. His ragged breaths plastered the black hood against his nose and mouth, and I suppressed an involuntary shudder at the memory of how that felt.

"What does that mean?" he squeaked.

"It means, okay. You'll do anything I want."

"Yes!" He sagged in his bonds, panting and trembling. "Yes! Anything you want! Just name it. Anything."

"You're going to pack up your rifle, and you're going to go and shoot the guy that sent you." I leaned closer and lowered my voice. "And if you try to warn him, or if you don't do the job... I'll find you. And I *won't* kill you. Not for a very..." I trailed a fingertip over the exposed skin of his throat. He flinched and whimpered as I finished, "...*very* long time. Got it?"

"I g-got it. I promise. I'll do it. You c-can count on me."

"Good." I headed for the door, then turned and fired a trank dart into his chest.

He sucked in a breath, probably to scream again, and collapsed.

I slipped out and closed the door behind me as the other three came out of the observation room.

"I'm not getting him out of that pool of piss," Holt said. "These are A. Testonis." He indicated his glossy leather boots with pride.

Hellhound guffawed. "Ya only got one testoni? That explains a lot."

Holt drew himself up. "'A' is the designer's initial, you dumb shit. These boots are the finest Italian leather money can buy."

Hellhound jerked his chin toward his own well-worn footwear. "Well, these are the shittiest boots the army can pawn off on me, so I'll go get him. Bit a' piss ain't the worst thing I ever waded through."

He went into the room and released the prisoner, effortlessly hoisting the limp form across his shoulders in a fireman's carry. Kane had retrieved a wheeled cart from down the hallway, and Hellhound dumped his burden onto it.

"Where do you want him?" Kane inquired.

I gave him a smile. "Back in the house. We'll get the RCMP to meet you there. If you don't mind taking him up to the bedroom, that's probably the best chance for him to remember to take his gun with him before he runs. Police can grab him as he leaves the house. I don't want them standing right there when he wakes up. That might be a little too obvious even for a dim-bulb like Zimm."

"Consider it done."

"Thanks." I turned to Holt. "Can you arrange that with the RCMP? I need to make a pit stop before we get on the road to Drumheller." He nodded, and I added, "By the way, you're driving. My car's in Calgary and my truck's at home."

CHAPTER 43

The small observation room at the RCMP station was overheated and crowded with Holt, me, and Noonan's bulky partner, whose nameplate read 'Rice'.

Rice wasn't a talkative sort, which suited me fine. After offering us a cup of coffee, he seated himself and didn't speak again. We stared at the monitor in silence.

I used the opportunity to do some secret breathing exercises, trying to convince my hammering heart that being surrounded by police uniforms and shut into a tiny room wasn't scary at all.

Much.

Trapped-trapped-trapped!

Shut up.

Breathe...

Inside the interview room, Margaret sat at a table facing the camera, looking far calmer than I felt. Every now and then Noonan asked a desultory question, but it was clear that he didn't expect any answer other than the one Margaret supplied each time in an emotionless voice: "I want my lawyer here before I answer any questions."

I eyed her with a deepening sense of my own inadequacy. Only a few weeks ago I'd been questioned by the police, and the memory made me cringe inwardly. I hadn't asked for a lawyer. I'd gotten defensive, lost my temper, and generally been a complete idiot. I was just damn lucky the Regina police had been patient and understanding. Agent or not, I could have ended up in prison.

Trapped...

The arrival of a suit-clad woman in the interview room dragged me out of my toxic marinade of fear and shame. She offered a handshake to Margaret and a formal nod to the constable before seating herself beside Margaret. "Constable, would you explain why my client has been detained?"

"We have reason to believe Ms. Young may be able to provide some information about an attempted murder."

"I'll need some time to confer with my client."

Noonan nodded and left the room, and our monitor went dark.

Holt sighed and stretched out his legs, crossing his arms and sinking his chin onto his chest.

I glanced at my watch. After ten PM already. God, this was going to be another damn long night. Fatigue ached in my bones and I slouched lower in the uncomfortable chair.

The click of the monitor roused me from a doze and I dragged myself upright, rubbing gritty eyes.

"Please go ahead with your questions," the lawyer said.

"Ms. Young, do you know Aydan Kelly?" Noonan asked.

Margaret glanced at her lawyer. "Yes. Slightly."

"But not well?"

"No."

"But you invited her to a party at your home tonight."

"Yes."

"Why?"

Margaret glanced at her lawyer again. "I wanted to get to know her better. I moved to Silverside nine months ago and I'm trying to make some new friends."

"Why did you move to Silverside?"

"For work."

"And your work is?"

"I'm a private investigator."

"So you moved to Silverside to investigate someone," Noonan said. "Who were you investigating?"

This time Margaret looked worried as she conferred with her lawyer. After a short whispered discussion, she replied, "Aydan Kelly."

Shit. If I hadn't noticed her following me for the past nine months, how many other times had I been oblivious to being tailed?

"So you didn't actually want to be friends with her," Noonan clarified. "You were investigating her."

Margaret frowned. "No, my investigation is over. I'm terminating the contract at the end of this month."

"Have you given notice to your client?"

"N-No. Not yet."

"She's probably telling the truth," I whispered to Holt. "She told Lola she was planning to get rid of her last client and retire."

"Shh." He leaned closer to the monitor, listening.

"So you've been investigating Ms. Kelly for quite a while," Noonan observed.

"Nine months," Margaret confirmed.

"Who's her damn client?" I demanded.

Holt made a sharp palm-down silencing gesture. "Shh!"

"Who is your client?" Noonan asked.

Shit, could he hear us? I mentally reviewed what I'd said so far and relaxed. Nothing too rude or embarrassing, thank God.

"My client records are confidential," Margaret said.

"You're allowed and required under the Privacy Act to disclose the identity of your client in a police investigation," Noonan replied. "Who is your client?"

Margaret leaned in for another murmured conversation with her lawyer before responding, "Lawrence Harchman."

Adrenaline scorched my veins. Harchman again.

But if he'd been spying on me for the past nine months, why had he waited this long to make his move?

The constable's voice brought my attention back to the interview. "Why did Mr. Harchman want you to investigate Ms. Kelly?"

"He said Aydan had been harassing him ever since they made a series of porn movies together."

Constable Rice jerked around to stare at me.

"I didn't!" I hissed. "They were faked!"

Holt glared at me. "Shhh!"

Margaret went on, "He wanted to keep tabs on her so she couldn't sneak up on him and disrupt his business or personal life. He hired another private investigator from Calgary to document their interactions anytime Aydan approached him, and my job was to alert the other investigator whenever Aydan left Silverside."

"More money than brains," Rice muttered.

Holt didn't shush *him*.

Noonan said, "That sounds like easy money. Why would you terminate the contract?"

"As I got to know Aydan better, she just didn't seem like the type to harass anyone. I got curious and started digging."

Pink tinged Margaret's cheeks. "I watched some of the porn videos, and I think they were faked. Mr. Harchman was definitely having sex with someone, but it wasn't Aydan. The woman's face looks a lot like her, but their body types are completely different."

Which was a polite way to say that virtual-reality 'me' had boobs the size of volleyballs.

"Thank you," I mouthed, avoiding another round of Holt's shushing.

"That changed things," Margaret continued. "If the videos are fake, then maybe it's Mr. Harchman who has an unhealthy obsession with Aydan. Even though I've never seen him here in Silverside, I'm uncomfortable with the thought that my reports might be used to help him stalk Aydan. That's why I'm quitting the job."

"How did Mr. Harchman choose you for this job?"

"He found me on the AAPI website. He contacted me and asked if I would be willing to set aside all my other clients in return for a long-term contract on a generous retainer that would include relocation and living expenses. I wasn't the first investigator he had contacted with this offer." Her serious expression softened into an almost-smile. "The others he called weren't willing to give up all their clients, but I was considering retirement anyway. I had been thinking of getting out of Calgary, and this was an opportunity to try out small-town living on someone else's dime. It was a perfect fit."

God, she was convincing. Her voice was confident, her gaze level. I instinctively trusted her.

Stop that.

The constable prompted, "So you took the job, and reported regularly to Mr. Harchman."

"I only submit a written summary to Mr. Harchman once a month. My main contact is with the other investigator. I call him whenever one of Aydan's vehicles passes the camera hidden in a roadside shrine on the highway, just west of the turnoff to her farm. I monitor the camera with a remote app on my phone, and regularly swap out the battery in the camera. Those are my only duties."

I let out a secret breath of relief. She hadn't been following me everywhere. I hadn't missed a tail. And that explained why her phone seemed to be constantly dinging. She'd been a busy woman for the past nine months.

That also explained where that roadside shrine had come from. I hadn't heard about anyone being killed on the highway near my place, but I hadn't bothered to dig into it, either.

Note to self: Investigate *everything* new in your vicinity, no matter how unimportant it seems.

"But of course you mentioned to Mr. Harchman that you had invited Ms. Kelly to your party," Noonan said understandingly. "So he would know he wouldn't have to worry about Ms. Kelly coming to Calgary tonight."

Margaret straightened, her brows snapping together. "Of course not! That would be a violation of Aydan's privacy. And mine."

"But yet, there was a sniper across the street with a rifle trained on your door," Noonan persisted. "You and all your guests were safe inside. Ms. Kelly was the only one he could have been waiting for."

"Wha-" The word quavered out on a gasp and Margaret blanched sheet-white. "A *sniper?*"

Damn, if she was acting, then she and the hitman were in serious competition for that Oscar.

"Do you have him in custody?" Margaret squeaked.

"Yes."

"Thank God!" She fell back in her chair. "How did you find out he was there? Have you told Aydan?"

"How would he have known about your party?" Noonan countered. "Who did you tell?"

"Nobody! I personally invited each of the women, that's all. Maybe one of them said something to someone else..." Margaret's voice trailed off, and her colour came back in a flood. "Oh, no. Oh, *damn!* I-"

"Ms. Young!" her lawyer interrupted. "Constable, may we have a moment?"

The constable rose and left the interview room.

Before our video monitor blinked off I glimpsed Margaret whispering tensely to the lawyer, her face flushed with what looked like fury.

CHAPTER 44

Holt leaned back in his chair and stretched out his legs. "So. Harchman again. Think Young's lying?"

I sighed and slid lower in my chair. "If she is, she's really good. I haven't noticed any tells."

"Me, neither," Holt confirmed. "But the questioning's barely started. And she sure lost her cool a minute ago. Hope the lawyer doesn't-"

He broke off as the observation room door opened, wafting in a merciful breath of cooler air from the corridor.

Noonan poked his head in the gap. "Do you have any questions to add yet?"

Holt and I exchanged a glance, and I replied, "No, I don't think so. It looks as though things might get interesting, though. Are you planning to tell her the sniper said Lawrence Harchman hired him?"

"Not yet. I'll see how her story goes before I give her any other facts." He gave me a disapproving look. "You do recall that Zimm's confession to you won't be admissible in court, don't you? You should have read his rights before you questioned him."

Holt snorted. "She's undercover. Reading rights might be a teensy bit of a giveaway. Besides, you caught him with a rifle pointed at a woman's door. You won't have any trouble getting him to confess."

"And even if he doesn't get convicted, it's okay," I added. "He's a small fish. The intel we got from him was more important."

Noonan gave us a resigned shrug and withdrew, and I pulled out my cell phone and dialled the analyst on call.

When Trish's crisp voice came on the line, I said, "Hi, it's Aydan. You're stuck on the late shift again?"

She chuckled. "I like this shift. It's when all the interesting things happen. What can I do for you?"

"Have you gotten anything off Zimm's phone records yet?"

"I've got the number that texted him the time and date of Ms. Young's party. Looks like it's a burner, so I'm tracing it back to where it was purchased. We might get lucky if somebody was dumb enough to buy it with a credit card. I'll keep you posted."

"Can you email me Zimm's phone records for the past couple of weeks?" I asked. "We'll want to check Margaret's phone and see if any numbers match up."

"Sure. On its way... now."

"Thanks. Got it," I added when my phone vibrated.

"Good. I'll give you a call if anything else comes up."

I thanked her and disconnected. Turning to Rice, I said, "I have a list of numbers from the sniper's phone. Where should I send a copy so you can compare it against Margaret's phone?"

"Send it to me. And Noonan." Rice gave me both email addresses, then rose and squeezed past us to the door. "I'll print out a copy and give it to Noonan in case he wants to use it in the interview."

He left, and I greedily inhaled the fresh air from the

corridor as the door opened and closed.

Silence fell. Holt and I stared at the blank video monitor. I suppressed the urge to fidget.

"Maybe Harchman isn't as dumb as you think," Holt said finally.

"He's dumber," I retorted. "Hiring a private detective to track me, and an amateur hitman to kill me. How did he think he wasn't going to get caught?"

Holt scowled. "He hasn't been caught. The only evidence we have is the word of a petty criminal, and it's not admissible in court. Unless we can get something concrete, Harchman's going to skate. Again."

As I slouched lower in my chair, he added, "Maybe Harchman's stupid like a fox."

"What the hell is that supposed to mean?"

"Think about it," Holt urged. "You said his wife acts like a bimbo but you don't think she's stupid. What if Harchman is faking stupid, too?" He leaned forward. "What if he's actually Volslav? His legitimate business interests and software apps are his cover, and everybody thinks he's too stupid to manage anything else. But he obviously knew about the ultrasound weapon back in November. He said he just made it up, and we believed him because-"

"Because we think he's a stupid little shit," I growled as shivers trickled down my backbone. "And he flushed Arlene Widdenback out by leaking information about the weapon to the media, and then he bribed Labelle to eliminate me and my arms buyer. We even went to his damn spa, for shit's sake! Now he's trying to kill me, but he doesn't actually care whether the job gets done, as long as I'm distracted while he sells his copy of the weapon. If I die, bonus. If I don't, I'll be too busy dealing with idiot hitmen and innocent private investigators and baseball-bat murders to realize what he's doing until it's too late."

"And Harchman could afford twenty mil," Holt added. "He's probably even figured out a way to get you arrested. What if the hitman turns around and tells the police you hired him to mail the package and shoot Margaret, and you threatened him if he didn't? It's basically the same story he told you, only with the names changed. Anybody would believe you planned to blow up Bill Harks, and it wouldn't be a stretch from there that you'd force your poor amateur hitman to kill the woman who was investigating you."

Nausea climbed my throat. "Then I end up in prison for murder, and Harchman's story about me as a stalker sounds perfectly plausible. So whether I live or die, Volslav ends up the only arms game in town."

Holt's gaze bored into me. "So is that why you didn't take the hood off when you were questioning Zimm? You didn't want us to see that he recognized you? And was that twenty mil a payoff to let Harchman sell the weapon right under your nose?"

"*Fuck off!*" I barked. When Holt eyed me in silence, I sucked in a deep breath and let it out slowly. "Look," I said in a quieter voice. "I know how badly you've been burned in the past, and I know it's your job to be suspicious and look at all the possible angles. But I promise you, I'm telling the truth. I didn't kill Bill Harks..." I hesitated. "Well, I guess I did, by refusing that package; but you know what I mean. I didn't send the bomb. I didn't hire the hitman. I didn't sell out to Volslav, and I sure as hell don't know where that bank account came from."

Holt shrugged. "I hope you're telling the truth." He crossed his arms over his chest and resumed staring at the blank video monitor.

"The lie detector will prove I am," I assured him. "Monday can't come soon enough."

And it was a damn good thing there wasn't a lie detector hooked up to me right now. Monday was shaping up to be the worst day of my life.

I copied Holt's pose, hoping my crossed arms would keep my terrified heart from leaping right out of my chest.

Fortunately, Rice returned before I could fixate for too long on the fact that I was confined in a tiny windowless room in a police station.

"Got a match on a phone number," he said, passing over a printed list with one number circled. "Zimm got a text from that number, and Young has been calling that number and receiving calls from it frequently for the last nine months. If it's Harchman..."

The video monitor flicked on, and he didn't finish the sentence.

Noonan was back in place, and Margaret's lawyer addressed him. "My client has information which she hopes will help straighten this situation out. Margaret, go ahead."

Margaret looked grim. "The name of Mr. Harchman's other investigator is Blake Fenler. We met once at Mr. Harchman's home when we were both hired. Before agreeing to work with Blake, I checked his credentials on the AAPI website and verified that he's a licensed investigator in good standing with the Association. I trusted him to maintain confidentiality and we compared notes often. I disclosed information about Aydan's friends and activities that I would never have disclosed to a client." Her lips tightened. "Blake Fenler was the only person besides my guests who knew I was having a party tonight, and that I had invited Aydan. And it was Blake who convinced me not to terminate my contract with Mr. Harchman until the end of the month. You should detain him for ques-" She bit her lip. "Sorry. I'm not trying to tell you how to do your job."

Rice was already on the line to the Calgary police.

In the interview room, Noonan nodded. "Thank you. We'll interview Mr. Fenler. What number did you use when you called him?"

Margaret recited the number from memory, the digits matching the number that had texted the hitman his instructions.

Rice flashed us a thumbs-up and passed the information on to Calgary.

Margaret's lawyer straightened as if working kinks out of her back from the uncomfortable chair. "My client has given you all the information she knows. Will you release her now?"

"Not yet," Noonan said politely. "I apologize for the delay, but we will have more questions." He rose and left the interview room, and our screen went dark again.

Suddenly I couldn't bear to be caged in the tiny room any longer. "I need a bathroom break," I announced, and lunged to my feet.

"Me, too," Holt seconded, and we headed down the corridor together.

When I emerged from the ladies' room, Holt was leaning against the wall a few yards away.

Politely waiting for me? Or guarding me in case I tried to flee?

He straightened and gave me a grimace. "It'll be a while if we have to wait for them to pick Fenler up. If they even locate him tonight. Let's go find some coffee."

I sighed and followed him down the corridor.

An hour later we reconvened in the stuffy observation room, and I stifled a groan as I lowered myself into the uncomfortable chair again. On the video monitor, Margaret looked as tired as I felt, but she straightened in her chair when Noonan entered.

"Did they detain Blake?" she asked.

"Yes."

The tense lines eased in her face. "Good. Has he said anything yet?"

"Yes." Noonan studied her in silence, and her relieved expression slowly tightened.

"What aren't you telling me?" she demanded.

"The Calgary police are interviewing Mr. Fenler now," Noonan said. "Mr. Fenler says Mr. Harchman dismissed him a week after hiring him, and he has never been in phone contact with you."

"*What?*" Margaret gaped at him. "That's a lie! He-"

Her lawyer leaned in to whisper hurriedly in her ear, but Margaret shook her head.

"No! I'm telling the truth! You can check my cell phone records. You'll see lots of incoming and outgoing calls to his number!"

"We do see frequent calls to the number you gave us," Noonan agreed. "That number isn't registered to Mr. Fenler. It's completely different than the one on his website."

"Yes, I knew that," Margaret persisted. "It's a prepaid phone. He knew he'd be getting a lot of calls from me, so he got it specifically for this job. He phoned me and gave me the number right after we started working together..." Her shoulders slumped as realization dawned on her face. "Oh, no. I've been scammed, haven't I?"

"Maybe. Or maybe you're lying about the terms of your contract with Mr. Harchman, and you've been giving him personal information about Ms. Kelly in the full knowledge-"

"*I haven't!*" Furious spots of colour burned in Margaret's cheeks. Eyeing her clenched fists, I felt slightly less guilty about my own reactions a few weeks ago. Apparently even the coolest of customers got bent out of shape when falsely accused.

Margaret's lawyer was whispering in her ear again and making calming motions.

I definitely should have gotten a lawyer back then.

I made a mental note to demand one if things went sideways for me on Monday. Which they almost certainly would.

But no lawyer in the world would be able to help me.

Shut up.

Margaret straightened again, her colour still high but her voice icy-calm. "I can prove I'm telling the truth. Let me make a call to that number right now, while you're listening."

That prompted another furious round of whispering from the lawyer, but Margaret gave her an adamant headshake. "If the Calgary police are interviewing the real Blake Fenler right now, then if I get an answer at this number, we'll know someone has been impersonating Blake to scam me. I want to do this. Let me have my phone."

"I'll be right back." Noonan rose and left the interview room, and the monitor blinked out.

A moment later, he stuck his head into the observation room. "Do you want to let her make the call?"

Holt and I exchanged a glance.

"I'd say 'yes'," I said.

Holt shook his head. "It could be a setup. If she tips

them off, we'll lose them. We need to know who's got that phone."

"We can trace the phone as soon as it connects," I argued.

"True..." Holt frowned. "Noonan, what do you think?"

"I can keep control of her phone. If we tell her to say she has connection problems before she says anything else, I can cut off the call without alerting the recipient if she deviates from the script."

"Okay," Holt conceded.

"Hang on, I'm going to get the Department involved." I hit the speed dial. "Hi, Trish, it's Aydan again. We're going to get Margaret to call that number you flagged. She says somebody's been scamming her, pretending to be another private investigator. Can you grab the trace info from the call?"

"Sure. Ready whenever you are."

Leaving the phone connection to Trish open, I turned to Noonan. "Okay, you're on."

He nodded and withdrew. Several minutes later our video monitor clicked on again, and we watched Noonan enter the interview room with Margaret's phone in his hand.

He explained the plan, cautioning Margaret that he would control the phone and end the call if he didn't like what she said.

Margaret eagerly agreed, and they rehearsed their script.

"He always chats for a few minutes at the end of a call," she told Noonan. "That's how he built the rapport that made me trust him, and elicited confidential information from me." She grimaced. "I should have known better."

"No, you shouldn't have," her lawyer said quickly. "You had no reason to believe there was anything suspicious going on. You did your due diligence when you met this man in person and checked his credentials. You've done nothing wrong."

"Tell him you don't have time to chat tonight," Noonan said. "Just stick to the script."

"I will." Margaret took a deep breath and let it out slowly. "I'm ready."

CHAPTER 45

Inside the interview room, Noonan pressed the speed dial button on Margaret's phone and she leaned forward, sucking in a breath. Noonan's finger hovered over the disconnect button.

After two rings, a male voice responded. "Hi, Margaret."

"Blake?" Margaret was frowning with concentration, but her voice sounded suitably uncertain. "Hello...? Sorry, I've got a bad connection. Are you there?"

"I'm here. Hello?"

"Oh, that's better. Sorry for such a late call. My guests are still here, but I just wanted to let you know that Aydan called two different times to say she would come later, but she never showed up. I doubt she's still at the office at..." Margaret consulted her wristwatch. "...One-thirty AM. I didn't spot her going by the highway camera, but I thought I should give you a heads-up just in case."

"Oh, darn." Fake-Blake's voice sounded chagrined. "And the party was going to be such a good chance for you cozy up and get a bit more information."

"Yes, well, you can't win them all. I'll try another time. Anyway, I have to get back to my party. Talk to you later."

"Hang on, while I've got you on the line... Have you heard anything more about that bomb? And is CRAPS making any progress on Eddy's case?"

Noonan shook his head warningly and Margaret let out a yelp. "Somebody just spilled wine on my rug! I have to go. I'll call you tomorrow and give you the scoop on everything. 'Bye."

Noonan disconnected and Margaret fell back in her chair, letting out a breath. "How did I do?"

I lost interest in Noonan's reply when Trish spoke in my ear. "Got the trace. The phone signal came from Lawrence Harchman's property."

"Got him!" I said with satisfaction. "Thanks, Trish. Start digging to see if you can make any connections between Harchman and Volslav."

"Will do." She disconnected.

I turned to Holt. "So far, so good."

He gave a noncommittal shrug as the door to the observation room opened again.

"Any questions?" Noonan asked.

"Nothing else I can think of. Holt?" I asked.

He shook his head and rose. "This could still be an elaborate setup with an accomplice on the other end of that call, but my gut says she's telling the truth. I don't see any reason to hold her based on what she's said so far. Kelly, do you want to observe any longer?"

"No, I'm ready to go." I stood and stretched, hiding my desire to lunge for the door and flee. "Thanks, you guys." I included Noonan and Rice in my nod of gratitude. "See if you can get anything else out of her, and if anything new comes up, give us a call."

"Okay," Noonan agreed. "Do you want us to pick up Mr. Harchman?"

"No," Holt and I said together.

"Not yet," I elaborated. "We're hoping to nail him for something bigger than murder. Let us see what other connections we can make." A thought struck me. "Oh. And, assuming you don't uncover anything that raises red flags... could you please ask Margaret to keep monitoring her camera and reporting to Fake-Blake as usual?"

"You sure you trust her?" Holt asked.

"I think so." I grimaced. "But it doesn't really matter. Unless something entirely new comes up in the rest of the questioning, she'll have to be released soon. If she's been lying all along, she'll tell Harchman everything and we're screwed anyway. But I think she's on the up-and-up; and if she is, I bet she'll be happy to help. She's got the background and experience to do a good job of stringing Fake-Blake along."

"That's what I thought, too," Noonan agreed.

"Great," I said with relief. "If she's up for it, could you please also get her to call Fake-Blake tomorrow morning like she promised, and spin a story about getting detained for questioning right after she talked to him? Word will already be getting around Silverside, and we don't want him to get suspicious if he doesn't hear anything about it from Margaret."

"But then he'll know his hitman has been arrested," Holt objected.

"Yeah..." I frowned. "I don't see any way around that, though. If Margaret doesn't call him like she promised and he doesn't hear from the hitman, he'll get suspicious, too."

"She could tell him she was detained and questioned but as far as she knows we haven't made any arrests," Noonan suggested. "Give the impression that we found the rifle but not the shooter."

I gave him a smile. "That'll work. He'll just figure his hitman is lying low, waiting for a chance to try again. Thanks."

Noonan nodded and we parted ways in the corridor; him returning to the tiny interview room, and Holt and me exiting into the blessed freedom of dark parking lot.

On the highway, I turned to Holt. "Can you drop me off at my place on your way by?"

"No."

I stared at the craggy profile illuminated by the dashboard lights. "Why the hell not? We'll be driving right by my road!"

"I'm not dropping you off," he said with exaggerated patience, "Because I'm staying at your place tonight."

After a moment, I closed my dangling jaw. "I thought we agreed you weren't doing the whole 'proposition Aydan' thing."

"Christ, Kelly, get over yourself!" He threw a glare my way before returning his attention to the highway. "I said I'm staying at your place, not sleeping with you. Dermott doesn't want you out of my sight."

"Well, bad news: I'm going to be out of your sight, because you're sure as hell not going to sit in my bedroom and watch me sleep. And you have to sleep sometime, too. Does Dermott expect you to stay awake until Monday?"

Holt stared out the windshield, his jaw set. "No, he expects me to sleep with you."

"*Seriously?*" My voice came out in a squawk.

Holt shrugged. "Why not? You sleep with Kane and Hellhound. Maybe even at the same time, for all we know. You've got a history of sleeping with your partners. And I'm your partner."

"I have *not*-" I bit off my furious retort, then drew in a deep breath and let it out slowly. "Okay, look. In the first place-"

"Save it," Holt interrupted. "I'm just telling you what Dermott thinks."

I regarded his expressionless profile for a few moments before curiosity overcame my indignation. "So what are you planning to do?"

He shot another irritable glance in my direction. "I'm planning to sleep wherever there's a place to sleep, a bed or a couch or the floor, or in my fucking car if I have to. And I'm going to trust you not to run off and leave me looking like an idiot."

"Of course you can trust me. Why would I run?"

Holt stayed silent.

I sighed. "Okay, I know you're not feeling very trusting right now, but you can count on me to stick around tonight."

"Not like I have a choice," Holt grumbled. "If you and your boyfriends gang up on me, I'm fucked anyway."

"Trust me, none of us want to fuck you." I grimaced. "In any sense of the word."

Holt growled something under his breath that I didn't catch, and I didn't ask him to repeat it. Instead I pulled out my phone and texted Kane and Hellhound to let them know we were on our way.

Holt didn't seem inclined to chat, so I closed my eyes and dozed for the rest of the trip.

When the monotonous hum of pavement under the tires gave way to the squeaky crunch of snow-covered gravel, I dragged myself out of my slouch.

Holt hissed, "*Shit!*" and drew his gun as he slowed the car.

I had spotted the distant shadowy figure beside the road, too. Pulse pounding, Glock in hand, I stared into the gloom at the limits of the headlights.

A moment later the bulky figure flung its arms up, then lowered its hands toward its head, elbows up. Then both arms to one side...

I burst out laughing and holstered my gun. "It's Arnie."

"How the hell do you know?" Holt growled. "Is that some secret signal?"

"Yep," I assured him, still giggling. "He's doing the actions to The Village People's 'YMCA'."

"Oh, for cr..." Holt holstered his weapon.

As we got closer, the headlights illuminated my favourite bearded face. We drew up beside Hellhound and I powered my window down.

"Hey, darlin'." He leaned in for a kiss, the frost in his beard leaving icy droplets on my chin.

"It's two o'-fucking-clock in the morning," Holt snarled. "What the hell are you pissing around out here for?"

"Didn't wanna communicate over an unsecured phone, an' I wanted to catch ya before ya got too close," Hellhound replied. "I checked the area with infrared an' night vision an' everythin' looks clear, but Kane an' I talked it over an' figured the two a' ya oughta stay in the bunker tonight. We're thinkin' that so-called sniper was more a distraction than a threat. Kane's got an ambush set up at the farm. We'll keep an eye on things here."

"Good plan," Holt agreed instantly.

"But-" I began.

"Good," Hellhound said. "See ya tomorrow, darlin'. Sleep tight." He kissed me again, then turned and strode back toward my farm.

Holt wasted no time in nosing the car onto the nearest crossing and turning back the way we'd come.

We were almost at the highway again before I found my voice. "That worked out well for you. Did you arrange that in advance?"

"Nope." Holt grinned. "But sometimes I win."

Waking up in the underground bunker four hours later was not one of the happier experiences of my life. I silenced the annoying alarm on my phone with a hand that felt too heavy for my arm, and dragged myself out of the bunk.

Holt's action-hero persona seemed to have deserted him. On the other side of the room, he pushed the pillow off his face and squinted at me with bloodshot eyes under rumpled hair.

"You snore," he grated.

"It was your idea to sleep there," I reminded him, and headed for the shower.

By seven-thirty AM we were assembled in my office. Spider looked as fresh as ever, Holt had apparently reconnected with his inner action hero somewhere between his shower and coffee, and I still felt like seven kinds of shit.

Dermott had also made an appearance before trudging down the hall to his office. I marvelled at his unprecedented dedication. He never came in on Sunday unless it was an emergency.

Then again, he was probably hanging around in the hope that I'd do something that would let him lock me up today instead of waiting until tomorrow. My only consolation was that he looked just as tired and grumpy as I felt.

"Did you hear from your boyfriends?" Holt asked.

I threw him a scowl. "They have names, you know."

"Whatever. Did you hear from them?"

"Yeah. Everything's fine at my farm. They'll be in town this morning, working on Eddy's and Pearl's cases." Flopping onto my couch, I reached out a hand toward Spider. "Let's get this done."

He dropped the tiny piece of circuitry onto my palm. "Are you sure about this? You look just as tired as yesterday." He flushed. "I mean, you always look good, I just-"

I waved him to silence. "Thanks, Spider, it's fine. Let's use a really unusual search term this time. Last time I followed the wrong oyster mushrooms and ended up God-knows-where."

"Okay, how about..." He hesitated. "Coulrophobia?"

"Um... okay. How do you spell that?"

"And what does it mean?" Holt put in.

Spider flushed. "It's a fear of clowns. C-O-U-L-R-O-phobia. Don't ask me why I know that."

"Your secret is safe with us," I assured him.

"Clowns are fucking creepy," Holt agreed. "Those big painted smiles..."

Spider shuddered. "Stop."

I checked my watch. "Let's get this show on the road. I want to make sure I have enough time to infiltrate the CIA's servers before Grandin's interview starts."

Before Spider had finished saying 'good luck', I was striding down the virtual reality corridors.

Holt's avatar popped into existence and hurried after me. "Do you even think you can do this?"

"It'll depend on whether they plug in the observation camera in the interview room." We strode into the virtual file room and I reached for his hand. "Wish me luck."

"Luck."

I vanished into the internet.

To my surprise, I found the CIA's servers without much trouble. Damn random internet connections; I never knew whether it would take seconds or hours to find my destination.

I trickled into their intranet and headed for the video controls.

The interview camera was stubbornly dark.

Dammit.

But I was early. Maybe they'd activate the camera when the interview started.

Time ticked away. I slipped a tiny tendril of consciousness down to the low-level machine language of the server, keeping track of the minutes.

Nine o'clock local. The camera still wasn't activated. Had the meeting been cancelled or postponed? Or was I missing it?

I concentrated on the camera. There were the software drivers. There was the hardware connection...

Suddenly I was looking at the inside of the interview room. Everett Marsh sat behind a table, alone. It looked as though he'd been there for a while. A Perrier bottle sat at the side of the table and a nearly-empty glass of bubbly water accompanied a crumpled sandwich wrapper in front of him. He sipped, then set the glass down and glanced at his watch before crossing his arms and sinking lower in his chair.

Waiting.

A few minutes later the door opened and two armed guards entered with Grandin between them in shackles.

Grandin was expressionless, his posture as arrogant as

always.

The guards seated him across from Marsh and stepped back a pace, still within easy reach. They clearly didn't trust Grandin any more than I did.

Marsh sat up straight and drained his glass. "Okay, Grandin, I have a few more questions for you." He set the glass down and reached for the bottle.

Grandin yelled and sprang.

The guards lunged for him.

Perrier splashed across Marsh's desk as he recoiled, still clutching the bottle.

A horrible scream tore the air and one of the guards collapsed, clutching his belly. Grandin sprawled on the floor beside him.

The injured guard's writhing grew feebler. The other guard pinned Grandin's motionless body. Marsh was on his feet, backing toward the door.

I let out a frantic voiceless shriek and rocketed back through the internet.

CHAPTER 46

Holt's virtual grip was still strong, thank God. My trip back to Sirius took milliseconds.

I blasted into the file repository, shattering furniture and walls. Holt threw himself to the floor as I scorched overhead, yelling, "*Spider!* Brad Wilson! U.S. Head of Weapons Research! Get him on the line, *now!*"

My virtual feet didn't touch the floor until I landed in front of the portal.

"DON'T JUMP!" Holt's bellow stopped me just in time to prevent me from flinging myself through.

"Thanks," I said, and stepped through at a decorous pace.

The usual sledgehammer of pain hit me between the eyes, but I didn't have time for it. I lurched to my feet and staggered toward the door, holding my head in both hands and squinting through one pain-slitted eye.

A moment later, a strong hand gripped my upper arm and Holt's voice spoke in my ear. "Where to?"

"Dermott!" I croaked. "Go, go!"

Holt dragged me forward, and I closed my eyes against the thumping pain and concentrated on moving my legs as fast as they could go.

We screeched to a halt before I'd managed to pry my

eyes open, and Dermott's voice greeted me. "What the *fuck?*"

"Brad Wilson," I panted. "U.S. Head of Weapons Research. Spider's getting him on the line now. Tell him there's a new weapon like the one we showed at the conference. In a Perrier bottle. Everett Marsh is involved. Grab him..."

Nausea overwhelmed me and my legs gave way, but I could already hear Dermott's voice on the phone.

Thank God.

I huddled in a miserable heap, still clutching my head and sucking air in an attempt to keep from vomiting.

"Breathe slower, Kelly." Holt's hands locked around my head and crushed the pain. "Slower. Deeper and slower."

I tried to obey. After a few minutes the pain and nausea subsided and my breathing evened out.

Groaning, I managed to open my eyes. "Thanks," I croaked.

He demanded, "What happened?"

I took stock of my position, slumped on the floor in Dermott's doorway. "Help me up."

Holt offered a hand, and I used it to drag myself to my feet. Trudging over to one of the chairs, I fell into it.

"Thanks for stopping me at the portal," I said.

"No problem. The way you blew through the the file repository, I figured you didn't have ten minutes to waste flailing and screaming because you went out too fast."

"Blind agony is an overrated pastime," I agreed. Spider hurried in, pale and wide-eyed, and I added, "Is Reggie here?"

"Probably. He's usually here early Sunday mornings. I'll check." He ran out again, and I concentrated on breathing.

Minutes later, Spider and Reggie returned, closing the door behind them. Dermott hung up the phone, and I faced four worried expressions.

"Everett Marsh just killed Grandin," I said. "Probably a guard, too. Ruptured something in his belly." I shuddered. "Maybe everything." Dragging myself back from the sound of screams, I focused on my report. "Marsh has an ultrasound weapon, disguised in a Perrier bottle." I turned to Reggie. "The bottle actually holds liquid. That's why nobody realized what was happening until it was too late. I think..."

Closing my eyes, I forced myself to play back the memory. Grandin leaping up with a yell...

After Marsh reached for the bottle.

"Grandin knew," I said with certainty. "He realized what the bottle was when Marsh picked it up, and he tried to duck the beam. Maybe he noticed something about the bottom of the bottle when Marsh swung it toward him, but he couldn't move fast enough to avoid it."

"Do you think the guards knew?" Dermott demanded.

"No. One was in too much pain to think, and the other jumped on Grandin. If he'd known what the bottle was, he would have known Grandin was already dead."

"Wilson's on it," Dermott said. "I didn't give him any details, nothing to make him think we know what just happened. But he hung up fast, so he knows it's urgent. If Marsh goes on a rampage in CIA headquarters with that weapon..."

We all exchanged sick looks.

"Well, we can't do anything about that from here," Reggie said practically. "Tell me more about the weapon."

I closed my eyes again, visualizing. "It looked just like a

real Perrier bottle. Clear green glass, the Perrier label..."

"How could it have been clear?" Holt demanded. "How did they hide the guts of the weapon?"

"I think..." I scrunched my eyes harder. "Come on, brain... Okay, the bottle was full. I could see the bubbles in the liquid. But..."

"Carbonated beverages don't have bubbles in the bottle until the bottle's opened," Reggie said.

My eyes flew open. "Right. The cap was off. Lying on the table beside the bottle. And the liquid spilled when Marsh swung the bottle around."

"So this weapon doesn't have the original flip-top rangefinder. What was the targeting system?"

"I don't know," I said slowly. "I don't think Marsh aimed it at all. It wasn't very accurate. I doubt if he meant to hit the guard."

Holt frowned. "But you still can't hide circuitry in a clear glass bottle."

"Unless it was micro-miniaturized and concealed by the label," Spider contributed. "But I don't think you'd be able to-"

"Mirror!" I interrupted.

Holt narrowed his eyes at me. "Speak English, Kelly."

"I think there was a mirrored cylinder inside the bottle. Smaller than the bottle, so there was room for a bit of liquid around it. If they concealed the circuitry inside the cylinder..."

"That would work," Reggie agreed. "The distortion of the green glass would help conceal the mirror, and the bubbly fluid with a convex reflective surface behind it-"

"Go somewhere else to brainstorm," Dermott interrupted. "I have to run this up the chain of command.

Out."

We obeyed.

In the hallway, Reggie said, "Call me if you remember anything else", and hurried for the stairs.

Spider looked at Holt and me. "Now what?"

I sighed. "I feel like I should be running to fix the emergency, but I guess there's nothing we can do from here. I'll go back into the network and look for connections between Lawrence Harchman and Volslav and Everett Marsh. And I'll see if I can get into Harchman's private network, but I doubt if I'll be able to. The last time we checked, it was completely separate from the internet. Oh, and I'll check Everett Marsh's stocks. It's pretty obvious that he's guilty now, but at least that'll be some concrete evidence."

"Maybe you should hijack another camera or two at the CIA offices," Holt suggested. "If it's a slaughter, we need to know."

A shiver shook me. "Okay."

We trekked back to my office in silence and I sank onto my sofa with a small groan. Spider opened his mouth, concern on his face, but before he could speak I tapped the fist I'd clenched around my network key.

"Coulrophobia." I gave him a tight-lipped smile.

He nodded, and I mentally stepped into the virtual reality void.

Holt materialized seconds later, and we headed for the file repository again. When we stepped inside, Holt glanced around the rebuilt illusion. No sign of my earlier destruction remained, and Holt let out a 'hmph' as he reached for my hand.

"Next time, aim higher if you're going to blow through

here," he growled. "You could have killed me."

"It's virtual reality. You wouldn't die unless you believed you had. You know that."

Holt's scowl deepened. "I might know that when we're standing here and everything's calm, but I've got real-life reflexes. A hundred and fifty pounds of fast-moving projectile will kill me. I'm not going to stand there and try to disbelieve it."

"Right. Sorry." I squeezed his hand and mentally thanked him for knocking ten pounds off my actual weight. "I'll aim higher." I faded into the internet before he could reply.

Much later, I crept back into Sirius and materialized in the file repository.

Holt's eyes widened, but before he could speak I growled, "Not a fucking word."

"You look great," he said. "Young and strong. Come on, let's go."

I must have looked as bad as I felt, because he kept up a running commentary during our slow trek to the portal. "This is such an easy walk for you. You're in such great shape..."

I couldn't quite regain my normal form, but at least none of my body parts fell off.

Stepping back into reality triggered a spate of my vilest invective, but Holt's powerful grip crushed the pain seconds later. Groaning, I hauled myself upright.

"So?" Holt demanded.

"So Marsh's winning stocks were all African gold companies. Shocker." My voice came out in a weary monotone. "The CIA's offices looked okay, so they must have stopped Marsh. I couldn't find Harchman's internal network, no surprise. I didn't find any other connections between Harchman and Volslav. I didn't find any other offshore bank accounts for Marsh. And I traced that deposit from Dymt Volslav back to an account that was opened with a deposit of twenty million dollars cash three days ago, and the account was closed as soon as the money was transferred to Arlene Widdenback's Cayman account. The address on Volslav's account was bogus."

"Or so you say," Holt said.

I glared at him. "I'm sure our analysts can confirm that for you."

"Actually, they already did," Spider said timidly. "Trish found that last night."

"Great." I dragged myself to my feet and handed my network key to Spider.

"Where are you going?" Holt demanded.

I gave him an 'I dare you to say anything' look. "To pee."

He didn't say anything.

When I returned, Holt and Spider broke off what looked like a heated conversation. Spider's cheeks were flushed, his jaw clenched.

"What's up?" I asked casually as I resumed my seat on the couch.

"What did you mean when you said you couldn't find any connections between Harchman and Volslav?" Holt countered.

I frowned and enunciated my words slowly and clearly. "I mean, I... couldn't... find... any..."

"Fuck off," Holt growled. "So you've looked at every file in the entire internet, and-"

"No," I said tiredly. "I just meant I hadn't found anything in the last two hours. I had all that other stuff to check, and I did it first because I knew looking for Harchman and Volslav would take the longest. Now I'll go back in, and Harchman and Volslav will be *all* I'm looking for. But I still might not find anything. Remember, Brock and Tammy and I have been looking for information on Volslav for months without success. The only new angle I have is this potential connection to Harchman."

Holt narrowed his eyes at me. "You say you've been looking without success. But somehow you found half a dozen generic words that started this whole clusterfuck in the first place. If you can find something that obscure, it's fucking hard to believe you can't find big, distinctive names like Harchman and Volslav."

"I told you, I don't know how or why it works. Or doesn't." I tried to summon enough energy to glare at him, and managed a myopic squint. "I'm doing the best I can. So are Tammy and Brock. If they can't find anything either, then there's no reason to believe I should be able to."

"Or maybe you're hiding stuff from them," Holt said. "Deleting every reference you find. And I know you can take thoughts and memories out of Mellor's mind. Brock and Mellor could have found all kinds of stuff, but they'd never know. And neither would we."

That was it. My last nerve.

Rage reddened my vision and I jerked forward so violently that even Holt The Magnificent twitched.

"*FINE!*" I bellowed in his face. "*If you don't fucking trust me, then ARREST ME!*" I shoved both hands at him, wrists together, still bellowing at the top of my lungs. "*Go on, DO IT, ASSHOLE!*"

Holt's shocked expression might have been comical if I hadn't been exerting every ounce of my will to keep from throttling him.

But his lapse in composure only lasted an instant before he raised a supercilious eyebrow and drawled, "Fuck, Kelly, take a chill-pill. Remember your anger management."

My fists clenched. "I'll give you anger management, you-"

"Aydan." Spider's anxious voice trickled through the fiery lava of my temper. "You're scaring me."

Still glaring at Holt, I drew a deep breath and let it out slowly. "Sorry, Spider. I promise I won't kill him in front of you."

Holt let out a derisive laugh. "I'd like to see you try."

The fact that he was right did nothing to improve my temper.

"Bullets," I ground out. "The great equalizer."

Holt leaned back in his chair and waved a dismissive hand. "For fucksakes, get over it. I didn't mean anything. I'm just looking at all the angles."

"You accused me of *treason*," I growled.

Dermott appeared in the doorway. "What's going on here?" he demanded. His hopeful expression made me swallow my anger and paste on a bland face. He'd just love to see Holt arrest me.

Holt switched instantly to a cop-neutral expression, too. "Just batting some theories around."

"Oh." Dermott's gaze ping-ponged between the two of us. "What was all the yelling about?"

I leaned back on the sofa, feigning composure. "Just making a point."

Dermott eyed Holt, but when he didn't contradict me,

Dermott snapped, "Well, keep it down", and withdrew.

"And keep it together," Holt growled at me. "If you really want to end up in prison, you're doing a great job."

"At least I'd get more than four lousy hours of sleep a night in prison," I muttered, but my anger had subsided. I held out my hand to Spider for my network key. "Let's do this."

When I emerged into my usual pounding headache a couple of hours later, large warm hands locked around my head, gently chasing the pain away. My swearing faded into a moan of abject gratitude as I inhaled the delicious spicy scent that was Kane's alone.

Sudden embarrassment seared me.

Shit, I was still in virtual reality. Holt was never going to let me forget that I'd conjured up an imaginary Kane for a cuddle.

I opened my eyes to look for the portal, and my mouth fell open.

CHAPTER 47

"John?" My voice came out in a croak as I dragged my head up, breaking contact between the back of my head and his rock-hard abs. "Am I...?" I frowned around me through the remains of my headache.

Holt and Spider still occupied the same chairs. But Kane stood behind me, too good to be true. Still massaging my temples and shoulders with those glorious big warm hands.

A wave of disorientation shook me. "Am I in a sim right now?"

Holt frowned. "No."

The feeling of unreality persisted. "But if this was a sim, that's what you'd say in my imagination."

"It's not a sim." Kane's voice was deep and reassuring. "Try to put your hand through the sofa."

I tried, finding solid upholstery under my palm.

"But if the sofa was an externally-defined parameter, it would be solid..." I began, then stopped myself. "Forget it. What time is it? What's happening?"

I answered my first question with a glance at my watch. Noon.

"I'm sorry," Kane said. "I guess I shouldn't have..." He stepped back, taking his wonderful hands with him. "I can see why this was confusing for you. You seemed to be having a bad exit, and I reacted without thinking. Habit."

"I was having a hard time, and I appreciate your help." I gave him a smile as he came around where I could see him without craning my neck. "Thanks, but why are you here?"

"I signed him in," Holt said. "We need him."

"Okay..." I rubbed my temples, hoping to banish the confusion along with the residual ache. "What have I missed?"

"Did you find anything?" Holt asked.

Was he trying to trap me by getting me to disclose classified information to a civilian?

"Nothing new. Bring me up to speed on what's happening here," I demanded.

"I figured you wouldn't find anything new," Holt said.

Before I could snap at him, he went on, "There's probably nothing out there. It'll all be in Harchman's private network. That's where we need to be, and soon. If Volslav had a weapon here in Silverside for a demo on Friday night and Marsh had one in CIA headquarters just a few hours ago, that means there's probably more than one weapon. Unless they got it on a plane to Langley right after the demo here; but either way, we know there's a weapon in Langley now."

Queasy trepidation squirmed in my stomach. "Okay, and...?"

"And that's only a fifteen minute drive to the White House." Holt paused to let that chill sink in before continuing, "We've given the US the intel they need to deal with the threat, but as soon as the crisis is over they're going to want more details. If Harchman is Volslav, we need evidence, now. That means you need to get close enough to access their VR network. Harchman hates your guts and his guards will have instructions to keep you out, so we'll need to insert you."

"Right," I agreed. "But that has nothing to do with John. I'll sneak in along the creekbed like I did last time..." I trailed off, remembering that the creekbed would be under several feet of snow now.

"Yeah," Holt agreed sarcastically. "No problem."

I shrugged. "It's only a couple of miles. I can snowshoe."

"But once you're inside their perimeter, you'll need to come quite a bit closer to the building site before you can get a reliable network connection," Kane said. "And that means crossing the guards' regular patrol route. Remember the last time we did that?"

I grimaced. "Vividly."

We exchanged a glance, and I relived the horrible moment when I thought I'd sent him to his death.

Suppressing a shudder, I argued, "But this time I'll have night vision and infrared so I can easily avoid the guards. And it's no big deal to walk uphill on snowshoes."

"Except for the big fucking snowshoe-shaped tracks you leave behind," Holt pointed out. "You might as well send Harchman's guards an email and let them know you'll be dropping by, so they can pick you up at their convenience."

"Well, it's the only way in." I scowled at him. "They're sure as hell not going to let me in the front door."

Holt grinned. "No, but they'll let in Greg Holt, Realtor. Rich, single, and looking to..." He leered and made air quotes. "...*bone up*... my technique with the highly-qualified sex therapists supplied by Harchman's 'male wellness spa'."

"Ew. I really didn't need to know that you're planning to whack off in virtual reality." I glanced at Spider's crimson face. "Sorry, Spider. You probably didn't want to be thinking about that, either."

"I'm not going to be whacking off," Holt retorted. "I'm going to be your inside man."

I grimaced. "Enough with the double entendres."

He blinked at me, then scowled. "Get your mind out of the gutter. We need to infiltrate Harchman's compound. You can't go in alone because when you're in VR, the guards could walk right up and carry you off and you'd never even notice. They don't know me, so I'm the obvious choice for the inside man. Kane's cover is already in place as Arlene Widdenback's associate. So if the two of you get caught, which you'd damn well better not..." He gave me a glare. "You can maintain your covers long enough for me to get you out."

"John shouldn't be involved," I argued. "He's a civilian. And having him with me doesn't solve anything. Two sets of snowshoe tracks are twice as obvious as one."

"*No* sets of snowshoe tracks," Kane countered. "That's why you need me."

"Why, have you learned to flap your arms and fly in the past five months?"

Kane grinned. "I've known how to fly since I did my parachute training in the army. We're going to jump in."

I gaped at him exactly long enough for the words 'parachute' and 'we' to register in my brain. "I don't know how to parachute," I said flatly. "And I have no intention of learning."

"No problem," Holt said. "You don't have time to learn. We have to get in there tonight."

"Okay, so..." I frowned at them. "John's going in alone? How does that help? He can't access the network."

"That's right, I can't." Kane's smile widened. "So you

and I are going to tandem-jump."

This time my jaw flapped but no words came out at all. The queasy sensation in my guts tightened into hard knots.

"Don't worry," Kane went on. "I'm a qualified instructor. I've logged over a thousand jumps, and as my passenger, you don't need any skills at all. I once tandem-jumped carrying an eighty-five-year-old woman, and she loved every minute of it. It's very safe."

My words finally returned, in a voice like the thin creak of a twig about to snap. "Let me make one thing very clear. I am not going to jump out of a perfectly good airplane. I am especially not going to jump out of a perfectly good airplane in the dark, to land where there are sharp sticks hidden under the snow to impale me."

Kane frowned. "You're right, night-jumping into deep snow is more dangerous. But I've done it many times, and I'll be controlling the landing. You won't get hurt."

"I'm also not going to jump out of a perfectly good airplane so *you* can get impaled!" My voice was rising. "You have a son! Your responsibility is to him!"

Kane flinched, but when he spoke his voice was steady. "I also have a country, which I swore to serve. And I have you, whom it's both my duty and my desire to protect. Plus, there are no other agents who are qualified for tandem jumps."

"I bet Arnie could do it," I argued, mentally sidestepping the fact that I was talking about falling thousands of feet through thin air with nothing to save me but a bit of fabric on strings. "He must have taken the same parachuting courses as you. And I bet he's parachuted into a lot of dicey places for his job."

"He has," Kane agreed. "But he's never been trained as

an agent, and he's not qualified to do tandem jumps. I am."

"And Hellhound's going to be busy," Holt put in. "He'll be jumping with you so there's somebody else inside the perimeter to back you up."

"NO!" My denial wasn't quite a yell, but it was close. "I'm not putting either of them in danger! That is not going to happen!"

"You're not calling the shots," Holt said flatly. He turned to Kane. "Jump time's zero one hundred. Make sure she's ready." He strode out without looking at me.

An uneasy silence fell.

"Well, that got ugly fast," I said.

"I'm sorry you're upset, Aydan," Kane said. "But this really is the only solution."

I sighed and capitulated. "I know. We have to get into that network, and even if we surrounded the place with a strike force, they couldn't get in fast enough to keep Harchman from deleting his files. He's got an emergency kill routine that only takes a few keystrokes to activate."

"Maybe Brock and Tammy could go and stay as guests in the guesthouse," Spider suggested. "The Harchmans don't know them, and they could sit in their room and sift through the network to their heart's content."

Kane and I were already shaking our heads.

"I wish that would work," I told Spider. "But you know what Tammy's like. She'll talk to anybody, anytime, and say whatever pops into her mind. It would only take one slipup and they'd be in deep trouble."

"And Brock has no training as an agent," Kane seconded. "It would be completely irresponsible to risk Tammy's safety that way. And if they were captured and someone realized that she could be used as a decryption tool…"

Spider nodded, his brow furrowed. "I know. But it's just as dangerous for Aydan. Probably more dangerous, since the Harchmans already know her and hate her. I'm just... I wish there was another way."

I put on my best show of confidence. "Don't worry, it's old hat for John and me. We won't make the same mistakes as last time." I smiled at Kane. "Our team's back together again." I offered him a fist bump, which he returned with a smile.

But the troubled grey of his eyes told me he wasn't buying my act.

"Come on," he said. "Let's go and get you geared up with some snow camo, and then we'll meet Hellhound for lunch before we head out to Springbank Airport for a few practice jumps."

My knees started to quiver at the thought.

I forced a smile. "See you tomorrow, Spider."

"Okay..." He hesitated, then flung his lanky arms around me. "Be careful."

"Always," I assured him. "Or at least, as careful as I can possibly be while falling through thin air toward sharp objects."

He bit his lip, his face scrunching with worry. "That's not funny."

"I didn't think so, either," I agreed. "See you."

As I turned away, he exclaimed, "Wait! I just had an idea!"

Hope rose as I turned back to him. "I'm all ears."

"It might not be a good idea," he said hesitantly. "But... maybe you should take the other network key. The one that makes you pass out instead of giving you headaches. I know it hurts you more when you get tired, and..." He flushed.

"Your swearing was getting pretty loud already this afternoon. It might be hard for you to keep quiet by tonight."

Kane frowned. "I thought you weren't sure whether that other key was causing brain damage. And if Aydan's unconscious and we need to run..."

"But I wouldn't be unconscious for long," I argued. "I'd just be going into Harchman's network and checking a few files."

"Which could take hours," Kane replied. "We don't know how much data is in there. And if you have a one-to-four-ratio of unconsciousness to network time, that could mean you stay unconscious for half an hour or more. Not acceptable."

"But if the network connection gets broken the way it did last time, at least I'd be silent," I pointed out. "There's nothing like bloodcurdling screams to make a covert operation far more fun than it needs to be."

"True..." Kane didn't sound convinced.

"We'll take it," I told Spider. "Thanks. We may not use it, but it'll be good to have the option. We'll need that signalling device that gives me a blip in the network, too, so that John can signal me to come out if anything happens."

"I'll go down and get those for you and meet you in the lobby," Spider promised, and hurried out.

Kane and I followed him out and headed for Stores, where I was duly issued pants and a jacket in white and gray camo and a helmet. I seriously doubted the helmet would make any difference if I did a header into the ground from a couple of miles up.

When I expressed that thought, Kane said, "You'll appreciate the face shield when you hit terminal velocity. The windchill at minus twenty Celsius makes it about forty below."

"T-Terminal?" My voice came out in a quaver. "Why can't they call it something that doesn't sound like so much like death?"

Kane chuckled. "Don't worry, for a tandem skydive we'll only hit about a hundred and twenty miles per hour in freefall."

I licked dry lips. "Could we please not use the word 'hit' in the same sentence with 'a hundred and twenty miles per hour'?"

He sobered. "I'm sorry. You're actually nervous about this, aren't you?"

"Fucking-hell-yes!" My voice cracked and I swallowed hard.

Taking my hand, Kane looked into my eyes. "You'll be fine. It's normal to be nervous, but I'm pretty sure you'll love it as soon as you try it. There's no thrill like it."

"I'm a bookkeeper," I snapped. "We like safe, predictable routines. Not thrills. Especially not plummeting-to-death thrills."

"You'll be fine," he repeated. "I promise."

"Well, that's a pretty easy promise," I retorted sourly. "If I'm *not* fine, the only apology you'll need to make will be to a pile of strawberry jam wearing my clothes."

He shook his head. "That won't happen. Not on my watch." Laying an arm across my shoulders, he guided me down the hall. "Come on, you'll feel better after lunch."

"I seriously doubt that," I muttered.

CHAPTER 48

I couldn't give my lunch the appreciation it deserved. Eddy's juicy burger tasted like cardboard in my dry mouth, but I forced the food down anyway.

For the umpteenth time, I tore my thoughts away from hurtling to certain death and tuned back into Hellhound's report of their investigation.

"...an' Eddy says some stuff in the cellar looks like it mighta been moved." Hellhound eyed me expectantly.

"What kind of stuff?" I asked. "Would his staff normally go down there?"

"He only keeps stuff that ain't food down there, like napkins an' toilet paper an' canned goods. So yeah, the staff goes down there every now an' then." Hellhound shrugged. "Eddy said there wasn't anythin' obvious, he just had a feelin' things'd been moved."

"Nothing missing?"

"Not that he noticed."

I sighed. "Well, maybe that's where the murderer hid. You said it didn't look as though anybody had been upstairs?"

"Nah. There was dust on the stairs." He shrugged. "If anybody got up there, they flew."

Flying.

My mouth went dry all over again. I gulped my beer and changed the subject. "How about Pearl?"

"Cops released her, but she's stayin' with Lola. Doesn't feel safe in her house without her guns." He frowned. "I don't blame her. There were footprints in her house, from big boots. The guy that sneaked in musta had snow in his treads, an' when it melted an' dried it left salt outlines. Cops'll try an' match the prints, but everybody wears big boots in the winter."

I let out a breath. "Well, at least they're not trying to pin it on Pearl."

Hellhound shifted uncomfortably. "She ain't off the hook yet. The guy that got shot was a neighbour she'd had words with. The guy walks his dog through the park an' lets it shit on Pearl's property, an' she threatened to give him a buttload a' rock salt if she caught him again. That's why he was sneakin' around out there in the middle a' the night. Lettin' his dog take a shit."

Falling back in my chair with a groan, I pressed the cool beer bottle to my forehead. "I don't blame Pearl for being pissed off, but I wish she wasn't quite so outspoken. Do you think she did it?"

"Nah. But it ain't lookin' good for her."

Kane laid down his napkin. "Don't worry, Aydan, we won't give up on Eddy and Pearl. But we need to get on the road now. It'll take us two and half hours to drive to Springbank, and I want to get a few jumps in before we lose the light."

My hand clenched involuntarily on my beer bottle.

"Drink up," Kane encouraged as he rose. "I'll get the tab."

As he headed for the bar, I chugged the last of my beer.

Then I snitched Arnie's beer and gulped the last of it, too.

Arnie's face softened, and he took my hand and stroked my quivering fingers. "It'll be okay, darlin'. Kane's the best. You'll be fine."

"No, I'll be falling thousands of feet, screaming all the way, and probably shitting my pants. I'm not sure whether to hope we land safely, or hope we smash into the ground and die on our first jump so I won't have to do it twice."

Kane returned, tucking his wallet into his pocket. "All right, let's go." He turned to Hellhound. "We'll likely finish up at the airport around five, so we'll meet you at my place around six."

"'Kay." Hellhound rose, still holding my hand, which was a good thing because my trembling knees seemed to need a bit of help. When I sidled out from behind the table, he took me in his arms and placed his lips next to my ear. "I know you're scared shitless, darlin'," he said gently. "An' I know you're gonna do this anyway. An' that makes ya the bravest person I know." He drew back and pressed a kiss to my lips, then stepped back with a smile. "See ya later."

Feeling like a child seeking reassurance on the first day of school, I took Kane's hand and managed a dry croak.

"Let's roll."

Preoccupied by fear, I didn't take in much of the long drive. Even though I'd used the washroom before we'd left Blue Eddy's, I was squirming with urgent need by the time we got to Drumheller half an hour later.

I overcame my embarrassment and asked Kane to make a pit stop. "Just need to return some of Eddy's rental beer," I said lightly as I got out of the Expedition.

When I needed to stop again in Calgary, I had no excuse. I did what was necessary before slinking back into the vehicle, avoiding Kane's concerned gaze.

After the orientation and briefing at Springback Airport, I darted into the bathroom yet again. Perched uneasily in the cubicle, I stared at its dismal walls and tried not to think about what I was about to do.

But I couldn't hide in the bathroom forever. And there was no other way for me to get inside Harchman's perimeter.

And a lot of people might die if I didn't do this.

When I emerged from the washroom, it was with my head high and my shoulders squared.

Kane was waiting across from the door. He straightened, giving me a worried once-over. "Are you-"

"I'm fine. Let's do this."

Hiding the trembling of my knees as best I could, I strode beside him out into the long rays of the sun, already on its journey toward the horizon.

It was cold inside the plane, and the last vestiges of my body heat fled despite Kane's body pressed against my back in the harness.

The touch of his gloved hand made me twitch. "This time we'll be doing a nice easy jump from ten thousand feet above ground level and we'll open the canopy at five thousand," he said over the roar of the engine. "It'll take us a few minutes to get up to altitude. Here." He handed me a chocolate bar, maybe hoping it would distract me from what we were about to do.

I wasn't distracted. "So you're saying we'll fall five thousand feet before we find out whether we're going to die. A mile. Straight down." Shivers seized me.

Kane put his arms around me with a gentle squeeze that

was probably supposed to be reassuring. "Eat your chocolate. And don't worry-"

I cut him off with a sharply-raised hand. "No more reassurances. It's not helping. But I'm doing this no matter what, and I'll either live or die. If I live, I'll do it again. And again, until I either die or get into Harchman's."

He leaned closer, placing his lips next to my ear and lowering his voice. "Aydan, I've seen you under live fire, and you weren't this frightened. You don't need to worry so much, this is a much safer-"

I waved him to silence again. "No more reassurances." I bit savagely into the chocolate bar.

Far too soon, the hatch was open. Icy wind rushed in like an eager predator.

Checking the altimeter strapped to his wrist, Kane secured our shoulder clips and moved us toward the door.

My feet glued themselves to the floor of the plane.

Kane nudged me forward, and my planted feet skidded a little closer to the gaping maw of wind and nothingness. My hand shot out and locked onto the side of the door.

Kane reached over and tugged gently at my wrist, and my grip tightened. I strained instinctively away from the abyss, shoving back against the unyielding wall of Kane's body. The wind roared its hunger. My heart hammered so hard Kane could probably feel it through my backbone.

He tried unsuccessfully to nudge me forward again, then moved around me, turning us sideways to the door.

"I'm not going to give you any more reassurances," he said firmly in my ear. "I know you're committed to doing this. But if you don't let go of that handhold, you could injure us both. Now, cross your arms and hold onto your shoulder harness with both hands."

Focusing all my will, I managed to loosen my grip.

As my hand released, he flung us out of the plane.

Blind terror seized me as the wind punched us, snatching us away from the safety of the plane.

Down.

Down.

I was screaming. Unable to stop, barely able to draw breath.

Frigid air tore past and suddenly I was belly-down, the slowly-turning earth below rushing up far too fast.

Even though I knew we were in the correct orientation for a tandem dive, the fact that Kane had put my body between his and the murderous ground felt like the worst possible betrayal.

Both my hands clenched like vises in the fabric of Kane's jacket. My back arched in an attempt to wrap my legs around him, too.

Still we fell.

Something was wrong.

Our parachute hadn't deployed.

Gonna-die...

A sharp jerk made me scream again with the tiny bit of breath still left in my lungs.

My harness had broken.

Falling...

The wind roaring up my nose slowed.

Sucking huge terrified breaths, I dared a glance downward. Kane's and my boots dangled together, far above the runways of Springbank Airport.

Okay, maybe my harness hadn't broken. My courage sure as hell had.

"Better?" Kane said gently into the relative quiet broken

by the flutter of the canopy above us.

I couldn't unstick my tongue from the roof of my mouth. I managed a jerky nod.

His chuckle vibrated my back. "Good. When you stopped screaming, I was hoping it wasn't because you'd passed out."

Violent tremors rolled through my body. I couldn't feel my feet or hands or face, only icy numbness. We fell.

The ground was zooming up, faster and faster.

"Legs up," Kane reminded me.

I jerked into a fetal curl, fighting the constriction of the harness. Not even close to the relaxed position Kane had demonstrated earlier, but my only instinct was to get as far away as possible from the death-dealing ground.

We were falling too fast.

We were going to-

A tug on the harness slowed us miraculously, and Kane's body flexed behind me as his feet touched down.

It probably would have been a perfect landing, but I was still curled into a terrified ball. Kane staggered forward and fell to his knees as my dead weight pulled him off-balance.

"You can put your feet down now." Amusement warmed his voice as he unclipped my harness.

I hunched forward and vomited.

For long minutes I was oblivious to everything except the spasms that wrenched my body. I retched over and over until nothing remained but dry heaves that wrung piteous whimpers from my throat.

At last the spasms ended and I drew my first full breath. Then another. Kane's hand made gentle circles on my back as he murmured comfort.

With trembling arms, I eased myself back to sit on my

heels.

Our pilot came over bearing a steaming paper cup and a sympathetic expression. He handed the cup to Kane and mercifully left me to my humiliation.

"Can you hold this?" Kane asked, offering me the cup.

I tried to answer, but only a tortured croak emerged from my throat. I nodded instead, and reached for the cup with both shaking hands.

I used the first sip of tea laced with cream and sugar to rinse and spit. The next sip went down uneasily, but stayed put. After a few minutes of silent communion with the tea, I straightened from my slump and managed scratchy-throated words at last.

"Help me up."

Kane obeyed, and I wobbled in his grip for a moment before my legs deigned to cooperate again. I gulped the remainder of the cooling tea, and kicked some snow over the mess I'd made.

"Let's go again," I croaked.

"Are you sure?" He eyed my tremors with concern.

"Yeah. We're losing the light. Have you got another chocolate bar?"

"We'll get you one before we go up."

The next jump was just as terrifying as the first, but at least I didn't scream all the way down or puke. By the third jump, I remembered to flex my knees on landing the way Kane had showed me, and we touched down lightly.

When Kane unhooked me, I gave him a grin and fist pump. "Nailed it!"

An answering grin spread across his face. "You're

starting to love this just a bit, aren't you?"

I shook my head. "Successfully suppressing my screams is not the same as 'loving'. But at least we should be able to get down at Harchman's without alerting everyone inside a five-mile radius."

"That's good." Kane glanced at the setting sun. "I want to do one more jump before we lose the light completely. This time we'll start higher and open the canopy lower, like a modified HALO."

"What makes you think we'll get any kind of halo?" I demanded. "With the thoughts I was having on the way down, pitchforks and eternal damnation are far more likely."

Kane laughed. "H-A-L-O. High-Altitude-Low-Opening. That's how the military deploys personnel over hostile territory. They start at a much higher altitude than we will, and open lower because there are enemies on the ground watching for them. I don't expect any hostile fire tonight, but I also don't intend to fly directly overhead and bail out at an altitude where we can be readily spotted by the guards. So, modified HALO."

"You're the boss," I said uneasily, and followed him to the plane.

CHAPTER 49

By the time we got to Kane's house, I could barely hold myself upright in the seat. Tremors vibrated my hands.

"I'm sorry it'll just be pizza tonight," Kane said as he pulled into his garage. "I'd love to cook you a proper meal, but when Hellhound's in charge of supper..." He shrugged.

"Pizza will be fine. In fact, pizza will be magnificent," I assured him. "I'm starving."

He tactfully didn't remind me of the ignominious reason why my stomach was so empty, and we went into the house in silence.

Arnie met us at the door, smiling. "Look what the cat dragged in." Peering down into my face, he frowned. "Ya look kinda rough, darlin'."

"She did fine," Kane said. "She's a natural."

"And he's a liar." I shot him a smile to soften my words. "I screamed like a slasher-movie victim. I puked. I would have shit my pants, if I hadn't already shit my way through every bathroom between Silverside and Springbank."

Arnie chuckled, but sobered into a concerned frown. "Pizza gonna be okay? Maybe toast'd be easier on your stomach."

"Nope, a giant greasy pizza sounds like pure heaven to me." I sniffed the air hopefully. "Is it here?"

"Just got here. Haven't even opened the boxes yet." He nodded toward the kitchen, and I hurried in.

Over hot delicious slices, we reviewed our strategy for the evening.

"The only thing I don't like about Holt's plan is what happens if we can't..." Kane glanced at Hellhound and finished obliquely, "...achieve our objective. If we don't find anything, we don't have any justification to deploy the strike team."

"But if we don't find anything, that means Harchman isn't Volslav," I pointed out. "So we should be okay even if his guards catch us. We got caught last time, and all Harchman did was call the police."

"True," Kane said dubiously. "But he hadn't hired anyone to kill you then. If we get caught this time, he'll likely kill us." He shifted his shoulders in an uncomfortable shrug. "If we're lucky. If we're not..."

"But if we get caught, we have Arnie and Holt and the strike team to get us out," I argued, hoping to reassure myself.

"Which will blow our cover, and Harchman will probably wipe his servers." Kane frowned. "The strike team is a last resort."

Hellhound nodded. "Yeah, an' that's somethin' else I ain't crazy about. Last time, some a' the guards were hired guns an' the rest were just rent-a-cops. I don't mind offin' some asshole if he's gonna kill me, but I don't wanna take out some poor bastard gettin' paid shit for basic security. An' I can't tell the difference 'til it's too late."

I gulped another bite of pizza. "Even the basic security guys are dangerous enough. They're all armed, and there's at least one that's so terrified of bears, he'll shoot at anything that moves whether he can see it clearly or not."

The other two swivelled to look at me.

"How did you come by that piece of intel?" Kane inquired. "We didn't run across anything like that the last time we were there."

"Um, I sneaked in along the creek a couple of other times." I concentrated on my pizza. "At night. Pretending to be a bear."

"Alone? Without backup?" Kane's eyes glinted dangerously.

"Holt knew where I was."

I crossed my fingers to dilute the half-truth. Holt had been much too far away to help me and he hadn't known what I was doing; but he *had* technically known where I was. Or my general vicinity, anyway.

Hellhound broke the tension with a chuckle. "An' now I know why my parka needed washin' that time ya borrowed it."

"Yep," I agreed with relief. "I made a great bear on all fours with your duffel bag stuffed down the front of your big parka."

"So you've used the same access route at least three times." Kane was definitely not chuckling. "It's a miracle you didn't get caught. We can't use that route anymore."

"No, it's okay," I assured him. "I told Tawny I'd sneaked in the front gate. And the guards were sure they'd seen a bear, not a person. I was close enough to hear them screaming like little girls. And I could hear their radio conversation."

"And they shot at you." Kane's voice was flat.

"And missed." I gave him a smile. "They're lousy shots when it's dark and they're scared."

Kane let out a long breath and scrubbed his palm over his face. "Moving on. Hellhound, I'd say you should just use trank darts unless you're sure you need lethal force. Even if we get surrounded at gunpoint, we can't know which guards are innocent."

"I fuckin' hate these jobs," Hellhound muttered. "All I want's a target I know I'm s'posed to take out." He sighed. "Okay, I oughta have a sight line to ya from my drop zone, so I'll keep my trank pistol handy an' switch to the rifle soon's I'm down. How're ya gonna move from there?"

Kane didn't reply, just glanced at me. Up to me to decide how much to tell him.

"We're not going to move," I said. "I'm going to do the same thing as I did with you a year and a half ago. I'll go into my, um... trance-"

"I get it now!" he interrupted, enlightenment dawning on his face. "Fuck, that piece a' circuitry ya were carryin'... that was your way into the virtual reality network, right? Ya weren't in a trance, ya were in VR. An' the signallin' thing talks to your network circuitry so ya know when to come out."

I sank my head into my hands with a groan. "You didn't hear that from me."

"Never heard a thing," he agreed. "But... that means you're gonna be in a lotta pain. Are ya gonna be able to keep quiet?"

I sighed. "I don't know. We have an alternative, but it makes me pass out. Sometimes for quite a while."

"Shit." Arnie eyed me, brow furrowed. "Is that... safe? Like, for your brain?"

"Nobody knows."

"Fuck. What if ya hafta bug out fast?"

"That's why we haven't decided whether to use the key that hurts me or the one that makes me pass out. If I'm blind with pain, I can barely move. If I'm unconscious, I can't move at all."

Arnie's frown deepened. "An' if somethin' fucks up with the original key, ya scream like somebody's rippin' your guts out and thrash like a rabid alligator."

I blinked at him. "That's... a vivid image. But, yeah. That's why we're thinking about using the one that makes me pass out."

"Use it," he said. "Kane an' I can carry ya as far's we need to, long's we trade off. It'll be safer an' easier to carry ya if you're unconscious an' quiet."

I nodded and tried not to think about that while we ran through our plans one last time.

Then the pizza was gone, and there wasn't much more to say.

Feigning composure, I yawned and hauled myself to my feet. "I'm going to try to get some sleep. If we don't have to leave for the airport until midnight, that'll give me a few hours at least."

"Good idea," Kane agreed. "Hellhound, you might as well sleep, too. I'll keep watch. I'm fairly sure we weren't followed here, but I don't like surprises."

"We'll split the watch," Hellhound said. "Ya want first or last shift?"

"Last," Kane decided. "If that's all right with you."

"Yeah. It's too early for me to sleep."

A few minutes later I was installed on a sofa-bed in Kane's office. I lay staring at the dark ceiling, listening to the noises of the unfamiliar house.

Strange bed. Strange house. Soon to be skydiving. I

likely wouldn't sleep, but I had to rest. I switched to yoga breathing.

In... Out... Slow like ocean waves...

The first quiet notes of Arnie's guitar drifted to my ears from the living room. His voice joined the guitar, a soft gravelly melody without words that wove a cocoon of comfort and reassurance around me.

My eyes dropped shut.

"Aydan." Kane's voice came from outside my door.

My eyes popped open. "I'm up." Suppressing a groan, I got out of the sofabed and straightened the clothes I'd slept in. After another trip to the bathroom, we were on our way.

Traffic was light on the outskirts of the city, dwindling to only a few cars as we followed the dark highway to the airport. We didn't talk, and I was glad of the silence.

I had thought my earlier trips in the airplane had been miserable, but they were nothing compared to this. The air got viciously cold as we climbed higher and higher.

Trying to distract myself, I concentrated on breathing evenly through the oxygen mask while I mentally checked my gear for the umpteenth time. The unconsciousness-inducing network key concealed in my bra. Combination night vision and infrared goggles in place behind my face shield. Bulletproof, bladeproof jacket under my snow camo. Abject fear in my heart.

Beside me, Hellhound was an eerie greenish zombie in my night vision, overlaid by the infrared display of a red blob fading to yellow, green, and blue at his extremities. I didn't bother to look at my own hands and feet. I already knew they'd show up as icy blue-violet. Shivers seized me.

"Base says Holt's in place," Kane said through my headset. "His room is bugged and he might be under surveillance, so he's using the covert protocol we agreed on. The tactical team is in place outside the property, and we have air support on standby."

That should have reassured me.

It didn't. I shivered harder. Kane hugged me close in the harness, but it didn't help.

"It's time." Kane's words sent an extra shock of adrenaline through my already-overloaded system.

As we put down our oxygen masks, Arnie gave my gloved hand a squeeze. "Love ya," he mouthed through his face shield.

"I love you," I mouthed back as we moved toward the hatch.

A moment later the dark wind claimed us.

I managed not to scream, but only because I knew it would blow John's and Arnie's eardrums through the comm link. Teeth clenched tight, I glimpsed Arnie hurtling through dark air beside us. Somehow that was more terrifying than falling myself. My eyes clamped shut.

The roar of the wind filled my ears and shoved icy fingers up my nose. I realized I had a deathgrip on Kane's jacket again when my arm moved with his while he checked the altimeter and GPS on his wrist.

Still we fell.

And fell.

Kane's body flexed and shifted above me as he steered us toward our destination. Or to our death. Maybe both.

I dared a peek between slitted eyelids and wished I

hadn't. The green-tinted ground was terrifyingly close, the roar of the wind almost deafening.

Arnie's sudden voice in my ear initiated a fresh surge of panic.

"Bogies headin' for my landin' zone," he said tightly. "Re-routin' to the alternate... fuck. Bogies there, too. Goin' to Plan B."

With a jolt, I realized I should have been scanning for guards, too. Too late now.

The jerk of my harness yanked a squeak of terror from my lips.

"Feet up," Kane prompted, and I obeyed as we swooped down toward the small clearing we'd marked on the map earlier.

Trees rushed up and a moment later our feet plunged into snow. My boots slithered on some unseen object and I lurched sideways, stifling a cry. Kane flailed briefly for balance before we toppled into a heap, accompanied by the clatter of the snowshoes strapped to his back.

"Stay down, don't move," he hissed. "If there are guards at Hellhound's original drop zone, they'll have a sightline to us."

I used every ounce of my willpower to lie stock-still instead of leaping up to look for Arnie. "What's Plan B?" I gritted.

"If he didn't find an alternate drop zone, he'll create a diversion when they spot him." Kane sounded grim.

Screams of fear and frustration and denial strangled in my throat. This couldn't be happening. Nobody had told me about Plan B.

But of course there had to be one. Arnie couldn't escape the laws of gravity, and he wouldn't draw attention to us by landing here.

"I'll contact Holt," Kane said shortly. "You get into the network. Don't waste..." He didn't say 'Arnie's sacrifice', but I heard it anyway.

I gave him a short nod and did the hardest thing I'd ever done.

I abandoned Arnie to his fate and stepped into virtual reality.

CHAPTER 50

I didn't waste time checking any of the sims in progress. Instead, I slipped invisibly into Harchman's data vault and dove into the first file directories I found.

Agonizingly conscious of time ticking away, I rifled through business emails, software code for Harchman's apps, and human resource files for the extensive staff. Nothing suspicious, dammit!

If Harchman was Volslav, where were his records? Even arms dealers had to keep track of their transactions, didn't they?

There weren't even any tantalizing encrypted partitions. I rocketed through file after file, all my senses alert. I only spent milliseconds on each file, but there were millions of them.

And while I was digging through cyber-mountains, what was happening to Arnie?

I yanked my mind away from horrible imaginings.

Where the hell were Harchman's bank statements?

At last I discovered them, in a folder named 'I'm rich'. God, what a smug little prick.

A fast perusal of the file dates left me vibrating with frustration. It was the same problem as Marsh's computer: The transactions I needed hadn't been issued in a statement yet. And I didn't have access to the internet to check Harchman's bank. When I examined his most recent statement, the number of digits left my head spinning.

Tawny's accounts were more modest: Tens of millions instead of hundreds. The reason for that became clear when I discovered a scanned copy of their prenuptial agreement. Tawny got a monthly allowance that exceeded my annual salary, but if she ever divorced Harchman, she got nothing.

I shook off my twinge of sympathy. She'd married him. Clearly the money was worth it to her.

And anyway, it didn't matter. I had checked everything. Tawny's files, too; in case Harchman was smart enough to do business in his wife's name. I still hadn't found any reference to weapons, Volslav, Everett Marsh, gold, or Africa.

Nothing.

Fuck, we couldn't have gotten this wrong, could we? Was Harchman really just a stupid little shit who'd hired a stupid little hitman?

And if we'd made a mistake, was Arnie suffering for nothing? What would the guards do if they caught a heavily-armed man parachuting onto their property?

Oh, please God, don't let them kill him...

Concentrate.

Maybe there was something in the sim archives. I couldn't imagine anybody being dumb enough to record illegal activities in virtual reality, but I had to be thorough. This was the only chance I'd get.

Queasiness shook me at the thought of what this operation was costing. The strike team, the helicopters, the air drop, the technology, all those man-hours. If we were wrong about this, Dermott would take all his fury and frustration out on me.

Clinging to the hope that Harchman was as stupid as I thought, I slipped into the most recent sim record, only to recoil.

Porn. Featuring Holt.

Of course, if he was under surveillance he had to play the part. He had a great body, but that was really more than I'd wanted to know about him.

I whisked to the next record wishing for brain bleach, but my wish was not to be granted. This one was porn, too. At least I didn't recognize the participants.

I flew through the sim records at top speed, catching only flashes of flesh in each before I moved on. When I finally discovered one where the participants were clothed, I had already advanced through two other sims before realizing I'd missed something.

Whisking back, I quivered with the electric shock of recognition. Harchman. And Rufus Zimm, the erstwhile hitman. Harchman was just as irritating in the sim as he was in real life. He lorded it over Zimm, acting as though he was granting him a tremendous favour. Zimm looked dazzled by the opulence of the room around him, and I wondered why Harchman had bothered with the sim instead of simply meeting Zimm in the real-life room.

Although maybe Harchman had a grain of sense after all. If Zimm decided to attack him for some reason, he couldn't be harmed in virtual reality. But if Harchman had any brains, he would have deleted the sim right afterward. Clearly he wasn't that smart.

I abandoned that sim and hurried through the next spate of porn until I spotted Harchman again, wearing a different and even more ostentatious suit, his shirtfront glittering with diamond studs. This time he oozed bonhomie, plying his guests with cigars and caviar while not-so-subtly reminding the two men that the cigars were Cohiba Bohikes that sold for eighteen thousand dollars a box, and the caviar was imported from Iran at thirty thousand dollars a kilo.

The dark-haired androgynous man in the European-looking suit declined a cigar and accepted the caviar with a gracious nod.

The other man declined both politely, and Harchman blathered on. The European man listened to his self-aggrandizing story with thinly-concealed boredom while the other man nodded deferentially, though he didn't seem obsequious.

"How fascinating," the deferential man said when Harchman finally had to draw breath. "And I know how valuable time is to such a successful man. Shall we proceed with our business?"

Harchman drew himself up, his puny chest inflating under the flattery. "Yes, of course. The reason I've flown you all the way here and given you an all-expenses-paid vacation in my exclusive spa..."

God, what a prick. But the other man's expression never changed from its pleasant smile.

Harchman burbled on about all the perks the man had received and what they would have cost if the man hadn't been his invited guest, but he finally got to the point. "...pleased to introduce you to my good friend, Dymt Volslav."

He gave the European man a chummy slap on the back. Volslav returned a thin unfriendly smile and reached over to shake hands with the other man, subtly moving his chair beyond Harchman's reach.

A gush of relief nearly swamped me. Finally, a

connection.

"It's a pleasure to meet you, Mr. Volslav," the deferential man said.

"The pleasure is mine," Volslav said in a warm voice with a hint of exotic accent.

Where had I heard that accent before?

Yana Orlov's had been similar. Another connection.

Volslav went on, "I wish to open an account with your bank, with a cash deposit of twenty million dollars."

The bank manager responded, "Certainly, Mr. Volslav. I have the paperwork here, and it would be my pleasure to open an account for you. How will you be transferring the funds?"

"Via armoured car. Please notify me when your aircraft is ready, and I'll send the car to the airport."

The bank manager brought a sheaf of paperwork out of his briefcase, and I withdrew from the sim with my virtual heart pounding.

So Dymt Volslav was a real person, and Harchman wasn't Volslav.

But opening a Cayman bank account wasn't a crime. I hadn't found anything incriminating either of them, except that Harchman had tried to have me killed; and I'd already damn well known that.

Dermott was going to be furious. And I'd never forgive myself if Harchman's trigger-happy guards shot Arnie because of this misguided mission.

But, dammit, my gut told me I was on the right track. There had to be something more here!

I flung myself into the next batch of sim records.

God, there was a lot of porn. There seemed to be an endless demand for Harchman's 'male wellness spa'. No wonder he was so rich.

I flew through sim after sim, but it seemed Harchman hadn't left recordings of any of his other business deals. Or maybe he'd deleted them already.

Shit, shit, shit!

At last I screeched to a halt and returned to another rare G-rated sim I'd overshot. There was Margaret Young meeting with Harchman, along with another man who must be the real Blake Fenler. Their conversation was exactly as Margaret had reported. She had been professional in her dealings with Harchman, clearly explaining what he could expect from her services and laying out her legal and ethical boundaries.

A tendril of warmth eased my worried heart. My fraud-radar had made me uneasy when I first met her, but it seemed I'd been right to trust her in the police interview.

I surfed onward through the sea of porn.

By the time I'd gone back a couple of years, I'd seen every sex act known to man and several that should have remained unknown. Dymt Volslav hadn't reappeared, nor had I seen any more of Harchman. Except in the nude, and that made me wish I could remove my brain.

And still, nothing incriminating. Elapsed time pressed on me with ever-increasing weight. Kane still hadn't signalled me to come out. Had something happened to him? Had I somehow gotten disconnected from my body, leaving me to wander eternally in virtual reality?

I couldn't stand it any longer. I would waste precious time lying unconscious when I left virtual reality, but I needed to check in with Kane.

As I turned to leave the sim repository, I realized a new sim had been created while I was in the archives. The cold hand of fear gripped my heart and squeezed hard. The torture sims I'd witnessed a year and a half ago still gave me nightmares.

But I had to know.

Hovering outside the sim, I breathed a fast three-word prayer: *Please be porn.*

I slipped invisibly through the virtual wall.

Even though I had braced for the worst, the scene still hit me like a physical blow. Arnie was bound and helpless, maybe unconscious. Or worse. His face was barely recognizable under the vicious punches the two guards kept hammering home. Pliers and boltcutters lay on the table, apparently unused so far, but terrifying in their potential.

Oh please, let Arnie realize he's in a sim. Floating cautiously closer, I visualized a whisper next to his blood-caked ear.

"Arnie, you're in a sim. You don't have to feel pain. Don't worry, we're going to get you out."

He didn't react. Another horrific punch hit him, and his head rolled loosely with the blow.

I could kill the guards without them ever knowing what hit them. But if I did, someone might notice in real life, and this horror-show would become Arnie's reality.

The sim flashed with a small electronic blip.

Kane's signal.

Biting back a frantic whimper, I rocketed for the portal and stepped through.

CHAPTER 51

I was warm.

Fuck, what had happened while I was unconscious?

My eyes popped open, and I recoiled with a yelp at the sight of Dymt Volslav. Beside me, Kane sat with his arms and legs securely bound to a sturdy chair. I recognized the steel-reinforced nylon ties the Department used. He wouldn't be able to break out of them.

"Tie her." Volslav's voice didn't sound nearly as pleasant as it had in the sim.

Two guards yanked me out of my slump in the chair, binding my arms and legs to it and yanking the ties tight.

There were already empty ties around the arms of the chair, and they dug into my wrists as the guards strapped me down. Had somebody else occupied this chair recently? Who?

My heart hammered as I frantically scanned the luxurious surroundings. Harchman's guesthouse. So Holt would be in the same building, thank God.

Assuming Holt was still free; and assuming he knew enough to look for us here. I knew this wing of the guesthouse all too well. It was secluded and soundproofed, and for good reason.

"Who are you and what do you want?" I demanded. It

might have sounded a bit more impressive if my voice hadn't cracked.

"Oh, good. You're conscious." Volslav smiled. "So I won't need him anymore." He swung up his gun and shot Kane.

One to the head, one to the chest.

Nearly point-blank range.

Kane's body jerked with the impact of the bullets before going horribly limp.

My heart stopped. My breath stopped.

Blood and brain and fragments of scalp dripped from the wall behind him. A slow pool of blood expanded on the floor under his body in the futile trickle of death.

No heartbeat to force it out. Only the sluggish seepage of gravity, draining his blood away like lost hope.

Maybe I screamed.

I didn't know.

I couldn't think.

At last, I realized Volslav was talking. "Ms. Widdenback." Fingers snapped in front of my face. "Ms. Widdenback!"

My eyes focused slowly.

"Ah, there you are." A smile spread across the androgynous features above me and violent hatred flared where my heart had once been.

Holt might have heard the gunshots.

Give him time to get here.

I pitched my voice to a growl that I hoped would hide the magnitude of my devastation. "Like I said, who the hell are you, and what the hell do you want?"

"Oh, you're cute when you're mad," Volslav cooed. "I'm Dymt Volslav. But that doesn't matter, because I don't actually want anything from you. Except to watch you suffer." The gun flashed up and fired again, and my knee exploded.

I screamed and doubled over.

But it didn't hurt as much as I'd expected. Maybe it was my fear and fury and adrenaline.

Or maybe...

My brain caught up at last. The guesthouse rooms were soundproofed, but not well enough to hide gunshots. And it would be damn hard to get bloodstains out of these expensive furnishings.

I was in a sim.

As the thought occurred to me, Kane's body flickered out of existence for an instant, then solidified again.

I didn't try to hide my cry of distress.

He was really dead.

If he had only been faking, his avatar would have remained in place regardless of my expectations or beliefs.

Maybe he hadn't known it was a sim. Or maybe, like Holt, he hadn't had time to disbelieve. It had all happened so fast.

Oh, God.

He was really dead.

I realized I was keening with terror and loss.

"Pull her up." Volslav's voice was ice-cold.

One of the guards yanked my head back by the hair.

"You stupid bitch." Volslav shot out my other knee.

I screamed and struggled, realizing as I did that the first set of ties on the chair had been for my avatar. But before I had opened my eyes and seen the sim, the ties hadn't been part of my reality. They couldn't hold my avatar until I believed they could.

They couldn't hold me now.

I fought the raging need to leap up and slaughter Volslav.

But it wouldn't help to kill him and the guards inside the sim. My physical body was probably guarded by men who weren't in virtual reality. If Volslav dropped dead, they'd kill me in real life.

I'd have to let Volslav kill me in the sim before I could safely exit into reality. And then I'd only have moments to act before they realized I wasn't really dead.

"You think you're brave?" Volslav fired again, leaving my left hand a mangled mess.

Dammit, I had been thinking so hard I'd forgotten to fake pain. I screamed some more.

"You stupid bitch," Volslav repeated savagely. "You couldn't even hire a decent assassin."

He shot my right hand.

Even though I couldn't feel the physical suffering, the emotional pain of Kane's death was more than enough to keep me crying and screaming authentically. I let it all out, thrashing and shrieking and wailing the agony of my grief in a way I would never allow myself in real life.

Grinning, Volslav fired more shots.

Feet. The shots came faster.

Elbows.

Shoulders.

Volslav's finger blurred, and for a crazy instant I glimpsed pink talons.

The shots stopped.

Exhausted, I let my avatar hang from its blood-soaked bonds.

"Well, that's no fun," Volslav said matter-of-factly. "Pull her head up."

One of the guard complied, and Volslav fired directly into my face.

CHAPTER 52

Letting my avatar vanish, I dove through the portal, blessing Harchman's specially-designed network keys that caused me neither pain nor unconsciousness.

Flashing a lightning glance through slitted eyelids, I let my body fall limp. The comfortable armchair supported my flaccid body. Good. My feet were still under me. I could move fast when the time came.

Kane's lifeless body sprawled in an armchair beside me, and my heart tore all over again.

No time to grieve.

Where Dymt Volslav had stood, there was Tawny Harchman.

Her over-the-top clothes and grossly inflated lips and boobs were incongruous with the cold decisive voice that issued from her lips. "Put their snowshoes on the bodies and dump them down by the creek. By the time they're found, they'll be frozen solid." Her lips curled. "Tragic accident."

"I'll get the laundry cart," one of the guards volunteered, and left.

I held desperately still, my mind rocketing through possibilities. The other guard was out of my reach, and he was armed. I had no weapon and I didn't know martial arts. If I tried anything I'd be dead in a heartbeat.

My only hope was to wait for the laundry cart. When they picked me up to throw me in, their hands would be busy and their guns would be close.

I took tiny controlled sips of breath.

In.

Out.

Fortunately, Tawny paid no attention to the two corpses keeping her company. She pulled out a cell phone and dialled, leaned casually against the wall and examining her long pink fingernails as if worried that she might have chipped her nail polish with all the trigger-pulling.

When the call connected, she didn't waste any time on niceties. "Do it tonight," she snapped in Volslav's exotic accent.

Her eyebrows crinkled in the nearest thing to a scowl she could manage with all the botox in her forehead. "Yes, *tonight*, idiot! What the hell did you think I meant when I said 'be ready'? What the hell am I paying you for? If I need to come down there..."

She didn't complete the sentence, and the rising pitch of the unintelligible voice on the other end of the line made it clear that her presence was a threat her hapless minion wanted to avoid at all costs. She disconnected with a small vicious smile.

The sound of the door opening nearly made me twitch. I could barely control my muscles. My tiny breaths weren't enough.

Air. I needed...

Fortunately Tawny and the other guard glanced toward the door, and I sucked in a huge grateful breath.

Tawny returned her attention to her phone with a single keypress, then glanced up again to stare at my apparently dead body with blank disinterest.

I held my breath.

The guesthouse's giant laundry cart rolled in and the second guard closed the door discreetly behind him. He plopped an armful of sheets down on the floor beside me and reached for my feet.

"Remember to take the fobs off them," Tawny reminded them.

The second guard's fingernail gouged the back of my neck as he peeled off the small device. He did the same to Kane's body, then came back to grip my shoulders.

"On three," he said to the guard at my feet just as Tawny spoke into her phone.

"I'm done with him. Shoot him."

Arnie.

Every muscle in my body galvanized as I shrieked, "NO!"

The guard behind me hadn't even relinquished his hold on my shoulders before his gun was in my hand. I fired blindly at the second guard as I lunged to my feet. He fell as my gun snapped over to fire at Tawny, but in the instant of silence between my shots, I heard Arnie's death knell from down the hall.

Two shots.

One to the head. One to the chest.

"*NO!*" The scream tore my throat. "NO-NO-NO-NO!" My finger convulsed on the trigger with each cry, hammering Tawny's body against the wall and following her down.

The guard at my feet attempted a feeble kick to my legs and I turned the gun on him again. One to the head. One to the heart.

Time slowed.

I'd forgotten the guard behind me.

I spun, finger on the trigger. Guard already on the floor. Large man bearing down on me-

I nearly shot him.

Then his arms were around me.

"John!" I flung my arms around him in turn. "*Omigod-I-thought-you-were-dead...*" My words dissolved into disjointed nonsense between sobbing gasps.

He was murmuring nonsense, too, his face pressed into my neck, the strength of his hug nearly crushing me. "Thank God, Aydan, thank God..."

We both drew a breath, pulling apart to stare at each other with anguished eyes.

"Arnie," I whispered and spun to run for the door.

"Wait!" Kane's hand clamped onto my shoulder. "You've only got one left in the magazine." He pulled me over to a polished sideboard where our weapons, gear, and outerwear were piled in a careless heap.

I flung down the guard's gun and grabbed my Glock.

Too little, too late.

But maybe Arnie was still clinging to life.

I tried to run for the door, but Kane's grip restrained me. "Stay focused," he hissed.

I sucked in a hard breath and let it out as slowly as I could, summoning the tactical skills I'd worked so hard to develop. "Okay." Another breath. "Okay."

We approached the door together. Kane raised his gun and jerked his chin toward the doorknob. I gripped it and met his eyes, nodding 'One-two-three'.

I yanked the door open and Kane surged through with the powerful fluid movements that bespoke a lifetime of combat experience. I followed, pivoting as a movement caught my eye.

Snatching my finger off the trigger, I let out a breath and lowered my weapon as Holt did the same.

"Tac team's incoming," he rapped out. "Helicopters should be here in-"

The powerful thudding of helicopter blades interrupted him and an amplified voice echoed through the building. "*Police! Lay down your weapons. Lie on the ground with your hands outspread. Police! Lay down your weapons...*"

"They shot Arnie, come on!" I yelled at Holt, and ran in the direction of the shots.

Holt and Kane pounded down the hall on either side of me, weapons at the ready.

When a guard popped out of a room ahead of us, his gun had barely twitched up before our three bullets struck the centre of his body mass, pitching him backward.

We didn't even slow as we bounded through the door. Me first, crouching and sidestepping to make room for the other two.

The second guard never had a chance. He was grabbing for his gun when our bullets mowed him down.

But we were too late.

The blood and tissue spattered on the wall and the slowly-widening red pool told the horrible story.

We straightened slowly from our crouched positions. The cottony deafness of close-range gunshots muffled my ears, pulsing in slow waves. The police loudspeaker was a distant buzz.

Kane came to me and I gripped his hand hard.

We moved together toward the sofa that hid the body.

CHAPTER 53

Kane and I shared a single agonized glance.

I braced myself for a sight that would haunt me forever, and we rounded the corner. My knees gave way at the sight of the bullet-ravaged face and body. Kane's strong arms were the only thing holding me up.

I tried to speak, but my voice wouldn't work.

My head was floating away.

I tried again. "Lawrence... Harchman...? Wh... what...?"

All my strength returned in a giant surge of renewed terror. *"Where's Arnie?"*

Hope flooded into Holt's face as he bounded forward. "It's not him?"

"No!" I wasn't sure whether I was laughing or crying. "Tawny said..." I couldn't catch my breath. "...she was... done with him... I thought... thank God..." I shook myself back to coherence. "We have to find Arnie!"

"The tac team will find him," Holt countered. "We need to stay put so we don't get accidentally shot."

I suddenly realized that sporadic bursts of gunfire were erupting outside. "But the innocent guards..." I protested.

"If they're innocent, they've laid down their weapons and they won't get hurt," Kane assured me.

Holt was talking rapidly into his headset. "...corrupt

guards are using radio frequency 5.41, so watch out for them. We're in the guesthouse, room..." He strode over to the door and cracked it open to peek at the number. "...fourteen. We'll stay here unless-"

"We have to find Arnie!" I interrupted. "They had him! They were torturing him!"

"Where?" Kane demanded.

"I don't know, I saw it in the-" Realization struck me. I could find out. I blurted, *"Be-right-back"* and dove into virtual reality.

There was only one active sim. Remembering at the last instant to turn invisible, I shot through the virtual wall.

Clamping my hand over my mouth, I managed not to scream or vomit. Arnie was unrecognizable. His blood-soaked body sagged in its bonds, his only movement caused by the brutal blows that still rained down on his inert form. The sim flickered and wavered, as though it was fading along with Arnie's life.

Instinct drove me at his nearest attacker, but somehow I managed to stop myself. Arnie couldn't survive much longer in the sim, but he'd die for sure if I gave away my presence.

I flung a frantic glance around the sim. None of the luxury of the guesthouse. The interior was painted cinderblocks, the furniture utilitarian. Where could it be?

Oh God, how far away was he?

I backed out of the sim, desperately racking my brain. How could I-

"Cameras!" I hissed, and flew down the virtual corridor. Blinking into invisibility, I tunnelled into the security server.

The surveillance camera feeds poured over me in a flood of moving images as I swam backward through the timestamps.

Back to one AM.

Forward.

Most of the cameras showed only empty corridors and night-still pathways. I surfed through the deluge of data, alert for any movement.

At last I found it, timestamped one fifty-five. Arnie had managed to evade the guards for nearly an hour, and they were clearly taking no chances. He was being marched along the path, hands bound behind him, surrounded by four guards.

Walking. They hadn't shot him, thank God.

But where had they taken him?

A moment of camera footage later, I knew.

I blasted back to the portal and sprang through.

When I jerked up to sitting position, Holt sprang back. "Christ, it's like the dead coming back to life!"

"I know where he is," I gasped. "Come on, we have to go right now! They're still torturing him and he can't last much longer!"

"Wait, let me clear it with-"

Holt's voice faded behind me as I lunged to my feet and ran for the door.

As I burst out of the guesthouse, one of the tac team members spun to face me. His automatic weapon jerked up, only to drop as Holt yelled a warning.

Kane sprinted hot on my heels and Holt brought up the rear, shouting, "Kelly! Fuck! *Stop!*"

I kept running, and he apparently decided to use his breath for more useful things like informing the tac team that we were coming through. His shouted commands faded into insignificance as I poured all my strength into running.

My boots pounded the flagged walking path, which was

mercifully clear of snow and ice. Down the hill, past the ostentatious gazebo that Harchman would never enjoy again.

Then we were running on the snowy path the guards patrolled, my gasps for breath louder than my footsteps. I tasted iron and my vision blurred. My legs were too heavy but I forced them faster.

Almost there.

A cinderblock guard building came into view and I redoubled my efforts. Kane and Holt kept up with me, both panting but still controlling their breathing.

Thank God. I might not make it.

The door to the building stood open.

I skidded to a halt a few yards away, chest heaving, gun bobbing uselessly in my weakened grip.

Holt threw Kane a look and received a nod in return. Kane spun and gave me a forceful hand signal. Stay here.

They ducked through the open door, crouching with guns at the ready. My legs gave way and I sprawled belly-down, training my Glock on the doorway with my elbows braced on the ground. The gun still shook with the wild hammering of my heart and the cold of the snowy pathway bit through my sweater.

Moments later Kane emerged, giving me a headshake and a frown.

"Wha...?" I struggled to my feet and hurried over on shaking legs.

"Nobody," Kane said.

Impossible.

I shoved past him. Past Holt, who was staring around the empty room.

"*NO!*" My desperate scream made Holt recoil a pace. "*WHERE IS HE?*"

Kane's gentle hand landed on my shoulder. "Aydan, calm down. Is this where you saw him last?"

"Yes." My voice was a bare whisper, my chest a burning void. "They must have moved him. Oh, God." Without much hope, I sought virtual reality again.

And found it. Faint, but there.

The sim was still active. I didn't look in.

Once again, the security servers swallowed me.

CHAPTER 54

"I know where he is, come on!" I lurched up from the concrete floor and ran for the door.

The trail in the snow began only a dozen yards past the guardhouse. Heart in my mouth, I read the sickening story in the two widely-spaced sets of footprints with a heavy drag mark between them.

My quivering legs could barely plod through the deep snow, and Kane and Holt quickly outpaced me. Without my night-vision headset, the faint moonlight rendered the snowy woods in gray and black, and the two dark forms ahead of me faded to invisibility.

The rapid crunch of their footsteps carried back to me as I forced my legs to rise and fall. Step. Step.

"Found him!" Kane's voice rang out, and I gasped a fearful breath. He sounded grim.

Oh no...

I hurried forward, every ounce of my attention focused on the approaching sounds of footsteps and exertion.

Oh, God, please let him still be alive.

Please, please...

A dark blob coalesced ahead of me, slowly separating into two men dragging a heavy burden.

"Arnie!" I plowed through the snow, throwing myself at

his motionless body. His face was ice-cold under my searching hands. "Arnie!" I sobbed his name, groping frantically under his collar.

"Aydan, stop." Kane's voice was gentle but urgent. "We have to get him to-"

"Got it!" I hooked a fingernail under the tiny adhesive patch on the back of his neck and pulled it off.

He stirred and mumbled.

"Arnie!" I patted his cheeks, then pressed my lips against his icy ones. "Come back, Arnie. It's over. You're safe."

"Darl'n?" he slurred. "'Zat you?"

"It's me. You're safe. It's over."

"'Kay, good." He went limp.

"Oh, no, you fucking don't!" I seized the front of his jacket and shook him with all my strength. "Arnie! Wake the fuck up!" Glancing up at Kane and Holt, I snapped, "Keep going! Arnie, *walk!*"

They dragged him forward, and he stumbled between them. Walking backward in front of him, I patted his cheeks firmly. "Arnie, you have to stay awake. Talk to me."

For a moment his head came up. "'Kay. Talkin'." His head drooped again.

"No, keep talking." I patted his cheeks again. "Tell me about... um..." What would get him talking? "Kathy. Is she settling in at your place okay?"

"Mmhm."

"No, you have to talk. What does she do all day?"

"Cook'n."

"What else, Arnie? What does she do?"

"Cleans."

"What else?"

"'Pol'gizes."

"That bothers you, right?"

"Yeah."

I shot a desperate glance at Kane, but couldn't make out his expression in the dimness. Surely we had to be almost back to the path.

"Come on, Arnie," I encouraged. "Tell me more about Kathy."

"Sings." His lolling head rose a fraction. "Great voice. Shy."

"You mean she's shy about singing?"

His head drooped again and he didn't respond.

"Arnie, talk to me. Tell me more about Kathy's singing."

Silence. He wasn't even trying to walk anymore. His entire weight was suspended by his arms over Holt's and Kane's shoulders, his boots dragging loosely in the snow.

"Get his feet," Holt grunted.

I obeyed, straining to hold the weight with the last of my strength.

At last we stumbled back onto the path. Minutes later we were in the guardhouse with the door closed and the heat turned to maximum.

We heaved Arnie's inert body onto a bunk. "Strip him," Holt snapped. "I'll find blankets and a medic."

Kane and I attacked Arnie's cold-stiffened clothes. "He needs body heat," Kane said. "And he'd probably rather have you cuddled up to him instead of me."

I nodded and stripped to my underwear, dropping my sweat-soaked clothes where they fell. When I lay down beside Arnie and took him in my arms, his frigid skin seared mine.

Holt came bearing more blankets, then left to find the

medic. Kane piled the blankets on top of us, even bundling one around our heads.

I wrapped my legs around Arnie's icy ones, running my hands up and down his cold back.

"John?" I asked from under the blankets.

"I'm here."

"What happened?"

He sighed, and a creak indicated he was sinking into a chair. "I don't know what happened to Arnie. He cut communication as soon as he realized he didn't have a good drop zone. He probably threw away his headset before he landed so they'd think he was alone. I don't know whether they caught him right away or not."

"No, it took them nearly an hour." I shook Arnie gently. "Arnie, tell me what happened when you landed."

His only reply was an unintelligible mumble.

"Arnie!" I shook him harder. "Talk to me! Don't go to sleep!"

"Not sleep'n."

"Good. Tell me what happened when you landed."

"Dogs. Trank." He fell silent again.

"That makes sense," Kane said. "I heard men shouting and dogs barking. He must have tranked the guards as soon as he was in range above them. That would have bought him time to get out of the drop zone. Then he must have drawn the guards in the opposite direction, because it was nearly an hour and a half before they found you and me."

"And that's when you signalled me?"

"Yes. You passed out, and I tried to carry you but the dogs caught me. I told the guards we'd been snowshoeing on the other side of the creek but you'd gotten hypothermia and lost consciousness and I was trying to get you to safety. They took us up to the guesthouse, and I actually thought we might get away with our little charade."

I shifted position, rolling my chilled side away from Arnie and pressed my warmer side against him.

"What's taking that medic?" I demanded.

"Holt will bring him as soon as he's available. There was a gunshot wound that was higher priority."

I hugged Arnie closer. "Arnie. Talk to me."

"Talk'n."

"How are you feeling?"

"'Kay." The word was a slurred mumble, so I didn't give it much credence.

"When did things go bad at the guesthouse?" I asked Kane.

"Almost immediately. Tawny and Harchman were both there. It sounded as though she'd persuaded him to go down to the guesthouse after the guards caught Arnie."

Enlightenment hit. "So that's what she meant. That's why... fuck, I just figured it out!"

"Explain," Kane demanded.

"I found sims of Harchman hiring Margaret Young; and the hitman; and introducing Volslav to the Cayman banker. I couldn't figure out why Harchman would do any of that in a sim, and then not delete the evidence. But I bet it wasn't him at all. Tawny must have created a construct of him so Dymt Volslav could open a bank account in the Caymans, because Volslav only exists in virtual reality..." I trailed off, letting all the pieces fall into place before I went on, "And Tawny wanted to get rid of Harchman. If the hitman killed me, she'd call the police and show them the sim videos of Harchman hiring the hitman. Harchman would get arrested for conspiracy to murder. But if badass Arlene Widdenback caught the hitman instead, and made him tell who had hired him-"

"Which was pretty well a sure thing, considering what an amateur he was," Kane put in.

"Right, that explains why she hired such an idiot. Tawny expected the hitman to fail, and she expected me to kill Harchman for revenge. No wonder she was so mad. She thought Arnie was there to kill her husband, and he'd screwed up the hit."

Kane groaned. "Of course. She was expecting an assassin. That's why the guards were on the alert, and probably why she convinced Harchman to go to the guesthouse. To make him an easier target."

I snorted. "And to keep his blood off all that expensive furniture in their house."

A shiver shook Arnie. Had I imagined it?

"Sh'took me t'see'm," he mumbled.

"What, Arnie? She took you to see Harchman?"

"Mmhm." He shivered again.

"He's shivering!" I cried jubilantly.

"Good," Kane said. "I have hot coffee here as soon as he's alert enough to drink it."

"I bet she planned to make a sim of Arnie killing Harchman, and pretend it was a security video," I said. "That's why she needed camera footage of Arnie and Harchman face to face. So she could fill in the murder later."

"Sent cops 'way," Arnie said. "Train'n ex'cise."

"That makes sense," Kane said. "When the innocent guards caught an intruder, they would call the police right away. But Tawny needed to pin Harchman's murder on an assassin, so she had her own guards pretend it was just a training exercise. That kept the police away, and later she could have pretended that the guards had accidentally allowed in a professional assassin instead of the trainer they were expecting." He let out a humorless chuckle. "And then she got a chance to kill her competition in the same evening. She must have been thrilled."

"I thought she *had* killed her competition." I shuddered. "How did you survive? When your body flickered in the sim, I thought for sure you were dead."

Arnie was shivering in earnest now. I hugged him tighter, my heart lifting when his arms came around me in return.

"I messed up," Kane admitted. "I knew right away I was in a sim because the chairs didn't match the ones in the guesthouse. I made myself invisible and floated up to the ceiling while imagining a construct of myself in the chair." A rueful note tinged his voice as he went on, "At least, I thought that's what I'd done. After Tawny shot the construct, I realized it was only her expectations and yours that were maintaining it. When you both stopped believing I was alive, the construct disappeared for an instant before I could imagine it back. I was just hoping you knew you were in a sim. When she was shooting you and you were screaming like that, I thought..." His voice faded into a gulp.

"Sorry," I said. "I knew it was a sim, but I couldn't tell you."

"F-fuckin' sims," Arnie muttered, shivering violently. "M-mind-f-fuck."

"Can you drink some coffee now, if we help you sit up?" I asked.

"Y-yeah."

Kane unwrapped the blanket from our heads, and we got Arnie's shoulders propped up.

"I'll pour. You drink," Kane said as Arnie tried to reach for the coffee cup. "Keep your arms under the blankets."

"S-so d-did ya f-find-" Arnie broke off to swallow a gulp of coffee. "...F-fuck, too sweet."

"You need the sugar," Kane said firmly. "Here." He held the cup to Arnie's lips again.

Arnie swallowed another mouthful, shuddered, and finished, "F-find what ya w-were lookin' f-for?"

My heart sank. "No. I don't even know whether Tawny was the head of the Volslav or just upper management. I didn't find any records at all."

"Oh." Kane's shoulders drooped. "So we don't know how many ultrasound weapons there are, where they're stored, where they were manufactured or by whom, whether they've sold any on the open market, who else was involved, the extent of Volslav's operations, why Volslav paid you twenty million dollars-"

"Stop," I interrupted. "You're just depressing me."

"I hate to say it, but here's an even more depressing thought," Kane said soberly. "Before she shot you, Tawny... Volslav... said 'you couldn't even hire a decent assassin'. When he hears that, Dermott will probably think Volslav paid you that twenty million to do his... her... dirty work."

I groaned. "Don't want to think about it."

Kane switched topics, turning to Hellhound. "Your sim was still active when we found you, so the men who were torturing you must still be hiding somewhere. Do have any idea where?"

To my surprise, Arnie emitted a rusty chuckle. "F-fuck me."

"Maybe after you've warmed up a bit," I teased.

He grinned. "Th-that'd warm m-me up."

"So will this." Kane held the cup to his lips, and added, "So, I'm assuming that wasn't meant as an invitation?"

Arnie shook his head and swallowed his mouthful. "N-Nah, I just f-figured it out. Th-those guys were whalin' on m-me earlier an' I f-figured it was a f-fuckin' sim." He squeezed my hand under the blanket. "An' then Aydan c-came an' whispered in m-my ear so I knew. B-but they didn't have any r-reason to keep b-beatin' on me. They n-never asked me anythin'. I b-bet I k-kept the fuckin' sim alive m-myself. I b-bet they chucked m-me in a snowbank an' f-fucked off long ago, an' I j-just kept b-believin'.'"

I let my head fall against his shoulder. "Shit. That explains why everything was flickering and fading. You were the only person keeping the sim going, but you were passing out from hypothermia."

The door opened and Holt and the medic rushed in on a gust of icy air. They slowed at the sight of Hellhound sitting up.

The medic's strained and blood-spattered face relaxed. "I see he's conscious. Is he oriented to time and place?"

"Yes," Kane assured him. "He started shivering about ten minutes ago, and now he's not shivering quite so hard. We've been giving him hot sugary coffee."

"Good."

After a cursory examination, the medic pronounced Arnie out of danger and departed hurriedly. I sent up a hope that all his other patients had equally good outcomes.

Holt eyed me eagerly. "So? What did you get?"

When I didn't answer immediately, the light went out of his eyes.

"I found a couple of sims that proved Tawny was framing Harchman so she could get her hands on his money," I offered without much enthusiasm. "And one that proved Tawny was playing Dymt Volslav in virtual reality."

"And?" Holt demanded.

I sighed. "And nothing. That's it. That's all I found."

His face hardened. "And now that's all *we'll* find, because you've got twenty million reasons to make sure Volslav's ass is covered."

Kane's brows snapped together and he opened his mouth for what was likely to be an angry retort, but I silenced him with a weary gesture.

"No, that's all we'll find because that's all there was. And the lie detector will prove it."

Holt's jaw hardened. "Well, good. Because you're getting on a helicopter to Silverside, right fucking now." He jerked his chin at Kane and Hellhound. "You, too. Get dressed. Your ride's waiting."

Kane began, "But our vehicles are at Spr-"

"Tough. Move it."

CHAPTER 55

I huddled miserably in the centre seat of the helicopter, shivering in my sweat-clammy clothes despite the outerwear I'd retrieved from the guesthouse before boarding. Kane and Hellhound sat on either side of me. In front, two heavily-armed members of the tactical team kept a watchful eye on us. A third occupied the side-facing seat behind us. They had relieved us of our weapons, and the empty holsters at my ankles felt cold and exposed.

Fatigue and despair dragged my shoulders into a slump. So many reasons for Dermott to bury me. Any one of them would have been enough. Together?

"I'm so fucked," I muttered.

Nobody heard me over the noise of the rotors, and I shrank into myself and tucked my chin to my chest. When I closed my eyes, nightmare memories flashed in my mind.

Half-dreaming, I dozed and woke with violent twitches and cries of terror. Kane and Hellhound patiently soothed me, and each time I resolved to stay awake only to drop into the clutches of my next nightmare.

Volslav's grinning face hovered in front of me, his gun firing again and again.

Tawny's bullet-ridden body slid down the wall, leaving crimson streaks...

I bolted upright with a cry and our guards twitched their weapons up.

"I've got it!" Excitement electrified my blood. "I know where Volslav's records are!"

"Settle down, darlin', you're freakin' the guards out," Hellhound said gently.

"I need to talk to Holt!" I turned to the guard. "Can you get him on the radio? It's an emergency."

"Our instructions are to take you to-"

"Yeah, fine, but I have to talk to Holt right away!" When he hesitated, I added, "Look, it's not a secret! I can yell into your phone if you hold it two feet away, but I really have to talk to Holt right now! It's a matter of national security!"

That was an exaggeration, but it tipped the balance in my favour.

A few moments later, Holt's voice came through the speaker. "Holt."

"It's Aydan. Is Tawny's body still there?"

"Not your concern. You're off the investigation."

"Fine, but you need to get to that body and check her necklace. I bet it's got a flash drive in it!"

"You *bet?*" Skepticism dripped from Holt's voice.

"I bet you a bottle of your super-expensive single-malt scotch."

"You can't afford that bet. It's three hundred bucks a bottle." But he sounded as though he was considering it.

"*You* can't afford this bet," I countered. "Because I know I'm right."

"I'll check." He disconnected.

"What makes you think it's in her necklace?" Kane asked.

"I was just running everything through my mind." In a nightmare, but I didn't bother to mention that. "You know how fancy and expensive Tawny's clothes are, and she always wears... wore... tons of big blingy rings and jewellery."

Kane nodded, and I went on, "She always wore that necklace along with her other necklaces, but it's so understated I didn't really notice it before. Volslav was wearing the same necklace in the sim. That clean unisex design worked with his European look so it didn't occur to me until just now, but the necklace was the only thing that was the same between Tawny and Volslav. If I was going to carry top-secret data around, I'd make sure it never left my body. I bet Tawny was so used to always wearing that necklace that she didn't even realize she'd recreated it on Volslav in the sim."

"That makes sense," Kane said. "I hope you're right."

I hunched into myself again, and let the rotor noise swallow my words. "Me, too."

At Sirius, only Kane and Hellhound were diverted down to the secured area. I did my best to mask my surprise and increasing nervousness.

I had expected to be chucked in a cell and abandoned. After all, it was four in the morning. Dermott never came in before nine.

As I stood stiffly in the lobby waiting for my guards to finish at the security wicket, I crossed my fingers for luck and sent a brief prayer skyward just to make sure I'd covered all the bases between superstition and religion.

Please, let Stemp be back in time to do my lie detector interview.

He would be fair. I still might not be able to conceal that I knew Hellhound had killed Fitzgerald, but at least I'd have a chance.

The thought of that interview shortened my breath and made my already-quivering knees weaken.

"Come on." The guard's gruff voice made me twitch.

Plodding between them up the stairs, my heart sank lower and lower. Only one thing awaited upstairs.

Dermott's office.

Or maybe...

Hope dawned. Maybe Stemp was already back. Unlike Dermott, he would be alert and involved no matter what time it was. Maybe that's why I was being ushered upstairs at such an ungodly hour.

As we rounded the corner, my heart sank. Stemp's office was dark, the door closed. Down the hall, light poured out of Dermott's office.

I drew in a long breath and let it out slowly. Okay. Dermott wanted to debrief. But he couldn't do anything without the lie detector. There was still time for Stemp to come back and rescue me.

When we entered, Dermott looked up from his computer. His usually-florid complexion was paled by fatigue and his bloodshot eyes suggested he'd been here all night.

Great. A tired, pissed-off Dermott. So much more reasonable than a well-rested Dermott.

He jerked his chin toward the chair across from him. "Sit." Transferring his scowl to the guards, he added, "Wait outside."

Deciding that the best defence was a good offence, I waited until the door closed and asked, "Did Holt find a flash drive in Tawny's necklace?"

"Yeah." Dermott's scornful glance shrivelled my hope.

"Guess you had to report that, didn't you? You knew we'd find it anyway."

Biting back the urge to snap at him, I asked, "What was on it?"

"Wouldn't you like to know?" He gave me a nasty smile.

"Yeah. I'd like to know." I stared him in the eye.

His smile widened. "Well, thanks to you, we now know about your deal with Volslav."

Somehow I managed not to sink my head into my hands. "I don't have any deals with Volslav."

"Except that twenty million," he taunted. "And now I know why you didn't mind reporting it. You knew we'd seize it, but the other twenty million would be yours to keep."

"What other twenty million?" I demanded. "I keep telling you, I have no idea why Volslav created that account for me and deposited the money!"

"Oh, so that's not your signature on the bill of sale transferring the building and equipment of Sirius Dynamics to Volslav? With twenty million as a deposit and the other half payable on title transfer?"

I gaped at him.

Grinning, he went on, "Funny, our handwriting analysis says it's an exact match to your signature. No wonder you've got that high-powered lawyer working on transferring Sirius to you. You were going to make out like a bandit."

After a moment of stunned silence, I found my voice. "I have no idea what you're talking about."

"We'll see about that." He picked up the phone. "Bring the lie detector." He disconnected.

My stab of fear must have transmitted itself to my expression.

Dermott leaned back in his chair, smirking. "You

weren't expecting that, were you? You figured your buddy Stemp would be back in time to fake your interview and let you off the hook. Well, guess what, bitch? That's not going to happen. The lie detector came back a couple of hours ago, and we're doing your interview right here, right now. By the time Stemp gets back, you'll be buried so deep you'll never see the light of day again."

CHAPTER 56

I tried to squelch my terror while the tech fastened the lie detector's crown of electrodes to my forehead. If only Jack had been here, at least I wouldn't feel quite so alone and exposed.

But she would be fast asleep right now, unaware that her invention was about to send me to prison for the rest of my life.

The tech left and Dermott eyed the console, looking smug.

"All right, let's start with the basics. Is your name Aydan Kelly?"

My heart thumped.

"Yes."

Green light. True.

"Do you also go by Arlene Widdenback?"

"Yes."

The red light flashed. Lie.

Adrenaline surged into my veins. Had he rigged the lie detector to give false readings?

Dermott directed a puzzled frown at the machine.

Okay, maybe he hadn't been expecting that, either.

"It's a cover identity," I suggested, wishing my voice didn't sound so weak. "I don't really go by it. Maybe you could phrase the question differently?"

"Okay. Do you use the name Arlene Widdenback as a cover identity?"

"Yes."

This time the green light flashed.

Dermott relaxed and swooped in for the kill. "Did you know Volslav had transferred twenty million dollars into your bank account?"

That was an easy one. "No."

The yellow light flashed. Invalid pairing. The machine was as confused as I was.

I stared at it, paralyzed. Dermott had messed with it somehow. He was railroading me.

But he didn't look as triumphant as I'd expected. His brows drew together, and he rephrased the question.

"Did you know in advance that Volslav was going to transfer twenty million dollars into a bank account in your name?"

"N-no."

This time the light flashed green. I eased out the breath I'd been holding. Dermott's frown deepened.

"Did you sign a bill of sale or any other contract with Volslav?"

"No."

Green light.

"What the fuck?" Dermott demanded. "Your signature is an exact match on that bill of sale!"

Somehow I managed to keep my voice steady. "That probably proves it's a fake. You know as well as I do that if you write your own signature ten times, it'll be a tiny bit different each time."

He scowled and fired the next question at me. "Did you

sign a bill of sale or any other contract with either or both of the Harchmans?"

"No."

The green light shone again, and I dared to relax just a fraction.

"Did you ever make any kind of unwritten agreement or deal with Volslav or either or both of the Harchmans?"

"Um... yeah, Arlene Widdenback had that deal with Lawrence Harchman for half the proceeds from the porn videos."

Dermott smirked. "Right, I'd forgotten about that. Other than your porn-movie deal, did you ever make any kind of agreement or deal with Volslav or either or both of the Harchmans?"

"No."

The green light blessed my answer.

Dermott asked several other questions in the same vein with different phrasing, but each time the green light saved me.

"Okay," he said, sounding disappointed. "Did you make or send the bomb that killed Bill Harks?

"No."

"Did you have it made or sent?"

"No."

"Did you know it was going to be sent?"

"No."

"Did you know or had you met Rufus Zimm before we captured him?"

"No."

Green lights all the way.

After another spate of questions that made it clear I was innocent of any wrongdoing with Volslav, the Harchmans, or

Zimm, Dermott eyed me without expression for a few moments.

Then he picked up some papers from his desk. "Okay, we'll do your requalification interview."

As we worked our way through the standardized questions, cautious hope wormed into my heart.

Maybe I'd misjudged Dermott. Maybe he really was trying to act in the best interests of the Department. After all, an agent with a security clearance as high as mine was a huge risk. If Dermott truly believed Stemp was playing fast and loose with regulations and giving me special privileges, I could see why he'd be eager to nail both of us.

And he still had ample opportunities to nail me. Even if I could edge around the moral and legal ambiguity of not reporting Arnie's murder confession, I had no leg to stand on when it came to my investigation of Eddy's and Pearl's cases. As transgressions went, it wasn't quite as damning, but it would be equally dangerous to my freedom. If my interference in my friends' cases proved that the Department couldn't trust me...

"Did you know Arnold Helmand was going to kill Richard Fitzgerald?"

"No," I replied absently, then sucked in a breath. "Wait, hang on! I'm not answering any questions that aren't related to my requalification!"

"You just did." Dermott gave me a smug smile, obviously proud that he'd used the rhythm of the standard questions to disarm me before he threw in a big one.

Luckily he'd phrased the question just right. I *hadn't* known in advance what Arnie was going to do.

Hiding my quivering insides with hard tone, I shot a pointed glance at the glowing green light. "Okay, so you've got your answer. And unless you have more questions that are actually sanctioned by the Department, we're done here. You know better than to ask mission-specific questions."

"That wasn't a mission." His eyes narrowed. "You were relieved of duty at the time. Technically a civilian. I can ask anything I want."

I scowled back. "You can ask, but I don't have to answer."

His vicious smile was back. "Okay, so here's a Department-sanctioned question: Have you done anything to violate your oath as an agent? Like, say, hiding evidence of a murder?"

"No," I snapped. I hadn't hidden evidence.

The green light shone and Dermott's brows drew down. "Okay, I'll rephrase that. Have you done anything to violate your oath as an agent?"

The standard question.

The one I'd been dreading.

Eddy's voice echoed in my mind. *'My lawyer made sure I knew it's not illegal to just not talk to the police.'*

But technically, I *was* the police. It was my duty as an agent to report that confession.

"What's the matter?" Dermott taunted. "Cat got your tongue?" His voice went hard. "Answer the question. Have you done anything to violate your oath as an agent?"

My shoulders slumped. I was opening my mouth to admit the truth when Dermott's own words came back to me. I'd been relieved of duty. Technically a civilian.

And it wasn't illegal to just not talk to the police.

"No," I said with far more confidence than I felt.

The green light shone, and Dermott's jaw dropped. "Bullshit! I know, Holt knows, and *you* know damn well that your fucking boyfriend killed Richard Fitzgerald in cold blood!" Red suffused his cheeks as his fist clenched. "And you know damn well that it's your duty as an agent to report something like that! Don't you?"

"Yes."

The green light shone again, and his eyes narrowed. "Oh, you tricky bitch. I see the loophole. The standard question says 'your oath as an agent', but you were technically a fucking civilian." Dermott lunged to his feet to loom menacingly over me. "So answer me this," he ground out between clenched teeth. "Do you damn well know that your fucking boyfriend killed Richard Fitzgerald?"

"I'm not going to answer that," I said, but despair chilled my heart. Refusing to answer a question was an automatic fail.

All signs of temper gone, Dermott gave me a cocky smirk and sank back into his chair, linking his hands behind his head. "Go ahead and refuse to answer," he said happily. "I'll ask you the same damn thing in front of a tribunal. And you can refuse to answer or answer and fail, but either way you're going to prison." He leaned in. "Come on, bitch, make my day. Just give me a nice little red light. Do you know that your boyfriend killed Richard Fitzgerald?"

I clenched my fists, trying to prevent myself from lunging over the desk and punching him right in his self-satisfied grin.

And the lightweight band around my ring finger squeezed gently.

"No," I said calmly.

My boyfriend hadn't killed Richard Fitzgerald.

My husband had.

Dermott gaped at the green light.

I added, "And before you decide I'm exploiting a loophole, I'll give you this statement, too: Arnold Helmand has been my boyfriend for the past year and half."

"Is that true?" Dermott asked in a deflated tone.

"Yes."

Green light.

His eyes narrowed. "Kane's your boyfriend, too."

"Yes."

Green light.

We eyed each other in silence.

"So as far as you know, neither of your boyfriends killed Fitzgerald," he persisted. "Is that true?"

"Yes."

Green light.

"Fuck. So you really don't know who killed Fitzgerald," he said heavily, but it didn't sound like an official question. Fortunately.

"How the hell would I know?" I demanded, hiding my fear in indignation. "Fitzgerald was a crime lord, a pedophile, a rapist, and a murderer. Lots of people probably wanted to kill him, and I have no way of knowing who did. I was in a hotel six hundred kilometres away when it happened. You've asked your questions a bunch of different ways, and my answer's not going to change."

I almost added, "So can we move on?" but I pressed my lips together instead. Don't look too eager.

For a long moment, Dermott scowled at me in silence. Then his frown eased as though a new and pleasant thought had struck him.

"Okay," he said. "Let's move on. Did you use Department resources to investigate criminal cases involving your friends, even though there was no connection to any active Departmental investigations?"

My heart plummeted so fast and hard that the thump sounded in my ears and my chair quivered.

Dermott sprang to his feet. "What the fuck was that?"

An instant later the security alarm blared.

Okay, so maybe that thump hadn't been my heart.

As the security alarms continued to shrill, I quivered on the edge of my chair. I should be running to see what was happening.

But I was unarmed. And Dermott would probably take a dim view of me fleeing just when the questions got dicey.

Well, dicier.

One of the guards stuck his head in the door, radio in hand. "Breach in the east tunnel!"

Dermott made a violent 'scram' gesture. "Help them contain it! Go, go!"

The two guards ran.

As their pounding footsteps receded, Dermott drew his weapon and pointed it at me. "If this is your doing..."

"It's not!"

Dermott blinked, then apparently remembered I was hooked up to a lie detector. "Is this your doing?"

"No!"

His next words hammered out at the speed of a machine gun. "If I give back your weapon, will you help contain the breach and come back here and finish your interview right afterward without harming me or anybody else from the Department?"

"Yes!"

He barely glanced at the green light. "Come on!" He ran for the door.

I yanked off the band of electrodes and grabbed my

Glock from his desk. My exhausted muscles rebelled, but I forced my legs into a run despite the pain and leaden weakness.

Arnie and John were below in the secured area.

And something had just exploded down there.

CHAPTER 57

The clamour of the security alarms punished my eardrums as I dashed out of Dermott's office. I instinctively turned for the stairs, but Dermott's shout made me spin in the opposite direction.

"Here!" Standing in the doorway of the electrical room, he braced the door open with his foot and beckoned. "Hurry up!"

What the...?

I shook off my confusion and ran over. As he grabbed my arm and jerked me inside the tiny room, my adrenaline spilled over into paranoia. Was he going to attack me in here?

Snatching a key on a chain from under his shirt, he unlocked one of the electrical panels and flipped a couple of breakers. Another panel swung open and he slapped his palm on the hand-shaped outline on a pad while leaning in for a retinal scan.

A beep sounded, but nothing else happened.

Dermott stepped back, grabbing my arm again to yank me forward. "Now you! It needs a director and an agent!"

I laid my hand on the panel and leaned close. Another beep sounded, and suddenly my stomach was floating up near my throat.

"High-speed elevator," Dermott explained as I grabbed for a handhold. "Comes out beside the Weapons Lab."

The elevator halted and my tired legs nearly buckled under the G-force.

I reached for the door handle, but Dermott threw an arm in front of me. "Wait." Unlocking another panel, he revealed a flat screen. A flick of the switch displayed multiple closed-circuit camera views.

Dust and rubble and the milling bodies of the tac team indicated the location of the breach, but the corridor outside our hideout appeared safe enough.

Dermott slapped the panels shut. "Release Kane and Hellhound and get them out through the time delay. Arm them and coordinate with security in the main lobby." He flung open the door and we ran in opposite directions, me toward the holding cells and him toward the gunshots and sounds of battle.

At each corner I skidded to a halt with my Glock at the ready, checking my routes ahead and behind. The corridors were deserted, but my blood pressure was nearing critical by the time I made it to the holding cells.

Kane and Hellhound were both pressed against the transparent barriers of their cell doors, tension in every line of their bodies.

Kane barked, "What's happening?"

"Somebody blew open the tunnel east of the Weapons Lab," I panted as I leaned in for the retinal scan, sending a silent thank-you to Command for updating security from the original numeric keypads. "Dermott wants you out and armed."

In seconds they were both free, and we ran for the stairwell. The suspense at each corner was worsened by the knowledge that I had to protect my unarmed companions.

Glock in trembling hand, I peeked around each corner, then herded them ahead of me, only to race past them again for the next corner.

When at last the door to the time-delay chamber closed behind us, I sagged against the wall, panting.

My tiny Glock felt like it weighed ten pounds and my legs were lead. Sweat poured off me, soaking my clothes and sticking my hair to my face.

"Ya okay, darlin'?" Hellhound inquired with concern. "Ya look like you're gonna keel over."

"I'm fine." I dragged myself upright and shouldered in front of him. "Damn, this chamber needs a closed-circuit camera. Who knows what we're stepping into?"

"Give me your gun," Kane said. "I'll take point this time."

"No."

"Aydan..."

"No," I repeated. "This is my job. If you get shot, it's my fault." When he opened his mouth to argue, I overrode him. "And I don't have children. Both of you, put your backs against this wall."

Kane looked mutinous but both men obeyed, flattening themselves on either side of the door.

The latch clicked open, and I crouched and sidestepped into the lobby, leading with my gun.

The guard in the security wicket made a convulsive grab for his weapon before relaxing as he recognized me. "Everything's clear here," he said. "Looks like there was only one breach in the tunnel."

"Clear," I threw over my shoulder to Kane and Hellhound, and they stepped out of the chamber. Turning back to the guard, I said, "Dermott said to arm John and Arnie. Do you have..."

I didn't need to complete the question. The guard dropped two Glock 10s and a handful of magazines into the turntable and spun them around to our side.

Kane and Hellhound appropriated them, pocketing some magazines and each jacking a round into the chamber.

"Where should we go?" I demanded of the guard. "Dermott said to coordinate with you."

"Looks like it's over." He pointed to his monitors and I leaned in to see Dermott and the security personnel emerging from the rubble with three limping prisoners.

"Unless it was just a distraction," I said grimly.

"Probably not. A pretty big group came through." The guard nodded toward the monitor. "Those are the only survivors."

I let out a long breath and trudged over to fall into one of the chairs. "Wake me if anything else blows up," I said, and closed my eyes.

"Sleeping on the job?" Dermott's unwelcome voice roused me.

I dragged myself up from my slouch and squinted at him through gritty eyes.

"She needs the sleep. Kane an' I were keepin' watch," Hellhound said with a look that dared Dermott to make something of it.

"Fine," Dermott said. "Kane and Helmand, turn in your weapons and wait here 'til I call you for your lie detector interviews."

Fear turned me rigid.

He was going to question Arnie under the lie detector.

Oh, God, no.

I sneaked a glance at Arnie, but his face was impassive. Avoiding my gaze.

Dermott was still talking. "After that, we'll do the full debriefing..." He consulted the lobby clock. "In three hours. Nine AM."

"What about Aydan?" Kane asked, his voice level but his glacial gaze daring Dermott to speak his vendetta out loud.

Dermott turned a bloodshot glare on me. "She's coming up to finish her interview." He transferred his glare to the security guard. "Don't let these two leave." He turned back to me. "Kelly, move it."

I plodded after him. My aching legs barely managed the stairs, and I wobbled precariously on the top one before righting myself.

The walk to Dermott's office felt like a death march. The weight of my despair increased with every step. I had no defense for snooping into my friends' criminal cases. And Arnie couldn't beat the lie detector.

It was over. We were both going to prison.

I half-sat, half-fell into the chair in Dermott's office, and my eyes slipped closed while he secured the lie detector's headdress around my forehead.

Chaotic images flashed through my exhausted brain. Tawny's cold stare. God, what a vicious bitch she'd turned out to be. Her minions would be relieved when they found out they were only going to prison instead of getting tortured and killed for whatever they'd failed to accomplish tonight...

My eyes popped open.

That was it.

The final connection.

"So." Dermott lowered himself carefully into his chair as though his back hurt. "Last question. Did you use Department resources to investigate criminal cases involving your friends, even though there was no connection to any active Departmental investigations?"

He didn't sound vindictive or angry or even smug. Just tired.

I straightened my spine and looked him in the eye. "No."

The green light shone.

Dermott passed a weary hand over his face. "I fucking knew it. This lie detector's fucked. I'll get it recalibrated, and we'll have to redo the whole damn interview."

Oh, God, no.

CHAPTER 58

"I'm not lying," I insisted. "The lie detector is working fine."

Dermott's usual belligerence returned. "Fuck off, Kelly! How stupid do you think I am?"

It didn't seem like a good idea to answer that.

Instead, I said, "I'm not trying to insult your intelligence. I'm just telling you that Pearl's and Eddy's cases were connected to Volslav."

"Bullshit." Dermott hesitated, then reluctantly asked, "How?"

"Via the tunnels."

"Don't play games with me. I'm 'way too fucking tired."

"I'm not playing games. I'm not lying, either." I hesitated. "You're right, I took an interest in my friends' cases. They're my friends, and I didn't want to see them wrongly convicted. But I didn't interfere with the investigations or the evidence, and I wasn't wasting Department resources. I had a gut feeling that something wasn't right with those cases, and that it was all somehow connected to Volslav."

Dermott massaged his forehead. "Bullshit." But he didn't sound certain.

"And now I know for sure," I told him with more

confidence than I felt. "Volslav created that bank account for me and faked the bill of sale because Tawny wanted to be sure that when she killed me, Sirius Dynamics would be hers. I bet she was using that drone on Monday night to figure out the extent of her new holdings."

"She was," Dermott agreed. "Holt called and said he'd found the scans from the ground-penetrating radar on her flash drive."

"So she knew where the tunnels led," I went on. "I haven't seen the scans, but I'm willing to bet that our tunnels go really damn close to the cellar of Blue Eddy's Saloon."

"They do." For a change, Dermott didn't sound hostile. "One of the original tunnel branches went to Blue Eddy's. When the Department took over Sirius Dynamics, we walled up that connection, but the wall is only about six feet thick there." He grimaced. "Was. That's where they broke through tonight."

"Makes sense," I said. "Bootleggers used to smuggle their booze through the tunnels during Prohibition. Pearl mentioned it during the CRAPS meeting, and said it would be fun to investigate. I bet Margaret mentioned it to Fake-Blake, who was really Volslav. And Volslav didn't want CRAPS poking around. Framing Pearl kept CRAPS from investigating the tunnels."

"That's pretty far-fetched," Dermott said slowly. "And there's no proof. And you couldn't have known the case was connected at the time."

"I didn't know at the time," I agreed. "But I suspected. I had reasonable cause."

Dermott grunted. "What about the murder at Eddy's?"

"That was probably an accident. But you'll have to ask your prisoner if you want to know for sure."

Dermott's head jerked up. "My prisoner? Which one?"

"The guy in the camo pants and big boots. I saw him on the security monitor when you were taking him to the cells, but it didn't register right away because I was so tired." A sluggish wave of fatigue coursed over me at the reminder, but I fought it back. "I've seen him at Eddy's every time I've been there this week. I didn't really pay attention because there have been so many other strangers around, but when I saw him tonight, I figured it out. He's been hiding in Eddy's cellar at night and slowly digging through to our tunnels. He's the one who killed Herman Lopez, and he shot the guy with Pearl's shotgun."

"Bullshit. You're just making that up to save your ass."

"I'm not-" I began, but Dermott interrupted.

"I'll settle this right now. I ran the evidence from Eddy's and Pearl's cases through our lab because I figured you'd try to pull a fast one somewhere along the line. The bat had been wiped clean, but there were a couple of partial prints." He picked up the phone and dialled. "Dermott here. Have you fingerprinted the prisoners yet? Good. Run their prints against the partials on that baseball bat from the Carlson case." He hung up and gave me a challenging stare. "What's your story now?"

Tired of fighting him, I shrugged. "I think I'm right. I think old Camo-Pants quietly let himself into Eddy's with a bump key last week. I think he was working away down there every night. I think Herman Lopez was cold and needed a bathroom, and either saw Camo-Pants sneaking into Eddy's or tried the door and found it was open. Lopez sneaked in, maybe went over to the bar to snag some free drinks. Camo-Pants got taken by surprise, grabbed the baseball bat, and killed Lopez. But then he was screwed.

Tawny had said he had to be ready at any time, and if the police found out a murder had been committed in the bar, the building would be locked down as a crime scene. Camo-Pants panicked and dragged Lopez's body outside and staged the murder there, then went back in the bar and cleaned up."

I stopped for breath, and Dermott snorted. "Fuck, you should write fiction. You're just making all this shit up as you go."

"I'm not done. When Tawny heard that Pearl was getting curious about the tunnels, she told Camo-Pants to deal with it. So he sneaked into Pearl's and framed her, because murdering her would have made the police ramp up a big investigation in town, and that's the last thing he wanted. I bet if you check his boots, the treads will match the prints at Pearl's."

Dermott's phone rang, making both of us jump.

He snatched up the receiver. "Dermott."

He listened, incredulity spreading over his face. "You're fucking kidding me." He listened again, shaking his head. "Okay, here's the next thing. Check the prisoner's boot treads against the prints from Pearl Swindon's place. Let me know ASAP."

Dermott hung up and faced me reluctantly. "You were right about the fingerprints. They match the guy you're calling Camo-Pants."

Somehow I managed not to mutter 'Thank God'. Instead, I said, "Tawny phoned Camo-Pants and told him to do it tonight. She thought she'd killed me, and she probably figured it was a perfect time to take over the building."

"That's stupid," Dermott objected. "If she knew she was getting the title to the building anyway, why would she risk breaking through the tunnel? She had to know a base this size would be manned."

"She probably did. She probably planned to have a huge team here by the time Camo-Pants broke through, and have the building secured with her own personnel by morning. If anybody official questioned it, she had the sale documents to prove she was the rightful owner. But I killed her before she could mobilize anybody except Camo-Pants and his cronies. And Camo-Pants went ahead anyway because he didn't dare disobey."

We eyed each other in silence.

"Where does Everett Marsh fit in?" Dermott asked.

"I don't know. I think he had a separate deal."

Dermott exhaled and leaned back in his chair. "Okay. I was just checking to see if you'd make up some shit for that, too. Holt actually found the answer on the flash drive. Volslav and Marsh had a deal. Marsh turned a blind eye to Volslav's arms deals, Volslav killed the African presidents and sold arms to the insurgents, and Marsh cleaned up on the shorted stocks. Your mother couriered information between them."

Bitterness filled my soul. "So she was in on the plot to kill me."

"No, she made a deal with Volslav to get you safely out of the country. In exchange, she'd pass information to Marsh via the diplomatic pouches. Your mother held up her end of the bargain, but Volslav double-crossed her. Decided to take you out instead of handing you over to dear old mum."

I let that sink in for a moment. I knew my mother had been a murderer, but at least she hadn't been trying to kill me. Did that make it better?

Too tired. I shook off the irrelevant thought and refocused. "So that's what the last inventory entry was, the one Marsh deleted. There wasn't any accompanying intel for his records, it was just the note telling him it was time to short his stocks."

Dermott shrugged. "Probably."

"Have you heard if they caught him?"

"Yeah, and they secured the weapon. He isn't talking yet, but they have more than enough evidence against him."

I sagged with relief. "Thank God. Was the rest of Volslav's information on the flash drive, too? Where they got the new weapons made, how many there were, who their buyer was, how-"

"Yeah," Dermott interrupted. "Everything was on there. There was only one weapon prototype. I've got teams on the way to raid the lab that built it, and we've already arrested the buyer who was staying at the Silverside Hotel."

"What about the drone, and the EMP weapon that knocked out my cameras at the farm? Have you found them?"

"Not yet, but when they're done securing everything downstairs, we'll question the prisoners. If your guess about Camo-Pants is right, he's probably got them-" His phone rang again, and he picked it up with a resigned gesture. "Dermott." His shoulders slumped. "Okay. Thanks."

He slapped the receiver back in its cradle and fixed me with a bloodshot glare.

"The bootprints matched, right?" I prompted.

"Yeah."

Silence fell again.

I had answered all his questions. Should I just get up and leave? What would he do if I did?

"Look." The sound of my own voice surprised me.

Was I really going there?

The words kept coming. "I know you're pissed off at me."

Yep, apparently I was going there.

"I'm sorry things turned out the way they did last month," I went on. "I didn't mean to make you look bad. I understand why you need to be suspicious of me, and Stemp, and everybody, and that's okay. But can we please put the vendetta behind us?" Exhaustion seized me again and my shoulders slumped despite my best efforts to sit up straight. "It's just too fucking much work to hold onto it."

Dermott's brows drew down as he mimicked my voice in an insulting falsetto. "*I didn't mean to make you look bad.*" He reverted to his usual growl. "Bullshit!"

I was just too damn tired.

"Ask me." My voice came out completely flat.

Dermott frowned. "What?"

I touched my crown of electrodes. "I can't lie to you. Go ahead and ask me if I meant to make you look bad. Ask me if I truly want to put this behind us and start fresh."

He glared at me in silence.

Looking for a trap. Or too arrogant to meet me halfway.

Or whatever.

When it became obvious that he wasn't going to say anything, I sighed and reached up to undo the clasp. "Fine."

"Did you intentionally make me look bad?" he blurted.

We locked eyes.

"No," I said quietly.

The green light shone.

"Do you truly want to put this behind us and start fresh?"

"Yes."

Green light again.

A slow, mocking smile spread over Dermott's face.

I braced my aching body for his insults and contempt.

His smile disappeared, leaving his usual scowl. "Fine. Get out of here."

I blinked. "What... what about my interview?"

"You passed. I'll let Command know."

I stared at him while his words slowly penetrated.

"Are you fucking deaf?" he barked. "Get out! And be back here by nine AM for debriefing. Send Helmand up next."

With trembling hands, I unfastened the lie detector from my forehead and let myself out.

I had passed.

Arnie wouldn't.

CHAPTER 59

I was trudging away from Dermott's office with my gaze focused a few inches in front of my feet when the sound of rapidly approaching footsteps made me jerk my head up.

Stemp halted, scanning my face. I thought I detected a flicker of concern, but it was quickly masked by his usual expressionless façade.

"In my office," he said, and led the way.

Too worn out to fear this new impending disaster, I shuffled after him.

He unlocked his office and motioned me in, then closed the door behind us and took a seat behind his desk. He activated a bug detector and showed me the green light. "Report."

"I just passed my requalification interview," I said flatly. "Tawny Harchman was playing Volslav with the help of virtual reality. She developed a new ultrasound weapon prototype and was demonstrating it to a buyer here. We caught the buyer and the CIA has the weapon, because Everett Marsh used it to kill Agent Grandin before he could reveal that Marsh was working with Volslav-slash-Tawny. Tawny killed Lawrence Harchman, and I killed her. Her men are in custody. Dermott and Holt suspect you of helping Volslav because you disappear overseas every time something with Volslav comes up."

Stemp sat in silence, apparently digesting my deluge of information. After a moment he said, "It sounds convoluted. I shall look forward to the debriefing." He hesitated. "So, Dermott and Holt are suspicious of me."

I sighed and slumped lower in the chair. "They're suspicious of everybody. Dermott even tried to coerce me into saying Hellhound murdered Richard Fitzgerald."

"*Did* he murder Fitzgerald?" Stemp's sharp amber gaze was like an icy knife-thrust to my gut.

Fortunately, I was too tired and dispirited to freak out. "How would I know? I was in a hotel six hundred kilometres away. Dermott was just trying to make me fail my interview."

"Indeed?" Stemp raised an eyebrow. "What makes you think that?"

I blew out a weary breath. "Oh, I don't know. Little things, like when he called me a treasonous bitch and tried to get Holt to arrest me. Or when he promised to bury me so deep I'd never see the light of day again." Before Stemp could respond, I added, "Anyway, it's no big deal. I passed my interview, and we talked a bit afterward. He might ease up on the vendetta now."

Stemp's eyebrows climbed nearly to his hairline. "You and Dermott talked? Civilly?"

"Yeah."

He leaned back in his chair. "Excellent. I was concerned that Dermott was losing his objectivity."

I snorted. "Dermott? Objective? I don't think we're talking about the same guy here."

"On the contrary, Dermott is usually quite objective. He has no loyalty to anyone, nor any regard for authority. He doesn't hesitate to point fingers and demand answers, loudly. He plays a critical role in the Department's ongoing security. I'm pleased that he is suspicious of me. He should be."

My jaw dropped. "Um... wha..." I stopped and tried again. "Is there... something you're trying to tell me?"

Stemp's dispassionate expression relaxed into a smile. "No. You can trust me, should you see fit to do so. I am merely saying that nobody should be above suspicion."

I let out a breath. "Okay. So... did everything go all right overseas?"

He lowered his voice. "Yes. But this cannot go on. If Dermott is suspicious, others may be taking notice, too. That is an unacceptable risk to my family."

"So what are you going to do?"

"Evaluate the repercussions of Tawny Harchman's death, and decide which of my plans to implement."

He had plans. Plural. Why was I not surprised?

But at least his little daughter would be safe.

And maybe, just maybe, he could save Arnie, too.

Letting out a tired sigh to hide the hopeful uptick of my pulse, I said, "Well, you'll get a lot of information in the debriefing. It's at nine. And you should also know that Dermott is going to question Arnie and John under the lie detector now."

Stemp frowned. "Why is he questioning them outside the debriefing?"

"No idea," I lied.

"Hm." Stemp glanced at his wristwatch. "The debriefing will be postponed until thirteen hundred. Go home and get some sleep."

"But Dermott-"

"Is no longer in charge. And also needs sleep."

Somehow I managed not to collapse as relief collided with reality. "I can't go home. I don't have a vehicle. My car's in Calgary, and Kane's and Hellhound's vehicles are at Springbank."

"You may all leave your keys at the security wicket. I'll arrange to have your vehicles brought back." Stemp reached into his pocket and handed a set of car keys across the desk. "Take my vehicle. I'll expect it, and your team, back here at thirteen hundred."

He was overriding Dermott. Cancelling Arnie's lie detector interview. Oh, thank God.

I accepted Stemp's keys and hid my soaring hope in a dispassionate tone. "Should I still send Arnie up for the lie detector interview?"

"Yes."

My heart thudded to the bottom of my belly and lay there, bruised and broken.

Arnie had been so damn close to salvation.

But not close enough.

I should have known Stemp would never compromise his ethics or the Department's security.

"Thank you for lending us your car," I said mechanically, and dragged myself to my feet.

When I emerged from the stairwell, Kane and Hellhound rose from the lobby chairs and hurried over.

"Ya okay?" Hellhound asked worriedly.

"Yes." I could barely force words out through my exhaustion and despair. "Passed my interview. Dermott wants to interview you now."

Arnie's chin came up, and he squared his shoulders. "'Kay."

I flung my arms around him as though I could pull his body inside mine and carry him to safety.

He hugged me back, then kissed me tenderly before disengaging. "Love ya, darlin'." He turned and strode for the stairs before I could reply.

Kane's arm came around my shoulders, and I turned my face into his chest and hid in his embrace. He didn't offer any useless platitudes. We stood in silence, just holding each other.

After a long moment, I pulled away to trudge over to the chairs. Falling into one and closing my eyes, I did my best to shut out the misery.

"Hey, darlin', time to go." In my dream, Arnie stood in front of me, smiling and offering his hand to help me up.

I squeezed my eyes shut, clinging to the dream.

"Come on, darlin'." A whiskery kiss made my eyes pop open.

"Arnie?" My voice was barely a whisper.

He grinned. "Rise an' shine. We're done here." Behind him, John stood smiling, too.

"But... the interviews...?" My brain felt as though it had been scooped out and replaced with sticky porridge.

"Kane did his while ya were sleepin'. We're both done. Come on."

Fearful hope rose as I took his hand and hauled myself upright. "So... we can go?"

"Yep. Debriefin's been postponed 'til one."

I must still be dreaming. I clenched my hand around Stemp's car keys hard enough to hurt.

Arnie and John were still standing there smiling at me.

I held up the keys. "Stemp lent me his car so we can go back to my place and get some sleep." I headed for the security wicket as I spoke, and they followed. "Stemp says to leave our keys here, and they'll bring our cars this afternoon."

A few minutes later we stepped outside and the cold dark wind slapped me in the face. We hurried to Stemp's car and slid into the still-warm interior.

Sinking into the butter-soft leather of the driver's seat, I closed the door behind me, checked my bug detector, and demanded, "What happened? How did you pass?"

Hellhound shrugged, grinning. "I'm just an asset. I don't hafta do a requalification interview. An' Dermott only asked about stuff in this mission with Volslav. I told ya the Department didn't really wanna nail me. Dermott was only gunnin' for you." Hellhound's grin widened. "'Course, it prob'ly didn't hurt that Stemp was sittin' there through my whole interview, keepin' Dermott honest."

"My interview was the same," Kane agreed. "Their questions were strictly to determine whether you had any known connections to Volslav, and to confirm that you truly believed Pearl's and Eddy's cases were related to Volslav's case."

"So..." I couldn't quite make myself believe. "Everything's... okay?"

"Yep. It's all good, darlin'," Arnie assured me.

I had to say it out loud to make it real. "It's over. We're all safe. And Eddy and Pearl are completely exonerated." When both men nodded and smiled, I fell back in the seat, staring up at the roof liner to hide the moisture in my eyes. "Oh, thank God." I let out a long breath, suddenly realizing how tired I was when every muscle in my body relaxed.

"Good Lord, I'm bagged. I could sleep right here."

"I'll drive if you like," Kane offered.

"No, it's okay. Stemp gave the keys to me, so I'm responsible." I started the car and steered out of the parking lot. "And anyway, I'm going to stay awake by telling you all the details that got filled in since we last talked."

My story took the entire length of the drive. As we pulled into my lane, I finished, "So it was just my luck that Dermott's a traditionalist. He has enough trouble accepting that I have two boyfriends. It never occurred to him that I might be married and still have a boyfriend on the side."

"I still feel bad that ya hadta lie for me," Hellhound muttered.

"I didn't lie. The lie detector said I was telling the truth."

"Yeah, but technically ya lied for me. It ain't right."

I sighed. "Would it have been right if Fitzgerald had tortured and murdered Kathy? Or you? Would it have been right if you'd let him live so he could kill and brutalize even more people?"

Kane chimed in. "Would it have been right if Aydan had told the truth and gone to prison?"

"So there wasn't any 'right' solution." I pulled into my garage and turned the car off, then reached over to gently shove Arnie's shoulder. "You're just going to have to live with the guilt."

He chuckled. "Okay. I know when I'm outnumbered."

The warm safety of my house felt like a welcoming hug. As we shed our boots and jackets at the door, Arnie turned to me with a smile. "Well, darlin', guess that means it's divorce time."

A small pang arrowed through my heart.

Kane's perceptive gaze flicked from me to Arnie. "I'll go

and make up the guest bed," he said, and vanished down the hall.

Hellhound pulled a sheaf of papers from his parka pocket. "I got the forms right here. We don't even hafta go back to Vegas, we can just mail 'em in."

"Oh." My voice came out small. "Good."

Anxiety rose in Arnie's eyes. "What's wrong?"

"Nothing." Compelled to honesty, I added, "Don't take this wrong, but... I'm sad to be divorcing you." He stiffened, and I hurriedly added, "But only because divorce makes it sound like I want to be rid of you, and that's not how I feel."

He didn't relax. His worried gaze searched my face.

I put as much reassurance into my voice as I could. "Don't worry, I'm not backing out of our deal. Give me the papers and I'll sign them right now."

He hesitated, still frowning. "Are ya sure?"

"Of course I'm sure. That was our deal."

"But it ain't really what ya want."

"Yeah, it is... kind of. I mean, I don't want to be married; I just..." Abandoning the attempt to explain feelings that I hadn't even figured out for myself yet, I gave him a smile. "I just want you to know I love you. And that's why I'm divorcing you." I wiggled my fingers in a 'hand-it-over' gesture. "Now give me the papers. We can get John to sign as a witness."

It only took a few minutes to skim the forms and sign them where yellow sticky-notes had been affixed. As Arnie had promised, his signatures were already in place. I handed the papers back, and he accepted them with a troubled expression.

"Aydan... ya know I'd do anythin' to make ya happy, right?"

"Yes. You proved that. I can't think of a bigger sacrifice you could have made for me."

"It wasn't a sacrifice," he said seriously. "An' if I thought it'd make ya happy to stay married, I'd do it. But I don't think it'd make ya happy."

"Why not?"

"'Cause someday ya might want a real marriage to a guy that'll be a proper husband to ya."

"I won't."

He let out a rueful chuckle. "Oh, yeah? Last week I woulda sworn on my own grave that I'd never get married. An' we woulda both laughed our asses off at the thought a' marryin' each other." He turned out his hands, palms up. "But here we are. Ya never know what's gonna happen."

I sighed. "I guess you're right, but we never would have done it if either of us thought it was going to be a real marriage."

"Yeah, I know. An' I get what you're sayin' about the divorce, too." He touched my cheek tenderly. "An' that's why we gotta do it now. I know ya, darlin'. If we stayed married an' later ya changed your mind... You'd be thinkin' it'd hurt me if ya asked for a divorce, an' ya wouldn't do it. I'd be livin' my life same as always, but you'd be trapped." He looked into my eyes. "Tell me I'm wrong."

I gazed up at him, imagining the scenario he'd painted. "I... You might be right."

"I know I'm right, darlin', an' ya wanna know why?"

"Why?" I asked absently, still imagining how awful it would be to ask him for a divorce if I had said I wanted to stay married. No matter how little he claimed to care, that would feel like a betrayal.

"Ya said Dermott was a traditionalist, but so are you.

Usually I can see the sparks flyin' between you an' Kane, but soon's we were married..." Arnie snapped his fingers. "Gone. Just like that. Ya hugged him an' said ya loved him, but ya never once kissed him on the lips. Never once looked at him like ya wanted to back him up against the wall an' fuck him silly. Ya turned off a whole part a' yourself even though ya knew I didn't want that from ya."

I stared at him, recognizing the truth in his words.

"Aydan..." Arnie gently took my hands. "We ain't gettin' divorced 'cause I don't wanna be with ya. It's 'cause I love ya, an' I don't ever want ya to suffer because a' me."

"You wouldn't make me suffer." I clutched his hands to my heart. "I know you wouldn't."

"Nah, but you'd make yourself suffer, an' I couldn't stop ya." He brought our clasped hands to his lips and kissed my knuckles. "Tell ya what, darlin'. If ya ever get to the point where ya don't feel like ya gotta give up part a' yourself for your husband, then maybe we can talk about gettin' married again." He was still smiling, but his eyes were somber. "But by then you'll know ya deserve somebody a helluva lot better'n me."

"You're wrong there, because there's nobody better than you." I reached up to kiss him. "But you're right about the rest of it. Thanks. I'm not feeling sad about the divorce anymore."

"Good, 'cause ya know it doesn't change a damn thing." He smiled and slipped his arms around me. "We still got our rings, an' those are the promises that count."

I cuddled into the warmth of his embrace. "Always."

Book 17 is available!

Visit my Books page at dianehenders.com/books for progress updates and announcements.

A Request

Thanks for reading!

If you enjoyed this book, I'd really appreciate it if you'd take a moment to review it online.

Here are some suggestions for the "star" ratings:
Five stars: Loved the book and can hardly wait for the next one.
Four stars: Liked the book and plan to read the next one.
Three stars: The book was okay. Might read the next one.
Two stars: Didn't like the book. Probably won't read the next one.
One star: Hated the book. Would never read another in the series.

You can help prospective readers by writing a few sentences about what you liked or disliked about the book.

Thanks for taking the time to do a review!

About Me

Before I started writing fiction, I had a checkered career: technical writer, computer geek, and interior designer. I'm good at two out of three of those. Fortunately, I had the sense to quit the one I sucked at (interior design).

When my mid-life crisis hit, I took up muay thai and started writing thrillers featuring a middle-aged female protagonist. ('Walter Mitty', you say? Nope, never heard of him.)

Writing and kicking the hell out of stuff seemed more productive than more typical mid-life-crisis activities like getting a divorce, buying a Harley Crossbones, and cruising across the country picking up men in sleazy bars; especially since it's winter most months of the year here in Canada.

It's much more comfortable to sit at my computer. And Harleys are expensive. Come to think of it, so are beer and gasoline.

Oh, and I still love my husband. There's that. So I stuck with the writing.

Diane Henders

And here's my "professional" bio, in case you need something more suitable for mixed company:

Diane Henders is the Kindle best-selling author of the NEVER SAY SPY series: Sexy thrillers packed with tension, laughs, profanity, and sometimes warm fuzzies.

The first book in the series, NEVER SAY SPY, has had over 450,000 downloads to date, and stayed on Kindle's 'Women Sleuths' Top 100 list for 60 consecutive months.

Diane enjoys target shooting, gardening, auto mechanics, painting (art, not walls), music, and martial arts; and loves food and drink almost as much as she loves her husband. They live in the wilds of British Columbia, Canada, where they get all the adrenaline rush they could ever want by growing fruit trees in bear country.

Want to know what else is roiling around in the cesspit of my mind? Drop by my blog and website at dianehenders.com, check out the extras, and don't forget to leave a comment in the guest book to say hi – I love hearing from you! Or you can connect with me on Facebook at:
https://www.facebook.com/authordianehenders.
See you there!